The Paragraph Ranch

For Jerry and Nancy —

Kay Ellington
and
Barbara Brannon

Happy Trails !

Kay Ellington

Booktrope Editions
Seattle WA 2014

Barbara Brannon

Cover Design by Greg Simanson

This is a work of fiction. Names, characters, businesses, places, events, and incidents are either the product of the author's imagination or are used fictitiously. Any resemblance to similarly named places or to persons living or deceased is unintentional.

Print ISBN 978-1-62015-461-8

EPUB ISBN 978-1-62015-471-7

DISCOUNTS OR CUSTOMIZED EDITIONS MAY BE AVAILABLE FOR EDUCATIONAL AND OTHER GROUPS BASED ON BULK PURCHASE.

For further information please contact info@booktrope.com

www.facebook.com/TheParagraphRanch

www.ParagraphRanch.com

Library of Congress Control Number: 2014914342

for Ruth

Contents

Prologue

Alice
Thursday, May 1, 2008

IN FIFTY-FIVE YEARS on the home place we ain't never missed putting in a crop, and I don't intend to miss one now. No matter what them three say. Why, we planted cotton the week Wilton got back from Korea. And the year it snowed the first of May. And the time when Dee Anna was six months old and we carried her out here in a apple crate.

There's something about a fresh plowed field that gets to you. Makes your heart ache. All them even rows, perfect and clean, not a weed in sight. Terraces purty as a picture. Sun coming up over the breaks, wind a-blowin' across the plains, fe'lark singing in that mesquite tree there.

He used to say this place was too sorry to run cattle on and too dry to farm. But we made it. Some years we nearly went broke, some years we had a little to put by. It's harder these days, what with all the talk of irrigation running out. And harder now they don't let you catch your own seed and you have to buy it from the farm supply. How anybody can own a patent on a plant God Himself invented is beyond me. Nothing ever stays the same, though, does it?

I'm gonna sit here and finish this Thermos of coffee and listen out for Hector on the tractor. And then I guess I'll drive on back to the house.

I'm all right, Wilton. I can manage.

I won't let you down. I promise.

1
Gone to Texas

*At the heart of every story lies one of two universal plots.
Number one: Someone takes a trip.*
— *G. H. Templeton*, **The Working Writer**

THERE WASN'T A SOUL in eleven hundred square miles of Caprock County, Texas, willing or able to take on the care of Mary Alice Bennett, not for love or money. Of course, who in their right mind could blame them?

That's what it felt like to Dee, anyhow, who was beginning to wonder whether her mother's reputation hadn't leaked to every home health agency in West Texas. She repeated the words in a tone of rising frustration. "Six *weeks* waiting period?"

"For full-time assistance, yes," said Mitzi Autry, coordinator of Helping Hands, the only organization in the Claxton phone book that could see her on such short notice.

Dee, usually so poised and in control in the college classroom, was ready to strangle the woman. "By then my mother will be back on her feet and won't *need* help! What do your patients do?"

"Mrs. Kaufmann, in cases like this, like I said, the family usually pulls together and takes care of their loved one without outside assistance in the short term."

"Bennett. It's Bennett-Kaufmann. But we can't right now." Dee's words rushed out like a runaway train. "My sister's a realtor in the Metroplex and has her own issues to deal with. My brother Buddy—maybe you've heard of Buddy Bennett's All-Star Football Camp?—well, that's not going to happen. I live fifteen hundred miles away and I have a writing fellowship in Massachusetts that I can't miss. Mrs. Bennett's grandchildren, including my own daughter, aren't likely to drop what they're doing to spend the summer looking after an invalid in an old farmhouse without central air. And there's no one else." She pushed a wayward strand of straight brown hair back behind her ear, tried to calm down and get a grip. "And besides that, you don't know my mother."

Mitzi drew back, pursed her lips, and scanned the computer monitor. "Hmmm. Maybe you're in luck," she said, clicking the mouse and making a note. "One of our clients passed away yesterday." She looked back up at Dee and reddened. "I didn't mean it that way."

Dee was beyond worrying about decorum. Too much was riding on this. "So you might have someone available?"

"One girl who can come part-time three days a week, but that's it."

"We'll take her," Dee replied. She said a silent thank-you to the universe. They would manage. Mama would be okay, all things considered. And she wouldn't have to change that airline ticket to Massachusetts after all.

*   *   *

Out on the Abilene highway in the rental car, Dee thought back over the past twenty-four hours. She was mortified at her display of pique at the agency. *That's not who I am.* But not so mortified she couldn't feel a huge sense of relief.

Just as she'd wrapped up the last day of her fiction workshop in North Carolina Thursday morning and given the student writers instructions for their final assignment, her phone had rung with Penny's number. Even at a convenient time Dee didn't relish an encounter with her domineering older sister. But no call from Texas in the middle of a workday ever bore good news.

Mama was in the Claxton hospital, Penny'd said. A car accident. At Penny's stricken tone, Dee's blood ran cold. She shooed the students out and shut the door. *Not another parent . . . not so soon . . .*

"Omigosh . . . how—how bad is it?"

"We're not sure what happened—it's bizarre. Hector found Mama all bruised up layin' in a bar ditch beside the road, out by the turnoff to the farm. . . . don't really know yet. Buddy called to tell me they took . . . emergency room—" Penny's voice crackled unevenly over the phone then cut out altogether for a moment. Dee guessed she was driving, somewhere in the microwave wilderness west of Dallas.

"But she's okay? Is Buddy with her?" Their brother wouldn't be prone to histrionics, at least.

" . . . Buddy had a call from Brother Roy, who was at the hospital visiting Mrs. Archibald when he ran into Hector."

"Hector found her . . . Brother Roy?" What did the man who farmed Mama's land, the preacher, and her third-grade teacher have to do with things? "Did you or didn't you say she's *alive?*"

"Yes, that we can be thankful for," said Penny, coming in more clearly now. "Buddy said something about broken bones. It's a good thing Hector did find her—otherwise, they might not have known how to locate next of kin."

"Next of kin? Is it that serious?"

"Nobody knows yet. You ought to think about how soon you can get here. I can't handle it all. You did say you weren't teaching this summer, didn't you?" Her sister's words jarred her.

"No—yes, I mean, no, I'm not." Dee hadn't yet discussed the writing fellowship with anyone but Abby. Her daughter was the only one she could trust not to shoot the opportunity down until it yielded some surer success.

Penny dictated instructions as usual. "Buddy's headed to Claxton as soon as he gets out of his P.E. class and finds a substitute. You better go ahead and book a flight. We have got to talk about Mama's situation— and the farm. *If* she gets through this."

That phrase hit her in the gut. Dee knew the bulk of responsibility had fallen on Penny last year, looking after their father as he'd lingered in long-term care. Their brother, tied up in playoffs, hadn't been much help. It couldn't have been easy, and she owed Penny that much understanding. But Penny would never know what Dee had sacrificed herself, as a single parent. And she surely wouldn't sympathize about the precarious state of Dee's checking account and credit card balances, or appreciate how crucial this residency was to her career's survival. Any thought of the approaching publish-or-perish deadline turned her stomach inside out. She *had* to make this work—or seven years' worth of teaching, and everything she'd given up in her personal life, would be for nothing.

"I'll see what I can do. Why don't you call me back the minute you know more?" said Dee. "Maybe things aren't as bad as they sound."

Penny's voice eroded into melodramatic sobs. "You be praying for us. I don't know if I can go through this again."

Dee had grasped one thing: what *this* meant. She couldn't risk leaving unfinished business with another parent either. Of course she loved her family . . . but why did they have to make it so hard? Would they ever forgive her for the choices she'd made? She clicked the call off, forced back her own tears, and dialed her department chair's number. Whatever was going on . . . she had to get *home*.

Home was a topic that always stirred mixed feelings for Dee. With the adult Bennett children, family matters were like a high-stakes game of rock, scissors, paper—and Dee, nine years younger than Penny and seven younger than Buddy, never seemed to come out on top. When they were children their parents had pushed them all to work hard, earn good grades, and be both competitive and honorable. Growing up on a farm, no one could get away without pulling their weight—literally. Dee remembered dragging a tow sack of cotton twice as tall as herself while the older kids, much faster pickers, left her behind. They took games like checkers and 42 dominoes seriously. They joined 4-H and school clubs, bringing home medals and blue ribbons. Around the house they learned to make do with whatever the year's crop would bring, for Wilton and Alice Bennett never had a credit card, never bought a vehicle new, never put up a Christmas tree.

But Dee had wanted more from life and was determined to get it. At eighteen she'd moved out the day after high school graduation, started college that summer, and never looked back.

So she couldn't explain to her family why, at thirty-nine, even with an advanced degree, a steady job at a respected East Coast college, a place of her own, and a promising new relationship, she hadn't reached a comfortable level of achievement or stability. Why things had turned out so badly between her and Jacob. Why she'd let Abby go. Why no one could let her live it down.

She packed her suitcase and made mental notes: *Call Rob, cancel kayaking weekend. Call Jake, get number for Abby's new iPhone. Pack manuscript.*

*   *   *

"Your mother's still in surgery, but we have every reason to believe it's going smoothly," Dr. Taylor told the Bennett siblings gathered at the nurses' station, in a temporary wing of the hospital away from the noise and dust of a major renovation project. "Dr. Kim is done stabilizing the broken wrists and is applying casts now." He hadn't been certain about the cause of the accident either, but he was clear about one thing. "Alice Bennett's a tough old bird, and she'll pull through. But she'll be incapacitated for a while, and you kids"—he'd said the word with a straight face—"need to look into long-term care options." Ron Taylor was a Claxton native who had come back home after medical school, taking over the local family practice. A boyish-looking thirty, he was doctor to nearly everyone in town though half the age of most.

Dr. Taylor reviewed the chart on the countertop. "We'll have your mother sedated when she first comes out of surgery," he said, "so be prepared—she may not be quite herself. Try to keep her from getting riled up again, for everyone's sake. But otherwise, she's very lucky."

"So, no internal injuries, nothing life-threatening?" asked Buddy, arms crossed and towering over the doctor.

"No, nothing like that, but the ant bites could certainly have been life-threatening. It took us a while to realize your mom was allergic. From the pattern of welts on her torso, it looks like she may have fallen right into a bed of 'em."

Dee winced at the image. She conjured up a scene from a horror film, insects swarming over the victim's skin. "Is she going to be okay, then?" she asked. "Long term?" *Incapacitated,* he'd said. What, exactly, did that mean?

"That depends," said Dr. Taylor. "She's going to need extensive therapy and rehabilitation for the broken bones."

"Where would that be, in a rehab hospital?" asked Penny, who was entering notes on her smartphone.

"Oh, no, it can easily be done outpatient, under supervision. In her own home, or wherever you choose."

The three Bennetts avoided one another's gaze.

Dr. Taylor noticed their uneasiness. "Having an aging parent requires making some difficult decisions about caregiving. Medicare—Mrs. Bennett is on Medicare, right?—will cover some home health visits, but not round-the-clock care. Or maybe you'd like your mother to come stay with one of you. If so, we can work out a transfer to a facility near you. Just let us know. Seems like y'all have a lot to discuss." He paused and took a longer look at the male in the group. "I just realized. Are you Buddy Bennett the football coach?"

Buddy's blush was visible even under the wind-toughened skin of his face, and Dee and Penny smirked. "Yep, that's our brother," said Penny.

"I thought so," the doctor said. "I was pretty sure I'd seen you on TV."

"The second winningest coach in Texas high school football," Dee and Penny chanted in unison, teasing him with the phrase the sportscasters never failed to use.

"Where do you coach, again?"

"Darrell, between Fort Stockton and Monahans," Buddy answered.

"That's right," Dr. Taylor said, "Darrell Dust Devils, great mascot name." He finished marking the chart and left them with his best wishes, humming under his breath the "Dust 'Em Devils" fight song many West Texans knew by heart.

Dee's cell phone buzzed in her pocket. The screen flashed with a brief message from Rob back in North Carolina. *So sorry about yr mom Call when u know more. Anything I can do?* She appreciated his solicitousness—a good sign things between them might be going somewhere. Five years younger than Dee, Rob was a texter, not a talker. That was okay with her today—Dee didn't have a moment, or the battery life, for a conversation. In haste, she realized, she'd left the charger in her campus office.

*   *   *

Over breakfast in the makeshift hospital cafeteria the next morning, after taking weary turns at Mama's bedside overnight, the siblings discussed a plan of action. Dee's legs ached from being folded up in the wooden armchair, and she detected a slightly rank odor from the gray knit hoodie she'd alternated wearing and using for a pillow.

"At least it's just bruises and a couple of broken bones," she said. "Whatever happened, it surely could've been worse."

"Worse? At least? Did you hear her talking out of her mind all night?" countered Penny, who'd already freshened up her makeup and blonde hair and looked as though she could be showing a million-dollar house at any moment. "I thought she was going to get us all sued, calling the nurses such names. And that poor Asian doctor—"

Buddy waved his arms across the table between his sisters like a referee calling time out. "C'mon, we should be glad Mama'll get to go home at all. Dee's right, it could have been much worse—although I still can't understand how it happened."

"Maybe a mean streak a mile wide gives you protective superpowers," Dee said. She meant it to be funny.

Buddy ignored her. "So Dee, what are your travel plans?"

Penny raised an expectant eyebrow.

"I left things open-ended," Dee replied. She knew where this was headed. "I have some end-of-semester chores, but I think I can do them from here."

"That's good," said Penny, "because as you may or may not recall, I'm right in the middle of preparation for my commercial license. I *can't* not finish this. Plus, I would sure hate to cancel the dress fittings for next week. We worked too hard to get Madison's wedding planner on board, and her father and I don't need things to fall apart now." They all knew it was a balancing act for Penny to stage the wedding of the century for her eldest daughter—while making sure her ex picked up the tab for the whole show.

Dee nodded. "What about Mama staying with you during her rehab?"

"I bet you'd like that, Dee—just wash your hands of the whole thing. You know good and well she wouldn't go for it. I like to've never heard the end of complaining the last time she spent a weekend with us."

"I can't see it happening," Buddy agreed, between bites of sausage-and-egg burrito. "You know if we had any medical facilities in Darrell, she could come stay with me and Roxanne, but I think it's risky to be so far from a hospital. And it still wouldn't solve the problem of having someone with her round the clock—school's not out until June, and summer camp starts right after that."

"Look," said Dee, "I realize nobody else on the planet can run a sports camp, and Maddy's got to have nuptials to rival the Bush daughters'. But there's something I haven't had a chance to tell you all. I do have summer plans. I was selected for a writing fellowship in Massachusetts that starts the first of June."

"Is that like a job?" Buddy said. "I mean, do you get paid? Or is it just an honor?"

"Room and board," Dee said defensively, "but it's a pretty big deal. Plus, it'll be close to Abby in Northampton. We'll have a chance to spend some time together during her summer break. And it gives me access to research libraries and time to finish my book."

"Ah, yes, Dr. Dee's eternal work-in-progress," Penny said.

"Don't get snarky," Dee said. "I don't go out of my way to diss Realtors-with-a-capital-R."

"Maybe because we actually make money," her sister retorted.

"I knew I could count on you both to understand," Dee said, shaking her head and throwing her napkin onto her plastic plate.

"Listen, we want you to get to do your thing," said Penny as they all rose to leave. "But the reality is, someone has to help Mama. And what do you think she would say, after what she's been through?"

Dee knew exactly what Mama would say. Family obligations always came first. "Let's just see what works out," she said. "We have some time to see how she fares."

Penny backed off. "Well, right this moment we have some details to take care of. Dee, why don't you check on the home health care and the house, while I stay here with Mama?"

"Works for me," said Buddy. "I'm going to talk with Sheriff Kreidler and get a look at the car."

"Y'all come back upstairs with me and see how she's doing before you go," said Penny.

Dee rubbed her forehead wearily. Buddy talked as they walked together down the corridor, following detour signs around orange construction cones and dodging teams of workers in hard hats. "We do have to get serious about selling the farm," he said. "Mama's got no business living by herself out in the country, and this just proves it."

"She's got no business living by herself anywhere, now," added Penny.

"You know she goes ballistic at the mention of the term 'assisted living,'" Dee reminded them.

"We all have to do what we have to do, whether we like it or not," was her sister's unbending response.

As they stepped off the elevator they heard a commotion from the direction of Mama's room. Buddy broke into a run, but before he could reach the door a young-looking nurse slammed it closed and stood outside. She bit her lip to keep from crying. "I am a professional. I can handle this. Just give me a second."

"What, what?" demanded Penny. "Oh, my God, has she—"

"I was only trying to move Mrs. Bennett so she wouldn't develop bedsores. It's all okay." The nurse drew a deep breath and opened the door again.

The dragon's roar issued from the cave. "Rape! Rape! Some pervert is in here trying to feel me up. Get the cops!"

"Mama, Mama, settle down," shouted Penny. "We're all here. Me and Buddy and Dee. You're not well. It's just the nurse doing her job."

"What are all these people doing in my house? I was out plowing," Mama said loudly, then corrected herself. "Out *checking* on the plowing. I was down by the turnrow, seeing if them terraces had been throwed up good. Wilton—"

Maybe Mama did have a stroke, Dee thought. It had been a full year since Daddy last planted cotton. Or maybe Alzheimer's was setting in.

"You're in the Claxton hospital, Mama," said Buddy in a soothing tone. "You were hurt. These doctors and nurses are looking after you."

The vitriol subsided. Mama lay on her back, both arms immobilized in traction like those of a cartoon accident victim. Dee thought she'd get used to the sight of her mother in the hospital bed, but she felt a wrench in her heart all over again. Alice Bennett's face was bruised and grossly swollen, and her lips were cracked and scabbed. Angry lesions peppered the parts of her arms not covered in bandages. The back of one suspended hand was taped to an intravenous line. Her hair, normally a neat silver bob, was frazzled and matted. She stared up at the ceiling like a lunatic.

"Dammit, I can't see a thing without my glasses," Mama said, more quietly. Dee worried about her mother's state of mind. Despite her acid tongue, Mama had never held with cursing.

"They were broken in the accident, apparently," explained the nurse, who had regained her composure.

"You keep a spare pair at home, don't you, Mama?" asked Dee, looking for the quickest excuse to exit. "I can bring them tonight."

"Go on, y'all, I've got this," said Penny, exasperated. "Go on, now."

Dee sighed. "Is there anything else I should bring Mama from home?"

"Underwear, pajamas, toiletries—just use some common sense," Penny replied. "If that's not asking too much of someone with a PhD."

2
No Place Like Home

*Create an unforgettable sense of place, through close
observation, powerful imagery, and precise description.*

THE MIDDAY SUN was beating down ferociously by the time Dee
finished with the health care agency and drove out to the home place.
Dee felt about ready for a meltdown herself, after all the drama.

The Bennett farm was situated ten miles north of town on a two-lane
road paved with caliche. Dee followed the twisting drive up over the
red-rock breaks. She gritted her teeth and gunned the accelerator in
the rental Hyundai to get up the hill, maneuvering carefully to avoid
old washouts and ruts.

The farm house stood on a rise near the edge of the eroded breaks,
affording a view of rolling farmlands to the south and east. The rugged
country toward the north was punctuated by oil pumpjacks and gas
wells. A steady breeze blew across the plateau from the west but did
little to cool the air.

The Bennett half section had been planted in cotton every year since
Wilton Bennett inherited it in 1953, and for decades before that. It was
dryland cotton, irrigated only from what sporadic rainfall could be
captured in the long rows and ditches. The crop was completely dependent
on the vagaries of nature for its success or failure, both of which Wilton
and Alice had experienced their share of.

A good-sized corner of the farm was unsuited for cultivation due
to its uneven terrain. Ravines strewn with sandstone boulders cut into

the caprock and led into a draw at the bottom, where mesquite, hackberry, and cottonwoods clustered thickly around a mostly dry stream. Too little land to run cattle, Wilton had always said, but too rough to farm. He'd let that part go to cover, allowing a few scrawny head of beef to forage for whatever they could find. Calves were fattened and hauled to the livestock auction in Abilene for sale.

Dee shifted into low gear to top the hill. She was pleased to see that Mama's hollyhocks were blooming. But grass grew knee-high all the way to the kitchen door. The grapevines, with their hard, pellet-sized fruit, were starting to overwhelm the arbor Daddy had fashioned from chicken wire draped over clothesline poles unused once he'd installed a gas dryer. Makeshift cow pens—rusted box springs upended and fastened to fence posts—stood empty.

The wood frame house, its painted windowsills and eaves scarred by hailstorms, was complemented by a barn and numerous smaller outbuildings and shaded by two large, weathered mulberry trees. On the north side, protected by a shelterbelt of tall cedars, stood a row of peach trees, their rangy limbs propped by two-by-fours and their emerging fruit glowing like little suns among the branches. In the back yard, a storm cellar with heavy metal doors was nearly concealed by weeds. Farther away stood a water tank and a pump once driven by an old-fashioned windmill. Though the pump ran on electricity these days, the windmill's creaking vanes still turned, its gearbox attached to a crankshaft long broken. A sorry testament to the machine that had settled the West, thought Dee.

It was Daddy's Ford pickup, though, parked under a mesquite tree and covered in bird poop, that ultimately got to her. Dee cut the car's engine. As she stepped out, a blast of wind nearly tore its door off the hinges. The West Texas wind could be ferocious, especially in spring, when it often darkened the skies with brown dust. She walked over to the truck, picking her way through dry weeds that crunched under her soles.

It was as though Wilton Bennett himself had decided to go rest under the tree and never get up again. Dee laid a hand on the truck's hood and exhaled a long breath. Maybe this place *was* too much for Mama. How could one seventy-three-year-old woman possibly look after all this? Much less plant a crop, or even gather the fruit that grew of its own accord?

Dee knew exactly where her sister's sentiments lay on that score. Penny made no secret of the fact that she didn't like Mama staying by herself, especially this far from help or a neighbor. Now it looked like they should've listened to her. But five months earlier, when Daddy lost the battle with cancer, Mama had begged them not to make her move. They hadn't pushed the issue.

From where Dee could see at the top of the rise, the fields looked to be freshly plowed. Buddy had told Mama not to fool with planting a crop this season, just let it be and he'd take care of it next year. Maybe it was time for them to consider some winter wheat or sorghum anyway, he'd suggested. As for Hector, he'd get along fine for a season—plenty of farms would be glad to hire him on.

Dee walked back up the hill to the house. The crape myrtle at the corner of the porch looked lifeless, and weeds had taken over what used to be the kitchen garden in the back.

The house wasn't locked. She wasn't surprised. Dee let the screen slam behind her and pushed the heavy east-facing door open to admit the slanting light. Dust motes sparkled in the pattern cast on the linoleum hall floor. She checked out each room of the rambling house just to be sure nothing was amiss. You never knew.

She went to the bathroom—the only bathroom—to freshen up. She pulled the string on the light fixture over the mirror and studied her reflection. As an infant she could fit in the large porcelain basin to be bathed. Now, nearly as tall as her father, she stood eye-level with the old beveled mirror. The bead-board wainscoting still held the scent of the pine-oil cleanser her mother used, and mingled in she could detect hints of Ivory soap and Aqua Velva.

The cool tap water felt good on her face. The clothes she'd left North Carolina in wouldn't do for another minute, though, and she went to the car to retrieve her suitcase. Alone on the ridge, she could hear the doves cooing in the branches, the putt and rumble of a tractor's engine across the highway.

She'd been all too eager to leave this place for good. When she was growing up her friends in town hung out at the Dairy Queen or the roller rink on Saturday nights, lived in brick ranch-style homes with fashionably paneled dens, had their own stereo systems, and bought their dresses from Gray's on the square or even Neiman-Marcus. Dee wore clothes her sister sewed, and she'd been to Dallas only once in her young life.

Besides, back then Mama and Daddy seemed to have their hands too full to devote time to Dee. There was Penny's senior-year pregnancy, hushed up with a speedy marriage. Then Buddy's college football injuries. Penny's divorce and her return to the home place with a toddler in tow. Ten-year-old Auntie Dee's childhood ended abruptly as her parents grew into grandparents for Penny's children, then Buddy's.

Dee had turned to books for solace and companionship. The small Claxton Public Library became her second home after school. By eighth grade, she'd read almost every volume on its shelves. She joined the yearbook staff, excelled in English, earned a scholarship to Baylor, and left Claxton for good. These days she visited once a year or so, usually over a holiday or long weekend.

So why, Dee wondered now, was she the only one of her generation not ready to let this place go forever?

Dee brushed her hair back in a ponytail and changed into a cotton shirt and capris. She lay down on her old bed, just to rest for a moment— and promptly succumbed to sleep.

*   *   *

The telephone startled her back to reality, and she jumped and ran for the extension phone on the kitchen wall. "Bennett residence, this is Dee."

"Mom?" came a voice half college sophistication, half little-girl worry.

"Oh, Abby, I'm so glad to hear from you! Gosh, I've been trying and trying to reach you. Gramma Alice—"

"It's okay, Dad told me you called him looking for me, and I already got the scoop from Aunt Penny. You should check your phone every now and then."

"I'm sure it's dead," she said, reaching for her purse.

"I'm glad Gramma Alice isn't," Abby quipped. "I'm glad she's all right."

"It's not good, though, honey. It really changes everything for her."

"Do I need to come?"

"No, no, you don't need to take your mind off finals. Aunt Penny and Uncle Buddy are both here."

"I'm really sorry—I can't imagine Gramma Alice being hurt. She's always been so strong."

"Me either, sweetie. She wasn't—well, she hasn't been quite herself, and I don't think you'd want to see her like this. We'll wait and see how things progress." Dee let her words trail off indefinitely. "What else is up with you?"

"Well . . . I have a new job that I really like."

"Great, where?"

"At the food bank, just off West Street. It's walking distance."

That paycheck wouldn't make much of a dent in living expenses, Dee thought, but she held her tongue. "Your father told me you'd moved off campus."

"Yeah . . . there's a reason for that."

Dee waited for the other shoe to drop. It always did. "How are classes? Did you hear about your scholarship for fall yet?"

"Mom, I know this is not great timing, but . . . I'm not going back to Smith in the fall."

"What, why?" Dee started to pace around the kitchen. "Are you transferring?"

"No, I'm staying in Northampton. Just not going to school."

"You're right, it's not good timing. But you're wrong—you most certainly *are* going back." Dee could feel it happening. At times like this she grew imperious and inflexible. After everything she'd given up for Abby's sake, *this* was what she got in return?

"Mom . . . I only called to check on Gramma. And you. We can talk about it later, when you come up."

"Damn straight we'll talk about it later." Dee slammed the phone into the cradle, then squeezed her temples between her hands.

Why did she do this? She instantly regretted her reaction. Why alienate her only child, her talented, headstrong daughter, every time she managed to track her down and begin a real conversation? It seemed she could deal with only one demanding generation at a time.

"Shit, shit, shit, shit, *shit!*" Dee stomped through the kitchen, raising her voice with every step.

There was a sudden knock on the screen door. "*Hola,* anyone home?"

"Here—I'm coming." Dee went to the door, embarrassed.

"Hello, I'm—" the visitor said.

"Of course, Hector, I remember." She opened the door and offered Hector Ortiz a handshake. "I'm Dee, Alice's youngest."

"Yes," Hector said. "I saw you at your father's funeral, but you were busy."

"Right. Please, please come in. We've been . . . under a lot of pressure." Dee remembered her manners. "Would you like a glass of water? I don't know what else there is."

"Thanks, no. I just finished talking to your sister about Miz Alice."

"Come have a seat and tell me what happened."

Hector, dusty from the tractor, remained standing. Dee leaned against the kitchen counter. "Well, strange thing," he said, "your sister said maybe a truck done run into her. But your mama, she didn't say nothing about that when I found her. She was really in bad shape. I went back down there yesterday afternoon; I didn't see any skid marks or nothing. Only the tracks where she ran off the road—I can show you. And there weren't no paint smears on the car."

"We keep wondering if she blacked out or something."

Hector nodded, "Maybe. I hope she'll be okay. And if there's anything I can do for your family just let me know."

"Sure. And I hope your family is well, too."

"We are fine, thanks. Better get back to planting. Good rain this year, could be two bales to the acre."

"Hector . . . did my brother talk to you about the planting?"

"Oh, no, Miz Alice and I worked all that out. We got all the seed and everything." Hector winked. "She said she knows more about cotton than people give her credit for."

"Well, thank you for doing that, Hector." Dee said. "I guess I'll spend the night here—so don't worry if you see the lights on." She could at least get the sheets and dishes washed before Mama came home. It wouldn't take much effort—Alice Bennett had always kept a clean and uncluttered house, and aside from dealing with the ever-present West Texas dust there wasn't a lot of extra housework to be done.

The screen door slammed again as Penny walked in behind them. "You go right ahead. You couldn't pay me to stay in this sweatbox. I booked a room at the Stagecoach Inn for the weekend. Hector, didn't you say you were going to check on those terraces?"

Hector nodded good-bye and headed out the door.

"I didn't expect to see you here," Dee said to Penny. Whenever Penny and her family visited, they chose an air-conditioned motel in town over the Spartan climate control of the home place. Buddy's kids generally did whatever Penny's kids did, especially if it involved a swimming pool or video games. It was unspoken, though, that Dee and Abby, on their short and infrequent trips, would stay at the home place. Dee was sure they suspected she couldn't justify a hotel bill on top of airfare.

"Mama's sleeping again. Buddy came on back to the hospital after checking on the car. The police had it impounded, but the insurance man said the damage looked minimal."

"That's good, but—"

"In the meantime, I thought if we wanted to get serious about listing this place, I could get some measurements and start looking at comparables."

"Slow down," Dee said. "So was there a wreck or not?"

"The agent said there was no indication of impact from another vehicle," Penny said. "It's looking more and more like Mama just ran off the road. This may be the end of driving for her."

"I get it. But as for the house and farm, it might not be smart to try to sell right now," Dee countered.

"Our brokerage has been blowing and going—you may not realize I sold five *million* dollars' worth of real estate last year."

"That's the Metroplex; this is a hundred miles from the nearest Starbucks."

"I don't know about Claxton, but I'll find out," Penny said. "It always pays to have a real estate agent in the family."

"Maybe so," Dee replied, taking a long look around the room, trying to imagine it as others would see it. The red leather wagon-wheel-design sofa that Daddy had given Mama for their fortieth wedding anniversary still looked good as new. The high-backed armchair had seen better days. The plain white walls, adorned with family portraits and an assortment of grocery-store promotional prints, would impress no one. "Buddy's sleeping at the hospital again tonight?" she asked.

"Yes, and we'd better get back out there to help Mama with dinner. Before some orderly decides he's had enough and stuffs a pillow over her face."

*   *   *

As they reached the third-floor ICU room, Dee and Penny could hear a grating voice behind a clear partition and a series of curtains. Mama was talking loudly, and that was either a good sign or a bad one.

"Festus," Dee heard their mother say as though the character from the old *Gunsmoke* TV show were right there in the room.

Buddy said something she couldn't make out. Penny knocked on the glass as they entered, and said brightly, "How're you feeling, Mama?"

"Like hell. Like pure-tee hell."

"Must be the drugs," Buddy explained. "Shhh, Mama, don't wear yourself out."

Mama spoke again. "Wearin' a hat . . . like Festus," she repeated, more insistently.

"Hey, Mama," Dee said as she pulled back the curtain. Her mother's vulnerability led Dee to reach over and caress her forehead. "How are you doing?"

Mama shook away the hand and turned her head in Dee's direction with some difficulty. "I didn't realize I had died," she said.

"So glad you're better, Mama." Dee tried another tack, soothing her arm. "Thank goodness."

"No," Mama replied, turning her gaze back toward the ceiling, "I must be dead, because Dee Anna Bennett only shows up when there's a funeral."

"She's still sort of out of it," Buddy said. "I don't think—"

Penny finished his sentence. "I don't think she's fully conscious. She's still not really aware of the casts and all. Dee, why don't you visit while we grab a bite? Come on, Buddy."

"Mama, I'm going to sit with you for a while," said Dee. "Don't talk if you don't feel like it."

Mama didn't miss a beat. "That Jew from Jersey didn't come with you, did he? And what about Abigail?"

"You know Abby's in college, Mama. And you know Jacob and I aren't still—"

"I didn't like him no way."

"That's ancient history. Let's discuss something else. Have you remembered anything more about the accident?"

"Warin' a brown cowboy hat." Agitated but unable to turn over, Mama moved her head restlessly from side to side. "In a green pickup truck. That Oriental doctor—"

"Asian, Mama. Dr. Kim is Korean."

"—she said I might of broke these wrists by holding onto the steering wheel real hard in a crash. But I also might have done it falling. Said I was covered in ant bites and almost died. Guess I must've laid there a while."

"You don't remember more? What about your car, did you hit something?"

"The car . . . that's funny, the police were askin' me about the car too. And Hector."

"Hector? You were going somewhere with Hector?"

"Now Dee Anna, you know I wouldn't never ride nowhere with Hector. I was comin' out to check on the cotton. I was so glad to see . . ." Mama trailed off into silence. Dee held her breath and listened to make sure the monitor's beeping pattern hadn't changed.

Mama turned, with effort, and mumbled again. "Hector got me out of the ditch. A green truck."

This wasn't going anywhere, thought Dee. They all knew Hector drove a blue El Camino out to work the farm. Mama wasn't making any sense, and there was no need to stress her further. "It's okay. We just want you to get well. We're thankful for Hector too, and we're sure glad you're here in the hospital where they can look after you." *Until Monday, anyway.*

"Festus wore a hat. A hat like that. And Nolan Ryan."

＊　　　＊　　　＊

At eight p.m. it must've been ninety degrees still, Dee thought, as she raised windows on opposite sides of the house to let a breeze circulate. The old evaporative cooler didn't help much, and she'd probably have to leave the windows open to sleep. The thought crossed her mind that, before her father's illness, her mother had probably never spent a night alone there. Did it worry Mama to sleep with the windows open now? Or did she just keep them closed and suffer? Dee couldn't remember ever hearing about a violent crime in Claxton. Sure, there were domestic disturbances, and sometimes burglaries, but nothing scarier than that, and, as Mama would always remind them, what would anyone want to steal from an old farmer's homestead anyway?

Dee noted that the place was not as isolated as last time she'd been home—certainly not as much as when she'd grown up. A double-wide with a swing set out back now sat in the field at the bottom of the hill, across the road from the mailboxes. She took comfort in the fact that it looked to be occupied by a family and not some felon cooking meth. She wondered if her mother had met the new neighbors. Down the road the Echols house was vacant, though—Mrs. Echols had moved to the senior apartments in town after her husband died, Dee recalled.

When Dee walked to the kitchen, the floor creaked loudly. She jumped even though she knew to expect the sound. The breeze ruffled the pages of the calendar supplied by the Caprock State Bank, and Dee remembered to take care of one chore Mama would've done without fail each evening. Picking out a stub of pencil from the last, skinny kitchen drawer, she drew an X through the date, as well as the two before it—signifying days without rain. There was a green pencil in the drawer, too, to track rainy days. Most of May awaited, clean and unmarked as a spring field. Dee went ahead and penciled in "Dee in Mass." in the block for June 1. She underlined it and added *Abby.* The afternoon's conversation still stung.

She took down the phone, dialed the number Jake had given her and, tethered by the cord, headed to the refrigerator and poked around the shelves. She could sure use a nice glass of wine or a stiff vodka gimlet right about now . . . but in the teetotaling Bennett house there wasn't a chance of either.

"Hi, Mom," Abby answered instantly, her tone already forgiving.

"Hey, I just wanted to say I'm sorry about how I reacted earlier today."

"It's okay. I know you're stressed. Do you know when Gramma Alice's coming home?"

"Maybe next week. She's in traction and pretty bruised up . . . and she's going to need some help out here." Dee lifted the lid on an expired carton of cottage cheese, sniffed it, and threw it in the trash.

"How about home health care?" Abby asked. "Too expensive?"

"No, that isn't really the problem . . . but there's only one part-time person available to help right now."

"Well, that's something," Abby said. "Besides, if I know the Bennetts, you're all too stubborn to fail. You'll find a way."

"Speaking of finding a way," Dee said, as she pulled a box of macaroni noodles out of the cabinet and started water boiling on the stove, "what's this about your not going back to school this fall?"

"Mom, Smith College is just not me," she began. "There are two kinds of students here. Angry political types who don't shave their armpits, and blue-blood Smithies who clerk at the Supreme Court in the summers and whose great-grandmothers have buildings named after them."

"Okay, how about U Mass?" Dee said, setting aside her dismay.

Abby let out a long, exasperated sigh. "I just don't know if I'm college material," she continued. "The academic life works great for you and Dad. Did he tell you his news, by the way? He made chair."

"Great," Dee said weakly.

"If it makes you feel any better, he was pretty pissed too when I told him I wasn't going back," Abby said. "He practically demanded that I move back in with him and Melissa."

"Ouch," Dee said, burning her hand on the scalding water as she poured the noodles into the pot.

"What are you doing?" Abby said.

"Making dinner," Dee replied.

"What does the picture on the box look like?"

"Very funny, Miss Organic Holier-Than-Thou," Dee said. "I'll have you know I'm cooking something from scratch."

"Do tell."

"A pasta dish."

"Oh, you're boiling macaroni," Abby replied. "At least put some butter and parmesan on it. A dash of cayenne will also kick it up a bit."

"I fully admit it. You're a better cook than I am."

"That's why Chuck and I want to start our own restaurant," Abby said.

"Who's Chuck?"

"Just a friend," Abby replied, "but we have a lot of the same interests, and . . ."

"If you want to open a restaurant, then why not go to culinary school?"

"Mom, some of us don't want to spend our lives in classrooms. Sometimes the best classroom is just living."

"Sometimes you have to get credentials to *make* a decent living," Dee snapped. "Be realistic."

"I *am* realistic," Abby replied coolly. "Not idealistic."

"I'm sorry, sweetie," Dee said. "I'm tired. I have a lot on my mind, and I've got to get some rest."

"I understand, Mom. Keep me posted on Gramma Alice."

"Will do. Love you, honey," Dee said.

"Same here," Abby said, and hung up. The silent chill on the line did nothing to alleviate the stifling heat of the kitchen.

Dee found a two-liter of generic diet cola in the pantry—previously opened and flat. She poured herself a glass and took her bowl of macaroni elbows into the living room. She located the remote beside Mama's recliner, flicked on the TV, and recoiled from its sudden loudness. She reminded herself Mama would need to have her hearing aids checked. At least the satellite dish Buddy had given her parents was an improvement over the four channels they used to pick up with the roof antenna. Now, she figured Mama stayed tuned to the game shows and the Weather Channel.

She heard the front screen door slam, swing back, and slam again. Had the day's anxieties made her jumpy, or was the wind picking up again? She crept into the kitchen, found a flashlight in the pantry, and took Mama's cast-iron skillet from the stove. She tiptoed through the hall to the front door. She grabbed the knob and jerked the door open, frying pan raised.

A big yellow dog of no certain breed sauntered in, wagged its tail, and lay right down in the hallway. Dee, chiding herself for her fears, tried to usher him back out. But the dog was having none of it. He plopped to the floor, put his nose between his paws, and remained as steadfast as if he'd belonged there. Mama certainly didn't take to pets—so whose was this?

"What are you doing way out here, fella?" Dee asked. She reached for the tag on his collar. "Chester," it read. But there was no number or indication of an owner. She tried again to drag Chester out the door. But he only scratched and whined more. Dee gave up and let him stay. She latched the screen, closed the front door, and turned the old-fashioned lock behind them.

Through the open windows she could hear the coyotes howling. The sound wasn't unfamiliar to her—it just took on an eerie tone when there was no one else in the house. She patted the side of the red couch, and Chester came obligingly to her side. With the dog for company, she finished off her impromptu meal and fell asleep in front of the TV dreaming of Festus plowing the farm in a green pickup truck. Maybe tomorrow would bring a solution.

3
A Stake in the Ground

*Introduce elements of surprise into your plot early on,
to build tension and keep readers turning the page.*

DEE WOKE AT A QUARTER TO SIX to the sounds of the weekend news show and Chester whining at the kitchen door. She let the dog out and stood on the porch to admire the beauty of the sky. It had been many years since she had been up this early on her family's farm, and the purple dawn behind the silhouettes of the mesquite trees filled her with a renewed sense of awe.

She had missed the sky out here, she had to admit. Nowhere was the horizon as full of promise as in Texas. You could see forever.

When Dee had first taken her full-time teaching job at North Carolina's Walter Raleigh College in 2001, well before national rankings cast the genteel institution into the spotlight, the college's leafy rural campus was a haven for renowned writers-in-residence. The college had been better known for its scenic beauty and laid-back lifestyle than its academics. Compared to the dusty plains of West Texas, Walter Raleigh was an enchanted forest. And in a climate where jobs for new PhD's in English came along less often than a two-bales-to-the-acre crop, Dee had been grateful for the position. She'd been especially grateful it hadn't been in Texas. But sometimes, living in the green East, Dee felt a strange depression, as though the clouds and trees were closing in on her. She never told anyone how much she longed for open space and an empty spring field.

She made a pot of coffee and brought a cup back out on the porch, where she sat down in her pajamas, watched the sunrise, and jotted a description in her journal. She thought about the years she'd labored to write something worthwhile, and to teach her students the craft even as she was learning it. But she was stuck. A year-round course load sapped all her time and energy. Until the fellowship, which had certainly come at an opportune moment.

"We're in high cotton now," Pritchard had said. "*High* cotton." That was just the way he'd said it that afternoon, leaning back and lighting a cigar even though smoking had been banned in campus offices long ago. Dee couldn't tell whether he was being serious or sarcastic.

He'd sailed the magazine across his desk to her, inviting her to peruse the page with the rankings. "America's Twenty-five Most Underrated Creative Writing Programs." There it was, the money shot of Raleigh College's Old Main framed by moss-draped live oaks. Beneath the factoids and the praise for alumni authors was an alphabetical rundown of faculty, in which her name appeared second from the top: *Dee Bennett-Kaufmann, PhD, Assistant Professor.* As department chair, *J. Keith Pritchard, MFA,* came first.

Dee had passed the piece back with sincere congratulations, even if it did upstage her own good news. She showed him the award letter and told him about the residency. "It means I won't be around to teach the intro sections this summer, of course," she said to fill the silence while he read it. *For the first time in my seven years here,* she didn't say.

His expression had stuck with her. A wrinkle of a smile. Was he pleased? Or mocking her? "We-ell," he'd said in his Georgia drawl, "Dr. Dee's in high cotton too."

*   *   *

She was just getting dressed when she heard the screen door rattle. Buddy's husky voice came through it. "Dee, you here?"

"There in a minute," she yelled, zipping her jeans.

"I brought donuts."

"Well, good, because I made coffee and there's not a thing to go with it." She ushered him into the kitchen and pulled out two brown mugs, yard-sale finds from the seventies. "How's Mama?"

"Good news is," Buddy said, filling his cup, "that she's feeling better. Bad news—"

"Is that she's feeling better," Dee finished his sentence. "And she's pitching a fit to go home."

"Exactly," Buddy said. He ran his hands through his salt-and-pepper hair and gazed at his frosted cruller as if it were a playbook with directions written in code.

"Penny's there now?"

"Yes, she was feeding her breakfast. We still haven't figured out what to do—me and her both have to be back at work Monday." He yawned and stretched his lanky arms wide.

"Good donuts," Dee said. "These come from Wilson's?"

"Yes and no. It's still called Wilson's Bakery, but the Wilsons sold it to a Vietnamese couple last year."

"Winds of change are blowin'," Dee said. "When I stopped at Allsup's yesterday to gas up the rental car, it took me aback to see beer and wine in the cooler."

"I know. Hard to think of Claxton finally going wet," Buddy said.

Dee took a bite of a maple glazed. "So, what's the ETA on Mama's car?"

"I dunno, a week or so," Buddy said, "Why?"

"I need to turn in the rental this morning. Is the truck still drivable?"

"Should be. How are you with a stick shift these days?"

"Fine," Dee lied.

Wilton's '82 Ford F-150 had been fitted to run on propane, and when the original muffler had gone out, he'd replaced it with one from a junkyard. The old pickup was noisy as well as temperamental.

"Why don't you drive it a bit just to make sure it shifts okay?" Buddy said. "Then I'll bring you back out here after you return the car."

"No, I'm sure it's fine," Dee said.

"Chicken," Buddy taunted her.

"All right, all right, have it your way." She got the keys and went out to crank the truck. Buddy hopped into the passenger seat beside her. When she went to release the clutch the engine backfired, but on the second try she got it started. Dee shifted the truck into first. It lurched forward, jerking their heads against the gun rack in the back window, and jumped five yards before she could shift it into second.

Buddy snickered. "Are you sure you can do this?"

"Yes," Dee said, her lips pursed in determination. "I can handle it for a few days if I have to."

"Dee, I teach driver's ed," Buddy said. "You can't fool me. Let's work on this together, and I'll have you comfortable with the stick before I leave."

"Okay, okay," Dee said, "if you insist." It took the greater part of two hours for Dee to get the basics down. Ornery parent, strong-willed child, high-and-mighty sister, know-it-all brother—what was one more irritation in the mix?

*   *   *

When Dee and Buddy returned to the hospital, they could hear Mama's voice all the way down the hall, clear as a bell. "I am *not* selling my house and my farm. Penny, are you intending to dump me in that nursing home?"

Dee, suddenly furious, summoned Penny out into the hall. "Are you trying to kill her?" she said under her breath.

"What do you mean?" Penny said. "We agreed on this."

"We agreed to start making plans ourselves," Dee said. "But Mama will need her familiar surroundings to recuperate."

"You don't understand how bad off she was physically—even before this accident," Penny said. "You're never around. You don't know. And how long *are* you going to stay this time?"

"As long as it takes." Dee spat out the words.

"I'll believe it when I see it."

"Let's just take it slow," Dee pleaded as they returned to Mama's room.

Though still groggy from the medications, Mama spoke firmly. The position of her bound arms lent her a certain aggressive determination as well. "I want to make this perfectly clear: I do *not* plan to go to no old folks' home. It's my house, and I'll make the decisions when the time comes."

"Actually, that's not quite true," said Penny. Buddy and Dee turned to see what was coming next. "Did you ever look at Daddy's will after he died? I talked with him about it. He said he was going to put the farm in our names—us three—so the government couldn't take it when you got where you couldn't live by yourself."

"Stephanie Jean Bennett, what on earth are you talking about?" Mama struggled to raise her head, but the effort of straining her injured arms against the traction was too much, and she lay back against the pillow again.

"Just read it, Mama—you'll see it's true. You have a lifetime tenancy. But you don't own the property. If the three of us agree, we can sell at any time. And we think the time is now."

For once Alice Bennett was at a loss for words.

"You're kidding, right, Penny?" asked Dee.

"No," said Mama slowly, "I imagine she's telling the truth. Wilton always took the safe way. He didn't have an ounce of financial gumption, even if he did make sure we had a roof over our heads."

"Listen, Mama," said Dee, "no one's going to the nursing home." She forced the words out. "*I'm* going to stay with you at the farm, and you'll be able to do your rehab right here in Claxton." Penny and Buddy both turned to their younger sister. It was their turn to be struck dumb.

"I don't aim to go into no rehab either," Mama said. "Makes me sound like one of them movie stars who get in trouble with drugs and such."

Dee stood firm. "Either I stay and you do what the doctor says—or I pack up tomorrow and let Penny sell the place right out from under you. Which one's it going to be?"

Penny and Buddy waited to hear how this was going to play out. Mama glared but ceased the complaining. "How long?"

"You've got three weeks to get well. Then I'm headed for Massachusetts to see Abby—and to spend the rest of the summer at a writing fellowship."

"Writing fellowship. Hmmph. What is that, a bunch of eggheads holding hands around a typewriter and singing Kum-Ba-Yah?"

"Your choice, Alice Mo-Malice." Dee invoked the name she'd called their mother behind her back when she was a teenager. "Take it or leave it."

4
Toilet Training

*Show the reader what is happening through dialogue
and action, as in a stage play; do not tell it as though
you were reading the news on the radio.*

BY SUNDAY AFTERNOON Mama's condition had improved considerably. Sedation and sleep had done wonders, and the swelling in her face and arms had subsided. The slur in her voice was mostly gone. She was even pestering the nurse to find out if the hospital TV could get *Dancing with the Stars*. Buddy was making some headway spoon-feeding Mama carrots and mashed potatoes in small bites.

"I'll handle the front end," Buddy had told Dee when it came to Mama's feeding. "You handle the back end." Dee had thanked him sarcastically.

"She's sounding more like her old self," remarked Penny.

"Except with Tourette's," Buddy whispered to Dee. "I keep waiting for her to get us all sued for harassment." Dee sighed. Granted, their mother's bigotry was bred in the bone, but she usually had the wherewithal not to show it in public. They were discovering that under the influence she was liable to say anything.

Buddy persisted with the spoon once more. "Mama, you have to eat."

Mama shook her head. "I'm not hungry. It's okay. I've had enough. Besides, Dr. Taylor says he's sending me home tomorrow, once that chink doctor comes and puts my hard casts on," she informed them all. "They went ahead and took out the catheter this morning."

"Mama, please," exhorted Penny. "Your doctor is Koh-*ree*-an."

"All I know is, she's got slanty eyes and an attitude."

"Can you just manage 'Asian' then?"

"Whatever—I gotta go pee."

Buddy hastily pushed the call button, and they all stood waiting awkwardly in the small room. Soon a male aide, rotund and black, with dreadlocks and a sunny disposition, appeared.

"My mother needs help going to the bathroom," Dee explained.

"I ain't going with *him*," Mama said. Her vision was back in full working order, too.

"Miz Alice, I can show one of your daughters how to help you, if you'd like," he said in a Caribbean lilt.

"Okay, but I'm not going with you," Mama replied. "What's up with the pigtails? You look like a overgrown pickaninny."

Dee started to apologize, but he waved her protest away. "No worries, mon. Sticks and stones, you know."

Penny and Dee each waited for the other to volunteer. "Little sister, I'm leaving shortly—so you better learn how to do this," Penny said.

Dee gritted her teeth as the aide showed her how to grasp Mama's armpits to steady her, and she walked her to the bathroom.

"Do you have children, ma'am?" he asked Dee.

"A college-age daughter."

"Then you know how to diaper and clean up a baby. It's no different with a parent. You do it all with love," he said, again with the beatific smile. Dee wondered whether he really loved his job that much—or whether he had partaken of the patients' prescriptions.

As she gently eased Mama down on the toilet, her mother ordered them both outside. "I got a shy bladder. I'll call you when I'm done."

"It's just a different kind of potty training," the nurse said. Dee flashed back to Abby as a toddler, Jake doing his turn with child care during the daytime hours, Dee at night.

Just then Mama said loudly, to no one in particular, "I wish they hadn't sent some fat Negro up here to take care of me. Nobody takes any pride in their work anymore. I can remember when nurses wore white uniforms, white hose, white caps, all starched and pressed. Now, they all look like inmates in them slouchy scrubs. The very idea that they'd send some colored boy up here . . ." Mama's voice trailed off. "You can come on in, I'm done."

Buddy excused himself to call Roxanne and the boys.

As Dee wiped her mother's nether parts with a moistened cloth, she heard high-heeled footsteps from down the hall and a knock on the door.

"Well, Auntie, I didn't mean to catch you with your drawers down," came a voice from Dee's past.

"Good Lord," said Mama, her backside to the open door as Dee struggled to rearrange the hospital gown. "Ruby Lee?"

Ruby Lee Ransom Martinez Bargeron, née Bennett, was a redhead these days, Dee observed. The last time Dee had seen her cousin was freshman year at Baylor. Ruby Lee, blonde at the time, had been engaged to a singer in a country and western band called Backroom Banjo. Ruby Lee and her beau had taken Dee out to a club she technically wasn't old enough to enter.

"I saw Buddy out in the hall, doing his best to avoid any of these female problems," Ruby Lee said as she swept into the room, talking and hugging Dee and Penny both in one seamless gesture.

Dee continued her methodical quest to get Mama back in bed. With the aide's help, she carefully replicated the traction, pretending to study the bed's complex mechanisms while Ruby Lee and Penny caught up on the news.

Best Dee could recall, Ruby Lee was almost a decade older than Penny, which would put her, hmmm, pushing sixty. The ensemble of leopard-print capri pants, leather tank top, glittered full-length peacock-design shawl, and three-inch purple slingbacks obscured Ruby Lee's age by at least a decade.

"What are you doing here, Ruby Lee?" Mama asked. Dee felt relieved that Mama was assuming her customary role of hostess and acting more normal.

"Barge and I have just been to an estate sale in Sweetwater, and I heard from Aunt Donna that you were in the hospital so I thought I'd stop and check on you," Ruby Lee said, settling herself comfortably into the only chair in the room and never missing a beat.

"Who's running your store while you're gone?" Mama asked.

"We left Pearl in charge," Ruby Lee said as she surveyed the room. "Little sister's gotten to be real good help."

"Wow, I haven't seen Cousin Pearl since we both graduated from high school," said Dee.

Ruby Lee, always quick about social matters, said, "You all have got to come to Poplar Grove and visit us when you're feeling better! Business is really picking up, what with all the oilfield activity and the new wind energy project everyone keeps talking about. In fact, Dee and Penny, y'all look like you could use a break this minute. Why don't you go get a Coke or something, and tell Buddy that all the hygiene issues have been taken care of?"

Come to think of it, Dee realized, she was starving. She hadn't had much more than noodles and a donut since she'd arrived. "Good idea," she said.

"Well, okay," Penny agreed.

In the corridor the sisters ran into Mama's doctor giving instructions to Buddy.

"Doc says Mama can go home tomorrow as long as she has someone there to look out for her," Buddy told them.

"That's great," Penny replied.

"I'm releasing her on condition that you work with Helping Hands on the rehabilitation therapy," Dr. Taylor reminded them. "You remember she'll need constant care for three or four weeks. Maybe longer."

"My sister will be there around the clock," Penny assured him. She cast a sardonic smile in Dee's direction. "We always know we can count on her."

*   *   *

On Monday morning—after letting the faithful Chester back outside—Dee showered, then hosed down the truck and coaxed and cursed it into town, arriving at the hospital in time to intercept Mama's meal tray.

Mama was still asleep. Dee gently nudged her. "Breakfast's here."

"Where's Buddy?" Mama mumbled, as she stirred, blinked her eyes, and motioned for Dee to get her eyeglasses.

"In Darrell, back at school," Dee said. "I'm going to be the one feeding you when we get home—thought we both better get used to it."

The large black nurse showed up with Mama's meds.

"Hello, Raul, how are you?" Mama said.

"Just fine, Mary Alice. And good to see you looking so gorgeous!" he replied, without a trace of irony.

"Raul's from the Bahamas," Mama said. "You remember my daughter Dee Anna?" Dee was struck with how Mama's manner could go from racist to gracious in a flash, but she'd always been that way. "He grew up on a sugar cane farm," Mama continued as he put a paper cup of pills and then some water to her lips.

Dee picked up the bowl of oatmeal and thrust the spoon in the general direction of Mama's mouth.

"Ha," Mama said, taking a bite of the cereal. "As soon as I get home, this contraption's coming off and I'm feeding myself."

"Now, Mama," Dee said, "you and I both know that's probably not a good idea."

"For several weeks, anyway," Dr. Taylor said as he entered on his rounds. "With wrist injuries like yours, we'll schedule you a checkup for X-rays, and then, when everything heals like it's supposed to, Dr. Kim will remove the casts. You won't have to be in traction once you leave the hospital, but we'll be fitting you with special slings to achieve the same effect."

"Sounds good," Dee said.

"Easy for you to say," Mama replied. "Try sleeping with your arms stuck out like this."

"We'll give you a mild sedative for sleep, Mrs. Bennett," the doctor said, "and we'll continue your painkillers, but we want to wean you off them soon."

Without Penny and Buddy to help, it took two nurses, one orderly, and Dee to maneuver Mama from bed to wheelchair, down the elevator, and into Daddy's pickup truck. Fortunately there wasn't much traffic on the Claxton courthouse square that early on a Monday morning, because the truck cut out every time Dee came to a stop. But it was only as they turned off the highway onto the farm road that Dee realized she hadn't given any thought to how she was going to get Mama out of the truck and into the house by herself.

As she slowed down to pull into the driveway, a red pickup passed them. Its driver waved, then did a U-turn.

"Who's that, Mama?"

"My new neighbor, Buck Turlock," Mama replied. "He lives in town, but he bought the Echols place, and he rents out that trailer house on it. He's got his finger in a lot of pies—a restaurant, and the tanning salon, and a bunch of other things, if I remember right."

"Oh, yeah . . . and didn't he date Penny in high school?" Dee said.

"Penny chased after him, but she never caught him," Mama said, chuckling. "He was a bit older than her. And even more conniving."

The red pickup pulled up beside them at the gate.

A husky man in a John Deere ball cap, Dickies work shirt, and Levi's stepped out. Dee rolled down her window. "Hey, Alice," the man shouted across her, "glad to see you're out of the hospital."

"Thank you, Buck. This is my youngest daughter, Dee Anna," Mama replied, leaning up as best she could, winded just from the effort it had taken to sit upright for the long ride.

"Y'all need some help?"

Mama started to shake her head no, but Dee replied quickly, "We'd really appreciate that."

Buck opened the gate for them and followed them to the top of the hill, where Dee parked as close to the door as the high grass would allow. Buck came around and opened Mama's door, then gently lifted her by her hips into the wheelchair that Dee had retrieved from the bed of the truck. Dee assisted awkwardly with her mother's immobilized arms. Between her and Buck, they managed to lift the chair up onto the porch and roll it into the living room.

"Thank you so much," Dee said, after Mama was comfortably seated on the couch with her arms supported on a pillow, and shook his hand. "I'm not sure we could have done it without you."

"Don't mention it," he said. "Glad to help."

"Would you like a cup of coffee?" she offered.

"Well, yes, ma'am, I would, if you don't mind," he said. "My first one's long since wore off."

"Have a seat, Buck," Mama said, motioning to Daddy's recliner. "I'm still purty weak and not much company, but we can visit a short spell."

"Looks like you and Hector have started on the cotton this year."

"He was fixing to plant that day I . . . that day of the accident," Mama said, "but I'm worried if we don't get rain soon, it'll just burn up."

"Ain't that the truth?" Buck said, and thanked Dee for the cup of coffee.

Dee excused herself to go unpack Mama's bag and get her medications set up, while Mama and her guest discussed boll weevil prevention and co-op gin politics. Mama complained about the hospital and the hot weather. But then Dee heard Buck say something that drew her back into the room.

"Well, Alice, when I found out you were in the hospital, I started wondering if this place might be getting to be too much for you."

Mama sat erect, reenergized and wary. Dee pretended to straighten a copy of *TV Guide* on the coffee table, but silently bristled at Buck's suggestion. This guy had some nerve to come in here and try such a blatant land grab. Dee started to intercede, but Buck kept talking.

"Not that I'm saying it is," Buck backtracked, registering Mama's reaction. "But maybe, if you ever decide you want to live the good life in town or something, you'd give me a chance to make an offer on the place."

Mama remained stoic.

"Down the road, you know." Buck continued to try to extricate himself from the mess he'd made.

Mama's lips were set tight. She managed a cool "We'll see."

Buck stood awkwardly and pulled his cap on hard. "Well, it's good to see you back home, and thanks for the coffee." He did a little bow of good-bye, and Mama acknowledged his gesture with a regal nod of her head.

"Thank you again for your help," Dee said as she walked him to the door.

Mama yelled after them, "Dee Anna, I have to go. It's urgent."

Okay, show time, Dee thought. "Be right there." She latched the screen door as Buck Turlock's pickup headed down the hill.

Mama and Dee's first foray to the bathroom was like a quick-step tango on *Dancing with the Stars*, minus the sequins. Mama rested her bound arms on Dee's shoulders, and they shuffled around the coffee table until Mama could get her balance. Dee guided her around the corner, switched sides to get through the doorway, then dipped her down onto the toilet.

Mama positioned herself, unsure what to use to prop her elbows on, while Dee pulled down her mother's elastic-waist pants. She left the room to give her mother whatever semblance of dignity could be preserved, and when she was done they performed the moves in reverse to get her to the couch again.

*   *   *

The morning's activities had been exhausting for both of them. In between warming up soup for lunch, doing repeat numbers of the bathroom dance, and getting Mama into bed for a nap, Dee at last tried to turn her attention to her professional chores.

First was the issue of Internet access. With sixty-odd composition exam grades to post plus the creative writing stories to read and her own magazine column to file, she was going to require considerable connection time. The local satellite communications company proved uncommunicative and unhelpful on the phone. After being transferred half a dozen times and holding for twenty minutes of the firm's maddening sales jingle, Dee learned that she would need to sign a two-year contract for service and order a special wireless card for her laptop computer—to be installed at the first available appointment ten days later. Dial-up with the phone company was more economical but no speedier on installation. Cable wasn't an option out in the country.

Frustrated and weary, she relinquished any hope of Internet at the farm. She'd have to find a way to get to town and try her chances there. Surely someone in Claxton, Texas, had heard of Wi-Fi?

Dee raised the living room window, stretched out on the couch, and soon fell into a fitful sleep. She found herself back in Jacob Kaufmann's philosophy course in the early nineties, students flocking from classroom to barroom—and some to bedroom, it was rumored—with the popular young professor. What a wild scene it had been back then, even at Baptist Baylor.

The dorm room was muggy with spring humidity, though a breeze blew through the open third-floor window. Casey Sparks, her roommate during senior year, was leaning out to make sure the smoke from her illicit joint went outside rather than in. God, they'd be *so* busted! Dee didn't partake—her Claxton upbringing had stuck firm—but Casey said the funniest things when she was high, and Dee couldn't help giggling right alongside her. Prince was playing on the boom box. *Party like it's nineteen-ninety-nine.* The door to the girls' tiny double room opened, and there stood Jake Kaufmann, exotic in his black leather jacket and dark curls, and instead of beckoning to Casey, the drop-dead-gorgeous blonde, he walked over to where tall, plain, brown-haired Dee Bennett stood on tiptoe lining up her books precisely on the shelf above her desk. *I was dreamin' when I wrote this, so sue me . . .* He laid his head against her shoulder blade, then reached his arms around her waist, sliding his hands under the wide rhinestone belt that was looped through her tight jeans, and right about that moment she heard a voice from the hallway.

"Dee Anna? Come here, I need you."

Dee shook herself awake from the bizarre fantasy and reoriented herself to her surroundings. Mama was calling her name. Must be bathroom time again. And what a crazy thing to imagine, Jake in their residence hall. She did wonder for a moment whatever became of Casey Sparks. She roused herself and went to Mama's room.

Dee thought back to the day she'd driven here with Jake, all the way from Waco in his vintage Karmann Ghia, so he could meet her parents. That hadn't gone so well. Mama and Daddy hadn't liked the idea of Dee dating Jake, not one bit. They didn't like his religion, they didn't like his age, they didn't like his looks, and they didn't like the way he carried on with their daughter. In a fit of pique Mama had flung herself on this same bed and lay there crying for an hour. Daddy sat on the old brown couch and responded in monosyllables to Jake's attempts at conversation. When Mama rose to cook a spiteful dinner of pork chops and watery mashed potatoes, Dee remembered, the pattern of the chenille bedspread still showed on the side of her face like an angry handprint.

But Jake had said he'd take her to places far away from Texas, and he made good on the promise. After skipping a wedding ceremony with either set of parents, they married in the McLennan County courthouse the week after her graduation, then flew to Paris with only what they could carry in their backpacks. There they visited the sites of the Enlightenment and the Revolution, went to museums on free days, wrote in their journals, and got drunk at the grave of Jim Morrison. They rented a third-floor apartment in the 2nd arrondissement and lived on baguettes and cheese and red *vin de table.* And by the time they returned to the States at the end of August, Dee was pregnant.

As if she'd tapped directly into Dee's reverie, Mama asked through the half-open bathroom door, "What do you hear from Abby?"

"She asked about you."

"She started up that restaurant yet?" Dee crossed her arms and leaned against the wall. It rankled that Abby always told any news to her grandmother first.

"I guess I'll see when I get there, won't I?" replied Dee.

"She told me about that writing fellership of yours too. Now, if you'll come take me to the couch, maybe you can help me get back to sleep."

Dee flushed the toilet and hoisted her mother to her feet again. "I didn't know you were having trouble," she said with concern, glad to be useful. "What can I do?"

"Just tell me about what you're writin'."

Dee rolled her eyes but complied. After getting Mama settled in with a pillow under her arms and a crocheted throw over her legs, she went to her bedroom and brought out the folder she'd packed in her suitcase. "In my line of work they say 'show, don't tell,' Mama, so I'm going to show you what a work-in-progress looks like." She undid the elastic band and set the four-inch-thick stack of paper, riddled with Post-its and paper clips, on the coffee table. "'G. H. Templeton: A Writer at Work.'"

Mama frowned. "So that's what you've been doin' for seven years?"

"Well, more than that, actually," Dee admitted, unsure whether her mother remembered that Templeton had been the topic of her dissertation. "But this isn't all I've been writing, of course."

"That's what I hear."

Dee had long ago given up talking with her family about her work, since their lack of enthusiasm always defeated her. She was sure Abby had told them about the magazine pieces and the awards. "Look, I don't get much time for research since I teach every summer. I can't just do this from my desk—I've got to travel to libraries and archives to fill in the gaps."

Mama was still glaring at the stack of papers like it might bite. "Lord, how big could the gaps be?"

"I guess it's hard to grasp," Dee said, forcing patience. "You recall that the story is about a woman who taught creative writing before it was trendy—in the 1930s? But since she wasn't very famous, it's hard to know much about her life or choices, or how she even became a teacher. In my dissertation it was okay to speculate and leave the answers for future researchers. Now, if I'm going to turn this into a book, I *am* the future researcher."

"Mmm," said Mama. "I see. Couldn't you just pick something easier, like Stephen King or Shakespeare?"

Dee sighed. Could she really expect to make her mother understand what that rush of discovery had been like? How it had changed her life?

It was back in the fall of 1999, when Jake had asked Dee—by then pursuing a doctorate and teaching three sections of freshman English in addition to handling a steady freelance editing gig—to come along with him to a lecture he'd been invited to give in Boston. They could leave Abby with a faculty colleague for a few days, he suggested, and surely she could get someone to cover her classes. They hadn't had a real vacation since moving from Waco to Chapel Hill, where he'd taken a tenure-track job and was immersed in cranking out his own book.

After the lecture they'd driven out to Concord and Worcester and Amherst in the rental car, then back to spend their last day in Cambridge. Massachusetts fascinated her. Not only the home of the early Colonial writers but the Transcendentalists, and Emily Dickinson, and so many centuries of history. And Harvard, whose walkways they wandered and libraries they explored.

In one of Harvard Square's closet-sized secondhand bookstores, Dee had come across a slim hardcover volume, missing its dust jacket, but with its title stamped in gold on the front and spine along with the author's name: *The Working Writer,* by G. H. Templeton. As a teaching assistant and freelance journalist herself, Dee was intrigued with the book, and though its 1939 publication date didn't bode well for relevance in the digital age, she bought it as a souvenir. For good measure, it had been signed by the author. Dee plunked down eighteen dollars for it, the rest of their week's dining budget.

But as she read the book on the plane coming home, its pithy, slightly antiquated prescriptions stuck with her. Templeton had compiled advice for a cadre of practicing writers who aspired to something higher than journalism, something not quite literature but just as engaging. He hit the right note with his essays on "A Sense of Place" and "Getting It Right." Not so much a textbook as a collection of brief lessons informing the writing life, the book became her touchstone. Dee found herself adopting parts of it for her classes and using its guidelines to improve her own work. And soon she realized she'd hit on a perfect topic for her dissertation: "creative writing" before its time.

Who was this G. H. Templeton? her adviser asked. No one he'd heard of. Dee launched a research plan that drew on her journalist's instincts but severely tested her sleuthing skills. Why did Templeton seem to have no other books to his name? Why was there no listing for him in the *Dictionary of Literary Biography* or *About the Author*? Why were his letters and papers not in evidence in any archive?

She stumbled upon the answer one day in the microfilm room, following a lead from the newspaper obituaries index. There, in the *Boston Globe,* a two-inch item from 1982: Gineva Templeton Jensen, born Boston, Massachusetts, 1908, a graduate of Abbot Academy and Emerson College (class of '29), essayist, writer of travelogues, and teacher of writing at Mills College, preceded in death by parents James Sprague Templeton and Minerva Jane Holland Templeton of Boston and husband Allan Day Jensen of San Francisco, California. If it hadn't been for the coincidence of surnames in the index she'd never have found it. G. H. Templeton was an unsung author—and a woman.

In relating the story to her mother, Dee left out most of the details. The more carefully you kept your counsel, she had learned, the less ammunition you provided for ridicule. "So do you see how perfect the Berkshires Fellowship is, Mama?" she asked, removing her reading glasses and placing the transcription of the obituary back on the table. "I can write all day and night if I want, and take the train into Northampton or Cambridge to work in manuscript collections whenever I need to. I have no teaching obligations except a critique of the other writers' work. Plus I'll be only twenty minutes from Abby."

No answer was forthcoming.

"Mama?" Dee repeated. Dee looked over to see that her mother made no movement from her sitting position, her immobilized arms propped on her pillow like those of a genie about to cast a spell, her breathing slow and regular and her eyes shut.

5
Helping Hands

Ignite your writing with interesting characters,
whose motivations may be noble, flawed, diabolical, or,
best of all, inscrutable.

DEE WOKE EARLY, just as the morning light was peeking through the bedspring fence outside her window. By eight o'clock she'd helped Mama out of bed, dressed her, brushed her teeth, and combed her hair. Chester the dog hadn't shown the previous night. Just as well, Dee thought, as she wondered whether he'd be safer out in the wild or facing Mama's wrath.

They sat down to a breakfast of oatmeal and coffee, which Dee alternated serving Mama and then herself. They expected the new home health worker at nine—and Dee was determined not to be found derelict in her duty.

At 9:15 the phone rang. "Hey, M. Alice Bennett?" the voice on the other end said.

"This is her daughter, Dee."

"Cool, this is Toni Tyner from Helping Hands Home Health, and I think I must have made a wrong turn or something. Are you guys really ten miles outside of town?"

"Yes," Dee replied. "Two miles past the gin off of FM 3425."

"Okay, cool, are you a white house on top of a hill?"

"Yes; are you nearby?"

"Okay, got it—I was right, I did make a wrong turn—I mean, I was wrong and made a right turn . . . well, anyway, I kept trying to call to verify the address, and then I had to come nearly all the way back to town to get GPS on my phone," said Toni Tyner. "There in a bit."

About fifteen minutes later, Dee peeked through the curtains in the hall entryway and could see a Volkswagen Beetle bouncing up the road and come to a halt in the front yard. A petite woman with spiked, nearly white hair, sporting polka-dotted scrubs, threw a cigarette butt on the ground and stubbed it out with the blunt end of her plastic clog shoe. Over her shoulder was slung a messenger-style bag. She picked her way through the grass, which seemed half as tall as she was, to the porch steps.

Before the visitor could waste time looking for the bell, Dee opened the door. "Glad you found us," she said as she showed the visitor into the living room. "Mama, meet your home health care aide, Toni Tyner— may we call you Toni?—and this is my mother, Alice Bennett."

Before the newcomer could say hello, Mama, with one glance over her glasses, blurted out, "Whew, do you smoke?"

Toni responded just as directly. "Yep, bummer, huh? Trying to quit." She sized up her new patient. "So, what happened to you, doll?"

"Long story," Mama answered.

"Gotcha," Toni said. "I bet you're sick of telling it."

Mama seemed to appreciate Toni's perceptiveness.

"As I'm sure Mitzi has told you," Dee said, "we're going to need help lifting Mrs. Bennett to go to the bathroom, getting her dressed, feeding her, and that sort of thing. It takes two of us just to help her stand up."

"Hon, why don't you have a lift chair? All my other clients in traction have them. That way the patient can raise themselves. I mean, you still have to wipe their butts and chins, if you know what I mean."

Mama didn't. "I don't need to spend money on nothing like that. This is temporary."

"No, you don't get it," said Toni. "Medicare will pay for it, if your doctor tells them to. It doesn't cost you a dime."

"Thanks for the suggestion, Toni. My mother and I will talk about it later."

"Okay, whatever," Toni said.

"In the meantime, why don't I show you around the place, and tell you where everything is?"

Toni turned to Mama and said loudly, "Don't worry, Allie, we'll have you up and boogyin' in no time."

Mama replied, "My hearing is fine. And the name's Alice."

"Oooohhh," Toni said. "Tough one here. Yes, ma'am."

Mama ignored the remark and returned her attention to Regis and Kelly on the TV set.

Dee took Toni around to the kitchen, Mama's bedroom, and the bathroom. She went over the physical therapy flyer that outlined Mama's finger and arm exercises. Dee grew annoyed that Toni was only half listening, stopping every few seconds to thumb-type into her fancy cell phone.

"Did you catch everything?" Dee finally said pointedly. "You might as well not bother with that. No one gets a signal out here."

"Whatever," Toni replied.

"I have to go to the bathroom," Mama said angrily, spitting out the words when they returned to the living room.

"No problem," Toni said, "I've got this one." Dee took notice of the dragon tattoos that covered both of Toni's arms as the slight woman easily helped raise Mama's 150-pound frame from the couch. To Dee's surprise, she accomplished this without inflicting pain or disturbing the casts, and led Mama calmly into the bathroom.

In a few minutes Toni escorted Mama back down the hallway and eased her onto the couch. Toni picked up her cell phone again. "Awesome. I texted Dr. Taylor's assistant, and she said the office will fax the Medicare authorization on the lift chair for you guys. Give me the word, and they'll bring it out on Thursday. I can show you how to use it."

"I wish you hadn't done that on your own," Dee said. "We're not sure it's the way to go."

"Will I really be able to get up and down by myself?" Mama asked.

"If I'm lying, I'm dying," Toni said, dramatically crossing her heart with her hand.

"If it keeps everybody and their dog from handling me like a sack of potatoes," said Mama, "then I'm for it."

"Fine," Dee said, but gave Toni a look to let her know that she was on warning.

*   *   *

The medical supply firm delivered the chair Thursday as promised. Toni arrived on time and showed Dee and Mama how it worked. Mama had regained enough mobility in her exposed fingers to press the chair's remote control with a bit of effort, and the seat slowly tilted enough that she could get to her feet on her own.

"See," Toni said, "this simplifies potty patrol significantly. Sure, we still have to help you drop your drawers, and do the cleanup on Aisle 1 and Aisle 2, but you get yourself there and that's half the battle."

Mama suppressed a smile despite herself. "Do you always talk that way?" she said to Toni.

"What way?" Toni replied, grinning. "Shoot, I'm on my best behavior for you, Allie Baby." Toni picked up the television remote. "Do y'all ever watch Tyra?" she asked as she flipped on the set and started changing channels.

"How about some coffee?" Dee said, expecting that, since she had showed her around the kitchen yesterday, Toni would make a pot.

"Love some. What about you, Alice?"

Dee went to make the coffee, and Toni and Mama settled in to watch the talk show. Dee, meantime, had a pressing problem to solve.

"Toni," she said, "I need to find a place in town that has Internet access. Do you know of one?"

"Not sure," Toni said. "Might try Java Jim's on the south side of the square."

"Do you think you could watch Mama for a couple of hours by yourself while I go into town and check my e-mail?"

"No problem," Toni assured her. "We're good, aren't we, Alice?"

"Thanks," said Dee. "I shouldn't be gone long, one way or the other. I'd give you my cell number, but it's out of commission until I pick up another charger. If anything comes up, just use the house phone. All the emergency numbers are right there beside it in the address book, including my brother's and sister's."

*   *   *

Dee's search led her to see Claxton in a whole new light. Like her mother, her hometown was aging—with new caretakers seeing it through the transition. Dee passed Pablo's Package Store and saw the Vietnamese couple through the window at Wilson's Bakery, and as she circled the courthouse square in first gear looking for Java Jim's, she felt a sense of sadness at the change in the makeup of Main Street. When she was growing up, there had been multiple shoe stores, a hardware store, a jeweler's shop, a barbershop and two beauty parlors, a fine department store and a not-so-fine department store, a five-and-dime, and a bridal shop where the gown for Penny's wedding to her first husband, the mechanic, had been purchased. By husband number two, the car salesman, Penny had moved to Dallas and the gown and the spouse had come from Las Colinas, but that was another story. Claxton's bridal emporium, in any case, was no more. Dee snapped back to the present.

Now the center of Claxton was occupied by bail bondsmen, finance companies, second-hand shops, a storefront church, and the coffee hangout. Vacant display windows had been decorated with Claxton High School colors and slogans like "Go Cougars Baseball: On to State!" Dee had wondered why everything Mama bought these days came from Walmart out on the highway. She had just assumed Mama was cheap—but now she saw that the options had become pretty limited.

After managing to coerce the pickup into a diagonal parking space, Dee headed into Java Jim's, laptop in hand. The coffee shop was empty at eleven in the morning. Two baristas stood with their backs turned to the counter. Dee could hear their conversation. "I was so wasted that I actually asked him—"

Dee coughed politely. Both employees turned around, startled.

"Can we help you?" the guy said.

"Do you have a Wi-Fi connection here?" Dee asked.

"We wish," the girl answered.

"That would be a 'no', I suppose."

One server nodded her head; the other shook his.

"Do you know where I could *find* Wi-Fi?" Dee said.

"Maybe they could tell you at the Radio Shack, which is one block up on the left." At least Dee now knew where she could buy a phone charger.

"Or the library—maybe they would know at the library," the girl said.

"The library!" Dee said. "That's great. Of course the public library would have Internet access."

"They do?" the guy replied.

"Yes, most likely," Dee said. "Thanks."

Dee cranked the truck again, backed out with some difficulty, and drove to the Caprock County Public Library, three blocks away. The library patrons' parking lot was completely unoccupied. Dee was relieved to see that she could simply pull in parallel to the curb, where she wouldn't have to struggle with reverse again when it was time to go.

Dee was also happy to see that the old single-story Austin-stone library building, her beloved after-school hangout, looked well tended and much as she remembered it. She rushed up the short flight of steps and through the heavy glass doors. A librarian was standing at the counter, ready to help her. What a blessing the public library was!

Before Dee could open her mouth, the woman asked, "Is that your truck?"

Dee thought the question odd, since the inquirer had obviously watched her get out of it—why ask something you knew the answer to?—but that sort of circuitous conversation was the West Texas way.

"You have to diagonal park," the librarian said. "We don't allow parallel parking."

Dee was flummoxed. "Oh. No one else is here. And I didn't see any markings."

"It doesn't matter. You need to re-park or leave."

"Okay," Dee said, elongating the last syllable. Rules were a necessary part of life—no one subscribed to that philosophy more strongly than Dee—but they should be logical and clearly stated. "Before I go to—" she used her fingers to make air quotation marks—"'re-park,' can you tell me if I can access the Internet here?"

"Do you have a library card?" the woman responded.

"No," Dee said, "I don't live here."

"You can't use the computers or the Internet without a library card."

"Then I need to get a library card."

"You can't get a card if you don't live here," the woman said, as another librarian emerged from the office behind her to greet the mail carrier and sign for a package. "But if you fill out this form, we can give you a temporary pass, which allows you to use the Internet for thirty minutes. You can do that after you re-park your vehicle."

Dee looked over as the other staffer took the slack of mail. "Cynthia?" she called out tentatively.

The librarian set down the mail and came around the counter. "Dee—Dee Anna Bennett?"

"Cynthia Vandever?"

"Well, it's Cynthia Philpott now," she answered, enfolding Dee in a long-lost-friend hug. "Gladys," Cynthia said to her re-park colleague, "Dee and I went to high school together."

Gladys seemed less than impressed. "She still needs to move her truck."

"Let's see," Dee said to Cynthia, "if I graduated in '87, that means you were class of '89."

"We were fine as wine in '89, y'all were just like heaven in '87!"

"Gosh, I had forgotten those slogans," Dee said. "I believe you were the only sophomore we allowed to work on the yearbook staff, weren't you?" She barely remembered Cynthia, but she'd say whatever it took at this point to be granted computer access. "You were always such a good writer. I guess that's why you're here at the library—with your own office and everything."

"Yes," Cynthia blushed, "I *am* head librarian. I mean, I'm not teaching at a university or anything like you are. We keep up with you in Claxton, Dee—you're one of our more illustrious alumni."

"What do you mean?" Dee said, genuinely surprised.

"I mean you have your PhD and you're living on the East Coast, and you're married to this Ivy Leaguer—"

Dee interrupted her. "*Was* married."

"I'm sorry," Cynthia said. "I didn't know."

"It was a while back. No big deal."

"But mostly I've kept up with your writing career. I've read a lot of your columns. Didn't you get published in the *Midwestern Review* recently, too?" Cynthia said. "I saw that on WordsWire.com."

"Yes, well, I had an essay published there once."

"And your mother said you had a book contract," she continued.

"Well, I'm revising my dissertation for publication, but that hardly—"

Cynthia gushed on without letting her finish. "So, I heard you're in town for a while to take care of your mother—I go to church with Mitzi from Helping Hands. How's your mom doing?"

"Better," Dee said.

"Sorry about Gladys," Cynthia whispered. "Don't worry about moving your dad's truck. You used to drive it in high school, remember?"

Dee grimaced and nodded. "Listen, Cynthia, I need some library assistance."

"Sure," Cynthia said, adjusting her glasses and sweater set.

"I need to use the Internet," Dee explained. "My students have to send in their final assignments by e-mail, and since I'm going to be here for a few days, I need to download them and take them home to start grading."

"Say no more," Cynthia said. "Come into my office and we'll get you fixed right up. If you have a flash drive"—Dee nodded to indicate she'd thought of that—"you can download everything here, then take your files to the printer out in the main reading room."

Dee threw a wan smile over her shoulder toward Gladys, who pointedly ignored it.

Getting into the university's remote-access e-mail program was easy once Cynthia set up a user account for Dee, and while Dee saved attachments and sent acknowledgments to each student, Cynthia said, "You know, I'm leading a writers' group, too."

"Really," said Dee, typing even faster.

"We only started back in March, but we've had very enthusiastic attendance."

"Good for you," Dee said, hoping she sounded sincere and attentive as she tried to make sure she didn't miss a download.

"I had a book of poems published."

"Congratulations—that's great." Her eyes focused firmly on the computer screen, and her fingers moved as quickly as she could manage.

"Well, I published it myself, really. It wasn't very expensive. But the account representative said it was one of the best self-published books he'd ever seen."

"That's terrific." Dee logged out and turned to leave, but Cynthia had her hemmed in.

"I was wondering if you would come speak to our writers' group while you're here," Cynthia said. "We meet Tuesday nights at six."

Dee earnestly considered the request. "I'd love to, but I can't leave Mama alone at night. We have Helping Hands only for a few hours during the day."

Cynthia contemplated Dee's answer, then clapped her palms together. "I know! We can come to your house. We're a small group, only seven or eight of us. It might be a good diversion for you, too."

"Well, I sort of have my hands full—"

"Besides, you're the closest thing that Claxton has ever had to a literary star."

It had been a long time since anyone had called Dee a literary star. Never, in fact. She found herself agreeing despite her better sense. "Okay then," Dee said, "I'll look forward to it. See y'all Tuesday night. You know how to find our place, don't you?"

It took Dee a good half hour longer to print out all the papers for marking and go through her inbox. Her feeling of triumph over Gladys and the Internet was short-lived when she considered the contents of her e-mail. Most were the usual sort. Spam, billing reminders, a note from Abby from a week ago telling her what she already knew by now about her daughter's future plans. A student asking for a reference. Rob. *Hope your doing ok. Kayak trip was great, but it sure wasn't as much fun at that B&B without you.* She gasped. She'd hardly given Rob a thought all week, and she typed out a quick response to let him know what was going on.

But there were two other messages that gave her even more pause.

Dear Professor Bennett-Kaufmann,

I'm writing on behalf of your editor, Susan Sterns, who is out of the country until May 26, to confirm that she has scheduled your book "G. H. Templeton: A Writer at Work" for next spring season. Since she has reminded us that timing is critical for you, and was unable to reach you before she left, I am attaching a tentative production schedule for the project. Ms. Sterns expects to check in with you upon her return. We both look forward to receiving your manuscript draft soon.

Best wishes,
Mason Walker, Editorial Intern

*   *   *

Dee, did your editor find you? Took the liberty of giving her assistant your contact info.

Hope all is well in Texas.
JKP

*   *   *

Dee felt conflicted as she left the library. She was immensely relieved to access her students' papers and avert immediate professional disaster. Yet she could clearly see the potential for a larger catastrophe, her career hanging on a precipice.

And maybe worse, she still had to go home and inform Mama that eight strangers would be showing up at the house next Tuesday night.

*   *   *

When Dee returned to the home place there was no VW Beetle in sight. Mama was alone in her chair in the living room, watching Dr. Phil on TV. Her face was a storm cloud.

"I wet my pants," Mama said sullenly. "I didn't know what else to do. I got myself up and walked down the hall, but I couldn't manage to get my britches down."

"What?! Where's Toni?"

"She left fifteen minutes after you did and said she'd be right back," Mama said, "but I haven't seen her since."

"Mama, I am so sorry. . . I don't know what's going on, but I'll find out."

Dee opened the back door to look around and smelled smoke. Under the grape arbor a patch of dry grass was smoldering, wisps of orange flame shooting up toward the posts of the makeshift structure and blowing toward the house. She ran to turn on the garden hose full force, wrestling it through the weeds until she could get the spray within range. She drenched the smoking sod for a good ten minutes. Walking over the charred ground, she found the remains of a Marlboro butt.

Just then the Beetle came bouncing up the hill. Dee threw down the hose and marched toward the car. Toni opened the door and stepped out with a sheepish gesture. "Man, I apologize," she began. "I had to go pay my power bill or they were going to cut me off. I didn't think it would take so long, and —"

Dee held up her hand to stop her. "Toni, you left Mama alone—*totally alone*," Dee said.

"Not for very long," Toni protested.

"She could have fallen, or worse. She was your responsibility."

"But—" Toni tried to explain.

Again Dee shut her up. "Not to mention that you started a wildfire. What on earth were you thinking?"

"Omigod," Toni said, "I had no—"

"We won't be needing your services anymore," Dee told her. "This isn't going to work out. We'll contact Helping Hands to make other arrangements."

The aide's mood swung from repentant to angry. "Fine, you can clean up that crazy woman's shit all by yourself," she said.

"Go, Toni—go *now*," Dee said, her voice rising.

"Gladly," she said, adding "bitch" before slamming her car door and bumping back down the hill.

Dee walked weakly into the house, wiping droplets of water from her green linen blouse. What if she'd taken just a little longer at the library? She couldn't think about the possibilities.

"I just fired Toni Tyner," Dee informed her mother.

"Good riddance," Mama said. "Best thing about her was this chair." She patted the armrest with her fingertips. "Don't need nobody in here anyway."

Dee went for a towel and a change of clothes to help address the next most pressing need. After tugging one pair of pants and underwear off her mother's bottom half and another on, and cleaning up the chair, Dee was not only wet from the garden hose but drenched in sweat as well. "Mama," she said, "I don't think I can handle what you need by myself—if something were to happen, and you were to fall, or . . ." Dee wasn't sure how to finish that sentence, so she said, "I just think it makes sense to get help if we can. Or maybe consider the rehab hospital."

"Is it you *cain't* handle it or you don't *want* to handle it?" Mama said.

Dee started to respond, but the phone rang and interrupted her retort. She dragged herself up off the floor. "Hello?" she answered.

"Mrs. Bennett-Kaufmann, this is Mitzi from Helping Hands. Our employee has asked to be relieved from her assignment with you. Is there a problem?" Dee could hear the chill in her voice.

"You bet there's a problem." When Dee laid out the story, Mitzi's tone softened. "So do you have anyone else who could help out—*without* burning down my mother's house?"

"Well, since you put it that way . . . there's a new girl who's just cleared screening. This would be her first assignment with us. She's very quiet and young and doesn't speak perfect English, though she does seem very capable. We'll try one more time, but our agency might not be a good fit for you," Mitzi said.

"I understand," Dee replied. "Let's see if we can't make it work this time."

"Her name is Teresa Rivera. It says here she does not have a car of her own, although I don't think that is absolutely critical in your case; she gets a ride to and from work assignments with family. She can start Monday."

Mama was less than thrilled when Dee relayed the news. "Oh great, just what I need, some hitchhikin' Meskin comin' into my house trying to tell me what to do. I guess beggars can't be choosers, though. I know you don't want the responsibility at all, so at least this gives you some relief."

"Mama, that's not true," Dee protested. "It's just that I have to finish grading papers and posting finals for my job, and I have to figure out a way to do that from here. But that won't keep me from taking care of you. I promised I would help, and I will."

"I know you'll be relieved when it's done," Mama said.

The only thing that gave Dee relief was knowing that in two and a half weeks she'd be out of here. Why had Mama always been so intractable? Why couldn't she be thankful for her good fortune? Why couldn't they just get along?

*   *   *

Mama had Dee put her to bed early, and Dee went back to the pickup to retrieve the papers she'd left in the haste of the afternoon's events. The wind had settled down some, and the sky was nearly black, the moon hanging like a single parenthesis mark in the sky. When she opened the truck, the door of the glove compartment bounced open. There were her father's leather work gloves—he really *did* keep them there, she thought—and a pack of Doublemint chewing gum, a tube of Blistex, and a Buck Owens cassette. All just as he had left them.

Dee sat in the darkened truck. Tears started to come, and once they came, they wouldn't stop. She wasn't sure what she felt—grief for her father, sadness for her mother's misery, or pity for herself. She didn't know what to make of her daughter's headstrong choices, either, how to advise or guide with so much distance between them.

As she climbed back up the stairs into the house, the phone rang. Abby, psychic.

"Hi, Mom, what are you doing?"

"I was outside sitting in PaPa's truck."

"Why?" Abby said.

"Well, I've been driving it," Dee replied.

"You, driving a stick shift? That I would like to see." Then, turning more solicitous, she said, "I just wanted to call and see how you're holding up."

It was therapeutic for Dee to tell all about the student papers, the library, Toni, the fire, missing her father. Abby howled at the way Dee portrayed the hapless Helping Hands worker. Dee had to admit that her daughter had a way of making people see the humor in even the grimmest situation.

It wouldn't be long till Dee would see her face to face again, and she would read whatever truth there was when she could look into her eyes. Until then, she'd have to take a deep breath and hold it together.

*   *   *

The old house creaked in a light wind that comforted Dee and unsettled her at the same time. She forced herself to buckle down to serious work on the student papers, stacking her printouts neatly on the desk within the lonely pool of light from a hobnail-glass lamp.

How long had this been her routine, at semester's end each December and May—how many years had she spent this same stretch of days and nights digesting the products of so many minds expressing so many thoughts and feelings and ideas? She dug in, determined not to be overwhelmed.

Dee had learned one thing herself: there were as many theories about teaching writing as practicing it. Maybe that's why she had latched on to Templeton's useful advice like a life preserver. Steering a sensible course between the tiresome anything-goes school and the rigid formula camp, *The Working Writer* grounded her. After earning her degree and advancing from part-time teaching assistant to adjunct professor at three colleges simultaneously, while trying to preserve some space for Jake and Abby, Dee turned often to the book for reassurance. She'd found the author's observations a wellspring of common sense, her style witty, urbane, as comfortable as a favorite pair of loafers.

She pictured Templeton's seminars, back in the more civilized mid-century. She conjured up an ideal scenario of dutiful students, spiral notebooks laid neatly on their wooden desks and fountain pens poised as they hung on their instructor's every jewel of wisdom.

Her students were nothing like that. Not that she expected them to be, but just a smidgen of decorum might've proved beneficial for all involved. Dee had nearly reached the breaking point—not only in her crazy-quilt teaching schedule, but in her sanity—in the spring of 2001 when a short-term vacancy in the English department at Walter Raleigh College morphed into a tenure-track job. Jake, that same semester, was offered his own opportunity of a lifetime. Dee had traded her personal life for her profession when she stayed—and let him go, taking Abby with him. She'd lived with that painful choice for seven years. Now she had to make it pay off.

6
Mothers and Daughters

Conflict—between characters, or within a character's own soul—is the essence of story.

IT WAS A GOOD THING she'd buckled down and made such steady progress on grading exams the night before, Dee decided, because Friday brought a stream of phone calls and visits.

First there'd been Brother Roy, who drove out to see his parishioner in the flesh so he could testify firsthand Sunday morning to the rest of the Second Baptist Church faithful that Alice Bennett was indeed much improved. Mama figured he was also fishing for more juicy details about how she'd wound up in the ditch, she told Dee, since she was certain that in a week's time rumor about her "incident" had grown to legendary proportions countywide.

Hector stopped by to tell Mama that he'd finished planting, the best news she'd heard all week, she said.

Jerry, the manager of the co-op gin, brought a tin of cookies and a get-well card signed by him and the bookkeeper, who had started out as an assistant in the 1950s, when Alice had handled the accounting for her father. The gin staff always remembered her at Christmas, long after he had passed away and she'd retired.

Penny called while Mama was napping to check on progress, and Dee gave her a report that included the home health aide's departure but omitted any mention of fire. Mitzi from Helping Hands phoned to confirm the new aide's schedule for Monday. "And you might appreciate knowing that Miss Tyner is no longer in our employ," she told Dee.

No sooner had Dee hung up from that call and finished helping Mama to and from the bathroom than the phone rang again. Dee deposited Mama on the couch and ran for the kitchen, catching the call on the tenth ring. She expected Buddy on his lunch hour, but a female voice with a flat Texas drawl nearly blasted her eardrums out.

"Well, I was about to decide y'all had skipped town. So—what are you two crazy gals doing next Saturday?"

"Are you sure you have the right number?" Dee asked warily.

"Yes, Dee Anna," said the caller, "it's your favorite cousin."

"Sorry, Ruby Lee, I didn't recognize your voice."

"Obviously! I'm so hurt! Now, how's Auntie Alice doing?"

"Improving slowly," Dee replied, and then added, at much lower volume, "physically—but emotionally, she's been better."

"Well, I have just the thing to cheer her up. Can I talk to Auntie?"

Mama was shaking her head in a vehement *no,* when Dee held the handset to Mama's ear. "She's right here and would be thrilled to talk with you."

"Hello?" Mama said weakly. Dee wasn't sure what Ruby Lee said next, but it must have been something wicked, because Mama lighted up and nodded her head. Her sullen tone was shifting to sunny right in front of Dee's eyes. In another sentence or two, she heard Mama say, "I told you I wasn't sure. You'll have to ask Dee Anna."

"What's up, Ruby Lee?" Dee said taking the phone again.

"Next Saturday, you remember we have our annual Poplar Grove Red Hat Society luncheon and pre–Memorial Day style show, and I would love for you and Auntie Alice to be my special guests. It's a lot of fun, and I thought y'all might need an excuse to get out of the house."

"A visit to Poplar Grove? I don't know," Dee said, drawing out her response, "Mama's kind of frail." Dee looked over at Mama, who was glowering at her and attempting to gesture with her elbows.

"I didn't say anything to Auntie Alice about this, but we can set up the table to accommodate her in a wheelchair, if that's easier."

"I just don't know. And I'm not sure Mama has anything suitable to wear to a Red Hat event." Mama nodded vigorously and tried to raise one arm to point to her head.

"And Barge is real good with the elderly," Ruby Lee said. "He can help you get her in and out of the car."

"Well, like I said, we can't tell if she's up for a road trip," Dee said. "I'll call you back when we know for sure."

"I'll be just fine," Mama said indignantly as Dee hung up. "Last thing I need is Ruby Lee Bargeron tellin' every soul in West Texas that I've got one foot in the grave and the other on a banana peel."

"Well, Mama, since your social calendar is starting to fill up, I'd better let you know about another event, before you hear it somewhere else."

"What sort of event?"

Dee explained about Cynthia and the writers' group.

"Lord God, Ruby Lee's style show and now a bunch of old coots trying to be authors. You know I can't feed a crowd here, in this condition."

"You don't have to provide refreshments, Mama. I think they usually meet at the library, and I'm sure they don't have food there."

"And where are all these folks going to park? Have you taken a look at the yard lately?"

Mama did have a point there. Dee would have to figure out something in a hurry. "Mama, she didn't really give me much of a choice. If I ever want to go back and use the computer again—which I'll need to do to post grades and send in this month's story—I'm going to have to count on her good graces."

Dee's parents had never entertained much when she was growing up, and the only consistent callers she could remember were extended family—aunts, uncles, cousins, mostly on Mama's side. A neighbor might stop by with a pie, or a visiting preacher might be invited out to Sunday supper, but in Dee's memory there had never been anything you could call a party at the home place.

Mama had always seemed to be too busy helping Dee's grandpa at the gin, while Dee's father wasn't inclined to invite company. Wilton was a man of few words who seemed to prefer the world of animals, plants, and gadgets. When they'd go to church or the annual electric co-op barbecue, Dee was struck with how hard it was for her father to make small talk with other farmers. When Dee would ask to have a friend stay over or maybe have a slumber party, he'd reply, "We have enough mouths to feed." It didn't take too many rejections to make her stop asking.

"What day did you say, again?" asked Mama. "Write it down on that calendar."

Dee did as instructed, also crossing out another day of no rain.

"Just get me out of the way before they all show up here," Mama said. "I don't want anybody seein' me like this. They might start makin' up stories about *me*."

*   *   *

Buck Turlock and his wife, Dianne, stopped by to visit Mama the next morning. While they were there, the Ford dealership called to say that the body department had finished with Mama's car. Buck generously gave Dee a ride to town to pick it up, while Dianne stayed with Mama.

On the way Buck said to Dee, "I hope I didn't offend your mother the other day, talking about buying her place and all. All I was trying to say was that if she ever gets ready to sell it, I'd like first dibs, with it being so close my own place." Dee paused, puzzled for a moment, before realizing that he meant the Echols farm.

"Mr. Turlock," Dee said, "Mama's just not ready to think that way yet. It's only been a few months since Daddy died, and right now, she's not ready to lose anything else."

"I understand," he said, as he dropped her off in front of the Wheeler Mims Ford sign. Dee retrieved the automobile and was thrilled to have a cool, cooperative ride back to the farm. She'd missed the familiar rhythms of her Subaru back home, but driving Alice's Crown Vic down the highway was like taking the helm of your own thirty-foot yacht.

Having the car back in the driveway seemed to lift Mama's spirits, too. She seemed to feel that it was the first step toward resuming a normal daily life. She looked at the gleaming light-brown sedan from the kitchen window, her elbow casts propped on the sink, and turned and remarked to Dee, "Looks good as new. Better, in fact, since it sure needed washing."

As she continued to stare out the open window, Mama said slowly, "I just now remembered something." She frowned and reached for the image that was coming to her. "I saw that green pickup coming—it was comin' over the hill, almost in my lane. I remember thinking, what in tarnation was somebody doing speeding like that, at that time of the morning with the sun right in their eyes—and I swerved off the road so he wouldn't run into me."

"Wow, that makes sense," Dee said. "You ran off the road, and that's why there was no collision! But why didn't the driver stop and render aid?"

"I don't know," Mama said. "I don't remember anything at all after that . . ."

"Maybe somebody was doing something that they shouldn't have. Maybe it was a getaway vehicle. Maybe there was a drug deal going down or something."

"I think you've been reading too many novels," Mama said. "Maybe they just didn't see me."

"Did you recognize anyone?"

"No," Mama said, "I don't think they were from around here."

"You said *they*—twice. So there was a driver and a passenger?"

"Now that you mention it, I guess there was—but I didn't mean that in the technical sense, Miss Professor."

"So, what were you doing that morning? Maybe you can remember some more."

"I do remember that much," said Mama. "I went out to check on the plowing. Hector was just about ready to plant. I wanted to check on them terraces myself."

Dee paused a minute, and then asked, "What made you decide to plant another crop, Mama?"

Alice looked at her youngest daughter and beckoned for her to walk her back to the chair. "You may not appreciate what it's like, and you probably thought it was awful, dirty work when you were a little kid with your nose stuck in a book, but cotton is all your daddy and I have ever known. Everything depends on how the crop makes that year—whether you can afford new tires for the car, or shingles to fix the roof, or enough groceries to get you through the winter. But it's also like startin' over with a clean slate every spring, the dirt all fresh and warm, and a few clouds that might bring rain. I would always go out and look over the fields before planting. I could just tell if the land was going to drain right, and if the rows had been laid out for the best yield."

"How'd you learn so much about farming?"

Mama laughed. "You spend enough time out there in all kinds of weather, you watch what time of year the plants come up, when the bolls burst, when the cotton's ready to pick—you can just tell. Nowadays they have gauges and instruments to tell you those things. Your grandfather ran the Claxton gin, you know, and I was there lots of times as a child, watching the trailers come in, watching when the cotton was graded. By the time I was in high school I kept all the account books for the gin, and I had a pretty good sense of what you had to make not to go broke. When your father and I got married, remember, he was a ranch hand—didn't know squat about cotton. He had to learn. Your aunts and uncles were around to help, and of course all the menfolk sat around at the Feed & Seed and talked about boll weevil eradication, and chemicals and irrigation systems and the like. We learned together."

"But it was Daddy's land to start with, wasn't it?" Dee started to suspect that there was more to the family stories she'd taken for granted than she had ever bothered to ask about.

Alice settled into the chair with a deeply exhaled breath. "Your daddy inherited his half of the section that had belonged to his father that had been a grant to *his* father. Texas gave veterans land way back then to encourage them to come out and settle the West. Wilton didn't give a hoot for farming like his daddy and granddaddy, though. He'd rather be off cowboyin'. He had some big dream of settin' up a ranch operation, which, of course, he never had the money to do. He let his brother pick which half he wanted and he took the other."

"And that's how Uncle Rupert ended up with the oil wells on his place?"

"Yep. Once they struck oil, him and Donna were comfortable for the rest of their lives—not rich, but they had whatever they wanted. While we scratched out our living year after year in cotton."

"I guess that's where Ruby Lee got her fancy tastes."

"And half of her husbands, who weren't nothin' but moochers."

"Speaking of Ruby Lee—have you decided yet about going to that style show?" Dee asked.

Mama sighed. "Well, I guess we might as well. If Dr. Taylor doesn't say no when we go in for the checkup, why, I suppose we'll plan us a little jaunt."

*   *   *

Mother's Day in the Bennett household, Dee recalled as she consulted the calendar the following morning, had always been a day of worship.

And not just at the Claxton Second Baptist Church, but at the altar of Alice Bennett's every wish. First the Bennett children would bring the cards they had made from construction paper and glitter, and the offering of wildflowers picked from the roadside. Daddy would present Mama with a mail-ordered box of pecan pralines from her favorite East Texas confectionery. Then, after Sunday school and church—where the boutonniered deacons would recognize the oldest mother and the newest, and provide a rose for each mom present—Wilton would drive them all to the Heritage House for a sit-down dinner of beef brisket or fried chicken. It was the one luxurious restaurant meal they could count on each year. After the feast, they'd return to the farm, where Daddy would resume his chores and Penny, Buddy, and Dee made sure that Mama did not have to lift a finger the rest of the day.

Things were decidedly more subdued on this occasion. Buddy and his wife called to see if Mama had received the flowers they'd sent; Penny called to say that her prayer circle was on top of the whole situation and she was sure Mama must be feeling better by now.

"Purty good, considering, but I'll sure be glad when I can get up and move without lookin' like a Halloween monster," Dee heard Mama answer as she held the phone up beside her mother's ear. "No, I'm not about to go to church in this condition. Me and Dee Anna are just going to take it easy out here by ourselves."

There was another pause while Mama listened.

"Yes, I sure appreciate them recorded books you sent," said Mama. "But I don't think we have the right machine to play 'em on. Mm-hmm." With her free hand Dee pulled a CD from the half-opened Amazon box on the coffee table. *Your Spiritual Path to Health and Happiness.* "I'll listen to it as soon as I'm feeling better," Mama said, rolling her eyes for Dee's benefit.

The thermometer was already past eighty and the air was still and close when Dee walked down the hill to retrieve the Sunday paper. On such a quiet morning she could hear the drone of a tractor-trailer's engine far out on the highway as easily as the call of a meadowlark among the hackberry thickets. Down the road in front of the double-wide on the old Echols place a blue-and-white van marked "Hope Fellowship" turned in, honked its horn, and idled until a blonde-haired girl in tank top, shorts, and flip-flops ran out and hopped in. Dee lifted a hand to wave but was too far off to be seen. She caught herself thinking exactly what her mother would have said: *Now, where are that child's parents, and why didn't they dress her properly for church?*

Outside the Bennett gate, beside the bar ditch, stood three posts: a rusted aluminum pole topped by a standard-issue black U.S. mailbox, a dark-green T-post to which the blue plastic *Claxton Daily Courier* tube was attached, and another post holding the white one for the *Lubbock Avalanche-Journal*. The *Courier* came six afternoons a week, but Alice and Wilton had subscribed to the big-city *A-J* on Sundays for as long as Dee could remember. As a kid she'd wondered how a newspaper in hot, dry West Texas came to be named after a snowslide, but this morning just pulling the fat roll of newsprint from its cubbyhole made her feel a little cooler. She fanned herself with the magazine section as she trudged back up the hill.

"Maybe you won't mind reading me the main stories," Mama suggested, since she couldn't hold the pages up for herself.

"What do you want first, the ag report or the funeral notices?" Dee asked.

"As long as you skip what's going on in Eye-rack, I don't care. That depresses me too much for Mother's Day."

"Agreed!" She shook out the paper and reached for the front page. "So tell me—have you met your neighbors at the bottom of the hill?"

"In the trailer house? They moved that in here about a month ago. I hadn't met the parents—just seen 'em drivin' in and out—but I stopped and talked to the little girl one morning when she was waiting for the school bus. She said her name was Stacey, and she had to start a new school when her family moved from Oklahoma. I think she said she was ten."

"Well, you shouldn't have to go far to borrow a cup of sugar," Dee said. She read aloud until Mama was sated with the news and requested the television be turned to "that good-lookin' preacher from Houston who tells people it's okay to be rich," then retired to her desk to review her notes for her upcoming stint in the Berkshires. She glanced at the alarm clock and wondered for a moment if she should just go ahead and call Abby. But no—she could wait. Let her take her own responsibility, her own time.

*   *   *

Dee had managed to learn plenty more about Gineva Holland Templeton Jensen, once that initial obituary clue turned up. Alumni files from Abbot, the famous Massachusetts preparatory school for women, and Emerson, the Boston liberal arts college, contributed a great deal about Templeton's early life. Letters home, and items in the school papers, portrayed young Gineva as a dedicated student, excelling in literature, classics, declamation, and music. The daughter of a well-to-do Worcester industrialist, she traveled widely with her family—to Europe after the war, to Mexico and the Caribbean, even to Hawaii, which was still a monarchy at the time. Upon graduation from Emerson in the spring of 1929, Dee guessed, Gineva must have expected to continue living in style as she sought her fortune—or a husband.

But when the stock market crashed that year, so did Mr. Templeton's financial empire. Gineva had to find work for a living. She became an avid motorist, and her most popular run of articles was a magazine series chronicling the breadth of the United States along the newly built Lincoln Highway, which she traveled alone. To guard her safety on the road she used only initials in her byline—a choice that did nothing to dispel readers' default assumptions of male authorship. Dee had tracked down some of these pieces in magazine indexes. Lively but not overblown, keen in description, accurate but subtle in capturing dialect. Good solid writing.

Upon her return to Boston in 1931, to judge by the carbon copy of a typed letter of application, Templeton sought to capitalize on her newfound celebrity. The Harvard Annex, through which the all-male university offered non-degree courses to women, had apparently advertised for someone to teach part of a new curriculum called "Creative Writing," and Templeton responded. But there Dee's research trail in the Harvard archives had stopped cold. There had been no record of any Templeton in the faculty rosters for that period, and no correspondence indexed by her name. The most critical gap in the story—a deal-breaker for any study that proposed to examine Templeton's contributions as a pioneer educator—remained what the subject had been up to from that time until her reappearance in California, at a women's college, twelve years later.

Dee's proposal to the Berkshires Fellowship had been her only hope for support in conducting further research onsite. And now that it was officially hers, she counted on it more than ever to discover the missing pieces in the puzzle.

＊   ＊   ＊

Later on their day of rest, Dee walked Mama out to the front porch to enjoy what was proving to be a beautiful evening. Not a hint of wind stirred over the rise, and no clouds or dust haze obscured the distant view. A mockingbird perched on the top branch of a mesquite tree, and the doves were cooing a chorus from somewhere in the thick green cedars.

"Looks like the birds will end up gettin' the best of the peaches this year," said Mama.

"Why do you say that?" asked Dee, who hadn't paid much attention to the timing of such things as a child. "When will they be ripe enough to pick?"

"Well, usually early July—but they won't make it that far if the birds get 'em first. Your daddy and I would put netting over the trees to keep the birds out."

"Is that something I can help with? Just tell me what to do."

"Oh, you don't want to fool with that old ladder. It's way back in the barn. I don't know if you can carry it by yourself."

"If I can lift an eleven-foot kayak onto the top of a Subaru, I think I can handle a stepladder," Dee countered. She went to retrieve it, choosing her steps carefully in the darkened barn. In the well house she found the netting, scads of tulle in a kelly-green color no bride should ever wish on a bridesmaid, folded and wound onto the cardboard bolt on which it had originally come. Woolworth's, twenty-nine cents a yard, the price sticker read.

Dee positioned the ladder and climbed it carefully, and with Mama calling out instructions from her lawn chair, unwound the net fabric and positioned it over the tree limbs. Dee shooed away a pair of mockingbirds with the empty bolt. She could see that already some fowl had pecked at the ripening fruit, leaving triangle-shaped indentions in the softer parts.

The job done, Dee sat down on the top step of the eight-foot ladder. The gaudily draped tree enfolded her as she held the cardboard across her knees. She gazed across the expanse of trees and outbuildings, and down the hill to the lights of the neighbors' houses beginning to come on, and beyond that to the faint, faraway glow that indicated the town of Claxton. In the evening sky, which melted from aqua to pink to violet as though one of those old-fashioned Christmas-tree color wheels shone on it, Venus emerged.

As she perched atop her throne, for the first time in a long time Dee felt—she searched for the word to capture her feeling of well-being, and the closest she could come was *absolved*.

Did a place have the power to do that? In the twenty-one years she had lived away from West Texas and her family, she had thought often about this hilltop farm—but usually as a prison she was glad to escape. She had so much to prove, first in college, and then after running off with Jacob. When Abigail was little they struggled to make ends meet on his salary and her part-time job as a copy editor. Rather than scrimp for day care, Jacob stayed home with Abby and taught night classes. By the time he returned home on class nights Abby was in bed; Dee was often asleep in her recliner, laptop computer left open to whatever document she'd been working on.

Then there were his student loans to repay, and her own graduate school expenses. Trips home to see her family in Texas or his in New Jersey were rare. By the time Dee had seen Jacob through the publication of his own book, and he started to move up the tenure ladder, she was deep into her own dissertation writing—the circumstance she had always held responsible, with considerable guilt, for the deterioration of their marriage. Somehow their schedules never seemed to mesh, and she felt them growing apart. They argued over big matters like money, or petty ones like whose turn it was to do laundry or what to have for dinner. He became distant and withdrawn; she grew irritable.

It was true she'd had little time or attention left for Jake or Abby at the end of a long day of teaching and grading. Why did it all seem to come so easy for him? He held court in his graduate seminars, left the grading to a teaching assistant, dashed off another scholarly article— keeping an open schedule and managing a multitude of tasks without wearing down like she did. So it was Jake who always saw to it that Abby made it to soccer practice or cello lessons on time, that she wrote letters to her grandparents, finished her homework. It was Jake who dispensed both discipline and advice. Who got to take her to the park, birthday parties, the dentist. Dee felt as much part-time mother as part-time professor.

The spring before Abby turned ten, Jake was tapped for an endowed professorship at Brandeis—his dream job, one that could forge his career path for the long term and solidify his position in the academy.

One that would provide the means for them to live in comfort at last. *Just think, Dee,* Jake had said, *private school for Abby, and you wouldn't have to work.* The prospect held promise. A way to salvage their family. Sweet relief.

But the instant Keith Pritchard dropped a hint to Dee that the Walter Raleigh College job would open up as a permanent position, she felt a surge of conflict. It wasn't true that when one door closed, another one opened, she'd told Jake in frustration; just as one door opened, another lured you in a different direction simultaneously. A perfect literary irony. Shakespeare, O. Henry.

Jake's reaction had caught her completely off guard. *You know, maybe you ought to consider it, babe. You deserve it. It might be worth a try.* Had he read her mind? Did he suspect that deep down she wasn't keen to trail him to another station—however lofty—where she'd have to start over again? Dee had a hard time reading him anymore.

What harm would there be in applying? he'd suggested. Dee wondered whether he was humoring her—or simply didn't think she stood a chance. Or maybe he really did believe in her and supported her ambitions. By the time she made her persuasive presentation to the Walter Raleigh search committee, she was certain the job was ideal for her.

We can make this long-distance thing work, Jake assured her. *Lots of couples do.* She should have suspected there was more to it. But she let herself believe him. She took the job and stayed behind. When he came home at Thanksgiving, it was with talk of divorce.

His desertion—for that was how she saw it—stung, but Dee didn't fight him for long. What use would there be in it? At worst he'd deliberately misled her, and left her and Abby to fend for themselves; on the other hand, she could be grateful he'd given her an easy way out. Whatever the case, she held herself, and her schedule and priorities, responsible for letting their relationship degrade to the point that he could treat her so callously. She cried at night in guilt and remorse, then tried to build up her confidence again by day.

That was nothing compared to the shock and hurt she felt when Abby, always willful and capricious, announced that she wanted to go live with her father in Boston. Dee argued, even pleaded, but in the end let her go. She consoled herself with the hope that Abby would be better off in Jake's custody. He'd been the primary caregiver all along: she told herself this during extended bouts of loneliness. She bought a house in the woods—a tiny, isolated two-bedroom lake cabin where she could try to escape the pain. She withdrew from any semblance of social life and retreated further into her writing. It was always Abby she ached for. Sometimes she could write—and sometimes she just couldn't.

Her family hadn't exactly been supportive. Alice and Wilton had been certain from the beginning the marriage would end unhappily, and when it did, Alice had plenty to say to Dee about it. Penny and Buddy offered unsolicited advice at every turn. Wilton just kept his mouth shut.

A loud buzzing erupted in the pocket of Dee's jeans at that moment, and she nearly tumbled off the top of the ladder. Catching herself, she reached to find the cell phone in her pocket, fully recharged but set to vibrate, ringing away. "Hello?"

The voice on the other end was disjointed, separated by cellular lapses. Dee hadn't realized her phone would pull in a signal at all, but maybe being on the top of the hill made the difference.

". . . just called . . . hope you're . . . love you."

"Abby?"

". . . Mother's Day . . . Gramma Alice doing . . ."

Dee stood up on the next-to-last step, as though reaching higher in the sky would help knit the signal back together. "Oh, I was just thinking of you, sweetie — I'm so glad you called!"

". . . get my card?"

"No, I didn't get a card yet, but that's okay—it's just good to hear your voice. More than you know." How much of her words carried back over the airwaves, she couldn't tell. "I love you too—you want to call me later on the house phone?"

". . . let you go . . . breaking up." Yes, Dee thought, but some bonds could transcend even the physics of space, and a wave could reach out and surprise you when you least expected it, from anywhere on the planet.

7
The Write Stuff

Gathering with likeminded writers to trade ideas and responses is one of the best ways to improve your work.

"WELL, MAMA, are you ready to give it another shot?" asked Dee the next morning. "Looks like your new helper's here." A Toyota pickup had made its way up the driveway and was turning around, about the same moment as they heard a knock at the door.

The new Helping Hands aide looked to be in her early twenties, Dee judged from her face, though it was hard to tell. Short and chunky, dressed in oversized black T-shirt, blue jeans, and black baseball cap, she could have passed for a teenager except for a demeanor of greater solemnity. She carried a student-style backpack but no purse. Her hair was pulled back in a ponytail under the ball cap, and the expression on her round brown face was stoic.

"Hello, I am from Helping Hands," she said, so softly Dee could hardly hear. "*Me llamo* Teresa. You mama need help?"

Dee brought Teresa over and introduced her to Mama, who eyed her warily. Teresa's expression remained steady. "What you want me to do first?"

"My daughter'll show you where everything is," said Mama. "You don't smoke, do you?"

"No, *no fumo.*"

"You're not behind on your light bill, are you?"

"Mama!" chided Dee. She motioned quickly for Teresa to follow her down the hallway, and after explaining that Mama might be a bit prickly, she went through the household routine as she had done with Toni. She was impressed when Teresa pulled out a spiral notebook and pen and began to make a list.

"Okay," Teresa said when she and Dee rejoined Mama in the living room. "Mrs. Bennett, we begin with your . . . shower?"

Dee went red in the face at the realization that Mama had been home from the hospital for a week—and not once had the idea of her mother's hygiene crossed her mind.

"That would be a nice change of pace," Mama said sarcastically, pointing her plaster-bound forearm in the direction of her unwashed scalp. "I think it's high time."

"Mama," Dee said, "I'm sorry. I forgot. I meant to—"

Mama rolled her eyes. "Do I have to think of everything around here? I was going to see how long you'd let me go on stinking."

Teresa pushed the button on the lift chair, helped Mama up, and walked her to the bathroom. Dee could hear the water running and the washcloth splashing. How could she have been so thoughtless? Maybe she'd had only herself to look after for too long. Or maybe she was just a total failure at helping others.

That reminded her: the Write Stuff members would be arriving tomorrow night for their class. What would she say to them that would strike the right note? She sat at the kitchen table and outlined some ideas on a legal pad. She felt comfortable enough teaching writers of any level, but it generally helped to know a little about their aspirations and skills before starting. She didn't want to choose a topic that was too elementary, or one that didn't interest them either. What would help them most, in the short space of one evening?

Half an hour later Dee looked up from her musings to see Teresa carrying a basket full of sheets and towels out to the back porch. "Have more clothes?" asked Teresa, hardly above a whisper.

"Come again?"

"More clothes to wash? I have changed the beds."

"Oh! Well, yes, I do, come to think of it," Dee said, realizing that laundry was yet another thing she hadn't thought of since she'd arrived.

With Teresa's aid Mama made her way down the hall, bracing herself against the chair rail for support. In a perky red blouse and tan slacks

Dee had never seen before, and with her hair combed into place and almost dry already, she looked younger and more relaxed than Dee had remembered in years.

"That's a nice shirt, Mama." Dee rose and followed to help.

"She look pretty in red," Teresa said softly, escorting her charge back to the lift chair.

"You look fit for a party!"

"No need to flatter me, Dee Anna, I still ain't comin' to that writers' group," said Mama.

"I know, I know," Dee said. "I thought I'd feed you your supper early, and then get you all comfortable in your bed with *Dancing with the Stars* before they arrive. And—I found something in the barn that you can use if you need me." Dee picked up an enormous cowbell from the table and shook it. The jangling sound could easily have been heard in any room of the house.

"Jezebel's bell!" she and Mama said at once.

"I'm going to hang it from a wire by your bed so that all you have to do is bump it with your elbow," Dee explained.

"You remember that ol' heifer?" Mama said, her face lighting up. "She was always gettin' out and gettin' knocked up or cut up by barbed wire. Your Daddy got the biggest bell he could find and hung it around her neck so he could hear her anytime he was out plowing."

"And Daddy never threw anything away," Dee said.

"Now I'm glad he never did. It makes it seem like he's still here."

"I know," Dee replied. "I look at the pig troughs or the fish tank or the rabbit cages, and remember how he'd get an idea that he was going to raise this animal or that, and then he'd take a sheet of aluminum or a rusted-out tire rim or a packing crate and made a shelter for them."

"Yep," Mama said, "when you live out here and don't have much, you figure out how to make do."

By the end of the day, Teresa and Dee had not only prepared two days' worth of meals to be heated up, but had the house in tip-top shape for company. Dee thanked her sincerely for taking care of Mama's needs and helping to bring order to their household.

"What time you meet tomorrow? I come to look after you mama," said Teresa.

"Oh, you don't need to do that on your day off, Teresa," Dee replied, "and besides, it's in the evening—the guests are coming at six."

"*Muy bien,*" she said, and turned away before Dee could say anything further.

*   *   *

The following morning, Dee was able to get Mama down the stairs into the car by herself with some effort, but she noticed that Mama drew in a short breath any time her casts were jostled. Nonetheless, mother and daughter were both optimistic as they made their way to town and parked in the handicapped spot at Dr. Taylor's office.

She couldn't wait for the examination to be over. She and Mama had agreed that to celebrate progress they planned to have cheeseburgers and milk shakes at the Lot-a-Burger, something Dee hadn't done since she was a teenager.

Dee and Mama eagerly related to Dr. Taylor the details Mama had recalled about the car accident. He listened intently as he checked her range of motion and felt inside the edges of the casts.

"So you're pretty sure you weren't involved in a hit-and-run, then?"

"I'm certain," said Mama. "I got plum out of their way. And I didn't—what do they call it—overcorrect, neither."

"Good for you . . . and good for your memory, too. I don't think you have a problem in that department—you just had a bad jolt, and then an anaphylactic reaction to fire-ant toxin. On that score, you're lucky. We'll never know whether you completely lost consciousness, but that kind of allergy can even cause cardiac arrest." He saw the worry on her face and scaled back the drama. "But you're on the mend now. More details may come back to you in time—and if you figure out who ran you off the road, we'll send a posse after 'em!"

After drawing a blood sample, he led her back to the X-ray room. It didn't take long for the digital camera to do its work.

"Mrs. Bennett," Dr. Taylor said as he brought up Mama's images on the computer screen, "it might be longer than we thought before we can get you back on the tennis court."

"Don't care about playing no tennis," Mama said. "Just how long before these dadgum casts can come off?"

"I'm not sure," he said. "Your bones are not starting to heal as quickly as I'd like. This happens with older patients—the blood flow doesn't get to the ends of their extremities. I want to step up the physical therapy, and Dee, you or someone will need to help her with it at least three times a day." He pulled an informational flyer out of a drawer. "In addition to the finger exercises, I'm going to prescribe a series for you to do with your shoulders as well and your feet and legs. The goal is to get your blood pumping."

Mama's spirit seemed to deflate like a tire going flat. Dee felt the same way but kept it to herself.

"I'm doing enough thurr-appy," Mama pouted, "and it hurts bad enough as it is. I don't want to do any more."

"Only way you're going to get better," the doctor said. "If all goes well, we'll have you lighting firecrackers by the Fourth of July. In the meantime, the best thing you can do is to get up and get moving—to not be sedentary. I know you have to be careful not to fall, but walk up and down the hallway of your house if you have to. Be as active as you can to keep your blood circulating."

*   *   *

In silence Dee and Mama chewed their cheeseburgers and sipped their chocolate malts, while arctic air and peppy fifties music blasted from the ceiling of the Lot-a-Burger dining room. "At least you're holding your own and not going backwards," Dee said. "I bet if we really work at your therapy, you'll beat the doctor's prediction."

Mama's competitive spirit and stubbornness responded to Dee's challenge. "You're right, Dee Anna . . . let's just show that Prissy-Pants Taylor. Ends of my extremities, my foot. But you're going to be leaving next week—and what'll I do on the days that Meskin don't come?"

"Let's cross that bridge when we come to it, Mama, and please don't call Teresa that. In the meantime, we've got guests arriving at the house at six."

"Oh, good Lord," Mama replied, "I wish you hadn't of reminded me. I was just gettin' to feeling better."

When they reached the farm, Dee helped her mother out of the car, and the two of them surveyed with dismay the overgrown grass and rampant weeds. It was even worse than Dee remembered. "What have you been doing about the grass since Daddy's been gone, Mama? And how about the trash that's piling up? Surely you're not still burning it."

Mama made a straw sucking noise that signaled the end of her malt and answered edgily, "You should have thought of those things when you agreed to Cynthia Vandever's cockamamie idea. There's not enough time to fix things up before this evening."

"I've mowed grass before, Mama."

"Not like out here you haven't—Buddy was always around to take care of it when you were little. The last couple of years, your father hired a man to come mow once a month. He'd just use the board mower on the tractor. But I haven't even bothered with it since . . . well, since Christmas. There's not time to get him to come now."

The wheels were beginning to turn in Dee's head. "So he uses Daddy's tractor?"

"Sure," Mama said. "In fact, he probably just leaves the mower blade on it. Don't get used for nothin' else."

"Daddy taught me how to drive the tractor when I was a kid," Dee said.

"Dee Anna, don't be silly," Mama said. "If it didn't start you'd have to charge the battery with the pickup. You'd have to go back to town and fill up a can with diesel. Hadn't been any fuel in the storage tank in years. And what if you turned the tractor over on yourself? We'd be stuck out here, both of us invalids, and I can't call for help."

"Mama, here's the plan. I'm going to sit you in the lawn chair on the front porch just like we did on Sunday," Dee said, as she eased her mother into the chair. "I'm going to get the cordless phone with the emergency button," she continued, "and if disaster strikes you can dial 911 with one of your fingers and shout to your heart's content."

"That's not funny," her mother said, as Dee went to change into jeans, work shirt, and a pair of boots she'd left in the closet years ago.

She returned with the phone and handed it to Mama. "It'll be fine," she said, yelling over her shoulder as she headed toward the barn. She pulled back the heavy door with some effort, and in the half-light located the can of diesel, which still had about a gallon in it. She took the hoe and rake over by the fence, along with Daddy's chain saw.

Dee approached the Massey Ferguson tractor, entombed in its corner of the barn in dust, cobwebs, and droppings, with apprehension. She inspected it thoroughly to make sure no varmints had taken up residence in it. She prayed that she didn't have to find the battery cables and jump-start it.

Buddy's stick-shift lessons came in handy when Dee climbed up into the tractor seat. She quickly found neutral, held in the clutch, turned the key, and heard a reluctant *grrr-grrr-grrr* before the engine fired up. She let up on the stubborn clutch as gently as she could manage and steered the tractor out of the garage with a few turns, but when she realized the platform was already lowered to the ground, she couldn't figure out how to raise it.

Mama spotted the problem from the porch. "The switch to the right of the fuel gauge," she yelled at Dee, who was kicking up dust in the driveway. "Raise it up, or you'll ruin the mower on the caliche. Shift to second and leave it there." Dee flipped the switch, and sure enough, the blade lifted enough to clear the driveway. Pretty soon she got the rhythm, figuring out how to back into tight spots and turn in a small enough radius to avoid taking out shrubs and flowers.

It took her a solid hour, but after the yard had been mowed, Dee stopped the tractor in front of the barn and hopped off. Gone was the tall brush, and even though the grass that remained was patchy and dry, she felt proud of her accomplishments. "It's an improvement, don't you think?" she called out to Mama.

Mama didn't answer immediately.

Dee came closer, wiping her forehead on her sleeve. "Mama? You okay?"

As soon as Dee was within earshot, Mama spoke quietly and deliberately. "Dee Anna, stop where you are and go get that hoe by the fence." It was a tone that left no room for argument, but Dee started to question anyway.

"Mama—"

"Go get that hoe and bring it over here. Now."

Dee did as she was told. As she clomped toward the porch, hoe in hand, Mama spoke quietly again. "Now walk over here toward the porch nice and easy."

"What's the matter?" Dee asked as she stepped carefully in Mama's direction.

"Take that hoe and get this snake," Mama whispered.

Dee's blood went cold when she saw the rattler stretched out on the porch, an arm's length from Mama's chair. She wasn't good at measurements, but if she had to guess, she'd say it was a good four feet long. It wasn't coiled to strike—in fact, it seemed to be napping—but that didn't make an ounce of difference to Dee.

"What do I do?" she whispered back.

"You got one chance to chop its head off. Make it good."

Oh, God, what if I miss? thought Dee. *I was never any good at golf.*

Dee raised the hoe with a steady motion, took aim, and brought the blade down hard. With a thundering whack she managed to separate a few inches of the snake's tail from its business end, but the reptile leapt into motion regardless. She took another swipe with the hoe, looping the snake around it and flinging it, writhing, off the porch toward the yard. It made for the weeds by the fencepost, struggling to make progress in a sidewinding pattern. Dee ran to the tractor, cranked it hurriedly, and drove to intercept the rattler's path. After running it over with the front wheels, she brought down the mower platform with a thud. She looked behind her and cut the motor only when she was satisfied that the snake had been puréed into a hundred bloody pieces, none of which would threaten them further.

Rubber-legged, she stepped off the tractor and walked carefully back to the porch, where she sat down, shaking, on the floor next to Mama.

"They're bad this time of year," Mama said.

"Omigod, Mama, what would you have done if it'd come closer?"

"Well, all I can say is, I've *really* got to pee now."

After taking care of the bathroom chore, Dee brought Mama back out to sit on the porch while she finished up weeding around the foundation. She was determined to leave no vegetation thick enough to harbor another snake.

"Did I ever tell you about the time I found one curled up with Buddy on the back porch?"

"Seems I remember something about that," Dee said, wishing once again in vain for a cold vodka gimlet, to hear this story with.

"It was a chilly spring morning and I was hanging out the clothes to dry," Mama said as Dee chopped and raked. "Buddy was just a baby, so I put him in a cardboard box on the porch with some blankets to keep him warm. When I went back to get some more clothespins, there was this snake curled up next to the box. Well, like you just did, I grabbed a hoe, and I took the head of that hoe and flung that snake on the ground and chopped its head clean off. About scared me half to death, and I was shaking just like you are. Buddy never woke up the whole time."

"How did you ever do it? Seems like farm life is so hard."

Mama shook her head, "Nah, what's hard is what *you* do. Have a boss telling you what to do, what to say, what to think, how to dress every day. Driving to work in traffic and finding a parking place. On the farm, if you're hungry, you go get some eggs from the chicken coop or pull some vegetables from the kitchen garden. If the weather's good for plowing, you plow. If it's good for picking, you pick. If it's not good for either one, you stay inside and wait until it is. It's not a bad life."

The smell of diesel wafted her way, conjuring up such a strong memory that she almost expected to hear her father call out from the barn, *Alice? I'm back. What's for supper?*

*   *   *

After she'd showered and dressed and set out chairs in a circle in the living room about five-thirty, Dee felt almost ready for the evening's gathering. What would these writers be like? she wondered. And what would they think if they found out she was a fraud—that she'd never actually published a book herself? Well, no matter, it was just once, a special favor to Cynthia. She heard wheels on the caliche driveway and looked up to see the Toyota pickup again. Teresa Rivera, dressed in ball cap and jeans just as the day before, got out on the passenger side and came to the door.

"I stay until your class is over . . . in case your mother needs me," Teresa told Dee. "What time should my father come back to get me?"

"Teresa, you don't have to do that," Dee said. "You know our contract with Helping Hands only covers daytime hours."

"We are here now. What time?"

"Well, the meeting is from six to eight," Dee said.

"*Ocho*," Teresa said to her father and waved him away. She carried her backpack over to Mama's chair and sat down next to her.

"Mrs. Bennett," she said, "you like to do therapy in bedroom or living room?" Teresa certainly knew how to avoid a "no" from Mama, thought Dee.

"If we really have to, then right here in the lift chair would work fine," Mama said.

"I go get the stress ball." Turning to Dee, Teresa handed her a package wrapped in foil inside a Walmart bag. "My neighbor make tamales, she make too many. Your writing class might want some."

"How nice—but you shouldn't have done that."

"Ma'am," she said, "can I . . . can I sit and listen while I take care of your mother?"

"Well, sure," Dee said, surprised. "I don't think the group would mind. I'll check when they get here."

*   *   *

Despite all Mama's protestations, it was apparent she wouldn't have missed the Write Stuff meeting for the world. Teresa found a chair in the back of the room and discreetly took out her spiral notebook and pen, while Mama held court from the sidelines and greeted each of the arrivals.

Cynthia called the gathering to order by asking each writer to tell his or her name and something about their writing goals. "We'll go around the room, and share as much as you feel comfortable with," she said. "We are so lucky to have with us Dr. Dee Anna Bennett-Kaufmann, of the creative writing faculty of Raleigh College and a Claxton native, to lead our program tonight."

Amid the polite applause Dee was almost sure she heard a snicker from Mama's direction when Cynthia used her full name.

"And I just want to remind you to finish those manuscript submissions and get them to me by the end of the week, for our next meeting," said Cynthia. "Okay, who'll get things started?"

A barrel-chested man in a Wrangler dress shirt and pressed jeans, wire-rimmed glasses and a handlebar moustache—the group's alpha writer, Dee guessed—stood up and removed his Stetson. "I'm J. D. Sandifer, and I'm a retired ag teacher from Claxton High School. Miss Dee, I think I might remember you from way back when I first started teaching, but I don't imagine you ever had any of my classes." She shook her head in agreement. "My goal is to be the next Louis L'Amour, God rest his soul. I want my book to show readers how exciting life out West can be."

One by one the others took turns with their introductions.

"My name is Frances Echols," said a short woman wearing a floral-print tunic and a good deal of silver jewelry. I used to live down the road here (hi, Alice!). I am working on what could best be called a gothic generational saga of a farm family in West Texas that has a rumored murder within the family that was never solved. It happened in the eighteen-eighties, back when Caprock County was nothing more than open range land, and the ranchers didn't like it when the homesteaders came in and—" She cut the synopsis short when the eyes of her peers shot in her direction. "Well, you'll just have to read the book. And, I belong to the Red Hat Club."

"Wendell Grover," said the balding man seated next to Frances Echols. "Retired Air Force pilot, originally from Bristol, Virginia, last assignment Dyess Air Force Base in Abilene. M'wife and I settled in Claxton because we like small-town life. I'm working on a historical novel set during the Civil War, which I hope to publish before the sesquicentennial."

"And when is that?" Dee asked innocently.

"Why, starting in 2011, of course. The fall of Fort Sumter in April 1861?"

Dee nodded—but she'd be a little more prepared with her inquiries next time.

Their leader was next. "I'm Cynthia Philpott, and I think you all know me as the head librarian at the Caprock County Public Library. I'm a graduate of Abilene Christian University. I write mysteries. My protagonist, Aunt Martha, is a librarian who not only aids law enforcement around the world as she visits missionaries and a large extended family, but continually helps justify the timelessness of the Dewey Decimal System as she solves crimes. I also sell Mary Kay, and I'm coordinator of the Rolling Plains Red Hat Club."

A dark-haired girl with black nail polish and multiple face piercings stood up. "Summer Jones. Age twenty-nine. And I do *not* belong to the Red Hat Club." Everyone laughed. "In my day job I'm the manager of the Subway sandwich shop. My thing is science fiction and fantasy. Right now, I'm working on a trilogy of identity theft and dark romance à la *The Golden Compass,* sort of."

"Thanks, Summer," said Cynthia. "Next?"

"My name is Margaret Strickland," said a slender woman in a polyester jogging suit who sported a silver hairstyle sufficiently lacquered to resist the wind. "I'm retired after forty-three years in the newspaper business."

Dee latched onto that. "Oh, were you an editor or reporter?"

"I actually handled the society section, events and weddings and obits, stuff like that—nothing fancy. But I sure came across lots of great material! Now I write romances, and some poetry. Most of my stories are set in Arkansas, where I grew up. But I just got back from Italy, after visiting my son who's stationed there, and I'm thinking about how I might could work that into my writing. My husband, Wes, is also getting ready to retire from the A-1 Auto Parts store. So maybe we'll travel to even more exotic places after that."

They continued around the circle. "Hi, I'm JoAnn Rinehart. I'm a paralegal—not ready to retire for a few more years. I'd like to think I could write like John Grisham, and I have several courtroom dramas in the works. In real life, though, I handle mostly wills and real estate closings." JoAnn's fellow writers smiled, appreciating the stretch of imagination her subject called for.

Then it was Dee's turn. Seated on the three-step stool from Mama's kitchen, she told them the essentials of her background and started things off the way she typically did with her new students, to pique their interest. "It's wonderful that you want to be writers," she told them sincerely. "But you are going to face one major challenge."

"What's that," asked J. D. Sandifer, "finding an agent?"

She laughed. "Well, make that *two* challenges. Let's back up a little bit. Several of you mentioned authors whose work you like or admire. You read their books religiously, right? So do scads of other readers—that's what makes those writers best sellers. They've managed to break out to commercial or literary success. They did what only a few manage to do: they, among all the possible authors and books out there, got *your* attention.

"Now swap places with them in your mind. If you want readers' attention, you're going to need discipline, learning, and some luck. Because these days, more people want to *write* books than want to read them."

She let them absorb that for a second and pressed on. "You've probably already started to figure that out, if you've ever sent out a query letter. How many of you have contacted an agent or editor before?" A few hands went up: J. D., Cynthia, Margaret. A couple of the other writers looked around as though they weren't quite ready to admit they had.

"You know that publishing a book is going to be a competitive game and an uphill battle. You may wonder if you'll ever get published." Yes, their eyes said, they all wondered that. Only JoAnn Rinehart sat back, arms folded, mouth set. If they weren't going to learn the secrets to getting published, her demeanor seemed to say, what were they here for?

"So let's not spend our precious time this evening focusing on publishing," Dee continued. "Let's not talk about editors, agents, queries, or, God forbid, advances and royalties. Let's talk about the real nitty-gritty: what you really love about writing, what you love about language, what you love about books. Let's talk about your *story*—and how you're going to get that down on paper."

Dee could see she had them with her. She had their attention now. But this gathering, somewhat to her surprise, was very different from the undergraduates she taught. When she led these writers in a discussion of "What Makes Writing Creative," they took notes. Lots of notes. They hung onto her words as gospel. They listened intently and jumped eagerly into discussions about the characters and plots they were constructing.

"Tell me about the law office where Chelsea works, JoAnn," Dee suggested. "Describe it right down to the coffeepot." JoAnn cooperated, proving herself extremely well prepared to answer the question. Wendell Grover's eyes had shone as he imagined, aloud, the last moments in the life of a young Confederate recruit. And when the evening's program wound down and Cynthia thanked her, the group applauded.

Dee stole a glance at her mother's face, but Mama had fallen asleep in her chair. Teresa, who noticed at the same time, gathered up her notebook, then gently woke her charge and led her to bed.

When the aspiring authors had all left for the evening, Dee sat on the front porch and watched the convoy of taillights make its way down the hill through the dusk. Teresa's father had arrived for her promptly at eight. The last one out—she couldn't tell who it was—lingered long enough to shut the gate and then moved on, turning onto the farm road and topping the rise.

She wished she had someone to talk with about the evening. J. D. Sandifer had been a hoot—part bluster, part self-doubt. Cynthia's Aunt Martha actually sounded like an interesting character. And the Grisham wannabe—what was her name, JoAnn? What was up with her, and why did Dee feel she hadn't connected? She dialed Abby's number on the kitchen phone. No answer—just voicemail.

She started to call Rob but decided against it. Not his sort of thing. For now, Dee just soaked in the still air, the last hues of the dying day, and the hum of cicadas in the mesquites. She'd text him tomorrow.

8
Calendar Girl

To build suspense, reveal bits of information gradually,
leaving something to the imagination as you go along.

THE ANXIETY AND SUCCESS of the Write Stuff presentation behind her, Dee worked like mad to read her university students' final assignments and turn in grades on time. Twice a year at semester's end, she dreaded these grading periods for the pressure she put on herself to be fair and refrain from acting on her personal tastes or biases. Every writer's approach was different, every subject was different, every style was different—and Dee felt jerked from one end of the emotional spectrum to another as she rode the roller coaster. Even though she didn't try to mark finals in the sort of detail she'd employ earlier in a term, when writers had the opportunity to absorb the comments and revise their work, she read each story twice to assure herself she was not guilty of snap judgments. Only caffeine—and Mama's unpredictably timed needs—broke the pattern and kept her going.

When Teresa arrived at eight on Friday morning, notebook and pen in hand, Dee had her marked printouts neatly stacked in file folders, ready to head to town. She gave Teresa explicit instructions—and the library's phone number—which Teresa dutifully recorded, along with notes about the lunch menu and Mama's medication schedule. Dee was wound so tight she thought her nerves might pop a spring at any moment, but Teresa's calm, careful demeanor helped set her mind at ease a bit.

"Thank you, Teresa. *Muchas gracias*. See you in a few hours, Mama. I'll bring a cake from Wilson's so we can all celebrate!"

At the library, Gladys the guardian of the Internet was back at the desk, while Cynthia was occupied on the phone. With the deadline for posting fast approaching—Eastern time, no less—Dee was beginning to get nervous once more.

"Hello, again," Dee said to Gladys, while craning her neck to catch Cynthia's eye.

"Can I help you?" Gladys said curtly to Dee.

"I'd like to use the Internet again."

"Do you have a library card?"

Dee realized that on her previous visit she'd left without taking care of that.

Cynthia, taking notice of the exchange, quickly got off the phone and strode over to meet Dee. "Gladys, I've got this one," she called out. "Come on back, Dee."

"Whew," she whispered. "Thanks!"

"No, thank *you*," Cynthia said as she printed out a temporary card for Dee. "The Write Stuff group couldn't stop talking about our meeting. Our listserv has been abuzz with chatter all week!"

"Oh, you're welcome," Dee said, her hand practically twitching, waiting for Cynthia to hand her the card.

"How's your mother?"

"Better."

"Did she get her casts off?"

"Not yet."

"How long are you going to be here?"

"A while longer, it looks like," Dee replied.

"Listen," Cynthia said, hesitating, "I know this is looking a gifted horse in the mouth, so to speak, but I got to wondering if you might be able to do a sort of quasi-critique of our writing? We have a small budget. We could pay you."

Dee eyed the library card that Cynthia was gesturing with and said, "Look, I'll make you a deal, but I'm not cheap. Here are my terms. One, unlimited access to the Internet when I come to the library. Two, limited exposure to Gladys when I come to the library. Three, parking privileges anywhere in the library's empty parking lot."

"You got it," Cynthia said, laughing, and handed her the card. "I was so hoping you'd agree! You go get your work done on the computer, and I'll grab their manuscripts for you to get started with."

Dee flashed her credentials in front of Gladys's nose as she hurried to the reading room to log on. Meticulously she entered each student's feedback and final grade, checked and rechecked the average and the letter grades, and hit the submit button. Only when she reached Zimmerman, Alan, could she sit back in relief and know that the school year was truly done. She allowed herself a moment to rub her weary eyes. All over but the shoutin'!

Commencement exercises, a week from tomorrow, would be only a formality for faculty marching in the procession, and a chance to bid good-bye to students who were graduating. By this time next week, Dee congratulated herself, she'd be on a flight home—and on Saturday evening, after graduation, on another to meet up with Abby in Boston. She could put all this behind her and get on with her life.

Cynthia came over and sat down beside Dee, handing her an armload of fat packets, each neatly fastened with a black binder clip.

"Wow," Dee said, as she flipped through the stack, "these are some pretty committed writers! I don't know if I'd have time to do thorough written critiques in the time I have left. What if we just workshop them?"

"Oooh," Cynthia squealed, "that sounds so literary. What do you mean?"

"Well . . . why don't you guys plan to come back to the farm for another meeting next Tuesday night?" Dee suggested. "A special session. You said you have computer files for all these?"

Cynthia nodded.

"Here's what you do," Dee said. "Make a masked copy—without the writer's name anywhere on it—of the first ten pages of each piece. Get a packet to all your members to read in advance, and have them write a single-page response to each one. I'll do the same, and we'll have a round-robin critique session just like in my Craft of Fiction classes."

"Oh, the group will be psyched!" Cynthia said.

"Well, we'll have fun." Dee thanked Cynthia again for the Internet help—and found that she really *was* curious to read what was in the stack of pages. By the time she drove to the bakery for the cake, stopped in at Java Jim's for a cup of coffee, purchased the only CD player in stock at the Radio Shack for Mama's audiobook, and returned to the library, Cynthia had the samples ready to go.

* * *

Mama was tuckered out, and Dee soon led her to bed. But no rest for the weary reader, Dee thought, as she retreated to her bedroom with a contraband slice of cake to read the newest batch of writing samples she'd inherited. She set Cynthia's pile on the desk and turned on the hobnail lamp with its yellowed parchment shade. Drawing a binder-clipped packet out of the batch at random, she folded back the cover sheet to hide the writer's name. She preferred to read her new students' writing blind, and she did her best to treat the Write Stuff pieces with the same objectivity. As if objectivity were possible, she thought . . . although she hated to admit it, a single grammatical faux pas or misspelled word was sometimes all it would take for Dee make a mental strike against the rest of a writer's work.

The first excerpt led with a powerful punch. *When your child dies inside of you—at your own hand—all of you that exists outside of your body dies.* It was a strong opening, and she read on. The writer had the courage to pull a Jay McInerney with that second-person sentence. *The doctors told you the baby might be severely retarded, unable to function. You thought you would be saving him from a life of misery and suffering. But were you really just protecting yourself?*

Someone was writing about abortion from personal experience, she guessed—unless it was the work of an especially impressive imagination. Who? The science fiction chick? She polled her memory. Three of the members had been men; that probably narrowed the pool. And all but Summer and JoAnn had been over sixty. Then she made herself turn things topsy-turvy: say that one of the men *had* written this piece? Separate the writing from the writer. You had to acknowledge that a story could spring from anywhere.

Dee finished the ten pages. Although it could've soft-pedaled the moral lesson and benefit from better development of turning points, it was a decent start for a memoir. If her instincts were right, its creator wouldn't have to go far for further research. She marked her feedback, circled one instance in which a sentence shifted to first person, and slid out another packet.

During the Depression, I was a one of a group of boys whose parents could no longer afford to feed us. They decided to let us seek a living on our own.

We hitched a ride to California where we found work in the strawberry fields. Most of us were kids, none of us old enough for a driver's license. We slept three to a bed, on cots, or mostly on the floor of dusty shacks. We picked from sun up to sun down six days a week. We earned a dollar a day and sent most of it back to our mommas.

Another memoir. Had the writer lived this, heard it secondhand, or made it up? The details were persuasive enough, though ten pages in, the writer hadn't introduced a conflict. *Maybe more effective told in third person,* she suggested, to free the writer from fact and let invention flow. *Figure out what your character wants most of all, and create an obstacle to that desire.* Intriguing stuff to work with.

Dee continued reading until she was down to the last crumb of German chocolate cake. She'd nibbled away at the writing samples until, before she realized, she had gone through half the folder. Not bad for an evening's work. She wondered if she had the stamina to make it through just one more before fatigue set in.

"Does an amoeba grieve when it splits itself in two?" X-Bot *messaged his droid lover W260 from his virtual prison in a parallel universe. If they did not find a way to close the gap in the space-time continuum—and fast—Dub Two might disappear from his world forever.*

Definitely the science fiction chick, Dee thought. No two ways about it. That ruled her out as a candidate for the first memoir. She chided herself for playing the guessing game—that wasn't the point. But she would be eager to finish the others in the morning, and then get back to her own work.

*   *   *

Teresa came early Saturday morning to help Mama get dressed and settled into the car for the ride to Poplar Grove. She seemed to Dee to be even quieter than usual, but she selected Mama's outfit with care and made sure her hair was neatly combed and sprayed in place. Together she and Dee managed to keep Mama standing long enough to pull the sleeves of a red cotton shirtdress over her wrists and button it all the way up the front. They chose a pair of flat-heeled ballerina slippers that would be easy for Mama to manage, and a pair of clip-on pearl earrings that Mama wore only on special occasions. From somewhere in Mama's closet Teresa had found a long, cream-colored crocheted shawl. When draped around Mama's back and arms, it nicely covered the casts.

"But what about a hat?" Dee pondered.

"I've got just the thing," Mama said. "Dee Anna, go in there in your bedroom and look up on the closet shelf. There's a hatbox from Gray's."

Dee returned with the box, which she remembered seeing somewhere before. But what was in it?

Mama removed the lid with her elbow and nodded at a jaunty straw picture-frame hat in the perfect shade of red to match her shirtdress. Teresa placed it atop Mama's silver hair and turned her to face Dee.

"Did you ever see that pitcher of me and your daddy at our fiftieth anniversary party, down at the fellowship hall?" Mama asked. Dee recalled it now—from a photo album in the buffet that she'd seldom opened. "Oh, my word, we were about to die of heatstroke that day, and the wind nearly snatched my new hat away before we could get inside the church."

"Mrs. Bennett *muy bonita* in red, no?" said Teresa, who stepped out the kitchen door and plucked one purple iris growing wild in the returning weeds, broke off most of its stem, and arranged the flower in Mama's hatband. The effect was flamboyant and perfect for the day's outing, and Mama looked ready to reign.

Teresa turned to Dee, her dark ponytail whipping around in the breeze, and said, "Call me when you leave Poplar Grove, and I will meet you here and help you get her out."

"Teresa, you don't have to do that," Dee said. She was beginning to wonder which of them was giving the orders—and which one carrying them out.

"If you want me to work for you," Teresa said, less timidly than before, "you have to listen to my good sense. We are making good progress. Call me."

"Okay then," Dee agreed.

*   *   *

For both Mama and Dee it was their first real venture out (not counting the doctor visit) since the accident. Although Poplar Grove, seat of Bracher County, was situated forty-two miles north of Claxton and had a population only half its size, Ruby Lee's Treasure Chest was a favorite shopping destination of Claxtonites. The smaller town had had something of an outlaw-and-red-light-district past, which it still celebrated with its Old West storefronts and Victorian embellishments. Romanticized vice was a great tourist draw.

Even though Dee had never before been to her cousin's retail establishment, it was impossible to mistake it. As they turned onto Main Street, she and Mama spied a grand old two-story building on the most prominent corner on town, painted in brazen shades of fuchsia and lavender. The name of the store, done in red script with a purple outline, covered the entire north outer wall. Dee was struck by the dimensions of the caricature bosom hinted at by the cursive capital R. She supposed that explained why whenever Ruby Lee said the name of her store, she thrust her impressive cleavage forward to illustrate it.

Though the parking lot was packed, a handicapped spot had been reserved with a personalized sign on it, and their tickets and the wheelchair were waiting at the front desk. Ruby Lee's long-suffering husband, Barge, helped Dee get Mama out of the car. Dee repositioned the shawl, letting the fringe hang down to cover the casts on Mama's arms. With the bit of rouge and lipstick Teresa had applied for her, aside from the wheelchair no one would've guessed Alice Bennett had been so recently hospitalized. And of course that was exactly how Mama wanted it.

A red-hatted usher showed Dee and Mama to their table right up front, under a gaslight chandelier converted to electrical bulbs. They spotted some of the Claxton Red Hat contingent, whom Dee recognized from the Write Stuff evening. Before the Cobb salads had been served, Ruby Lee, resplendent in lavender caftan and red beret, swept by to greet them.

"Ruby Lee," Dee said, "this is so kind of you. Mama has looked forward to it ever since you called. It's been, well," Dee paused, "we've had a bit of a time with it, stuck out there on the farm. If I can ever return the favor . . ."

"Well, there is one little thing," Ruby Lee said.

"Anything—just name it."

"I need a substitute for the style show. One of the participants has come down with a stomach bug and called in sick at the last minute."

"What do I need to do?"

"Be Miss November."

"Oh, God, Ruby Lee," said Dee. "You don't mean model? Anything but that."

"C'mon, it's no big deal. It's just a bunch of biddies in the audience, just us girls."

Dee started to protest—she hadn't waxed in weeks—but there was no opportunity to argue. Ruby Lee dragged her by the hand, away from Mama, and explained that she was going to borrow Dee while Barge visited with Mama a bit.

Mama seemed to enjoy being in on the fun. "Go ahead—Dee Anna and I have been connected at the hip for days. She probably needs a break."

"On one condition," Dee said, as Ruby Lee pulled her toward the dressing room. She reached over to a display rack and grabbed an outrageously large pair of rhinestone-studded sunglasses. "I wear these."

Ruby Lee laughed. "Suit yourself!"

Back in the dressing room, among all the twittering sixtysomethings tottering in their heels and dressing gowns, Ruby Lee handed Dee a Vera Bradley bag containing her outfit. "I've got just the thing for you. Size twelve, right?"

Dee grudgingly admitted to Ruby Lee's accuracy. Behind the flashy purple curtain she removed her street clothes quickly while the other robed models were already lining up—but she had a few minutes, since her month wouldn't come up till late in the program.

She was fully undressed when she reached into the bag for her robe and outfit—and was aghast to find that the swimsuit was a two-piece.

The suit was red, white, and blue paisley with a bow at the cleavage. Modest, to be sure—boy-leg trunks, flattering top—but she couldn't miss the disparity between her tanned-and-toned arms and her paper-white midriff and legs.

What could she possibly do?

To make matters worse, she also realized that she wasn't at all prepared for shoes—she'd worn her jeans and boots with a red dollar-store cowboy hat. *Well, you can't just do a thing halfway,* she thought. Donning her robe, she reached around the corner into the store's Western Room and grabbed a solution. She quickly finished dressing, added the accessory touches, and wrapped her robe back around her.

When her month was announced, she dropped the robe and strode out onto the red carpet, twirling a lariat in one hand and tipping the brim of her hat with the other. A pair of fancy dress chaps covered most of her untanned legs, and an oversized belt went a long way toward hiding her belly-button region.

After a surprised silence, the audience broke out in wild applause. Dee did her stroll down the carpet, trying her best to imitate a model's walk in the western boots, and then turned to go back. Only a few steps to freedom! As she looked over her shoulder and tilted the sunglasses saucily, she saw a camera flash—and realized with horror that there was a photographer in the room. And a male one at that.

She was so mortified she nearly tripped over her rope as she hastened back to the dressing room, bumping into Miss December on the way. What had gotten into her? Had she lost her mind, to listen to Ruby Lee?! All twelve models had to return for a curtain call, and Dee could only hope, as she gave the lariat a halfhearted twirl, that no one would recognize her behind the blingy Ray-Bans.

Afterwards, Ruby Lee rushed back to the dressing room and hugged her effusively. "You were great! They loved it!" she said.

"Why didn't you tell me there was going to be a photographer?" Dee wailed.

"Oh, that's just my friend Max. We always do a little story in the Poplar Grove paper."

Dee scurried to get back into her jeans and blouse, brushed her hair, and went out front to check on Mama, who was watching some of the Poplar Grove ladies enjoy their refreshments. Barge assisted her with a sip of tea at intervals.

Ruby Lee stood talking to a dark-haired guy in gray Stetson, black jeans, chambray shirt, and gray-streaked mustache. "Dee," she said, pulling her in, "let me introduce you to my dear friend Max Miller, the best shutterbug in the West." To Max she said, "And this is my cousin Dee from back East, who's a college professor. That's why we call her P-H-Dee," she said. "Get it?"

Dee was a bit chagrined to learn that her kinfolks said that behind her back, but Ruby Lee just seemed to think it all good fun.

Max grinned. "For an easterner, she does a pretty good cowgirl getup, don't you think?"

Dee was even more incensed to find that he had no trouble recognizing her as the model. "I grew up in West Texas, so it just sort of came back to me," she said.

"Nah, Dee's an artsy-fartsy type like you," Ruby Lee interjected, gesturing toward Max. To Dee she suggested, "Maybe you'd like to see Max's work sometime." To Max she suggested, "Dee's a novelist. She could probably do with a publicity portrait."

Now Dee was *really* on the spot. "I'm still working on my book. It's not a novel, though, more like nonfiction . . . and I'm going to Massachusetts to work on it . . . once my mother gets better . . ." Dee wondered why she was babbling, and finally just stopped talking.

"Here, write down your phone number for Max." Ruby Lee shoved a clipboard under her nose. Dee had no choice but to comply, and then Ruby Lee snatched the paper away.

About that time Miss February sidled up to the photographer. "I loved your coffee-table book about the quarter horses. Such power and majesty, don't you think?"

"Yes, ma'am," he replied. "I certainly agree."

"You'll let us know about the studio appointments?" Ruby Lee said to Max, edging between him and Miss February. Dee wondered what that was all about. A customer waving a credit card lured Ruby Lee to the next table, and Dee saw her chance. She began rolling Mama in the wheelchair toward the exit.

Just as she reached around to push the door open, Dee heard a voice say, "Let's go swimming sometime." She looked up to find Max Miller gallantly holding the door for them.

"Do you see a beach around here?" she shot back.

"I think I've just decided to put in a pool." He tipped his hat, shouldered his camera bag, and headed off to take more candids.

Out of earshot, Mama said, "If I didn't know better, Dee Anna, I'd bet that fellow was flirting with you."

"You don't say," Dee replied

"Well, you'd be a dang fool if you didn't flirt back," Mama said. "Or are you too googly-eyed over Rob the bean counter?"

Rob—she hadn't realized Mama knew about that. Abby, of course. But she did realize she'd forgotten to call him back on the land line this morning.

They were halfway to the car when Dee heard Ruby Lee's booming voice again. "Don't even think of sneaking out of here! I'll have supper at the house. Y'all go on out there with Barge and rest for a while. You've had an exciting day."

They were persuaded to stay not only for the evening meal but to spend the night with Ruby Lee and Barge, and Dee dutifully called Teresa to tell her that it would be Sunday morning before they would return.

For Dee it was a throwback to the long-ago days when she and Buddy and Penny would get together with their cousins in the summertime and tell tales. Dee, always the youngest in the crowd and elbowing her way into a circle of teenagers, felt like she was granted a glimpse into a grownup world she envied, and she felt a little of that urge to belong now. Even Mama sat up late with them, reminiscing about the good old days and commiserating about how much things had changed. Dee realized how much she'd missed company — family — like this.

"Now, who was that cute boy you dated sophomore year, Dee Anna?" asked Ruby Lee, as they did the kitchen chores away from Mama's prying ears.

"Good grief, I don't know —"

"Seein' anybody now?"

"Well, there's a guy back in North Carolina — a colleague, in the accounting department, actually — but I'm not sure it's going anywhere. We're mostly camping and kayaking buddies. That's how we met — through the college's outdoor rec program."

"What you do think of Max?"

Dee stopped her dish-drying and propped her hands on her hips. "You just never quit, do you?"

"You may be interested to know that Max has been trying to get a book of photographs published. Might be something there. He travels a lot on assignment, so you have to catch him while you can. I'm just sayin'."

"Thanks for thinking of me," Dee said, " but I'll only be here for another week."

"Does your mama know that?" Ruby Lee asked.

"I think she's counting on it," Dee replied. "We're about to drive each other nuts. And my coming out here to your show just proves it!"

9
Withdrawn

However carefully you have crafted your story,
be willing to revise radically.

THIRTY MINUTES BEFORE starting time the following Tuesday, Teresa arrived to help prepare for the writers' return. She went straight to the kitchen and put on a full pot of coffee, then brought a tray with cups and sugar and creamer over to the table where Dee had stacked her copies of the manuscripts. When everything else was settled, she took her seat, with her notebook, near Mama.

J. D. Sandifer was there first, accompanied this time by his wife, Pauline.

"I come along to keep Alice company," Pauline said to Dee. Turning to Mama, she explained, "I come by to see you at the hospital, but you was in ICU, so I couldn't get in."

Came, were, Dee thought, but smiled politely and nodded.

Mama, who seemed less than thrilled with the idea of Pauline's chatty companionship, replied, "We just need to sit in a corner and be quiet and let Dee Anna do her thang."

Margaret, the retired reporter–turned–romance writer, brought a bouquet of irises from her yard in a glass vase. "I hope you didn't find my prose to be as violet as these flowers," she said to Dee.

Frances, the family-saga writer, walked in right behind her. "Oh, Margaret, I never found your work to be violent."

"Purple in style, Frances," Margaret said, and in an aside to Dee added, "She's a little hard of hearing."

Wendell knocked on the door precisely on time, a satchel of background documents for his Civil War epic in hand. "Eighteen hundred hours on the dot," he said, and took a seat at the table between JoAnn and Cynthia. As Wendell pulled a sheaf of papers from his satchel, JoAnn commented to him about the barriers to research posed by Texas's privacy laws, and the pair launched into an impassioned discussion of the issue. Cynthia chimed in, mentioning the new restrictions on libraries after 9/11.

At ten after six, Cynthia announced above the chatter of the group, "Well, let's go ahead and get started . . . I don't think Summer is coming."

"What do you mean?" said Frances. "It was in the high eighties today."

Margaret turned to Frances. "No, she's talking about that girl from the Subway."

"Nope, I'm here!" Summer stumbled into the room amid aromas of garlic, grease, and sweat. "The Big Spring girls' soccer team stopped in on their way from a tournament, and we just cranked out thirty-three sandwiches in thirteen minutes." She pumped her fist in victory, and the group nodded in admiration.

"Okay," Dee said, "gather your chairs around the table. Glad everyone could make it. Now, have any of you ever taken part in a writing workshop before?"

The group went silent, and no one moved a muscle except for Pauline, who whispered something to Mama, who promptly rolled her eyes in Dee's direction.

"Well," offered Margaret, "we just look over each others' drafts and talk about what we liked, but no one really feels qualified to critique, if that's what you mean."

"No? Then I want to set some ground rules. First, has anyone here had a book on the *New York Times* best seller list?"

They all chuckled and shook their heads.

"Anyone at the top of the Amazon rankings?"

More laughter.

"All right," Dee said, "that means no one's an expert, and that includes me. So there are seven of you, and I want you to comment on one another's work as readers, not writers. For the moment, don't even get into grammar, punctuation, and all that. Just concentrate on the story. Does it grab your attention right from the start? Is there a conflict that cries out for resolution? Do you find the main character intriguing? What about the supporting characters?"

"Makes sense to me," said J. D.

"So. By now we've all read these excerpts, and we probably realize that the passages come from different places in longer works—some are taken from the beginning, but others jump into the middle, so see if you can make sense of the writing without the benefit of context. I want you to take each piece of writing on its own terms."

Dee concluded, "Most important, just remember that judgment is subjective, and not everyone will like everything—but treat the work of your fellow writers with respect. So if most of us say, 'It bothered me that the boy didn't get the girl,' give it some serious thought, but also bear in mind there might be six other readers who would say, 'I was glad the boy *didn't* get the girl.'"

Dee removed a stack of single sheets from a manila folder. "Here's a copy of what my students like to call Dr. Dee's Rules for Writing. They think they're being funny. But what we do during the semester is to consider every piece of writing in light of these guidelines—and figure out in what ways they are relevant, and in what ways they aren't. Many of these will be obvious to you even if you've never taken a writing class. 'Show, don't tell.' Sound familiar?"

Heads nodded all around.

"Now, we're going to shuffle that pile of excerpts on the kitchen table, and I will pick at random and read a few pages of each one aloud," Dee said. "We'll do it this way to avoid putting anyone on the spot. Just imagine you're listening to an audiobook. Afterward we'll discuss our reactions. You can claim your writing or remain anonymous, as you wish. Let's start."

Dee drew a packet out of the bunch and leaned against the tall kitchen stool to read. *When a man lusts for a woman,* she began, while a few in the group suppressed snickers, *it starts in the gut, and then kind of works its way down to the toes and back up again, sort of settling at the top of his chaps. Brendan O'Malley realized he had fallen asleep in the saddle not because of the sound of cattle bawling, but when he woke up dreaming about Daisy from the dance hall.*

Dee caught sight of Pauline Sandifer glaring at J. D. from across the room. She quickly scanned ahead and found safer sentences.

The smell of rain was in the air and lighting crackled across the dawn sky. Wilbur was already awake and breaking down camp. They knew they had to make Durango tonight with the herd if they had any chance of getting to Montana before September.

Wilbur's horse, Biscuits, knew the routine as well, and steadied himself for Wilbur's pack. There was something about a horse that comforted a man in the way a woman never could, the cowboy thought.

Pauline glared again.

The two cowboys urinated on the fire to douse it.

J. D. sort of slunk down in his chair, and Dee forced herself to keep a straight face. Mama gestured for Teresa to press her lift chair button. "Pauline and me are going to my bedroom to watch *Dancing with the Stars.*" Pauline nodded indignantly as she and Teresa helped Mama out of the room, and Teresa returned to sit on the sofa and listen intently.

"If writing was easy," Dee said to settle the group, "everyone would be an author. Sometimes you have to take a little heat for your art." Dee finished reading to the end of the page. "Remember, hold your thoughts and we'll discuss in a few minutes. By the way, that one was titled 'Biscuits and Me.'"

She picked another excerpt. "The Last Summer," from the pile.

You never know when The Last Summer will be, Hope thought, as she took the eye dropper from the hospice worker, and put some water into her mother's mouth. How quickly the cancer had stolen the season from them.

But the Big C, as Mom had called it, hadn't taken the memories. These days had been the best days of Hope's life, with long walks and long talks. She and her Mother had declared a cease-fire of sorts, and simply spent their time, cooking and eating, laughing, watching bad TV, and doing a little bit of drinking—the doctor had said red wine would be good for Mom's blood pressure.

When they found out that the time they had left was days not months, every night, Mom had Hope make a list of "questions to be answered now not later." At first the list was very serious, about wills, and memorial service preferences, and then it got silly, such as "Who was the first boy you ever kissed?"

Hope fought back tears as Mom murmured in pain.

By the time Dee reached the end of the submission, all of the writers except JoAnn—who looked around impatiently—had sat back in their chairs, subdued with sadness. Dee saw Frances reach over and pat Margaret's hand under the table. She was grateful that the next packet she drew out was upbeat and humorous, lifting the collective gloom. Nonetheless she appreciated how deeply the writers paid attention to each piece. They would really have the potential for helping one another, and she was glad to help get the ball rolling for them.

Dee read the remaining excerpts, and with the exception of the scene in which the robots waxed romantic, none of the manuscripts was greeted too harshly by the group. Even in the extreme cases fellow writers stuck to the rules and offered helpful criticisms.

"I know we had to rush through sort of fast," said Frances. "But I got a lot out of it. I can't wait to get back to my computer and revise my scene."

Summer added, "I never really understood about limited omniscient point of view. I think I'm starting to get it now."

"Too bad you're leaving us so soon," Cynthia said to Dee.

"I'll think about you all when I'm back in North Carolina," Dee replied sincerely. "I wish you luck."

Wendell shook her hand. "It's been great to have a pro among us." Dee accepted the compliment graciously, glad that he appeared unfazed by the comments she'd written on his draft. Or maybe he just hadn't had time to digest them yet.

Frances assured Dee that she would think about rewriting her brother's story in the third person.

J. D., who had gone to retrieve Pauline, was lingering with her in the back bedroom, where they were still talking Mama's ear off after the rest of the writers had bid goodnight.

*   *   *

After the Sandlfers departed and Dee straightened up the dining room, she went in to check on Mama—who was sitting straight up in her bed, still in her day clothes, snoring away, arms propped on a pillow in her lap. Dee turned off the television, removed Mama's glasses and placed them on the nightstand, brushed her hair back from her forehead, and helped ease her into a more comfortable position before turning off the light. What a day it had been for them both—and they had more to come as the end of the week approached.

Dee gathered her workshop materials into her briefcase and took out Friday's airline ticket. She noted a reminder on her calendar to drive into town and check in online for her late afternoon flight. She'd arranged with Ruby Lee and Barge to catch a ride to Dallas, where they had plans to visit the market and stock up on merchandise for the store.

Dee took her suitcase from the closet. She would do all her laundry tomorrow, and also write up a full report of notes on Mama's care and medications for anyone who might be helping out next. She made out a list neatly in her notebook: Update Mama's address book with new phone numbers. Send a thank-you note to Cynthia. Give Rob a call before she headed back (and remind him that she'd need him to drop off her cap and gown at her office after graduation on Saturday). E-mail Penny and Buddy her flight information. Tell Abby her anticipated arrival time and gate at Logan. Get her heavier jacket from home and add it to her suitcase. Thursday morning would be taken up with Mama's appointment in town with Dr. Kim, so it would be best to have everything in order well before then. Dee wanted nothing to detract from the precious few days she would have with Abby, or her stay at the visiting writers' quarters in the Berkshires.

She had washed her face and slipped into her pajamas and was just about to turn off her own light when she heard the clang of the cowbell. She rose silently and stoically, went to Mama's bedroom, helped her out of the bed into the bathroom, lowered her pants for her, and assisted her over the toilet. Charmin cleanup done and toilet flushed, Dee helped Mama into her nightgown and back to bed. They had developed a comfortable rhythm for a precarious and awkward situation. But thank God, she thought, they wouldn't need to do it for much longer.

Lying awake a few minutes later and thinking back over the Write Stuff group's interactions, Dee thought she heard a scratching sound at the front door. Yes, there it was again. And then she remembered — the big yellow dog who'd kept her company during her first nights alone in the house. She tiptoed down the hallway and eased the door open.

"Chester?" she whispered.

The dog responded with a friendly wag of his tail, and Dee couldn't resist. "Come on in, you rascal. But you're on your own again at daybreak, boy. Mama might send us both to the pound if she discovered you here!"

She'd leave here on Friday with some minor mysteries unsolved, she mused. Where did Chester belong, and why did he show up at such odd times? Who were Stacey's family, who lived in the trailer at the bottom of the hill? Which of the Write Stuff members had written the cancer story, which one the abortion memoir? And a larger one: Who had run Mama off the road in the first place? She figured she would never know.

She set the alarm for five and drifted off to sleep, the satisfied dog lounging at her feet.

*   *   *

Thursday morning came sooner than either of them could imagine. "C'mon, Mama, your friend Dr. Kim is waiting!" Dee urged, when her mother was still sleeping soundly at eight-thirty. "Don't you want to see how your bones are mending?" The sun shone valiantly through a thick layer of dust that hung in the air. The weather report said by afternoon they might see rain, but right now it was just dry, dreary, and windy. With Teresa on one side and Dee on the other, they dressed Mama and helped her down the steps into the car, a process that took a good ten minutes in the strong wind, but they drove into town in high spirits.

Dr. Kim took a long time examining the X-rays, holding first the left and then the right up to the light box and making notes on Mama's chart. At last she spoke. Dee glanced over at Mama's face and saw, in a single moment, everything Mama *hadn't* said about what was riding on this checkup. She started to get an inkling herself.

"Mrs. Bennett, your bones appear to be knitting back together in the way they should—the pattern is good, and I'm pleased with that. I'm also pleased with your muscle tone—you must have been keeping up your exercises."

Mama nodded warily.

"But it looks like healing is going to take a while longer. At the rate things are going, I think we will need to keep your wrists immobilized for another six weeks or so."

Mama nearly fell off the examining table, and Dee reached to steady her. "Another six weeks!" Mama said. "But Dr. Taylor told us—"

"I know it's not welcome news. I'm sure Dr. Taylor was looking on the bright side, and besides, orthopedics is not his specialty. It's really very hard to predict how any individual will respond. We want you fully healed before you put any pressure on these joints, so you don't reinjure yourself. I'm sure you wouldn't want that?"

"What I don't want is to keep on being dependent on somebody else for ever' little thing," said Mama petulantly. "I think I need a second opinion."

"You are certainly within your rights to do that, Mrs. Bennett. I want you to be satisfied that your course of treatment is the right one—that'll be important in your healing. You could probably get in with a specialist in Lubbock sometime next week."

Mama exhaled a long breath and looked in Dee's direction. "Wouldn't make no difference. Ain't nobody to carry me clear to Lubbock."

"But you have family so close by," replied the doctor. "You are lucky."

Dee was sure Mama didn't agree. She was thankful at least that Mama had refrained from insulting Dr. Kim again and appeared resigned to the prognosis. What real choice did she have, after all?

Teresa, gauging Mama's sullen expression when they returned to the waiting room, knew better than to ask for a report, but Mama said it all: "You're stuck with me for another six weeks, T'resa, so I sure hope takin' care of a broken-down old woman makes you happy."

Mama declined the opportunity to stop for a milk shake on the way home, and they all sat in silence as Dee drove.

Dee mulled her own options in her mind. Rehab hospital? They'd already reached a firm no there. Penny or Buddy? Still not likely. For herself, six more weeks . . . that would wipe out nearly the entire fellowship period, not to mention the visit with Abby, and the airline reservations. It might even threaten her chances with her book altogether. Maybe the Berkshires staff would change the dates for her. She'd have to get creative—fast.

When they got back to the home place, Teresa offered to make sandwiches for lunch before Mama's therapy session. But Mama refused, instead insisting on going straight back to bed. Dee and Teresa eased Mama down to the mattress, where she flung herself over so forcefully, face down on the bedspread, that Dee feared she'd do even more damage to her bones.

Dee didn't stick around for lunch, either, but instead drove straight back to town, to the library. She flashed Gladys her temporary computer permit and logged on to the Internet.

With a bit of research she found that if she changed tomorrow's Raleigh-to-Hartford ticket to depart directly from DFW instead, it looked like it would cost only a change fee plus two hundred dollars difference in fare . . . but the only available coach seat was on the 5:50 a.m. departure, and to get to Dallas in time, she'd have to leave almost immediately, rent a car one-way, maybe stay in a hotel for a few hours . . . and even assuming she could afford the extra hit on her budget, how would she get from the farm to the rental car office? She didn't know anyone who could do that kind of favor on short notice.

Who was she fooling? She had to agree with Mama. It was no fun having to depend on others for help.

What if Buddy and Roxanne could come stay with Mama on some of the week nights, and Penny and her girls could drive out to Claxton on the weekends? There was Penny's son Mark, the mechanic, but last they'd heard he was working on an offshore rig and wouldn't be back till August. Teresa seemed dependable, and that covered three days a week . . . even Buck Turlock and his wife were nearby a lot of the time. Maybe Cynthia could pull some strings with Mitzi and her Helping Hands staff.

She weighed all the possibilities and came to a decision.

She let out a deep breath and composed an e-mail. *Keith: Still in TX and won't make it for graduation Saturday. Mother's doing better but recovering slowly. I'll work out later travel from here. In the meantime, let me know if any questions come up.*

She hit Send, logged off, and went outside to make two calls to Massachusetts.

*　　*　　*

It wasn't lost on Dee that it was now possible—for the first time in her life—to buy an alcoholic drink in Claxton. She just didn't know where you might find one. She stopped in at the supermarket—the chain store with deli and pharmacy that had put the two local outfits out of business a couple of years ago—and bought a few items she knew were on Mama's list.

At the checkout she asked the clerk, "Say, I'm new here . . . can you tell me where there's a restaurant with a bar?" The young woman leaned around the partition that had kept Dee from seeing that she was well advanced in pregnancy and replied, "Well, I don't think I can help you with that myself, but I'll bet Jeff can tell you—hey, Jeff?" she yelled across to the cashier two lanes over. "Can you tell this lady where to find a bar in town?"

Jeez, thought Dee, everyone in the store thinks I'm a lush, at three in the afternoon. Jeff kindly came over to offer her a few suggestions. His best recommendation was Jesse Jane's Roadhouse, to which he gave her directions. Dee thanked him, pulled her recently acquired sunglasses down over her eyes, and tried to maintain her dignity as she left the store.

*   *   *

Jesse Jane's, a mile past the football stadium on the Sweetwater highway, did not exactly seem to be buzzing with excitement at that hour. Dee parked Mama's car at the far edge of the dirt lot and, still wearing her dark glasses, strolled over and opened the front door. It was inviting enough . . . and blessedly cool and shadowy, just the antidote she needed against the stifling Texas heat. She could make out a long, wooden L-shaped bar at the back, with a mirrored wall behind it and shelves full of potations in tempting shapes and colors. A small elevated stage occupied the other back corner. There were ample café tables and booths, too—just the sort of place she might've appreciated on a cozy evening with someone special.

Today, though, she headed straight for the nearest barstool. She was the only patron at the bar, it appeared, and it wasn't hard to get the bartender's attention.

"What'll you have on this fine afternoon?" the white-haired, middle-aged woman asked. "Not much of a crowd, with everybody getting ready to leave town for Memorial Day."

"Vodka gimlet, please." She pushed her sunglasses up over her head, using them as a hairband.

"Vodka we got. The second part, I'm stumped."

"Oh," said Dee. "It's not hard. Do you have lime juice?"

"Sure. I serve the best margarita in town."

"Well, make it with equal parts vodka and Rose's lime juice, over ice, squeeze in a little fresh lime juice, and garnish it with the rest of the lime. Raymond Chandler made his with gin, but vodka will do nicely."

"Raymond Chandler? He one of those Chandler boys that got busted with the meth lab?"

"Never mind. Just make it cold and quick."

"Are you new in town, or visiting?" asked the bartender as she mixed the drink.

Dee thought about it. "No and yes."

"Sounds complicated. I'm Jane, by the way. Welcome to Claxton."

"I was actually born here," Dee offered. "And I've been back staying with family for a while."

"Oh, well, then, I don't have to tell you what a new experience it is to have a drinking establishment in town. I moved down here from Lubbock when Caprock County approved liquor by the drink, and my partner and I renovated this vacant community center."

"Nice," said Dee, downing half the drink in one gulp. "Have you started to build up a clientele?"

"We have lots of regulars—roustabouts and oil crews, engineers, landmen, even a few bikers—but it's really not a rough crowd at all. We have a live band and dancing on Saturday night and karaoke on Fridays. You oughta come check it out."

Dee was about to demur when she heard the door open behind her and turned to see three figures silhouetted in the doorway. One of the men waved and called out to Jane as the group headed toward a dark booth opposite the bar.

"Speaking of, there are some of my guys now. Be right back." One of the patrons changed course and came over to where Dee was staring down into her cocktail.

"Well, if it isn't Miss November," he said. Dee turned to see Max Miller, the photographer, elbow propped on the bar beside her. "What, did that one little modelling experience drive you to drink?"

"Listen, Mr. Miller, that was a pretty dirty stunt for my cousin to pull. If those photos show up on any parts-store wall—"

"Whoa, don't get your chaps in a twist. I thought you were a very good sport. You rescued the show." Dee felt herself blush and was glad for the dark bar. "What're you drinking?" Max asked. "Can I buy you another?"

"Not unless you want to see me fall right off this barstool. It's the first drink I've had since I came to Claxton, and I think it's going straight to my head."

"Bad day or good day?"

"Bad."

"Mmm. Sorry. So . . . I've got to go wrap up some business with these fellows over here . . . you mind if I come back and join you?"

"Suit yourself. In the meantime, it's five o'clock somewhere." She raised her empty glass in a mock toast. "In Massachusetts, to be exact."

Jane took the men their drinks and peanuts. After a short while Max begged off and took a seat beside Dee at the bar, where she was well into the third gimlet. It didn't escape her notice that he'd ordered a Dr Pepper.

"Tell me about the bad day."

She did, starting with the doctor's news and Mama's dejection and working backward to fill him in about the accident, and her research plans, and winding up with Mama's dejection all over again. "When the doctor said she'd be in the casts for six more weeks, it's like all the spunk went out of her. All the determination to get well."

"But you're doing exactly what she needs to keep her healthy and happy. You should be proud of that."

"I might be, if I wasn't so resentful about it . . . and still wondering how I can have my cake and eat it too. I tried to change my summer plans, but no luck so far. And my sister and brother have their own obligations. We thought . . . well, I don't know what we thought, but it's clear that Mama can't be left alone at any time. Even with everyday tasks, she requires help, and if an emergency happened, day or night, she'd really need someone there. I think if we moved her to a nursing home she'd just wither up and die. And I'd have her haunting me for the rest of my life." Dee, becoming aware she'd been rambling, suddenly looked down at her watch. "Speaking of . . . omigosh, it's past six, and Teresa's ride gets there at five—omigosh, I'm late. She'll kill *me* if she's not already dead."

"Teresa who?"

Dee had a fleeting realization that she'd been vague about her antecedent. "Mama! I am in so much trouble . .

"Let me drive you. You've had four of those—and I'll bet they're a lot heavier on the vodka than the ice."

"You right 'bout that," she slurred. "If you're sure, c'mon, while I'm still in shape to give you directions."

They pulled up in the driveway at seven, the sun still high in the sky and the hot wind still steadily blowing. Teresa's father was waiting in his pickup with the windows rolled down. But the heat outdoors was nothing compared to the temperature in Mama's kitchen.

Alice was standing at the sink, cradling her immobilized arms, rocking back and forth and staring out the window, when Max led Dee through the side door. "Where on God's green earth have you been, Dee Anna Bennett?"

"I had a lot of things to care of. To *take* care of," said Dee. "Miller— Max—was nice enough to bring me home."

"From where, a distillery?" When Mama got agitated and tried to use her arms, she looked to Dee just like the robot on *Lost in Space*. Dee giggled and then began to hiccup.

"I don't see the humor in this a-tall," said Mama, fuming. "Teresa, you can go on home. We'll be fine."

"You sure, Mrs. Bennett? I can stay if I tell my father." She looked at Dee as if to seek permission.

"No," Mama said. "You've put up with quite enough for one day. Go on."

Dee stumbled over and collapsed on the red leather couch. Max said to Mama, "She really has had some hard things to deal with today, Mrs. Bennett, and it sounds like you have too. I can come out tomorrow and pick her up to get your car, after she's feeling better."

"After she's sober, you mean. I am so ashamed. You'd better go now too."

"Yes, ma'am—if you're sure you're okay."

"I'll be fine. I can manage."

*   *   *

Dee woke with an aching in the side of her head like someone was beating it with a brick. She opened one eye—the sun was shining brightly, but then, it had been shining the last time she remembered, too. She tried to move but found she was weighed down . . . she felt around to discern that she was covered by a heavy cotton quilt. She was on the red couch, still in last night's clothes and shoes. No wonder she was sweating already.

She ventured opening the other eye and could see Mama, erect in her chair, also wearing her same clothes from yesterday. What day was it, Friday? Right. She should be going over her checklist one last time, and waiting at the door for Ruby Lee. Tomorrow morning the Raleigh College faculty and graduates would be lining up for graduation on the lawn. And afterward—according to her airline ticket—she'd be on a plane headed north.

Dee stirred and tried to push the cover back.

"Got your suitcase packed? Mama asked acidly. "Or maybe you're too hung over to care."

"Mama . . ."

"I know I've gotten to be too much of a burden to bear. You just go on—you just call Penny and tell her to start lookin' into them assisted living apartments. Hand me that phone there. And I'll tell Ruby Lee you might need extra time gettin' ready. She'll be here in a half hour."

"Mama," Dee said, pulling herself slowly upright, "you don't have to do that."

"Well, if nobody else is gonna look after me, I'm gonna have to look after myself." Mama started to work herself up to a full-blown case of martyred self-righteousness. "It don't matter if it means I have to leave this home place. Nobody cares about some old widow-woman. Might as well just throw us away."

"That's not true—"

"You kids got better things to do than to help your own family. All those years your daddy and I thought we was raisin' you right, and now when there's the least hardship, you run off on some lark, as far away as you can go." Mama was on the verge of tears.

"*Mama!*" Dee practically shouted. "I'm not going anywhere. *You're* not going anywhere. I'll call Ruby Lee. I'm staying right here. I withdrew from the fellowship."

10
A Memorial Day Surprise

Number two: A stranger comes to town.

IT HAD BEEN A HOT, gloomy weekend at the home place. The only bright spot, for Dee, had been Penny's phone call to say that an important showing had come up at the last minute and she couldn't make it to Claxton after all. Mama's car had reappeared in the driveway, but Dee had not answered the knock at the door.

Neither Mama nor Dee knew what to say to each other, and without Teresa around to mediate and cajole, they'd simply gotten by with the rudiments of communication. If Jezebel's bell rang, Dee rose, went to her mother's room, and wordlessly assisted with toilet duty or fetched a glass of water. She served cold sandwiches and chips for lunch, and for supper she warmed up soup that Mama could sip through a straw. She devoutly wished for another of those kick-ass vodka gimlets from Jesse Jane's. At least it would dull the misery.

During Mama's lengthy stretches of rest or television Dee retreated to the desk in her room and tried to force herself to work on her book. She flipped through the files of notes, attempting to compose her thoughts or break through to a fresh way of telling the story. But most times she found herself staring at a blank page of her legal pad, doodling. Or she'd get out the laptop and try to write that way. After a full hour, she'd glance at the screen, to see that the only progress she'd made was another blue paragraph mark where she'd hit the return key.

*   *   *

While most of Claxton was preparing to enjoy their Memorial Day at the lake or packing a picnic cooler to take to the park, Dee clambered out of bed, splashed a little water on her face, and readied herself for another day of lifting and spooning and wiping. Mama was still sleeping, past her usual time, when Teresa arrived at eight-thirty. Dee was thankful that Teresa didn't mind working on a holiday—she'd had just about enough of the spiteful silence.

Just then the house phone rang. Teresa answered. "Someone name Abby for you?"

Dee took the phone from her. "Hey, sweetie, what's up? It's awfully early for you, isn't it?"

"Not when I've been on a Greyhound bus for the last forty-eight hours," she said. "Do you have any idea how many times you have to change buses to get from Northampton, Massachusetts, to Claxton, Texas?"

"You're in Claxton?" Dee rubbed her head. She wasn't sure she'd heard right.

"Come pick me up at the truck stop—the bus was late, and it just got in," Abby said. "I thought you could use another set of hands taking care of Gramma Alice at the farm. Since you had to stay and all."

Dee could hardly contain her astonishment and joy. Suddenly the despair of the past days fell away. Abby, right here in Claxton! "Why, that's—wonderful," she said. "But hon, what about your job?"

"I'll tell you about it in person, but it's no big deal. I'm just taking a break. I can go back whenever I want."

Among the half dozen things Dee noticed when she pulled into the parking lot of the truck stop where the Greyhound bus arrived once a day, she couldn't decide which drained her elation the quickest: that Abby was not alone; that the person accompanying her was older, and male; that her daughter had gained weight; that the pair were smoking; and that, as she got closer, she spotted a tattoo on Abby's neck, just below her right earlobe and framed by her curly brown locks. A *carrot*, for god's sake.

She said, instead, as she got out and ran to hug her, "It's so good to see you. Hop in."

"Mom, this is Ian," Abby said as they opened the back door and set their assorted bags on the seat. Dee shook Ian's hand and welcomed the muscular young man. She couldn't recall the name of the boyfriend Abby had mentioned so passionately over the phone in connection with the restaurant, but she was pretty sure that hadn't been it.

"Nice to meet you," Dee said.

"Ian can only hang out for a couple of days," Abby said. "He has an AmeriCorps job this summer, and he's on his way to New Mexico to learn to build adobe houses."

"Mm. Have y'all eaten?" Dee said.

"Y'all?" Abby said, and turned to Ian. "I used to get in trouble when I would go to visit Mom and say 'y'all.'"

"When in Rome," Dee said, trying to appear carefree, and then, suddenly, picked up on a distinct *meow* from the back seat. "What's that noise?"

"Oh," Abby said, holding up a carry-on that turned out to be a pet carrier containing an orange tabby cat. "This is Coriander—we call him Cori for short."

Dee pretended to fawn over the feline, but in her mind she was calculating how much credit she had left on her Discover card in case she needed to buy breakfast—or cat food—for them. She'd been hoarding her dollars for travel expenses.

"We're good," Abby said. "Let's go see Gramma Alice. How's she doing?"

"As well as can be expected under the circumstances. We'll see how much it sets her back when she finds out you're bringing a cat into her house."

* * *

"You're fat," were Mama's first words to Abby, followed by "Who's he?," "You do know that smoking's a sin," and "Don't even think you two're sleeping in the same bed in this house"—all said as Abby had reached over to hug her grandmother, and without missing a beat, replied, "Yep, but at least I can wipe my own butt."

Mama cackled at Abby's retort, and all the rancor seemed to recede from her. It was the first honest laugh Dee had heard from her mother in a long time. Abby and Ian settled onto the sofa next to Mama's recliner, while Dee brought in a chair from the dining room. Teresa had retreated to the kitchen, out of the hubbub.

Between Mama and her youngest grandchild there had always existed a no-holds-barred candor, a casual comfortableness that had skipped a generation. Not that their faux insults couldn't careen out of control, with one or the other of them ending up in tears, but for the most part, the pair navigated the high-wire bluntness strung between them with a deftness Dee had to admire.

"Man, the place looks like a dump," Abby said. "What happened to the kitchen garden? It's grown up with weeds."

Mama grew quiet. "That was PaPa's baby. He kept it up until he couldn't anymore . . ." Her voice faded away.

Dee saw the mortified look on Abby's face, and she intervened. "I tried to rescue the yard the other day with the tractor," she offered up to lighten the mood. Mama shook her head and closed her eyes in mock despair, leaving the impression that Dee's efforts had been a total debacle.

"Uh-oh," Abby replied, "you're lucky the house is still standing. Mom's never been very mechanical."

Now Dee fought getting defensive. She'd lived by herself for almost seven years and had found ways to keep her household functioning on a budget. Instead of setting the record straight, though, she introduced the visitors to Teresa, who brought fresh coffee for all.

"Teresa keeps me on my toes," Mama explained. "And my fingers." Dee marveled that Mama could switch on her good-natured side like a light bulb.

"That's great, Teresa, that you work helping people like my gramma," said Abby.

"It is my—my pleasure," Teresa said softly, searching for the right word.

"I-on,"—Mama pronounced his name like the particle—"what do *you* do for a living?" It was her not-so-subtle way of noting that he appeared to be older than his companion and should be out of college by now.

"I served in the Peace Corps for two years, and I've just returned from Indonesia," he said. "Now I'm in AmeriCorps, and I will be helping Native Americans build affordable housing. I'm working on a doctorate in anthropology, studying indigenous peoples."

"Hmmph," Mama said. "You should fit right in with this bunch of professional students."

Teresa tapped her wristwatch. "Ten a.m., Mrs. Bennett."

"I know, I know," Mama said, "Time for thurr-apy. Lord, I hate them exercises." She pushed the button on the lift chair, and Teresa helped her up.

"Abigail?" Mama said, invoking the formal name that she knew her granddaughter loathed.

"Yes, Gramma Alice?"

Mama wagged one cast-bound arm at her. "The Bible says it's wrong to deface your body. I don't believe in tattoos, especially some such silliness as a vegetable on your neck."

A plaintive *meow* came from behind the sofa before Abby could talk back.

"What the hell was that?" Mama was genuinely startled.

"My cat, Coriander. Don't worry—he's very gentle. And he's in a pet carrier anyway."

"Well, take it outside this instant," Mama said sharply. "In fifty years, I've never allowed an animal inside this house, and I don't intend to start now." Dee smiled wickedly inside, remembering the clandestine visits of Chester the dog.

Ian took Cori and a can of tuna to the barn, and Abby and Dee took their coffee to the kitchen table. When Ian reappeared in the kitchen doorway with two duffel bags, Dee calculated the lodging options in the three-bedroom house.

"Ian, you can put your things in my brother's old room, which is the one at the front of the house," she said. "However, the couch in the living room is very comfortable, and I'm sure you won't mind sleeping there."

"No problem," said Ian.

When he was out of earshot, Abby said to her mother, "I wish everyone would quit assuming I'm sleeping with Ian."

"Well, are you?"

"Only occasionally, if you must know. And no one is living together. We both have roommates, and it gets icky."

"Just a guess, but might he be living with an ex-girlfriend?" Dee said. "Or is she really an ex?"

"How did you know?" Abby said, her mouth gaping open.

"I teach college students. Post-adolescent angst is my specialty."

"Except when it's close to home," Abby said, almost under her breath, and then added, "Mom, I'm sorry. That was a cheap shot."

The kitchen phone rang again. Busy morning already, thought Dee as she answered it.

"Hey, good to hear from you," she said into the receiver. "How are things in North Carolina? I'm really sorry I had to change plans on you so suddenly." She mouthed an aside to Abby. *"Rob."*

Abby turned to Ian. "That's Mom's main squeeze. Rob the accountant. Great name for his line of work." Abby poured Ian more coffee while they eavesdropped on one half of the conversation.

"I think she's better," Dee said. "But the doctor's report was very hard on her. . . . Oh, I know it's been a long time already . . . . My daughter just arrived here a little while ago . . . . Yes, Ducky, I miss you, too."

Abby spewed coffee, laughing at Dee's lame attempt to be romantic.

"Sure, you can borrow the kayak again," Dee continued. "Someone should get some use out of it. And it would be great if you'd check on the house while you're there."

Abby whispered to her mother, "We're going for a walk so you can have phone sex with *Ducky*," and dragged Ian outside by the hand. Dee watched through the window as the pair opened the barn door and began to haul out the ladder, the yard tools, and Daddy's tool box.

Dee was listening to Rob wax philosophical about his recent keynote speech to the annual regional convention of CPAs when she looked up to see Teresa point to her watch and wave good-bye. Not sixty seconds later, she heard the cowbell from the living room. She excused herself from Rob mid-sentence and ran to answer the summons.

Dee took Mama down the hall to assist her with the familiar routine. As she helped Mama lower herself to the toilet seat, they were suddenly both startled to see Ian's face at the bathroom window. Standing on a ladder with a hammer and a caulk gun, he had begun to repair a broken shutter. Nonplussed by the necessary activities, he smiled and waved at Mama.

"Good Lord almighty," Mama said, "what does a person have to do to poop in private around here?"

"Good question," Dee answered, but Mama was not amused.

"Mom?" Abby was yelling from the kitchen. "Do you know where I could find the top part of the double boiler?"

"Just a minute," Dee shouted back, her nerves growing frazzled from being on call in different directions. She could hear pots and pans rattling.

"If she messes up my Revere Ware, she's paying for it," said Mama.

"Just put it on my account," Dee said testily. "I'm sure 24/7 home health care ought to be worth something."

The kitchen had always been Alice Bennett's stage, and she didn't give up the limelight willingly. She was an accomplished country cook who liked things done her way. When Penny and Dee were growing up and wanted to help, Mama would find a way to deploy them to housework or yard duty instead.

Alice's amply stocked larder reflected a post-Sputnik mindset: margarine, Crisco shortening, Miracle Whip, Thousand Island dressing, and Spam, plus varieties of Hamburger Helper, Jell-O, and canned condensed soup. Fresh ingredients from the garden were meant to be frozen, fried, preserved, or smothered in gravy. The aromas of cayenne and curry had probably never made an appearance, and nothing Penny had ever done to introduce gourmet dishes at family gatherings had impressed Mama. As for Dee, well, she'd missed the culinary gene entirely.

"I brought some of my own stuff for cooking," Abby said, as she unpacked a tin of spices, oils, garlic cloves, noodles, and fresh ginger root and placed them in the cabinet. "Teresa had this fryer cut up in the fridge, so I'm going to make Asian chicken soup for lunch."

"I like Chinese food," Mama said, returning with Dee to the chair. "There's a buffet in town that's all you can eat for $6.99. Daddy and I used to go there. 'Course some people claim they serve dog meat and roadkill there, but I never believed it."

"Oh, didn't you know that's what we're having for dinner?" Abby joked. "Won ton Chihuahua—tastes like *chee-kin!*"

Abby reached to fill a stock pot with water for cooking the chicken. But as soon as she pulled out the sprayer attachment, the faucet handle snapped off with a loud crack. Water shot up like a geyser, soaking everything within a five-foot radius and threatening to flood the living room.

"Oh!" shrieked Abby, wiping cold water from her forehead with the kitchen towel. Dee struggled to cover the broken fixture with the pot.

Ian, hearing the commotion, grabbed the pliers and came running, but Mama directed him back outside. "Ain't no cutoff valve. You have to shut it off out at the pump."

By the time he succeeded, both Dee and Abby were dripping from head to toe. They grabbed for each other to avoid slipping on the wet floor, but they both eventually collapsed, laughing like lunatics, in the puddle.

Mama laughed too, and Dee took that to signal forgiveness of last week's conflicts for them all.

*   *   *

As the four sat down to steaming bowls of savory noodle soup—a little later than they'd planned—Ian cautioned Mama about the faucet. "I've rigged it back for the time being," he explained, "but you really want to go easy on that handle until you can get a plumber out here to install a new one."

"Well, I'm mighty obliged. We'd of been in a pickle without you."

Abby asked, "Gramma Alice, would it bother you if we planted some herbs and vegetables in the kitchen garden? I know it's a bit late in the season, but as warm as it is, it shouldn't take long for plants to germinate."

"Now, who's going to take care of a garden?" Mama said.

"We all will at first." Abby looked over at her mother. "Won't we, Mom? But before long, you'll be able to again."

Mama brightened somewhat at the idea. "Well, just a few things— don't go overboard. Maybe some tomatoes. And peppers. Those are easy." She started to build up a head of steam. "Squash. Okra. Cucumbers. May as well plant some green beans—they'd come in by late summer. 'Course nobody knows how to set up a pole but me."

"Gramma Alice, the food bank where I work grows its own vegetables, and I found your seed stash in fruit jars in the barn. I can work magic with Kentucky Wonders and twine."

"The ground needs to prepared first," Ian offered. "We need some humus and organic fertilizer."

"And Ion, that war fence has got to be fixed before you plant a thing," said Mama.

"War fence?"

"Wire," Abby translated for him. "The deer will eat everything down to the roots if we don't set the garden fence back up."

"Guys," Dee said, "I have to go into town in the morning and check e-mail at the library. I can pick up what you need, if you'll stay here with Mama."

"Mom, I have my iPhone—you can check it here."

"You get a connection out here?" Dee said. "And you can type on it?"

Abby pulled out her smartphone and thumbed her way to Gmail.

Dee was impressed. "That could come in handy. But I need to sit down with a keyboard and log onto the university's intranet and all that. And I need to mail hard copies of papers to my office for filing when I get back. I'll swing by the feed store and get fertilizer on my way home. Do you think you'll be able to help Gramma Alice with bathroom duties?"

Abby looked at her grandmother mischievously. "Maybe, but she has to be nice to me. She has to let Cori stay in the barn. And she has to let me bring real butter into her house."

"I guess we all have to make sacrifices sometime," Mama said, her chin in the air.

Abby jotted down a short grocery list and handed it to her mother. "What you need to procure along with manure," she quipped.

*   *   *

While Mama napped and Abby and Dee took the opportunity to clean out and organize Mama's kitchen, Ian worked diligently around the house and yard, effecting a noticeable transformation. He was a wizard with a screwdriver and odds and ends of hardware, efficiently tackling a host of little problems like the sticking gate latch and the wobbly ceiling fan.

Dee looked for an opening to broach personal topics while she had her daughter's attention, but somehow with Abby she could never manage to be diplomatic. Standing on the stepladder at the end of a row of cabinet shelves, she paused with her cleaning rag. "Honey, I don't know how to say this, so I'll just come out with it."

"What?"

"Are you pregnant?"

"No!" Abby said, instantly offended. "God, no. Are you?"

"Not funny. And no, not much chance of that."

"Mom . . . knocked up at eighteen is the last thing I want to be. There are too many other things I want to do with my life. And you know Dad's been very up-front about the birth control stuff."

Dee knew what Abby said was true. Jake wouldn't have left that critical area of parenting to chance either. Her own awkward attempts to discuss the facts of life with Abby had occurred so long ago, she hardly remembered how much they'd covered.

"Okay. Then what's up with your job?"

"Just because I've gained weight doesn't mean people ought to assume I'm pregnant," Abby said with a pout. "I hated college, and I comforted myself by eating. But along the way, I also discovered healthier ways of cooking. In fact, I'm ten pounds below where I was."

"That's great," Dee said weakly.

"As for my job, you may have a hard time believing this, but I'm very good at it. The food bank is a part of the university co-op, so they always shut down for a couple of weeks between semesters." She caught her breath. "They're holding a spot for me until summer term begins. Kind of a leave of absence. Look, I'm not just paying lip service when I say that family's important to me. With Dad and Melissa's twins in kindergarten, I'm not exactly top of mind with them. Like it or not, you and Gramma Alice are pretty much all the roots I have."

Dee's heart melted, as it always did in the face of Abby's unabashed honesty, and also as usual, she was at a loss for words.

"I really do love you, Mom," Abby continued. "I came out here because I could tell you were having a hard time. And I'll stay as long as you need me. So now, why don't you tell me a little more about this book project?"

Dee came down from the stepladder and hugged her daughter long and hard. She exhaled a long breath. Maybe, just maybe, it would be okay.

They started on the dinner chores—chopping onions and peppers, crushing garlic—and soon the divine scent of sautéing aromatics filled the kitchen as Abby prepared their evening meal.

"So, you know what they say about publish or perish, right?" Dee said.

"I hear lots about it from Dad."

"Well, it's true. You reach a point where, if you want to keep your teaching job, you've got to show a strong record of publication. That means more than articles and essays and reviews and the like. It means a book."

"But if you've got a contract to publish your book, what's the problem?" asked Abby. "You've been working on this book about what's-her-name, Guinevere?—"

"Gineva Holland Templeton," Dee corrected.

"—for a long time now. What's so hard about it?"

"I ask myself that all the time." She considered how to address the simple question. "There are lots of ways to approach writing . . . if you write like most of my students do, it's a work of imagination, and you're free to take it in any direction you want. The direction it wants to go."

"Got it. That's what it was like in my high-school creative writing class."

"Yes. But scholarship has to be *right* as well as imaginative. It's like an enormous jigsaw puzzle, except that when you start out, you don't have all the pieces and you don't know how many are missing. You put together the parts that you can—and then you go searching for the others. When you find them, you might just have to mix it all up again, because it actually didn't fit together right the first time."

Abby added her own analogy. "Like a recipe where you have to fill in the blanks with other ingredients. Say you've got one avocado, one bottle of ketchup, a cup of brown sugar, and three sweet potatoes in the pantry. What else do you put with that to make something nutritious *and* good?"

"You've been watching too many cooking shows."

"So I'm guessing you're stuck filling in the last thousand pieces or so. Is that what you were planning to do in Massachusetts?"

"That, and revise the whole thing once I'm sure of the facts. Between the Boston area and central Massachusetts, there are an amazing number of libraries and archives . . . with information that might provide the missing links."

"I know. I get to use the Five College library system," Abby reminded her. "Pretty much anything you could want, at your fingertips. How often do you use the web for research?"

Dee gave that some thought. "I'm kind of hands-on. I like to see real letters, read real books."

"Hmm. Do you have any idea how much stuff has been digitized in the last few years? Honestly, Mom, I almost never set foot in the library building. I get books and articles right from my Wi-Fi connection in the apartment. I'll bet if you had access to more computer time at the library here in town, you could do a lot of searching remotely."

"You think so? There are a lot of unanswered questions. There's an entire stretch of Templeton's life that's just a black hole—after she applied to teach at Harvard, and then wound up in the Bay area in the 1940s. Either I figure out what happened during that time, and how it led to *The Working Writer,* or I have to fudge the most important part of her history."

"Remember how you came across Templeton's identity to begin with?" said Abby.

"Sure," replied Dee.

"Three names you just happened to spot in the same index. Three needles in a haystack. Have you thought about how quickly that would turn up in a web search today?"

"You might have a point," Dee admitted. She hugged her daughter again and brushed a curl out of her face. "You're pretty sharp for a kid with a carrot tattoo, you know that?"

After supper, Abby and Ian watched *Dancing with the Stars* with Mama while Dee did the dishes. Abby might just be onto something, Dee decided. She began to make a plan.

11
Distance Learning

Use your Carnegie Library and other reference resources to the fullest extent in researching the details of your story.

DEE DIALED THE LIBRARY promptly at nine, as soon as Abby and Teresa had Mama's morning routine under way. "Cynthia, it's Dee Bennett, and I have a proposition for you."

"What you do have in mind? We had such a great time last week at your place."

"Well, good, because . . . would you like to keep it going a bit longer?"

"Oh, I think that would be marvelous, and if I can speak for the rest of the group, sure!"

Dee explained her change in travel plans and her book predicament, and outlined what she had in mind. "Looks like I'll be here in Claxton for several more weeks—and I need lots of uninterrupted Internet access." She plunged in with her question. "Could I get a key to the library?"

Cynthia thought for a moment and said, "I can't give you a key, but here's what I *can* do. Gladys and the janitor, Grady, don't get along too well. Imagine that, huh? So Grady comes to work at four in the morning and puts in his half day before Gladys gets in at eight-thirty."

Dee started to get a sinking feeling where this was headed, but beggars couldn't be choosers.

"I can have Grady let you in when he's here," Cynthia offered, "but I can't have a patron on the premises without an employee on duty, and I'm sure you understand that."

"Fair enough. And that might work just fine, because my daughter will be here to help with Mama for a while."

"Oh, then she can come to the Write Stuff too! The more the merrier!"

Dee was pretty sure she'd have to work to be merry the next time the group met—if her mornings were going to start commencing before four. But one person, she was fairly certain, would be glad for the extended workshop. She'd look for an opportunity to pin Teresa Rivera down and see what had her so absorbed in that notebook.

*   *   *

At the feed store in town, not only did Dee find the soil additives Ian asked for, but the clerk steered her to nursery plants and herbs that would get their garden started much faster than from seed. While she waited for the cashier, her cell phone rang. Area code 413, Boston. Her publisher.

"Hi, Dee, Susan Sterns," said her editor at the university press, back from her sojourn in China. "So, are you here? Are you excited? How was the trip?"

"Well, there wasn't a trip . . . we had some issues with my mother's health here in Texas—and I hate to say, but I won't be coming."

Silence. Then, "Oh."

Once again Dee went through the chain of events that had led to her relinquishing the research opportunity of a lifetime.

"I understand, really," said Susan. "I was hoping you'd have some thoughts to discuss next Monday—I'm headed down to New York for BookExpo, but I'll be back and ready to chat then."

Dee cradled the phone with her shoulder and ear, fished around for her Discover card, pushed the shopping cart forward awkwardly with one arm, and paid the cashier. A pile of other cards spilled out of her wallet—UMass copy card, Boston Public Library, American Antiquarian Society, University of North Carolina Library System—and she had to gather them up while continuing to juggle the phone. The cashier did not look happy. "I'm sure I can be ready to talk by the first of the week, even if it's just by phone instead of in person," Dee said.

"Dee," Susan said, sounding hesitant, "I know you're under the gun with your department—you received the schedule from Mason, right? We're looking after your interests. Even if your contract does stipulate delivery of final manuscript by the end of August, we can be as patient as we need to be." She paused, then resumed with a softer tone. "But it's not your publisher who determines the outcome of your tenure review — it's your committee. I'm just here to help you publish the best book you can, on time."

Dear Susan. It was both a blessing and a curse to have such a supportive editor. But Dee knew she was right. It was her job, and not some faraway dream, that was on the line.

"No problem. I'll call you on Monday," Dee said, clicking the phone off. She steered the cart out the door and tossed the fertilizer into the trunk of the Ford.

*　　*　　*

When Dee returned to the farm, Mama was perched in her lawn-chair throne on the kitchen porch with a thin afghan over her knees to shield against a fresh breeze. Abby and Ian had begun to work miracles with the garden beds. The drooping wire fencing had already been set upright and reattached to the posts. Abby, in denim overalls, tie-dyed T-shirt, and Mama's garden gloves and straw hat, was filling the wheelbarrow with armfuls of dead grass. Ian wielded the hoe. Dee could hear Mama shouting, "No, if you do that, them cucumber hills will be shaded by the beans in the afternoon. Put the beans up against the barn."

"Look what I brought," Dee said, hefting the forty-pound bag of processed manure out of the trunk.

"Some good shit!" Abby exclaimed.

Mama scowled and chided her, though the cast frustrated her effort at finger-wagging. "Cussin's cussin', young lady, even if it is funny."

Ian helped Dee get the boxes of plants out of the car. "Wow, these are awesome. Good choices—Better Boy tomatoes will do well here. Pattypan squash, that's my favorite. So we need to set these in the ground before the sun gets too hot. Abby's going to go whip up some lunch for everybody. You want to help me plant?"

Mama didn't miss a beat. "Only thing Dee Anna's ever planted is her nose in a book."

Dee, who had been about to tell him she would be more useful rebuilding a jet engine blindfolded, replied, "Sure. Let me go change." For Ian's benefit, as she walked behind Mama's chair she stuck out her tongue in her mother's direction.

Ian showed Dee how to rake the manure and humus into the soil, how to lay out the garden rows to conserve water, how to leave adequate room for the squash and cucumber vines to spread. He explained which herbs preferred sun and which preferred shade. In an hour's time, working together, they had made considerable progress.

"Now, Mrs. Bennett," Ian called out, "I just need a pair of your old pantyhose."

"You one of them funny boys?" Mama shouted back.

"For the tomatoes. We're going to use pieces to tie these young plants to the stakes. They're nice and soft, and they'll keep the wind from blowing the plants over even when you set the cages around them."

"Well. Imagine that. When I was a girl we'd always cut up strips of old dresses to tie 'em up. Wilton, he would just plant the tomatoes next to the fence. The deer would eat what was on their side, but we still had enough on ours."

Dee went in and returned with the nylons and scissors. She got to work setting the tender plants, following Ian's example. As Dee was also learning, hair blowing in her eyes and sweat dripping from the end of her nose, there really was no graceful way to dig holes for a garden. You just had to bend over and kneel in the dirt.

As she set out the last tomato and struggled to pat the soil in place around its roots as neatly as Ian had, she heard a rustling in the brush behind her and a male voice, completely out of place, that made her crouch down even further and try to disappear.

"Morning, Mrs. Bennett," Max Miller called out to Mama. He carried a 35-millimeter camera on a strap around his neck, and he wore the gray wide-brimmed cowboy hat Dee had come to recognize. "I hate to bother you, but I'm looking for my—"

He didn't get a chance to finish. That moment the whirlwind broke loose.

Dee heard another rustling, this time fast and furious, and turned to see Chester the yellow lab bounding through the grass toward Max. The dog stopped short and sniffed the air for two seconds, then raced off toward the open door of the barn. No sooner had Chester blended into the shadows, barking madly, than Coriander the cat emerged, fur bristling, screeching toward the apparent safety of the enclosed garden plot.

Chester reappeared, gaining swiftly on the cat. Max ran toward the gate, camera bouncing over his shoulder.

Abby, barefoot and spatula in hand, appeared on the porch to see what the commotion was all about. At the sight of the big dog bearing down on her pet cat, she, too, dashed down the steps and into the garden. She went after Chester, shooing him with the spatula. Chester whimpered and sought refuge in Dee's arms, bowling her over flat onto the newly planted tomatoes. Cori escaped the way he had come and made for the porch. Ian quickly shut the gate to corral Chester in. Brown dust flew everywhere in the gusting wind.

When the melee settled, Dee eased up onto her elbows, which were covered in dirt and fertilizer like every other part of her. Max had managed to get hold of Chester's collar. He was reaching out his other hand to help Dee up when Abby stormed in between them, her curls flying.

"What the hell do you think you're doing, Mister?"

He backed off a step. "I came to—"

She gave no quarter. "Look what a mess you've caused in my grandmother's garden! You'll probably give her a stroke. You'll probably put her right back in the—"

This time he cut her off. "Wait, your grandmother?"

Dee had managed to get to a standing position. "Max," she said wearily, "my daughter, Abigail."

"Well—" Max waited for Abby to extend her hand, but that didn't happen. "It's a pleasure to meet you."

"You know this man?" Abby said to Dee.

"It's a long story." Dee turned to Max. "And this is your dog? What's he doing here?"

"It's a long story."

They all hushed when Mama yelled at them. "Listen, we don't have time for none of your long stories. You-all had better get up here in the house till this dust storm dies down. Besides, Abby, is that your casserole I smell burning?" Mama tilted her head toward the southern sky to call their attention to the dun-colored cloud moving in their direction. Ian had already gone for the water hose and had started to sprinkle down the wilting remains of the garden; Abby rushed up the steps and double-timed it back to the kitchen. Max dragged Chester, who looked wistfully over his shoulder at the house, to the barn and shut the door. Dee brushed off as much dirt as she could and scraped her manure-encrusted shoes against the edge of the bottom step. Only then did she look up to see Mama sitting in the lawn chair, seething, with Cori the cat curled in her lap, sheltered between her immobilized arms.

*   *   *

They all welcomed the lunch of Abby's scrumptious vegetarian lasagna—only a wee bit crunchy on top—and glasses of iced tea while they waited out the dust cloud. Teresa spirited Cori away and shut him in the bathroom.

Mama relished the unexpected opportunity to pump a guest for information. "You don't live around here, do you, Mr. Miller?"

"Just Max, please. No, ma'am, I live in town. I'm doing some nature photos on the Turlock place, and when Chester took off after a rabbit, I followed him across the draw. You can see that Chester wasn't the star student in obedience school. I apologize for the ruckus."

"It's all right," said Mama. "It was better'n the circus. Worth the price of a few tomato plants, don't you think, Dee Anna?"

"If there was film in that camera, I'm seizing it this time," Dee told Max.

"Film?" he teased her. "Where have you been since the dawn of digital photography?"

"*This* time?" asked Abby, ever perceptive.

By the time Mama finished relating the whole saga of the Red Hat Style Show, Abby and Ian were both howling. And Abby seemed to have warmed a few degrees toward Max.

The rattling of the dining-room windowpanes gradually lessened and the rustling of the tall cedars stilled for a while. After Dee and Max cleared and washed the dishes, she offered to drive him back to his truck.

"It's the least I can do to return the favor," she said quietly.

"When no one answered the door last Friday I thought maybe you weren't speaking to me."

"Well, just not to anyone."

"I asked Jane to follow me out here in your mother's car. Hope it was okay to leave the keys in it."

"I appreciate that, I really do. I wasn't fit for company all weekend. And then out of the blue, there was Abby, with her friend. I couldn't stay glum. She's the greatest frustration in my life—but also the greatest love." Dee's words surprised her. When had she ever said that to anyone, Abby included?

"I understand. Well, I should get back before Buck thinks I've been dragged off by coyotes. And your mother said you have company coming tonight, too?"

Dee let out a breath. "I'd plum forgotten."

"*Plum* forgotten? You might convince me yet that you're a Texan."

*   *   *

"Whoo, that wind is somethin' else," remarked J. D. as he stepped inside the Bennett kitchen, his stack of papers flapping crazily, and hung his hat on the rack. "Pauline decided to stay home tonight, Alice. She just had 'er hair done this morning."

Mama overheard him from her chair. "I wasn't fit for company noways," she said. "Teresa, will you help me to bed? All this activity today has wore me out."

"Don't get up, Teresa," said Abby. "I'll give Gramma Alice a hand, if I can figure out this chair. I'm pooped, too." As Abby worked out the right switch to raise Mama up and gathered the sections of the *Claxton Courier* from the end table, Frances blew in, assisted by a sudden gust.

"Well, Dr. Dee, we are pleasantly surprised that you are still among us!" she said. "But maybe your hot date last week made it worth sticking around?" She hinted for more.

That caught the attention of everyone, including Abby and Mama.

"Date?" Dee looked truly confused, but JoAnn, who had come in the door right behind Frances, explained.

"My friend Glenda's husband, Ray, was out at Jesse Jane's last Thursday and he said he saw Miller the photographer leaving with that professor woman," she said with a twinkle in her eye that let Dee know she'd been the subject of gossip. "And I don't know of but one professor woman that could be, do you, Frances?"

Dee laughed it off. "Goodness, JoAnn, I think you have your character's surveillance techniques down pat!" But Abby shot her mother a salacious look as she led Mama down the hallway.

Margaret turned to JoAnn and added, barely within Dee's earshot, "Well, I just hope Max is settling in and, you know, getting . . . *adjusted.*" JoAnn raised an eyebrow.

As Summer and Wendell and the others arrived in turn, Dee was able to restore their focus for a few minutes. "Since it turns out I'll be spending a few more weeks in Claxton, it's my good fortune to continue working with you. Shall we pick up where we left off last week and workshop an excerpt?" Dee said.

They took their seats, and Dee began to read. *Bradford yanked his hat down on his head and brandished his .44 caliber Army Colt. He pulled the hammer back. Three Union soldiers laid down their bayonets in front of him. It didn't seem sporting, but he had no choice, as he shot them one by one. Those Yankees had food on them, and he hadn't eaten anything since Florence, Alabama, two days ago.*

He pulled the hoecakes and ham out of their pockets, and ate hungrily and greedily. He'd take their shoes, too, if they'd fit.

The group offered some lukewarm remarks and gentle criticisms when she finished the excerpt from the Civil War epic. But Dee sensed they just weren't into it.

"I don't understand how one Rebel soldier by himself got three Yankees to surrender," said Summer. "Is that true to life?"

Wendell jumped to defend the piece. "Whoever wrote that probably did a lot of research at battlefields. It could've happened that way."

"Yes, but the writer didn't explain enough to make it convincing," she shot back. "We need to see the picture more clearly. What were the exact circumstances? What was the weather like? What time of day was it?"

Margaret joined the fray. "Did they still have bayonets in the Civil War? I didn't think—"

The men jumped on her at once, nodding. "Yes, don't you remember that famous picture from Gettysburg?" said J. D. "But the problem was, some generals were still stubborn about using the bayonet, and the results were disastrous for them. The Gatling gun was proving much more effective."

"Maybe we could all add our written comments on the pages," Dee suggested. But they would have no part of it.

"I don't understand why there has to be so much violence anyway," said Frances.

"Let's just move on for right now," Dee said. "We'll come back to 'The Eve of Appomattox' if we have time." She drew another manuscript from the stack.

The frost on the January grass sparkled in the pre-dawn of the streetlight, but Martha scarcely had time to notice its charm. She shivered and continued to dig through the dumpster behind the plastic surgeon's home.

Her niece would die if she saw Martha in her get-up as a homeless person, but she had to be unnoticed. She sighed and thought about all of the people in society who were there, but seemingly invisible. Sometimes she had wondered if she should have been a social worker instead of librarian. Sometimes she felt like there wasn't much difference.

Ewww, coffee grounds, mascara tubes, empty eyelash cases. Wait a minute, hadn't the surgeon said he was single and not seeing anyone? Size 13 shoe boxes? Witnesses had said it had been a woman driving the car who ran over the detective.

Might he be posing as a she?

There, that gave them all something to chew on. Or maybe because they all knew the piece was Cynthia's, they kept their mouths shut. Dee was thankful. She'd had enough of their gusting and griping tonight.

*   *   *

The lights were off in all the bedrooms, Teresa had left, and only after straightening up in the dining room did Dee wonder what had become of Ian and Abby. She tiptoed down the hall, first to check on Mama, who was fast asleep. She passed her own bedroom, and, peeking into Buddy's old room, found Abby snoring quietly underneath the light comforter. Ian was nowhere in evidence.

She returned to the kitchen and opened the door onto the porch. The wind had died down again to gusts, and she walked out into the yard to assess the results of the day's gardening. In the light of a partial moon, she made out an odd shape over near the well house. Stepping closer, she saw that one of the old cattle-fence bedsprings had been rigged atop a couple of empty barrels, like a camping cot on wheels, with a tarp strung above it that was flapping in the breeze. Lying on it, wrapped in an Indian blanket, with a duffel bag as pillow, was Ian's beefy frame, and in the crook of his arm Cori the cat was curled in a ball.

Dee sighed. The guy was honorable as well as resourceful. "Ian?" she said as gently as she could.

He opened his eyes wide and pulled a set of portable headphones from his ears. "Oh, hi, Dr. Mrs. Bennett," he said. "Um, I hope you don't mind if I borrowed this." He held up the case of the audiobook. *Your Spiritual Path to Health and Happiness.*

"I'm very glad it's getting some use," she answered. "Now, I know you have a bus to catch early in the morning. Why don't you come inside where it's warm and quiet?"

*   *   *

Physically and mentally drained herself, Dee lay on top of the covers watching the mulberry branches as the wind blew in petulant fits around the corner of the house and whistled through the loose panes. At some point she must have slept, for she dreamed she was flying away swiftly in the night air, looking down on the dusty old farm from a magic carpet that, on closer inspection, was an enormous Indian blanket.

Three-thirty, she thought as she woke and pulled on her jeans and whatever T-shirt was handy, was not an hour that should exist on the a.m. side of the clock. It belonged squarely in the middle of the afternoon, when sensible people were winding down their workdays and kids were boarding school buses to return home. How did farmers and ranchers get up in the dark every morning, much less go out in the cold to crank up the tractor or tend the stock? Definitely not the life for her. But she'd committed to give this early-morning research plan a try.

Abby had risen at that hour, too, to brew strong coffee and fill a Thermos for Ian to take on the bus to Albuquerque. Dee waited for their tearful and passionate farewell before shooing him out the door to the car. They made it to the Hi-Way Truck Stop just in time for the Greyhound's 4:10 arrival, and before its departure fifteen minutes later Dee thanked Ian sincerely for all he'd done to help Mama during his short sojourn. Not a bad kid, really, she decided as she waved good-bye and watched the bus pull onto the four-lane like a great ship steaming out of the harbor in the night.

*   *   *

Grady the janitor greeted her when she knocked at the library door. She nodded a hello and took her laptop and pad straight to the computer room, where Grady had finished vacuuming and left a single row of lights on for her. Cynthia had been as good as her word.

In the monastery silence Dee searched tentatively for answers. Her questions were many and complex. How did one even begin a systematic digital search? Her students relied on the Internet for everything—and were too quick to accept results that seemed satisfactory on the surface. She would have to dig deeper, if this machine was to yield up secrets from seventy years ago. If it was to shine any light into the cavern of her unfinished manuscript.

After a solid hour of desultory attempts she was surprised to come across a cache of correspondence, all scanned in high resolution, from one of the archives on her own list. In the folder with it was a nicely organized finding aid—a guide to the collection, showing the writer and recipient of each letter, and its date. Searching the list was a breeze, and it didn't take long for her to turn up a couple of relevant documents. She read and absorbed their contents. When she encountered any unfamiliar reference, she control-N'ed a fresh browser window and typed the term into the search engine. Wikipedia provided a starting point for any entity that was new to her. Bingo. It was that easy.

She sent some pages to the printer or flash drive, while others she read and noted for later. The research became like a treasure hunt in which each new nugget of information linked to another lead.

Without doubt the most valuable item Dee turned up in her first session was a rich and revealing oral history of a Mills College administrator whose long tenure at the California institution had overlapped Templeton's own. Readily accessible online once she looked in the right place, the transcript leapt to life on the page for Dee as though she were sitting beside the woman and conducting the interview herself. She learned about the terms of Templeton's hire: a new college president, taking office in 1943, had personally invited Templeton out to Mills and appointed her to the English faculty solely on the strength of a recommendation from someone at Bradford. No names were named, thought Dee, but she surmised it must have taken influential connections to engineer such an unusual arrangement, even given wartime shortages of personnel.

How had Templeton, an easterner by birth and education, become known in West Coast circles to begin with? And further, the speaker hinted at an unexpected change of direction in Templeton's career only a few years later: though considered a popular and gifted teacher, Templeton left the Mills faculty in the midst of unspecified circumstances in 1949. Dee already knew those dates from a research stint at Mills during her dissertation year—and she knew, as well, that there were no photographs of Templeton to be found in the college's yearbooks or faculty clipping files. There was more to that story, no doubt.

Dee sat back and rubbed her temples while files cranked out on the printer. There would be a lot to sift through in the coming days, a lot to analyze and place into proper perspective. Still a big puzzle to solve. But it was a start. Ideas and information began to merge, a tiny bit. A penlight shone into the cavern.

12
The Working Writer

*Whether you are an early bird or a night owl, set aside
a time in every day to write.*

DURING THE ENSUING DAYS of Operation Rooster Crow, as she
dubbed it, Dee's schedule fell into a regimented routine. Each morning
she left Mama, sleeping, in Abby's care, cowbell at the ready, and drove
the truck out on the dark, nearly empty highway into town. Each morning
Grady admitted her to the library with only a nod of his head. Four hours
later she emerged into the blinding sunlight, with pages of new notes
and answers and questions, just before Gladys's arrival at work.

Back at home, she would nap while Abby tended the garden and
Teresa took care of housework and Mama's therapy. Dee then rose and
showered in time for lunch, did Mama's errands and shopping, and
shut herself in the bedroom to work at her desk all afternoon. In the
midst of each writing session she felt utterly transported to New England
and San Francisco of the last century—without ever leaving West Texas.
She thrived in the surroundings of her imagination, mentally inhabiting
each newly revealed circumstance in a way that yielded clearer insights
into the next.

Of course it wasn't ideal, and the bitterness of having to cancel her
hard-won fellowship still stung. The Berkshires program administrator
had been sympathetic but unable to make alternate arrangements; since
the major part of the award involved free lodging, the living quarters
were booked for later weeks already. The best they could do was to
assure her priority consideration for next year.

Dee was coming to see how seductive this stay-at-home research could be—why it had become more and more difficult to pry her students away from their computer screens and force them into the college library. Still, for Dee, a special collections library was like the inner sanctum of a temple, a privileged haunt. Nothing could ever take the place of arriving at opening hour, securing your bag in a locker, and entering the reading room with blank paper and a supply of freshly sharpened number two pencils. Turning the pages of ancient leaves and letters and absorbing their mysteries was like handling holy writ.

But digital would have to do. Image by scanned image, Gineva Holland Templeton's missing years were taking shape in Dee's notebook and head. In a journal review of a recently published book about the Federal Writers' Project in New England, available online through one of the Claxton library's subscription services, Dee picked up a tantalizing clue courtesy of Google. Templeton's name was mentioned briefly among the contributors to the 1937 Massachusetts volume, known to be the most problematic of the WPA-funded state guides (the power brokers of the Commonwealth, it seemed, were not keen to showcase less flattering chapters in their history, such as the Lawrence mill workers' strike or the Sacco-Vanzetti case). Dee was immediately eager to learn more. If she could get her hands on the book itself, she might be able to tell how long, and how, Templeton had been employed by the project, and where she might turn for further evidence.

Furthermore, the complete run of Templeton's 1930–31 travelogues in *American Roadways* magazine was now available in a full-color online version. Dee was swept away with the author along stretches of "America's Main Street," the Lincoln Highway, from New York to Trenton to Philadelphia, Canton to Mansfield, Valparaiso to Joliet, Cheyenne to Laramie, Green River to Granger, Ely to Eureka, Reno to Stockton to San Francisco. Places Dee had never seen in modern-day America, this woman had visited solo before there was even a Holiday Inn. Templeton had interviewed local citizens all along the journey, their stories revealing a nation longing to claim its place as a global leader but unsure of its future. Like the celebrated photographers of the later Depression years, Templeton captured America's portrait in images as well as words. She had taken her own photographs, in all light and weather conditions, with a brand-new Leica Model C. She drove a Plymouth 30-U and carried with her a 1930 Remington Portable #3, the first typewriter model to feature an automatic paragraph indent key.

Dee had discovered these arcane details in the editor's note to the first installment of the series. The manufacturers of the camera, the car, and the typewriter, the editor explained, had donated their products to support the author's tour. The stunt had been conceived as a way to boost interest in leisure travel along the Lincoln Highway. But since Templeton shielded her full identity—at least in the magazine's pages—no photograph or revealing newspaper publicity turned up.

Dee discussed that quandary with Cynthia when she called her Friday to say how well the arrangement was working out otherwise.

"Hmm. You're certain you're not limiting your scope too much? Boolean operators can be tricky," Cynthia said in librarianese.

"I don't think so . . . I even take notes on my search terms as I go so I don't overlook something obvious."

"Good habit. Now, there was another item on the list you left for me—a book about the Federal Writers' Project?"

"Yes! It's the pits to be stranded so far from a major research library, but I wondered if you could pull any strings to get me a copy somehow. I'd be eternally grateful."

"I'm on it," Cynthia said. "And another thing—you haven't heard anything more from Wendell this week, have you? He e-mailed me that he wouldn't be at the writers' group, but he didn't say why."

*   *   *

On Saturday, following the final wee-hours library session of the week, Dee returned home and trudged up the steps to find Abby at the kitchen table, still in her pajamas, with a smirk on her face and a steaming cup of coffee poured for each of them.

"You have a message," Abby said drily, after finishing a bite of granola cereal.

"What? Who called so early?"

"A friend."

"Who? I don't have any friends."

"Hmm, that's not what your blue-hair writers say."

"Abby, don't be difficult. What message?"

"Your man friend called."

"Who, Rob?"

"Camera Man. Yellow-dog Man."

"Max Miller called? What did he say?"

"Oh, you *do* remember his name!"

"What, what?!" Dee was about ready to throttle her daughter.

"He said he was, um, in the neighborhood," Abby said between bites. "And wondered. If you wanted to come see some of the scenes he's been shooting." She rolled her eyes and smirked again.

"Lord, that took a lot to get out of you! So, where exactly in the neighborhood? What did he want?"

"Dunno. I guess he'll call back."

Dee groaned, yawned, and pushed herself up from the table. "I'm going to get some sleep. Next time he calls, tell him I just got back from California."

"Sure thing. But hey, was that a truck motor I just heard?"

"You've got to be kidding." Dee peeked out the kitchen curtain, then hustled to the bathroom to look in the mirror. It wasn't like she did the full facial-and-makeup regimen before her assignation with Grady the janitor. She brushed her hair, pulled it back in an elastic-banded ponytail, and held it in place with a spritz of spray. It was the best she could do on short notice.

She heard Abby open the door and invite their guest in.

"Morning, Max," Dee said nonchalantly as she returned to the kitchen. He smiled and returned her greeting—and she was immediately relieved to see that, rumpled and unshaven, he looked as scruffy as she felt. "What was this about being in the vicinity so early on a Saturday?"

"Sorry I missed you. I called on the off chance that you might be partial to sunrises."

"I am these days," she sighed. "What did you have in mind?"

"Come with me and see," he said. "That is, if Abigail doesn't mind my taking her mother away from the house for a couple of hours."

Abby piped up willingly. "Don't look at me, I'm just the hired help."

"Where are we going?"

"I'm still doing some work out on Buck Turlock's land," he said. "Come on, hop in the truck." She took a moment to change into shoes more suitable for the fields, and returned with her cap and sunglasses as well. He was an unpredictable one, this Miller guy, she decided. Liable to show up at the most unexpected times and places.

Max followed the dirt road behind the cow pen, down the hill, and across the Bennett back pasture toward a grove of mesquite trees. Dee could see a small tent set up beside a camp chair and a portable table, on which sat a Dutch oven and an enamel coffeepot. Within a ring of rocks on the ground were the damp remnants of a campfire.

"I made breakfast," Max said. "Coffee and honey biscuits. That is, if the raccoons haven't helped themselves."

"Do you sleep out here?" Dee asked.

"Sometimes—just me and my .22," he said, handing her a blue enamel plate with two hot, sweet biscuits, along with a tin cup of black coffee. "Make yourself at home for a sec. See that covey of quail? I want to get a shot."

A confused look came over Dee's face. She didn't know much about hunting, but she didn't *think* quail was in season yet.

"Photo," he said, pulling a camera from a bag in the tent and attaching a long lens.

Dee finished both biscuits and her coffee while she waited. She hadn't realized she was so hungry—or that buttered biscuits cooked by hot coals could taste so good. She closed her eyes and took in the full sensation of the breeze on her face. She could make out the pungent smell of desert sage and the more delicate notes of cedar.

"Sorry," Max said when he returned a full ten minutes later. "I also spotted a red fox stalking the birds. It's unusual to see them this time of year. You really have to take your time—and hope the wind doesn't give you away."

"You like outdoor assignments, don't you?"

"I grew up hunting with my father," he said. "Killing game for sport isn't my thing anymore, but I know a bit about animal behavior." He gave her a hand up out of the camp chair. "There might be just enough shadow from up here on the ridge to get a decent angle."

The sun was already well up in the cloudless sky as Dee hiked with Max to the top of the rise, where she watched him squat, check his light meter, and then lie flat to capture the view from the edge of a caliche embankment. The shutter clicked half a dozen times.

"Oh, well. Light's shot for now," Max said. He got up and sat with his feet dangling over the low ledge.

"But it's so sunny and beautiful," she said as she joined him. "What's wrong with that blue sky, and all the fields with the cotton starting to come up?"

"Too much light's almost worse than too little. It's not just about the light, but the *quality* of it. By midmorning, out here on the plains, everything's flat and washed out. Your eye doesn't necessarily perceive that, but the camera does. High contrast is what makes a great landscape. High drama."

She thought about that. "Same as in writing."

"That's what I wanted to talk to you about," said Max, turning his attention away from the distant point where the plowed rows converged on the horizon.

"What's on your mind?"

"Remember your cousin Ruby Lee mentioning the photography book I'm working on? She wasn't just blowing smoke."

"How far along are you?"

"With the photos, pretty much finished. The words, well, that's the problem. I can tell a story in pictures . . . but when it comes to the paragraphs between them, it's like I was telling you about the light— they're sort of flat and featureless."

"Did you write the text, or someone else?"

"I wrote it, if you can call it that," he admitted. "But I'm not happy with it. I was about on the verge of giving up, and then Ruby Lee introduced me to you, a real writer . . . and I wondered if you could take a look at it."

Yep, always that way, thought Dee. But she pushed that jaded thought out of her head. It was too beautiful a day for petty sarcasm. "I tell you what. I'm in the middle of a major project, and I have a deadline staring me right in the face. If I'm done next week—if I deliver this manuscript on time—I'm all yours. I'll read your book."

He smiled the friendly, laconic smile she was coming to recognize. "I'd be much obliged. And if you think you can improve it for me, I'll pay."

"One step at a time, Miller. What makes you think you'd like my writing, anyway?"

"Looked up your stuff online. Day hikes, wildflowers, old buildings— you've got a knack for nature too. It seemed pretty impressive to me. I especially liked that *Sierra* piece about the ponies . . . where was that?"

"Oh—Shackelford Banks!" she replied. "Have you ever been to the Outer Banks of North Carolina?"

"Never even seen the Atlantic Ocean—never lived anywhere outside of Texas, in fact."

"Well, then, we're even, because there's a whole lot of Texas I've never seen."

"But you grew up right out here, didn't you?" He indicated the home place behind them with a nod of his head.

"Yes—almost totally within the bounds of Caprock County. Mama and Daddy would take us up to the reservoir sometimes to go fishing with our aunts and uncles. And one time I got to go with my sister, Penny, to the Texas State Fair."

Max hoisted his camera again and focused as he spoke. "The fair's an amazing event—if you *have* to go somewhere there's crowds of people. I did a shoot there one time. Fireworks over Big Tex's head and all that." He let the camera rest again without clicking the shutter.

"I was only eight years old, and Penny was seventeen and had her driver's license and a job," Dee reminisced. "Mama let her take me and my brother all the way to Dallas if she'd pay our way. We stayed overnight with our aunt in Fort Worth for the weekend .... I thought it was so grand!"

"I guess it wasn't always pleasant for you, being stuck out in the country. Did your parents always farm?"

"My father worked on the farm all day, and he also helped out at the gin during cotton harvest. That's what he was doing the night I was born, in fact." Dee pulled her knees up under her chin and found herself, once again, just prattling on to this near stranger. But he kept the questions rolling, squinting in her direction in the sun in a way that made him seem honestly engaged.

"How's that?"

"Well . . . that year, in early November, when my mother was about at the end of her term, the cotton was starting to come in, and it was a huge crop. They were running the gin around the clock. On this particular Friday night the gin caught fire, and my daddy was there to fight it, along with my grandfather, who was the manager of the gin, and all the other men. Daddy had just come home for a bite of supper when my mother's water broke. They left my sister and brother at the farm by themselves, and Daddy got Mama into the old Rambler—but the brakes were shot, so he had to drive all the way to the hospital in Colorado City without stopping, until he pulled up under the awning, where he opened the car door and dragged his foot on the pavement to stop the car."

"Amazing. And then?"

"He left her there at the hospital, because he had to get back to the gin. By the next morning, when the fire was out and he came back, I had been delivered—and my mother was sobbing hysterically because they'd come to get information on her insurance, and it turned out to be a worthless policy Daddy'd bought from a fly-by-night salesman. They wouldn't let him take his wife and child home until he made a cash down payment, which of course he had to go back to Claxton again to rustle up."

"That's a great story." Max laughed along with her. "What an original entrance!"

"You can see why I might have been eager to exit. The West Texas part, I mean."

"You didn't stick around?"

"I packed up and left Claxton the day after high school graduation—I'd been accepted to Baylor, and I went ahead and started that summer. I haven't been back for more than three days at a time—ever—till now."

"I'll bet there's a story there, too."

"I imagine there is," she said, not to be coy but because she was suddenly exhausted. Her energy was sapped—and they hadn't brought water with them, either.

Her fatigue wasn't lost on Max. "I wouldn't mind hearing it sometime," he said. He shouldered his camera and gave her a hand up. "You up for another little hike? Let's get back to the truck and get you home."

The air from the open truck window revived her a bit. Drowsily, she watched the mesquite trees and fence posts unfold like a movie set alongside the road, with wildflowers lending their pastel hues to the décor and insects and field larks providing the soundtrack. She had a dreamy sense of those delicious moments when she'd followed this same landscape from the school bus, leaning against the glass with the wind in her hair and the endless future far, far down the road.

*   *   *

When she called her editor Monday afternoon, Dee was pleased enough with her progress on the research and writing front that her tone was jaunty and confident. "I'm cranking out the chapters, Susan—it's like I'm a revising machine. Literally on a roll every morning." She didn't mention just now many miles she'd rolled already.

"Well, don't you sound perky! I'm very happy to hear it. Do you think it's realistic for me to expect a draft in a week or so? I think I mentioned we have outside readers lined up to expedite the process."

Dee bit her lip but said, "Absolutely."

"Is there anything I can do to help in the meantime?" Susan asked.

Dee mentally ran down her wish list. Sure, ship the entire run of Works Progress Administration records out here from the National Archives. Get a speed-reader to plow through personnel files at Mills College. Persuade Little, Brown to make more of their publishing archives accessible. But she said with a laugh, "How about a ten thousand–dollar advance?" All miracles of the same magnitude.

*   *   *

Now that Tuesday evenings with the Write Stuff had become a regular occurrence, Dee looked forward to the change of pace as much as the writers seemed to relish returning for their critique sessions. But Wendell Grover was a no-show. Dee didn't feel familiar enough to call him, and Cynthia said he hadn't returned her messages.

"I already asked Sheriff K to ride by and check on him," she told Dee, "so we do know he's at home, and okay."

"I hope I didn't say something to offend him."

Cynthia waved her off. "Does the old codger seem thin-skinned to you? Let's just wait and see. We had one other writer who started out with us in the spring and hasn't been back. Circumstances change. We made it clear that participation is entirely voluntary—so no worries."

Whatever the case, Dee didn't want to lose one on her watch. It was a point of pride with her that her classes at Walter Raleigh had the lowest drop rate in the department. She wondered from time to time how her graduates were faring, since she'd missed them at the ceremony . . . but then again, not enough to e-mail and ask. The distance and separation had been healthy.

Cynthia had come to tonight's meeting not only with a boxful of materials for Dee, but an armload of files and books that she used as visual aids in a presentation about background research. Dee was impressed at how many truly useful tips Cynthia could offer for every sort of writing. She took careful notes herself.

"One other announcement I want to make before we wrap up," said Cynthia, holding up an informational flyer. "Some of you already participate in the Texas Writers Online group, I know. JoAnn, you're a member, right? And J. D.?"

They nodded.

"Well, TWO sponsors a series of writing contests around the state. And the deadline for the West Texas regional competition is June 15. There's a cash prize, and the winner is also recognized at the statewide conference in September. I hope you'll all consider submitting."

"I had a story get honorable mention a coupl'a years ago," said J. D. "But that's the closest I've come."

"So you see? You should all think about it. Dues are only twenty dollars, and you get a lot of other benefits for your money too. I'll leave the flyers here on the table—take one if you're interested."

While the writers filed out, full of excitement about the competition, Cynthia gathered up her workshop materials and described to Dee what was in the box. "I've located a copy of the Massachusetts state guide through interlibrary loan," she explained, "but it's not here yet. I'll let you know the minute it arrives!"

"Thank you—I owe you more than you'll ever know," said Dee. "What about photos? You said you'd check the Library of Congress and places like that."

"No luck there yet either. Or on the class reunion sites, which are generally very handy sources."

Dee had never actually seen the author's likeness. Not a single photograph had come to light—not even in the Abbot or Emerson yearbooks, which she had long ago checked in those institutions' archives. She mentioned this oddity to Cynthia after the writers had dispersed. Where else might she turn for information about Gineva Templeton the person? she wondered.

"How much have you delved into genealogy?" Cynthia asked. And when the answer was "not much," Cynthia promised to clear her schedule for the following day.

* * *

Dee stuck around after the library's public opening hours Wednesday morning, lingering in the ladies' room until she was certain Cynthia was on duty and she could avoid Gladys. In the head librarian's office, Cynthia set two cups of coffee on the desk and pulled up two chairs in front of the large computer monitor. "I thought you might need some fuel to keep you going," she said.

Dee agreed wholeheartedly and drank in the welcome aroma of brewed beans and caffeine.

"So, what we're going to do," said Cynthia, "is construct a family tree using this genealogical database. It might sound very elementary, but I'll bet you'll be surprised what will turn up."

"I've got the names of parents and spouse as starting points. But I don't know where they were born—biographical sources are about nil."

"Well, let's start making some logical guesses. I'm often called upon to help local history groups and even the Daughters of the Republic of Texas—and I have a few tricks to show you."

Within a matter of minutes Cynthia had pulled up U.S. Census records for Gineva Holland Templeton in 1910, 1920, and 1930. "That's as far forward as we can go, since the 1940 Census won't be made public until 2012. But look what you can gather already. Street addresses, parents' names and ages, occupations—you already had parts of that— and did you know you can also see where *their* parents were born?"

"Does that matter?"

"Watch," Cynthia instructed as she populated another search field with bits of data she'd just gleaned from the last hit. The results it yielded included a usefully narrowed set of records ranging from birth certificates and photos to draft registrations and death notices. "See? Allan Day Jensen—sounds like your gal's husband—died 6 September 1974, Oakland, California, aged 65 years. Let's open up a new window and search death notices in California newspapers at the time . . . and let's scroll down . . . no, not that Allan Johnson . . . or that A. D. Janson . . . but here you go, an obituary that names a brother and sister-in-law and a niece as survivors, in addition to his wife, Gineva. It says he was—wow, a jazz pianist."

"That's incredible! And I guess next you'll—"

"Plug in the relatives' names. Right." She keyed in several searches, along with the city given in the obituary. After a few tries a U.S. city directory listing appeared, giving a current California address and phone number that matched the brother's name. "And did you notice that middle initial G. in the niece's name?" Cynthia pointed out triumphantly.

"Um, yes—why?"

"Just a hunch. Could be totally meaningless, of course."

"Or maybe not! Hand me the phone—I'm calling right now," said Dee.

"Well—I'd wait a few hours if I were you. It's 7:30 on the West Coast, you know. And Gladys might give me a hard time about the long-distance, too."

"Oops. Don't want that."

"Give me a while to work on this some more while you go home and rest," said Cynthia. "Then call me after lunch. I'm totally psyched—getting to be a research assistant for a college professor!"

Cynthia delivered, in spades. Dee arrived at the library two days later to find a neat stack of printouts beside the computer. County property records for Allan Day Jensen; sundry news announcements for concerts in San Francisco, Marin, and Napa, including promotional photos of Jensen at the piano, with and without his band; a history booklet about the Jensen clan, of Danish ancestry, that indicated they had been fruit growers in California's Central Valley since before the Gold Rush. Dee was ecstatic about the incidental details, however little they illuminated her main subject.

She stuck around in town longer than usual, taking care of errands while waiting for a decent hour to make a phone call to the Pacific time zone. At the Lot-a-Burger, at eleven, she arranged her notebook and pad on a corner table and dialed the number they'd found for Arthur E. Jensen of San Jose, California. Dee's pulse raced with each ring.

"Heritage Oaks, how may I direct your call?" a woman's voice said.

"Oh—," stammered Dee. "I was trying to reach—Mr. Jensen."

"Jensen? Do you have a full name?"

"Arthur Jensen. I apologize if I've dialed a wrong number."

"No, that's right. But Mr. Jensen is not able to take calls. May I leave a message for the caregiver?"

Dee's hopes deflated. "Oh . . . yes . . . I suppose so." Dee explained that no, she wasn't a friend or a family member, but she hoped she could speak to someone about a research matter. Would the caregiver mind calling back? The receptionist was noncommittal but took down Dee's number at the home place.

Another dead end. Maddening. So many tantalizing tidbits, forming an intriguing backdrop. But where was Gineva in the story?

She was still pondering this question all the way home, where she opened the kitchen door at the farm to hear Mama criticizing Teresa in a bitter tone.

"Can't keep nothin' around here. Nothin'. My great-aunt's cake stand, that she left to me, and you've done broke it."

Abby spoke. "Gramma Alice, it was an accident. I heard it—I heard you bump into the doorway with your cast."

Teresa nodded, stricken but unable to defend herself. "I—I catch you—"

When Dee appeared in the dining room, Abby did her best to explain the situation while preserving everyone's honor. "Oh, Mom—the cake stand's broken, but I think Teresa knocked it off the buffet trying to keep Mama from falling. That's what it sounded like to me."

Teresa could only agree but managed few words. "*Si. Si. Lo siento.*"

Mama would not back down. "I'll never be able to replace it."

Dee bent down to pick up the pieces. "Let's see if we can patch things up. A little Super Glue might go a long way." Dee considered Teresa's presence a windfall and a blessing—and her persistence nothing short of a miracle, given Mama's mercurial temperament. She wondered how long Teresa would put up with the situation—or how long *she* could.

But then, these days were precious too. With Abby, with the progress on her work, with the writers—even with Mama. With Abby for company, Mama demanded little of Dee. Abby had been more than happy to take full command of the kitchen, and there was not a thing Mama could do except offer acerbic commentary about her preferred methods for preparing potato salad or cornbread or black-eyed peas. Maybe Abby was learning something as well, Dee hoped.

Teresa came reliably, always on time, always with her backpack and notebook, to handle therapy sessions and light housework, and her father picked her up at noon. In the evenings after supper Mama, Dee, and Abby sat in lawn chairs on the porch, drinking iced tea and watching the sunset glow on the clouds. Before Mama turned in they played 42, with Abby moving Mama's dominoes as she directed. Mama seldom lost a game. Dee was astonished at her mother's aptitude for laying down each piece for the maximum score—and for keeping mental track of dominoes played. Mama had always been good at the game, and Dee had forgotten what a formidable opponent she could be.

The last thing that Mama did before retiring each evening was to ask one of them to mark through the day's square on the Caprock State Bank calendar. The red X's marched on toward the day when, Dee feared, Abby would decide she was ready to return to her job, and their idyllic interval would be up.

*   *   *

"So, Mom, you've made great progress on your book, right?"

In a snap, Dee could see it coming. A question out of the blue as they finished their Sunday dinner, and she knew. "Progress, yes—conclusion, no," she replied.

"Wasn't the library a great plan, though?" The past-tense verb said it all.

"You leavin' us, Abigail?" Mama asked.

"Well . . . it's been fun hanging out, but it's about time I started earning a paycheck again. You and Mom both seem to be doing fine."

And that settled it. Abby would spend Monday doing garden and house chores while Dee put in one last day at the computer, and they'd drive Abby to the bus stop the following morning.

Was Mama really doing fine, Dee wondered? And was she? They'd managed not to kill each other so far. Surely they could get by.

Dee would need to tie up some loose paragraphs in her manuscript, fast. No, she hadn't answered all the burning questions, and the biography was far from complete. She'd had no return phone call from California. She had to be realistic: new information meant that answers were likely to be found not only in Massachusetts sources, but now in DC and California. And when would that ever happen? Her scope had broadened even as it had narrowed.

But she might just have enough to go on to make a convincing case. By having so much more of Templeton's own writing to comment upon, by having so many rich historical sources to cite—if she had to leave some empty stretches, still, maybe she could connect enough of the dots to make a worthwhile story. She would *have* to.

*   *   *

A restless wind shook the farmhouse windows, and Dee kicked the quilt off. She'd been dreaming that she was trying to help Mama up out of the bed, but Mama seemed to be howling in pain and Dee kept getting tangled in her bathrobe. The more she tried to assist, the more forcefully she was dragged out the door and down into the well, where she knew no one would find her. The water at the bottom of the well was not cool, but warm and growing warmer.

Waking from the nightmare, soaked in sweat and her heart beating like a drum, Dee looked over at the clock. In two hours she'd have to get up for good to take Abby down to the Hi-Way Truck Stop. Her daughter would board the 4:25 Greyhound and disappear from her life once more, for who-knew-how-long.

The moon shone directly through the screened window, too bright for sleep. Far off a coyote called, and another answered. Dee stared at the water stain on the ceiling and dreaded how empty the farmhouse would seem with just her and Mama, even with Teresa's occasional presence. She wondered how Mama had borne those months of being all alone out here after Daddy passed away.

Dee would try to keep her sadness to herself. She had always tried to spare her daughter the guilt her own mother imposed on her when brief visits would end. Mama, striking a tragic profile on the porch, would be sniffling and holding back tears, yet in her eyes was nothing but anger as she said good-bye to her youngest daughter. No hugs or kisses would be exchanged as Dee carried her suitcase down the steps and loaded it into the trunk of her rental car. Daddy would feel compelled to comfort Mama. No one ever felt compelled to comfort Dee.

Had Dee made Abby feel a similar remorse for wanting to live her own life? She hoped not; otherwise, what was all the sacrifice for? *So what if she wants to drop out of Smith . . .* the irony wasn't lost on Dee, as someone who had just backed out of a prestigious fellowship. But *I had to,* she thought. The circumstances had been beyond her control.

What was going on in Abby's heart and mind, Dee was sure she'd find out eventually. In her own time, she'd come clean. Hadn't she always? Dee turned her own choices over in her mind yet again. Should she have insisted on having custody of Abby when it might've made a difference? If only she knew then what she knew now. She didn't think Abby had been harmed by their long absences . . . but she could never be certain.

She got up in the dark to look in on Abby and Mama, then go to the bathroom. Outside the window a chime hanging in one of the peach trees made a disconcerting clatter in the wind. Through the tree branches, down the road near the turnrow, Dee thought she could make out red taillights in the field. What would anyone be doing out there at this hour? But she blinked and looked again, and the lights were gone.

Dee retrieved her laptop from her bedroom and sat for a while on the couch, trying to proofread footnotes by the light of the computer screen. That was all she remembered before dreaming she and Cynthia Philpott were sitting in front of a large computer monitor aboard a bus, where Abby was shaking her shoulder because they'd arrived at their stop.

She opened her eyes; Abby was indeed shaking her gently.

Abby was ready to go, with minimal baggage. Dee got Mama up and dressed as well. Silently the three made their way in the Crown Vic down to the turnrow and headed toward the highway. As the neon Phillips 66 sign came closer to view, Abby said, "Take care of yourself, Gramma Alice."

Mama sniffled, and Dee gritted her teeth. Dee parked the car and said, "Let's wait outside."

Abby got the signal—*I have something to say that I don't want your grandmother to hear*—and replied, "Okay."

As they stood in the truck-stop bay, Dee said, "Hon, you know I won't be coming to Northampton at all this summer. I couldn't arrange it once everything changed. And I still don't know how long I'll be here with Gramma Alice."

"I understand. And it actually works out well anyway," Abby said, with a hint of intrigue, just as the Greyhound bus pulled up.

"Why's that?"

"I'm going to Albuquerque instead."

The bus groaned to a stop, and two drowsy passengers disembarked.

"What? Why?" Dee asked.

"It's okay," Abby said, "Ian got me into AmeriCorps. We'll be fine. It's just for the summer. And I'm actually closer to Texas this way."

"Boarding for Amarillo and points east and west," said the bus driver over the speaker system, flashing his lights as a last call.

Dee started to protest, but there was no time, unless she wanted to make a scene. So she quietly handed Abby a couple of twenties, agreed to keep Cori for the time being, and told her to call when she got there, wherever *there* was.

*   *   *

The June morning was turning out perfect, weatherwise—no wind, no dust, just sunshine and blue sky. Buddy called to say he'd be driving up to see them on Friday afternoon and staying for dinner, though he was sorry to hear he'd just missed Abby.

The kitchen garden had been neatly weeded, and Dee and Mama stared out the window admiring it. "Look, Mama," Dee said, "blossoms on the tomatoes." Dee rose slowly to put on a kettle for tea and mix up a bowl of Abby's homemade granola to feed her mother.

"The house seems kinda empty with just us two old maids, don't it?" Mama said between bites, as Teresa came in the door. "Make that three."

"Well, if you're getting lonely, Mama, I have good news for you. It's time for the Write Stuff again tonight."

"Oh, brother," Mama said, "I have a better chance of getting a book published than them old coots. I guess you have to, though, since Cynthia lets you use the computer at the library. Whatever."

Teresa set her bag down and withdrew the blood pressure meter. She secured the cuff around Mama's arm and began pumping. "I will be back tonight to help," she said softly. "I can watch TV with you if you lonesome."

"No, no, I'll just stay out of the way and not be a bother," Mama said. "That way you won't have to take a break from writin' in that blessed notebook."

*   *   *

Wendell returned for that evening's meeting—forty-five minutes ahead of the appointed time, at that, catching Dee in the midst of sweeping the porch.

"Well, Colonel Grover, I wasn't sure if you'd deserted us," she teased him.

"Sorry I'm so early," he said, "but I made all the changes folks told me to, and I was hoping you could take a quick look at my chapter and see if I was on track."

"Sure," Dee said, "I'd be delighted! Come on in."

Wendell had her curiosity piqued before even setting foot in the door, which he did with a slight limp, Dee noticed.

"Did you hurt your leg?" she asked.

"Oh, no," Wendell answered, "not recently, anyway. Da Nang in '68, shrapnel injury. I was one of the lucky ones. Only flares up when the barometric pressure is down—so I suspect this means we should be getting some rain soon."

"So you were in Vietnam?"

"Yep. 366th Tactical, two full tours of duty."

Dee had always thought of the Vietnam War the way documentaries had captured it, with strong young men in camouflage carrying rifles in the jungle. But that was forty-some years ago, it dawned on her, and those young soldiers would now be retirement age.

"Well, I thank you for your service," she said as they pulled out chairs and skimmed his revised pages, which he'd typed on old-fashioned onionskin paper.

Wendell had taken the proffered suggestions of his fellow writers and not only incorporated them, but improved on them. His story had taken a major leap forward.

"Wendell, this is terrific," Dee told him sincerely.

"You think so?" He beamed widely, then snapped back into his usual stiff demeanor.

"So far, yes. You obviously put a lot of work into it."

"It took me about twenty different versions," he said. "I'd sit down to the typer-writer for four hours every day."

"You must have done nothing else for the past two weeks."

"Well, when you're a widower . . . ," Wendell said, trailing off as Dee looked at him with concern. "My wife died of a heart attack a year and a half ago."

"Oh, I'm sorry to hear that," Dee said.

"I was just glad she didn't have to suffer." Dee considered the blustering colonel more sympathetically.

"It's okay," he said. "My daughter and her family live in Abilene, not too far, and I'm active in my church. This writing project lets me go places and do things that I've always dreamed of—without ever leaving home, if you know what I mean."

"I do."

"And I've taken up metalworking, too. That's about as artistic as this old flyboy can get."

"You're doing great, Wendell, just great," said Dee. "Thanks for showing me."

They heard Teresa call out for help with the screen door, her arms cradling an enormous aluminum pan piled high with foil-wrapped bundles. "Is Miss Alice feeling better? I brought a surprise."

Dee jumped up to help her. "You didn't have to do that, Teresa."

"When my neighbor makes tamales, she makes enough to feed —" Teresa struggled for the idiom. "To feed the army!"

"Well, that's fortunate, since I'm here as its commanding officer," joked Wendell. They helped set the pan on the countertop as the rest of the group drifted in, drawn by the delicious aroma, and set out their pages and notebooks. Wendell took a paper plate and piled it high with tamales and fresh salsa.

Food for the body and food for the soul, Dee mused. She guessed that every member of the Write Stuff had been moved, by life experiences as important to them as Wendell Grover's, to create worlds that they could visit from time to time. It was that same capacity that had first attracted her to reading and then eventually writing, herself. Dee figured it was her job to be their tour guide on the journey.

J. D. arrived with a chocolate cake Pauline had sent for the group. "I'm going to have to join a gym if I keep hanging out with you guys," Dee said, as she thanked him for the cake and placed it on the counter beside the tamales.

As the writers took their places around the table, Dee made a last-minute adjustment to the evening's lesson plan. She had come to realize that with this bunch she should trust her instincts and go with the flow.

"As a warmup, I want us to talk for a few minutes about what each of you wants to get out of your writing," Dee said. "If you were to achieve all your writing dreams—then when the dust settled—an apt expression in West Texas!—where would you be? Be as realistic or as fanciful as you like. I think it's important for all writers to have a goal to visualize."

The members let her words sink in.

"I for one don't want to make sandwiches for the rest of my life," Summer began. "I realize that science fiction might not be the ticket out, but it makes me happy while I'm doing this dead-end job, and it gives me something to hold onto while I decide what comes next. And who knows, if I should happen to get published?"

"Same here," said Margaret. "I mean, I've had a decent career, but now that I have some free time, wouldn't it be nice to earn a little bit of royalty income? Still, if it doesn't, so what? If I write a book and the only people who read it are my friends and family, that's okay with me, if they enjoy it."

JoAnn jumped in. "Not me. I want to get a real book deal with a real agent and a real publisher. I know it's a racket, and I'm well aware the deck is stacked against us, but I don't want to be on the bench or the B-team. I want to sell books. No self-published, thousand-copy stuff for me, and I was hoping you might have a clue how to do that."

The writers looked at Dee expectantly.

"I do," she responded emphatically. "*Keep writing.* Don't get discouraged if it doesn't come easy, and continue what you're doing, critiquing each other's work."

JoAnn rolled her eyes at the stock answer. But it was clear that Dee had tapped into a topic the group really wanted to explore. The floodgates opened.

Cynthia said, "I've already met some of the published mystery writers from TWO. They're a great bunch, talented and dedicated and smart, and I'd be tickled to get to be a part of their life. Their books do respectably well, and they have their local fans."

"Same with the romance writers," said Margaret. "I mean, not everyone can be Jude Deveraux and sell zillions of books."

"If she was from the boondocks like us, there's no way that she'd sell that many," said Frances.

Margaret begged to differ. "Look at Jodi Thomas from Amarillo—she began writing after years as a schoolteacher, and now her books are on the *New York Times* best seller list! The romance writers are a tight group—at least the ones that I've met through the Southwestern Romance Writers Association. I'd be proud to get published like that, even if I never made it beyond my first book."

"Western writers are the same way," J. D. agreed. "I don't know how many copies they sell or anything, but they sure have a loyal following at the cowboy gatherings."

JoAnn, whose determined naysaying was beginning to remind Dee too much of the college classes she'd been glad to avoid this summer, called their attention to the differences between the genres they were describing and the mainstream fiction she aspired to. The discussion threatened to turn adversarial, and Dee steered it back to a more congenial track.

"Well," Dee said, "if you can conceive it and believe it, you can achieve it, as they say. I think there's something to that. Now, I don't mean to put anyone on the spot, but I would like to recognize one of you whose writing has really come a long way with the workshopping—so much that I'd like him to read part of his latest draft for you, if he's willing."

She turned to her Most Improved Player. "Wendell?"

*   *   *

Dee woke halfway from the haze of her morning nap the next day, when the house phone rang. Teresa picked up, but before Dee could pull the pillow over her head she caught a few words of the conversation on the receiving side.

". . . give her a message . . . from California? Jensen? Can you spell slowly, please?"

Dee was up in a flash, hurrying to the kitchen in bare feet. She pantomimed to Teresa that she'd take the call.

"Hello? This is Dee Bennett-Kaufmann. To whom am I speaking?"

The voice on the other end was female, the tone urbane. "I'm Arthur Jensen's daughter. I'll get right to the point: my father is indisposed, and I would like to know more about your reason for contacting him."

Dee shook off the mental fuzziness and summoned her most professional and solicitous manner. "I'm an admirer of Gineva Holland Templeton."

"I see. As am I." There was a long pause, and Dee wondered whether she had chosen the wrong approach. "You wrote your dissertation on

Templeton in 2001. I assume you're looking to turn that research into a book. Am I somewhere near the mark?"

Dee, astonished, replied, "Yes, but how did you—"

"Google, my dear. It works both ways. Now, if you'll tell me a bit more about what you know, and what you *want* to know, I'll see if I can be of service."

Dee exhaled and pulled up a stool at the kitchen counter. She grabbed a pen from the drawer and the closest paper to hand, the back side of a recipe card for Buttermilk Pie. She proceeded to describe how she'd stumbled upon Templeton's book, how it had inspired her teaching and writing, how she had searched for more. "But I've never been able to fit the pieces together," she told Templeton's niece. "I hope you can help."

"Let me think about it. I assume there is some time pressure?"

"Yes," Dee admitted as evenly as she could. She didn't want to scare off a valuable source now. She gave the woman her e-mail and cell phone details. "And while I have you, do you mind—I don't think I got your name?"

"Elsa Jensen," replied the voice smoothly. "Elsa Gineva Jensen."

*   *   *

At four the next morning, an e-mail was waiting. Dee plunged in. Good god, she thought, Elsa Jensen must have typed nonstop since their conversation. The text scrolled on forever.

Dear Dr. Bennett-Kaufmann,

I commend you for perceiving the influential role Gineva Holland Templeton played in American letters, though through no fault of your own your appreciation is necessarily incomplete. I will try to remedy that omission, but understand that I am obligated to preserve certain confidences. I of course am biased; you will take this into consideration too, no doubt.

You wonder what led Templeton to her ground-breaking concept of "creative" writing, and further, what led her to so abruptly abandon it.

Let me paint a picture of Gineva for you. I had the delight of knowing her for more than thirty-two years, from my birth in 1949 until her passing in 1982. Our Jensen line were few in number, and close, and with her husband, Allan,

Gineva visited Arthur and Corrine and me at our farm in San Jose almost every week during those happy years. We traveled frequently, too, always the five of us together: two couples and one child who was doted upon by all.

Gineva was the adventuresome one, planner of excursions, researcher of arrangements, seizer of opportunities. But that is not to say she was impetuous; no, she carefully calculated her decisions and made the most of the results. Allan was more likely to follow a whim or turn on a dime, but she gently brought him back in line. She steered his musical career adeptly (you know already that he was a popular jazz pianist), helping negotiate engagements and fees, arrange publicity, and, well, keep him out of trouble. She was witty, quick with a joke or a pithy observation, but profound when a conversation or debate demanded wisdom. I think of her in hindsight as the Dorothy Parker of California.

She was not tall in stature, but she was robust in build, descended from strong Yankee forbears, and she exuded good health and capability. I'd have to guess five-five, a hundred and forty pounds. (I still keep some of her Chanel suits, but I cannot fit into them!) Her most striking physical feature, though, was the luxuriant chestnut hair that she wore styled in bangs or waves, without fail, to hide the right side of her face.

I will tell you, as it was told to me, the circumstance of her early years that accounted for this habit, and for her lifelong refusal to be photographed. (As far as I know there exists no portrait. Not a single one.) Gineva was born with a disability—a severe strabismus causing her right eye to turn inward at a drastic angle. Not only was the condition disfiguring, it was disturbing to those looking at her face, and likely to impair her vision if not corrected early. Surgery was indicated, though risky. Gineva's parents chose that route. The operation was successful, but a subsequent infection cost the child her eye, and very nearly her life. She was eventually fitted with a prosthesis. (I have her first one, as a keepsake too.) As Gineva grew older, she determined to mask her condition—not because she was shy or vain, but because she became aware of the chilling effect of her glass eye on others. She found ways to cope with diminished eyesight: she learned to drive an automobile, she read and wrote diligently, and most of all, she became adept with a camera. (An ideal apparatus for someone with monocular vision, when you think about it.) I believe that what some would have described as a deformity shaped, even sharpened, her powers of artistic observation.

There, now you know.

About Gineva's education, you already know a good deal. She had the benefit of excellent schooling, and to all accounts acquitted herself well. I gather — as you may too from an assessment of her early writings — that she tended to engage more with places than people. You will not find among her preparatory or college record a long list of social organizations or charitable activities. You will find evidence of interests in travel, in automobiles, in astronomy. She told me once that she dreamed of being an airplane pilot, but this was one endeavor closed to her on account of her partial blindness. She loved music — especially the new jazz and swing tunes of the twenties and thirties — and danced enthusiastically.

You guess correctly that James Templeton's failed investments and precarious finances led Gineva to seek employment soon after her graduation from Emerson College in 1929. The situation became dire, in fact. Having declined earlier offers to teach school when she had no pressing need to work, by late that year she found few opportunities available even for a promising college graduate. Marriage prospects were slim, since she hadn't cultivated a circle of friends, either. But Gineva was always resourceful. She approached American Roadways, with only her powers of persuasion, some college magazine clippings, and an unconventional story idea. It was her idea to solicit sponsorships, too. They bought it.

American Roadways provided Gineva — or G. H. Templeton, as she signed her pieces — a huge break. Other freelance assignments would come her way as a result — scores of them, all documented in her scrapbook of clippings. (I am attaching a full bibliography to this message.) As important, though, was a chance acquaintance she'd made near the end of her cross-country journey. Taking the Richmond-to-San Francisco auto ferry on the Lincoln Highway in mid-March 1931, Gineva met Allan Jensen, a young man about her age, who was traveling over to play an engagement at the Sir Francis Drake Hotel. She caught his show that night. They became casual friends; they kept in touch, following each other's careers.

Upon her return to Boston by air, Gineva was not as dismissive of teaching as an occupation. She enjoyed the writing life but, perhaps cautioned by her father's financial downfall, coveted the security of a steady paycheck. During those early years of the Great Depression she supported herself as a part-time lecturer at Bradford College and private tutor, supplementing her income with newspaper and magazine features. She honed her interview and descriptive skills, learned to write quickly and accurately, scrupulously met deadlines. I am convinced she developed good listening skills, too, as she sought to deflect attention from herself and focus it on her subject. These capabilities she used *as the basis of a practical course at Bradford called "Writing for Work and Art" (I have scanned a copy of the typed syllabus and attached it for you.)*

She did not talk much about those years. I believe they were lonely and demanding. Her father died in 1933 and her mother soon after; you have those dates in your genealogical records. She had few friends and no romances. I venture into the realm of speculation when I suggest that this isolation led her to believe she could pull off a victory for her sex within the domain of Cambridge's elite, and exclusively male, ivory tower. She was known professionally only from her byline. It was an opportune time to storm Harvard's castle walls.

While Harvard had been offering non-degree instruction, somewhat reluctantly, to women since the late nineteenth century in a separate program, the faculty were all men even in the 1930s. Responding to a job posting in summer 1934 for an instructor of writing, she made a favorable enough impression to survive the screening process. "The dean extended by cable an employment offer, and I accepted in kind," she wrote in a document of October 5, 1934 (a deposition, perhaps?). "I presumed he found the credentials of G. H. Templeton sufficient to teach Creative Writing 33 in the curriculum of the Harvard Annex. Upon attending the first faculty meeting before the start of the term, however, I found myself dismissed as speedily as I had been hired, without making a single mark on a chalkboard," she wrote.

Here, again, was a turning point. If the academy could offer nothing more substantial than desultory schedules and discrimination, to hell with it. (I can quite picture her saying this; she did not shy away from strong language.) The following year the Works Progress Administration initiated a series of relief projects to support writers and publish useful guidebooks. Gineva was hired on as a "worker-writer" for the Federal Writers Project, producing entries for the Massachusetts state guide. Although the undertaking was fraught with political pitfalls, and opportunity for advancement was limited, she found the work rewarding and suited to her temperament and talent. It was through this experience that she began to outline the practicalities of her profession that would eventually be compiled as The Working Writer.

The book enjoyed some success in its 1939 printing, a copy of which you said you own. But soon afterward, the nation turned its attention to war, and one author's advice regarding an occupation many considered dispensable, or even frivolous, slid into obscurity. In 1940 Gineva even attempted a sequel aimed at the creative-writing student, "The Writer's Apprentice" (its title a play on a popular film of that year, as you may recognize), but that project never it made it past the manuscript stage. By 1943, the Massachusetts writing project was drawing to a close, and once again Gineva faced unemployment. The situation worsened when a difference of philosophy between Gineva and the volume editor grew to a full-blown dispute, and Gineva's prospects in the Boston market dwindled.

She needed a fresh start, and she found it on the opposite coast. With the encouragement of her longtime friend Allan Jensen and a glowing recommendation from a Bradford colleague, Gineva landed a teaching position at Mills, the women's college in Oakland, California. Years later, she loved to describe her drastic removal: "I slid the key under the landlady's door, packed up my typewriter, and shook the Boston dust off my feet." She never looked back.

In Oakland she found renewed vigor. She had come to the Bay Area on the cusp of a transformational time—of edgy art, radical ideas, free expression. In the Berkeley coffee shops and San Francisco clubs, even in the verdant neighborhoods of old Oakland, Gineva forged a new identity. Reconnecting with Allan, she became drawn into his Bohemian circle. I venture to say she made true friends for the first time in her life. They were nothing like her Boston family or colleagues.

You would no doubt be surprised to think of Gineva as a grande dame of the Beat movement. Yet that is the best way I can describe it. As the New York iconoclasts migrated to San Francisco, they inevitably gravitated to Allan Jensen's haunts. There would be Gineva, listening avidly to the talk and the music, because she understood what it meant to be spurned by the establishment. Her carefully cultivated style lent her an air of exoticism, too, I suppose. As for drugs, she remained aloof from that scene; she'd looked after her own welfare for too long to get caught up in destructive excesses. But whenever one of the newcomers needed a sage and sympathetic ear, or a sounding board, or an audience, it was Gineva they turned to.

Now that I have told you this, you might detect coded signs of Templeton in the Beats' writings. You would not have recognized her there otherwise; the Beats, whatever their individual sexual orientation, famously gave women scant attention.

In 1949, Gineva and Allan married. Allan's brother Arthur, younger by two years, had been married to Corrine for a decade when I came along that year. We lived a surprisingly sheltered life even in the heady mix of those times, and I remember as a child meeting Kerouac, Ginsberg, Burroughs. And Ferlinghetti, with whom I still stay in touch.

The most difficult question, I suppose, is why Gineva quit writing, herself, when she moved west. I always thought she could have done anything she wanted. She was surrounded by rich culture and events; she circulated among literary lights. Once she married into the comfortably well-off Jensen family, she no longer had to scratch out a living from hand to mouth. Or maybe that is exactly why.

She was the most sensible, yet sensitive, person I ever knew. I loved to hear her tell stories of her adventures. She left me a wealth of memories when she died, and yet she took many secrets with her. She took her way of seeing, which is what I miss most.

I have rambled despite my intentions. But you may quote me, for whatever benefit it may add. I hope these revelations have shed some new light on your subject; they are all I can share at present. The shadows, one way or another, are always with us.

With my best wishes,
Elsa G. Jensen

Wow, Dee said aloud in the quiet library, startling herself. There would be no rest today—not until she had absorbed every ounce of this material and woven it into her manuscript. Not until she had integrated enough of this new knowledge to form follow-up questions. She leaned her chair back against the wall and thought, *I have hit the fucking mother lode.*

13
A Manuscript Mailed on Friday

The only writers who need concern themselves with deadlines are those who expect to be paid.

DEE AWOKE AT HER ACCUSTOMED HOUR, three-thirty, but pulled the quilt back up to her chin and lay in bed, listening to the predawn silence. Too early to get Mama up, but she didn't know how she could go back to sleep. She had hardly slept already, after yesterday's marathon session. Today would be the day.

She went through the list in her head. File backed up to flash drive and also e-mailed to her university address? Check. Bibliography verified against footnotes? Check. Summary written, revised, proofread twice? Check. As soon as it was light, she'd make coffee, get Mama into the car, and drive to the library. She would compose a brief e-mail to Susan, being careful to strike the right note between apology (for tardiness) and triumph (for the new information she'd been able to turn up in this draft), attach her Word files, and hit Send. She went over the list again in case she'd overlooked something vital the first time. And then again.

In the dark she pictured the scene. Although she'd never actually set foot inside her editor's office, she'd visited plenty of others. There would be Susan, brushing her dark hair out of her face and adjusting her purple-framed glasses, sitting down to her computer with a steaming Starbucks skinny latte. The music of workday Boston traffic would be in full swing far below. A polite ping would announce the arrival of Dee's electronic message. Not as dramatic as a white box with a cover letter and a neat stack of rubber-banded typescript pages, the way things were done in the old days, but a whole lot faster.

Dee had figured first thing on a Friday was more favorable timing than Monday morning. Assuming, of course, that Susan hadn't taken off already for a long weekend at the Cape . . . oh, shoot, that was a possibility . . . well, the die was cast now. This milestone had been too long in coming.

As the hour approached and Dee listened out for the jangle of Jezebel's cowbell from Mama's room, the first pink tint of morning fell on her desk and lampshade. Soon an odd *plink, plink* noise punctuated the still dawn. It increased in intensity then faded away, then came again. Dee struggled to place it.

She sat straight up in bed, where she could see out the window. *Rain!* It hadn't rained in so long she'd forgotten what it sounded like. Mama heard it, too, for the bell began to clang repeatedly, and Dee ran to her room to help her mother up.

"I don't know whether to praise God or build a ark when it rains after this long," said Mama, gesturing for Dee to fetch her glasses and bathrobe, "but I know the cotton'll be glad for it."

"As long as it doesn't keep us from getting to the library before Gladys arrives. Let's get you dressed and out to the car before it gets worse."

"Go let all the windows down first," Mama ordered. "But be quick about it. My bladder can't wait long with this going on."

*   *   *

By the time they reached town, the rain was indeed coming down harder. Dee had the car's wipers going full speed but still had a hard time seeing in front of the headlights. She pulled into the library lot and parked beside the curb, as close as she could to the front door.

"You'll be okay here for a few minutes, won't you?" she asked Mama. "We can't get those casts wet. I won't be long."

And she wasn't. Log into the university e-mail server, plug in the flash drive, write the message she'd already crafted in her head, attach, send, log off. Done.

Within that short span, by the time she came back out the door and Grady locked it again behind her, the shower had passed to the east of town, leaving the brick-paved downtown streets steaming and the rising sun peeking through gaps in the clouds.

Dee pulled into Wilson's to get each of them a donut and coffee. She spared no expense this morning, springing for creme-filled.

As they turned back toward the highway, the Ford's tires splashed water up to the doors at every intersection. When they reached the railroad underpass, however, which dipped down to cross a normally dry stream, the torrent was six feet wide and touching the two-foot mark on the flood gauge.

Dee came to a stop and turned to Mama. "Wow . . . what do we do now?"

"Let's take the back way," said Mama. "We can come around by the far side of the field and see if the cotton got any rain."

They nibbled on their pastries and sipped coffee as Mama gave expert directions for every turn on the long, two-lane farm-to-market roads that crisscrossed Caprock County's eastern half. They came at last to a low bridge where the water spilled over the side. Dee remembered the draw from her childhood, but she didn't recall ever seeing it during a flash flood. She nervously made the crossing, even though the overflow was only an inch deep, and when she accelerated up the hill and over the rise on the far side, she was astonished to find that they were looking west at the Bennett cotton farm—and off toward the north, projected against a gun-metal sky, at the brightest double rainbow she'd ever seen.

Wouldn't Max Miller have loved to get this shot? she thought. Inspiration struck. She slowed and rolled down the window, pulled her cell phone from her purse, and aimed its tiny lens toward the sky. She clicked and saved repeatedly.

Mama leaned forward for a better view. Dee was so mesmerized by the sight, she hadn't realized she was stopped smack in the middle of a public road when a pickup truck, approaching from behind, blinked its headlights and then pulled around to pass her. It sped around the curve and disappeared.

Mama turned her head quickly. "Thar it is!"

"I know, isn't it beautiful?" replied Dee. "It could almost make you love—"

"The green pickup truck. I saw it!"

"*What* green pickup?"

"I knew I wasn't seeing things," Mama said, troubled, but with a tone of certainty. "That truck that just passed us. Can we catch up with him?"

Then Dee understood. The truck Mama had described in the hospital. Could it really have figured into her accident? Dee rolled up the window and hit the gas. She rounded the turn, and the road became straight again. But there was no vehicle in sight.

"Mama," Dee asked, "are you sure?"

Mama seemed lost in thought. "I was headed the other way . . . going sort of slow, after I'd been settin' out here looking over the fields . . ."

"And he sped around you like he did just then?" Dee scoped out the road ahead of her, glancing down each of the turnoffs as they passed.

"No . . . I think—I think, yes, by golly, he was coming from the *opposite* direction. I got a good look at the truck as I was goin' up the hill on the other side of that bridge we just crossed. He was nearly over in my lane, and I could see that the sun was right in his eyes, and I sort of moved over to the shoulder . . ."

"Okay . . . what next?"

". . . and just as I topped the hill I saw something coming at me that made me run plum off the road. I nearly peed in my britches. I remember plain as day!"

"What was it?" Dee asked excitedly. They might really be onto something here.

Mama let out a long breath. "I can't recollect. I don't know whether I blacked out, or hit something—it's a complete blank. Something big was headed toward me. Huge. I knew I was going to die right then and there. That's all I remember."

"You said he. Was there a man driving the green truck?"

Mama thought about it for a second. "Two men. Two men . . . the one doin' the driving was squinting into the sun." She sat back in the seat to rack her brain some more. "It's no good. My mind's not what it used to be."

They'd driven a good five miles down the highway by then. The pickup was long gone, Dee was sure. And what if they could've gotten a license plate, anyway? She wasn't sure she'd know what to tell the police if they did. That six weeks ago her mother thought she saw a green truck, but there was no collision involved, and then some mysterious phantom appeared on the highway, and there was no evidence of any of it?

*   *   *

When Mama and Dee returned home, hoping for some rest before Buddy's arrival, Cori the cat was behaving strangely, roaming anxiously and meowing loudly. He darted between them as Dee led Mama into the kitchen door. Unused to the indoors, he skittered across the floor and took off down the hallway.

"What's wrong with that dang cat?" Mama barked.

"I'm not sure—maybe he didn't like the rain," Dee offered, helping Mama onto the bed and slipping her shoes off. About the time she eased Mama back on the pillow the cat came tearing into the room and leapt onto the bed.

"Jesus! Put him back in the barn. He's about to drive me batty. Put him to use—maybe he'll catch him a mouse."

Dee put out more food and tried to examine Cori for injuries, but he was not to be consoled. That was all she needed, Dee thought—Abby gone for only seventy-two hours, and already Dee had let ill befall the poor animal. At last she cornered him and dispatched him to the barn for time out. She lay back on the red leather couch, her eyelids drooping, and covered her head with a pillow. Not even the unearthly caterwauling prevented her from falling into a deep, well-deserved sleep.

*   *   *

Cori was still howling at noon, when Dee got Mama dressed for Buddy's visit in her newest slacks ensemble—specially chosen, Dee guessed, to forestall any impression that she was incapable of caring for herself. Mama had also been very particular about the house cleaning that week, and had made sure Dee swept the porch and reopened the windows and Teresa dusted every inch of every surface.

Dee heard her brother drive up and guided Mama out to the porch to greet him. He sauntered up the steps carrying a cardboard box full of white Styrofoam cartons and singing, "School's—out—for—the summer!"

"Hey there," Dee said. "Funny, I don't remember you as an Alice Cooper fan."

"I'll do anything to celebrate the end of school these days. Kids get louder and crazier every year." He called out, "You ready for lunch, Mama? I brought brisket from the year-end football fundraiser." Buddy turned to Dee again. "Speaking of loud and crazy, what kind of critter do you have caged in the barn? I can hear it all the way up here."

"It's Abby's cat," Mama replied, "and I think it's gone out of its mind."

Dee explained to Buddy about Abby's unannounced visit — and equally abrupt departure. "I'm sorry you missed her, but you know when she gets an idea in her head, she doesn't waste time acting on it. She would've been happy to see her favorite uncle."

"Only uncle, coincidentally," he added. "So do you think you'd better get that cat to the vet or something? I'll take it if you want me to."

"No, no, you stay and visit with Mama," Dee said. "Is there a still an animal hospital in town?"

Mama answered. "There's only one veterinarian's office — two doctors, husband-and-wife team. From India, Banga-la-desh, or someplace like that. They're in the old Sears catalog store on Third."

Reaching the voice recording of Nehi Behal, D.V.M., and Mital Behal, D.V.M., which said they'd be back in the office that afternoon, Dee retrieved Cori's travel carrier. "Come out here and help me get him," Dee said to Buddy, a cue that she needed to talk with him in private.

"What's up?" he asked as they headed toward the barn.

"You remember back in the hospital, that first night, when Mama said something about a green pickup truck? She saw it this morning, out near the Abilene highway."

"Really?" Buddy said. "I thought that was all a bunch of hooey. Her talking out of her head."

"There's more. Spotting the truck seems to have jogged her memory. She says on the morning of the accident she was coming over that big hill — you know the one, where the highway crosses the draw? — and the pickup was in her lane. It may have run her off the road. And she talked about something bigger in the road — an animal, a vehicle, I don't know."

"An animal? Like a deer or a coyote?"

"I got the idea she meant something *really* big. But that's all I could get out of her."

"You think there's anything to it?"

"I don't know what to think. She certainly seemed convinced. And another odd thing: this morning, when we left, the gate at the road was standing open. I remember because I had to get out in the rain to close it."

"Could it have been Teresa?"

"She's never been careless about the gate before. I just want to make sure there's no burglar or axe murderer on the loose, you know?"

"Well, it could've been Hector or someone else with a legitimate reason. About the truck—maybe I can ask Ed or Sheriff K if they know who drives a green pickup. Did you get a make or model?"

"Come on, what do you think? I wouldn't know a Dodge from a dodgeball, and Mama didn't get a good look. But I'd feel better if you'd look around while you're here. Maybe drive down to the turnrow and check things out."

"I'll do that on my way out," Buddy said. "But let's capture that cat in case it's really a zombie in disguise."

Dee rolled her eyes. "You really have been in high school too long."

*   *   *

The former Sears catalog building was located south of the square in a block that had been abandoned by major retail about the time Dee started high school. The Cougar Bookstore, the drugstore, the dry cleaners, and the town's main grocery store had all moved at the same time when a new strip center was built on the Abilene highway. The five-and-dime shut down completely, bowing to chain-store competition. A down-market drugstore took the place of the locally owned firm. The circa-1920 Caprock Oldsmobile dealership had held on longer than most, but eventually it merged with the other GM franchise in town, and its new models had been moved from the old-fashioned storefront showroom with its tall windows out to the blacktopped lots beside the four-lane.

Third Street's anchor tenants now included a wig shop, a tanning salon, a martial arts training center, and a used furniture store, though the roster had changed often.

Dee found a parking space with no difficulty. She grabbed Cori's carrier and rushed to the vets' office only to find a neatly lettered note taped to the locked door. *We will return as soon as possible.* A plastic suction-cup sign with clock hands was set to "Back at 2:00."

With half an hour to kill, Dee stood and considered her options. It was too hot to leave the cat in the car. She turned to walk down the block, carrier in hand. She could always window-shop, she supposed, although she didn't know why she might need a wig.

Two doors down, in the plate-glass window of the long-departed Oldsmobile dealership, a sign stopped her midstride. *Windstream Galleries.* There was Max Miller, his back turned, hanging a group of landscape enlargements alongside a selection of bridal, graduation, and family portraits. On an easel nearby stood the group photograph from the Poplar Grove Red Hat Style Show, and prominently visible on the front row—in sunglasses, chaps, boots, and all—was a figure that made Dee turn crimson.

Before Max could catch sight of her, she whipped around the way she'd come. Cori chose that moment to let out a netherworldly screech.

Dee was halfway to the drugstore when she heard footsteps catching up to hers.

"Hey, don't you speak, or did that cat get your tongue?"

Busted. She turned around as though she had no idea he was there.

"Oh, hi," she said, trying to subdue the wailing animal. "I didn't know you worked—had a—studio—here—downtown."

"Yep. Work here, live here. Whaddya have there?"

"Oh, ah, here? Yes. I'm sure you haven't forgotten Coriander. My daughter's cat. Abby's . . . gone, left for Albuquerque, on the bus, and he's howling in pain and—and, well, I'm bringing him to the vet. I don't know what's the matter with him."

Cori writhed and clawed at the door of the cage.

Max approached and looked inside the carrier. "I think I know what's wrong with your cat."

"Really?" Dee said.

Max nodded, and purred to the cat, "Aww, it'll be okay, girl." He turned to Dee. "I'm pretty sure your him's a her."

"What?"

"Never had a cat before, have you?"

Dee started to say something defensive but thought better of it. "I guess not. I've never given the issue much consideration."

"Trust me," Max said, smiling devilishly. "I know when I see something in heat."

Dee had a Cowboy Wilbur moment, and she wasn't sure whether she liked it or not. But she was suddenly even more aware of Max's freshly shaven face, his pressed jeans and oxford shirt, boots, green eyes, mustache, short-cropped dark hair.

"The Behals went out to the rodeo grounds," Max said. "It'll be a while. Can I offer you and your cat some water?"

Dee found herself nodding as though in a trance and following him through the door. His studio looked more like an art gallery than a place to have a portrait taken, she thought. The large open room was subdivided by partitions and illuminated by contemporary stage lights. Empty frames were stacked against half-painted walls, and ladders and toolboxes filled a back corner. And what was up with the Red Hat portraits?

"Pardon the mess," he said, returning with two plastic bottles and a bowl. "It's a work in progress."

"A gallery, here in Claxton? How—how wonderful!"

"Well, it was more my wife's idea than mine, but—" She couldn't disguise the fleeting puzzlement on her face, and he backtracked. "My late wife. She was an artist in San Antonio."

"I'm so sorry," Dee said, flustered all over again.

"No, *I'm* sorry just to blurt that out," Max said, pretending to fiddle with Cori's cage as he slipped the bowl to the cat. "She had her eye on a place on the Riverwalk. The plans were drawn up before she died. Afterward, it seemed best to start over somewhere else. That's been five years ago—and you see how far I've gotten."

Dee looked away, concentrating on the photographs on the walls. "The space is a beautiful tribute." He nodded quietly in agreement as she explored.

Besides the corner where the portraits and Red Hat photos were displayed, the only other finished section of the gallery appeared to be a back wall where a series of black-and-white landscapes, matted in stark black frames, hung in a row as straight as the West Texas horizon. They depicted an array of wind turbines, giant three-blade windmills like the ones Dee had seen along the interstate when she drove in from Dallas.

She broke the awkward silence. "What are these?"

"They're part of a commissioned series on the Turkey Run Wind Energy Project, south of here. In due time it will be the largest wind energy installation in the country. I've been hired to do promotional stills—for annual reports and calendars and such—but I'm also doing a traveling exhibition of art photographs."

"And you've been working on this for a while?"

"Almost a year now. It's what brought me here."

"Wow," said Dee as she admired the images. "They're like nothing I've ever seen. I mean, the photos *and* the windmills."

"The wind turbines make a pretty striking picture. You should see them up close."

"That would be something," she said, nodding. "But I guess I won't really have an opportunity before I leave—especially if you and I are going to have a look at your book before I go." She was struck, suddenly, by the impending shifts in the lives that mattered most to her: Abby on a winding path, then her book, a reality at last, and Mama . . . in this quiet moment, in the still of a sun-washed studio, she could envision the changes coming, just as surely as she could feel the potential energy of those windmill blades that would not remain stationary for long.

Coriander let out a howl that startled them both and echoed off every wall of the gallery.

"Come on, you little hussy," said Dee to the cat. "You've caused enough grief for one afternoon."

"Call you about the book project next week?" asked Max.

"I'll look forward to it," Dee said, looking over her shoulder and struggling to calm the cat, only to run smack into the doorframe on the way out.

*   *   *

"Well, that's the second package I'm glad to be rid of today," said Dee as she shut the door of the home place behind her, happy to have left Cori in the care of the Doctors Behal. "Now, you said there was barbecue?"

No one answered. Buddy and Mama occupied opposite ends of the couch, Buddy looking like he'd brought home a report card with straight F's and Mama glaring at him like she was about to put him on permanent detention.

"What, did everybody drink a bottle of cod-liver oil or something?" asked Dee.

Mama turned her glare toward Dee. "So are you in on this, too, Dee Anna?"

"No, Mama," Buddy replied, "I haven't had time to tell her."

"Tell me what?"

"Penny and I arranged for an appraiser to come look at the farm next week," he said.

"Oh, jeez, Buddy, why didn't you at least talk with Mama about it first?"

"That's exactly what I came to do today. I mean, what's going to happen when you leave?" Buddy asked. "We have to get started now."

"I'll finally get some peace and quiet, that's what," Mama said. "You kids are smothering me. And you can't wait to sell this albatross and get your cut of the proceeds."

Dee was speechless. It had never occurred to her that Mama thought that way. But then, who could ever tell what Mama really thought?

"Mama, you know it's not about the money. We'd be lucky to make enough to even keep you in groceries," said Buddy.

"Teresa will continue to come for a few hours each day during the week," Dee finally said.

"I'll be glad when we're done with that Meskin and I can take care of myself."

Buddy ignored Mama and said, "It does sound like Teresa's a big help, but is that enough?"

"Not right now," Dee admitted.

"I've had it with all of you," Mama said, pushing her lift chair button and leaning on her casts to stand up. "I wish you'd all go on, and let me die in peace." She hobbled into the kitchen alone and peered through the door at the garden.

"Mama, I'm leaving that man's business card on the countertop," said Buddy, as he rose to leave. "The appointment time is written on the back." He tried halfheartedly to give her a hug on his way out the door.

Mama turned away and walked slowly toward the hallway. Dee followed and helped her to bed, without another word passing between the two of them.

Dee made herself a cold barbecue sandwich for supper and sat alone at the kitchen table to eat it. When she finished, she stood and walked over to the calendar, and picked up the green colored pencil to mark an X for a day of rain. Only then did she notice the date. It had been Friday the thirteenth all right, no two ways about it.

14
Dryland Farming

*If you encounter a dry spell, rest briefly and appraise
your progress. Then pour yourself a drink and put the
next sheet in the typewriter.*

DEE STOPPED BY the grocery store on Tuesday morning for coffee,
tea, and milk and wistfully looked for the *New Yorker* summer fiction
issue, but no such luck. She had a moment of certainty that her mind
was going to mush as she stood in line perusing the celebrity-tabloid
headlines in two languages. A different cashier had been on duty—the
pregnant one was probably off on maternity leave by now, she calculated.

Had she really been here in Claxton for six *weeks*? Sometimes it seemed
as though she had never left—as though twenty-one years had compressed
to nothing and she was still a high-school senior counting the days
until graduation.

Dee returned from her grocery-and-e-mail run to find two surprises:
Buddy's silver Suburban in the yard and, as she walked into the kitchen,
his head in the oven.

"Oh, no, don't pull a Sylvia Plath on us now," Dee said suspiciously.
"Were we expecting you?"

Her brother backed away from the appliance and stood up with
some difficulty. A smear of burned grease streaked his forehead. "Huh?"

"Never mind. I just didn't know you were coming."

"Igniter's about to go out," Mama explained from her tray table in
front of the television, where Teresa had brought her a bowl of cold

cereal for lunch. "The fellow who knew how to fix it went to work in the oilfield, and his son's a no-count drunk who doesn't show up half the time when I call him."

"I thought I could get it repaired before the appraiser came this afternoon," Buddy added, gesturing with the wrench in his hand.

"Cheerios are good for your choler—*choles*terol," Dee heard Teresa remind Mama, who had turned up her nose at the uncooked meal.

"I don't need nobody like you telling me what to eat," Mama said.

"What do you mean by that?" Teresa said, uncharacteristically snappish.

"Nothing," Dee intervened, then said under her breath, "Buddy, just admit it. You're here because Penny called you."

He looked at her sheepishly.

"She pitched a fit, didn't she? She didn't think Mama and I could handle the appraiser by ourselves."

"Look," Buddy said, softly, "I'm sorry. You know how she is. Besides, no harm done. I think I fixed the igniter. What's wrong with having an extra set of hands?"

Dee started to object but Buddy motioned her to lower her voice. "Dee, she's going to have to sell the place, I tell you. I've been looking at her bank statements, her savings in the gin credit union, everything . . . she doesn't have enough for living expenses and apartment rent otherwise."

He handed her a brochure. *Autumn Breeze—Patio Homes for the Golden Years.*

"Penny give you this too?" She put it back down with a sigh. It was too soon for Mama to give in to old age, she thought. "We've got it under control, and it won't be long till she's mobile again—"

"Can you honestly tell me that you think that she should stay out here alone even after she's healed up?"

"Maybe not," Dee said, finally admitting it to Buddy and herself. "But she could if she had help."

"And you see how well that's going," he said, and stuck his head back in the oven.

*   *   *

The farm appraiser arrived promptly at three, shortly after Teresa had gone for the day. Jimmy Don Jerrell, a short, stooped man of indeterminate age, was from nearby Roscoe and did a bit of farming himself from time to time.

Mama was ensconced in the recliner with Dr. Phil turned on full blast.

"Looks like you got a good start on your cotton crop, Mrs. Bennett," Mr. Jerrell shouted toward her. She nodded, never looking at him, but mashed the remote with the edge of her cast to turn down the volume a notch. "It won't be long before you have squares."

Mama turned down the TV a couple more notches, threw a knowing glance his way, and nodded a bit more vigorously.

Mr. Jerrell pressed his advantage. "It's hard to make a go without irrigation these days. But your skiprow plan seems to have worked out well."

"Haddn' it, though?" Mama turned to him, forgetting to be morose. "My late husband, Wilton, always thought that was too risky. I wanted to try it that way this year to see if it'd increase yield."

"Well, I think you're smart to do it. Say, would you mind giving me a little tour of your home?" he said. "Of course with the help of your son and daughter."

"Shoot," Mama said, pushing the lift-chair button and using her elbows to push up to the walker, "I ain't no invalid."

As Jimmy Don Jerrell extolled the virtues of sudan versus sorghum, it wasn't long before Mama was trailing him like a puppy from room to room while he opened doors, flipped on light switches, took measurements, and checked appliances. Buddy had managed to fix the oven igniter just in time.

Mr. Jerrell was almost finished making notes on his clipboard and was getting ready to leave through the kitchen door, when he turned and asked her, "Could I trouble you for a glass of water?"

Buddy ran over to the cabinet, grabbed a glass, and twisted the faucet handle with a flourish.

Dee could see it coming, like a slow-motion movie. She had wanted to yell, "Gently, Buddy, *gently*, or you'll—" But it was too late.

The handle detached and the sprayer attachment went off like a Water Wiggle in the kitchen, and Buddy was useless against it. A three-hundred-pound fullback he could have taken one down in one swoop. But the malfunctioning faucet and squirming hose eluded him.

Dee rushed in to assist but succeeded only in soaking both Mr. Jerrell and Mama.

"Cain't you just turn off the valve under the sink?" shouted Mr. Jerrell.

"There's never been one," replied Buddy. "Let me run outside and shut it off at the pump."

Once the waterworks subsided and Buddy arrived with the mop, Dee got each of them a hand towel and did her best to dry off her mother's casts. Mr. Jerrell kept apologizing for asking for a glass of water.

Dee handed him a bottle from the fridge for the road.

Mama simply thanked him and went back to the couch, smiling almost imperceptibly.

Dee found her mother's expression infectious. Maybe no one else would even want this old claptrap of a farm.

*   *   *

Where had the time gone? Dee thought as she saw JoAnn's Malibu pull into the driveway. She quickly fluffed up the throw pillows on the couch and arranged the extra chairs around the table.

She grabbed the brown envelope from her bedroom with all of the writers' assignments and flipped through it frantically for the pieces that they hadn't read last week. Cowboy Wilbur, latest chapter. Seen it. Cynthia's library detective. Read it. Ah, here was one they hadn't yet workshopped, along with new installments from several of the stories that were now as familiar to her as her own work.

Just in time. She could hear Teresa call out "Hello?" as the door opened. "I'm back, Miz Bennett. You ready for your exercises?" Everyone seemed to arrive at once, full of energy.

"Okay, gang," Dee said. "Ready to critique your most recent submissions?" She caught her breath, drew out an excerpt from JoAnn's novel *The Barrister,* and began to read.

Kip Larson was too hung-over to go to trial and he knew it, but he would never get into the witness protection program if he didn't take the stand today. Worse, he'd be dead before you could say, "Howdy y'all" if the Ft. Worth Mafia had their way.

Besides, if he didn't go, he might never see Marsela again. What were the chances that he would run into the assistant DA at a hotel bar in the Stockyards? Of all the women you might pick up in the Metroplex, who knew that he'd encounter the one working for Carlo aka Bubba the Butcher Morganti? Dee smiled. John Grisham, Texas style. Someday she might even see JoAnn Rinehart's name on a dust jacket in an airport book rack. She kept reading.

They made it through two other manuscripts—a chapter of the Civil War epic and a flash fiction piece that carried Cynthia's trademark expressions—before taking a short break. When they reconvened, Dee picked up the story she'd spotted earlier. She immediately felt more relaxed with the smooth lyricism of the writing. "This one's called 'The Swimming Lesson,'" she announced to the listeners.

"I don't remember reading that one," said Margaret. Other heads shook as well.

"Well, maybe it was omitted by accident. Let's keep going," Dee said as she held it up to read.

I spent the day with my grandfather begging the tourists for pesos. Normally this would make me sad. My grandmother would sit squat-legged near the border crossing at Presidio with a beat-up styrofoam cup, pretending to be blind. My job was to empty the cup when no one was looking and to bring her food and water when the street was empty.

But today I was not sad. Today was the day that my brother Jesus and I were going to cross the Rio Grande. It had been the worst drought in years. All of the gardens had burned up. The only good thing about the parching of the land was that the river was now so low, downstream from Ojinaga, you could swim it.

As Dee paused to turn the page she caught the sigh of the wind outside. In the room, her audience had turned quiet. All eyes and ears were attuned to the reading.

I had been cleaning motels all summer and had saved enough money to bribe the constable, and Jesus was out of jail. At sunset we set out for the muddy, snake-infested ravine, three miles from my grandmother's shack near Ojinaga. My cousin Juan gave us a ride, all three of us holding on to each other on his motor scooter in the dark.

The water stank. In the distance we could hear dogs—or were they wolves? With our pockets full of dollars traded to the cab drivers for pesos, Jesus and I waded into the water, waving good-bye to our cousin.

It was a baptism for a new life, freedom, money and prosperity. We had family across the border who would help us adjust.

Asustada? my brother said to me, grinning, as he dog-paddled in the deepening water. But I was not afraid, even though we both knew he was a better swimmer.

In the middle of the river, with the bottom well beyond our feet, we heard a helicopter and saw searchlights illuminating the waves. Jesus ducked under water, and I hid myself under a floating tree.

I held my breath for as long as I could, and then came up for air. I looked for Jesus. He must already be ahead of me, I thought, and I kept swimming, swimming, and whispering Jesus, Jesus, Jesus. My arms were tired. I was weary, but I could see the bank. I was sure Jesus was on land, hiding to tease me.

Wearily, I could finally feel my feet touching bottom. I stood up, fighting the current, and walked to the bank.

I hid in a culvert all night until Jesus came.

My heart made my throat scream when I saw his body wash up on the shore.

I tried to revive him but it was no use. There was nothing left to do but to take the dollars and wallet from his pocket, and walk to the truck stop outside of Presidio where they had a phone booth. My aunt would be waiting for my call, but my heart was heavy with what I had to tell.

Everyone sat, silent and still, when Dee reached the end of the last page.

"Did you catch the use of the word 'had'"? Margaret said. "That was backstory that should have been part of the main story."

"But what a story it was," JoAnn countered. Dee caught, for the first time, a tone of genuine engagement in JoAnn's response.

"Folks," Dee held up her hand. "Let's hold our thoughts until all of the stories have been read."

"That rocked," Summer said.

"I don't know," grumbled Wendell. "What's that part about waiting until Jesus came supposed to mean?"

"And a body washing up on shore? Horrid," said Frances.

Dee gave them her most severe professorial glare over her glasses, and they were again subdued. They had time to make it through two more pieces, including a portion of Summer's sci-fi epic.

Teresa closed her notebook quietly and disappeared down the hallway toward Mama's room. J. D. rose, too, and declared that he thought he'd better get back home to Pauline. Wendell left with a perfunctory wave to no one in particular, and the women filed out.

Dee spotted Teresa heading out the door last, her backpack slung over one shoulder. "You're going?"

"My father is waiting."

"Teresa . . . it was your story, wasn't it?"

Teresa paused. "I thought the writers were supposed to be ano—how do you say—anonymous?"

"It was very good. Whoever wrote it."

"I have to go," Teresa said, and let the screen door slam shut behind her.

"Bring it back if you want me to read the rest," said Dee into the empty night.

*   *   *

As Dee dropped off to sleep that night she dreamed she was swimming upstream in cold water, in a river that ran through the heart of the desert.

15
Living off the Land

*If you want to write about the world,
go out and observe it.*

THE FOLLOWING DAY, Dee took the next available time during Teresa's work shift to make good on her promise to look at Max Miller's book—meeting its creator in town partly because she wanted to be free to concentrate on the work at hand, and partly to avoid Mama's prying eyes. She needed a clear head and a professional environment.

On a folding table in the middle of his light-filled studio, Max spread out large sheets of drawing paper to which he'd affixed full-color photographic prints and taped slips with paragraphs of text. It was a coffee-table book in the making. "So here you go, Professor," he said. "First time I've tried my hand at anything like this."

Dee took her time turning the oversized pages, taking in the distinctive ways Max had captured a place she'd never found particularly inspiring. Dramatic cloud formations framed multi-hued sunsets. A bright green stripping machine, working by headlights in the late fall evening, harvested cotton against a red dusk. A flock of wild turkeys took wing from tangled cover. A ribbon of blue flowed between banks of russet clay at the base of a snow-rimmed canyon.

"Impressive," she said, and she meant it. Though she didn't consider herself an expert—and certainly not an art critic—she judged Max's work to rank among the best landscape photography in her experience.

Clearly he knew how to compose and light a scene to evoke a response and keep the viewer turning the pages.

The written word was another matter, however. Max was right; his project cried out for an editor. She took out her notebook and uncapped her pen.

"What do you think?" he asked, as eager for the teacher's feedback as any of her students.

"Give me a minute."

Dee chose a page with an image that particularly moved her: grain elevators towering above a small-town railroad siding like Manhattan skyscrapers in the slanting, golden light. By the time Max returned with a brace of cold bottled Cokes, she'd taken his workmanlike description and woven it into a lyrical paragraph about the ways America's food moved from rural farm to urban table.

"I'm not certain about the specifics," she explained as he read it over her shoulder, "but you get the picture."

"I *do* get the picture," the photographer quipped. "Whatever it costs, you're hired."

She smiled. "I'll have my people get in touch with your people." She'd ask JoAnn the paralegal to write up a simple contract. She was beginning to relish the assignment already.

"Now, I understand your time's short and your days are spoken for," said Max. "Do you think we could work at your mother's place and whip this into shape before you depart for civilization again?"

"You got it, Miller. Give me your manuscript on a flash drive, and I'll start reading right away—before I hear back from my editor and have to get back on my own book. We can touch base daily as I go through it." She smiled again. "We're practically turning into a publishing enterprise out here, don't you think?"

*   *   *

The prospect of a regular visitor besides the Wrong Stuff, as Mama had taken to calling them, seemed to improve the somber mood that had hung over them since the appraiser's visit. When Max wrapped up his working session with Dee on Friday, Mama took the initiative of asking him to come out for supper with them the next night. To Dee's knowledge, it was the first dinner invitation Mama had issued to anyone but immediate family since Daddy died. Not even the preacher had rated that.

"I'd be pleased, Mrs. Bennett," said Max with a wink, "—that is, if my editor says we can take a break." Dee started to panic at the thought of preparing a Saturday-evening meal without help, but Max saved the day before she had to admit to her culinary clumsiness. "What's more, why don't I bring some steaks for the grill? Don't worry about the fixin's, either. I make a mean baked potato."

*   *   *

Max wasn't exaggerating, Dee thought as she finished cutting the last morsel of rib eye on her mother's plate and helping her get her fork slowly to her mouth. His loaded twice-baked potatoes earned Alice Bennett's highest praise. Mama swore that his peach cobbler—made with fresh fruit from a u-pick-'em orchard near Abilene, he explained when pressed—could hold its own at the county fair. He even brought his guitar, regaling them after the meal with Mama's Bob Wills and Hank Williams favorites as the sun sank low on the horizon.

Max told behind-the-scenes stories of previous Red Hat Style Shows at Ruby Lee's and even shared a little gossip about Ruby Lee herself. "We go *way* back," he chuckled. "I used to do the publicity shots for that band . . . what was their name? But I think that was two husbands ago."

Mama was practically floating on air when Dee tucked her in after dark. "Dee Anna," she said, whispering conspiratorially, "this may be your last chance to get a good man. Don't screw it up by trying to high-tail it out of here in two weeks."

"Mama! What makes you think I don't already *have* a good man?! But I'm not 'high-tailing' it anywhere, anyhow," Dee assured her. "You're making great progress. I'm not leaving until you can handle things on your own again."

"I don't know if you can stay *that* long," Mama said wistfully.

Max was washing up the dishes when Dee returned.

"I'll do that," she said. "I can manage kitchen duties as long as they involve water and not fire."

"Cool customer, huh? And here I thought you showed such promise as a hot model."

She popped him across the leg of his jeans with the dishtowel. "Let's just leave that part of my sordid past alone, shall we?"

Afraid he might catch her blushing like a teenager, she slipped away to wipe down the dining-room table and turn off the overhead light. Outside the window the shadows turned to blue and purple, the cicadas began their evening song, and the moon rose behind the old bed-frame fence. Dee struggled to remember what the moon looked like over the lake back home. And she hadn't thought of Rob in days.

*   *   *

"Grab your boots, we're going to do fieldwork today," Max instructed Dee Wednesday morning when he arrived for their editorial session. "Come on—I'm showing you what makes outdoor photography so much fun." It had rained a little overnight and the day was fresh and clear.

Dee made sure her mother was settled in with Teresa's regimen before taking off with Max in his truck. He drove her north to a part of the county where the highway crossed a narrow fork of the river—usually narrow, that was. Stopping the truck on the shoulder of the road beside the bridge, he took out his large camera bag and tripod. "Oh, and would you mind carrying this?" he asked Dee as he reached to retrieve a Browning twelve-gauge from the rack in the cab.

Dee hesitated as though the gun might bite.

"Don't worry, it's not loaded," he assured her, handing her the ammo case from under the seat. "But never take someone's word for that in any case."

"Don't worry, I wouldn't," Dee assured him.

Max broke down the gun's action to show her where the shells would go, then slung the gun over his shoulder. "I got it. If you're not comfortable with firearms, I'll swap you for the tripod. But I don't come out here without some protection against snakes or wild hogs."

"Snakes?" Dee rethought the prospect of the gun.

"One of the hazards of getting close enough to wild animals to photograph them," Max reminded her, "is how close they can get to *you*."

"I think *I* might not mind knowing how to shoot that thing while you're occupied with the camera," Dee said.

"Consider it done. Come on, we have a bit of walking to do first."

They slipped through the fence and trekked through hackberry and agarita and mesquite brush above the riverbank, following the swollen watercourse until the terrain began to rise and the stream tapered off.

"There's a spring hidden up here in the side of the canyon," Max explained. "Years ago, buffalo would've come to water here . . . today there are still antelope and coyotes and small mammals. Plus the variety of plant life is incredible—and there's something else I want to show you."

They reached a large outcrop of boulders where Max laid down his gear and climbed up. He helped Dee crawl up and over several more rocks, until they came to an opening in the cliff face. He pointed to the underside of a sheltering ledge.

"Can you make out the designs?" he asked.

"Umm . . . I see a lot of scratched lines, if that's what you mean."

"Look more closely."

Dee could see, upon careful inspection, that there was a pattern to the lines and curves pecked into the surface. "Wow—petroglyphs? I've never seen them except in books."

"You won't see these in any book, either, since they're on private land. Probably a good idea, too—artifact hunters would destroy a site like this in no time. So I have an agreement with the landowner. I don't reveal the location—or even publish shots that would raise curiosity— and he lets me take photos of any wildlife I can track. Forty square miles of prime game land, and I'm the only one with permission to be out here."

"Pretty special, Miller."

"Yes, it is. Puts the whole project in a different perspective, wouldn't you say? But I also wanted you to see it for yourself. There are feelings no photograph can capture."

Dee mulled over that for a while as they sat in silence on the tallest rock overlooking the water. She saw Max reach a forefinger to his lips, then nod his head ever so slightly in the direction of downstream. She turned her eyes to see a large mule deer—a doe—accompanied by a spotted fawn half its size. The pair of animals felt their way across the sandy edge of the stream to the spring, where they bent down to drink.

Max reached slowly for the camera hanging around his neck and focused his shot. The deer went about their business. Max gave Dee the thumbs-up as they scrambled down from the rock.

"It's a waiting game," he explained. "You learn what you can about the habits of animals, then go to the places they live at the times of day you're most likely to see them. It's a little late by now, of course, and we were lucky. So—you ready for a sandwich and a different kind of shooting lesson?"

They spent the better part of the afternoon tramping through a flat meadow near the river, where Max hung their soda cans from a tree limb as plinking targets. By the time they were ready to pack it in and head back, Dee had put aside most of her trepidation about the gun.

"Okay, so now I think I can manage in a pinch," she said, pleased with her emerging survival skills. "As long as the hog or rattlesnake or whatever will just be courteous enough to stand still in one place while it's attacking me."

*   *   *

They arrived back at the home place as Teresa was silently setting the table for supper, placing the dinner plates with exaggerated care. Mama, still seated in her recliner, wore a sour expression.

"What's up?" Dee asked when no one greeted her or Max—or extended him a dinner invitation.

"I'll tell you what's up," said Mama. "That durned Meskin broke my good cut-glass tea pitcher, puttin' hot water in it right out of the refrigerator. It made a holy mess all over the kitchen. I swear she hadn't got the sense God give a prairie dog."

"Mama, I'm sure you can get another tea pitcher. You can't get another Teresa."

"I'm calling the agency so they can take it out of her pay."

"Mama! You're just lucky that Teresa's willing to make meals the way you want—you'd be starving by now if you had to depend on me."

"When you leave I don't want to be stuck with her," she said churlishly.

In the kitchen, a cabinet door slammed with some force.

Max took that as his exit cue. "I'll walk you out," Dee said to him, noticing that Teresa had already removed the extra place setting from the table before gathering up her backpack and notebook and heading out the door.

Teresa turned away from where her father was waiting in his truck, but she did not look Dee in the eye. "I'm sorry about the pitcher. I can replace it. But she . . . she said things."

"What things?" Dee was alarmed even if not surprised.

"Mrs. Bennett . . . does not always say things that are true."

Dee let out a long breath. "Please don't worry. We'll work it out. You understand that my mother is—from a different generation? A different place?"

Teresa left without waving as the truck drove away.

Dee turned to Max, who was politely pretending not to notice. "Thanks for a wonderful day," she said. "I learned a great many things."

"Me too," he said. "And one of them is that *I* don't want you to go, either."

She felt a shock as though someone had doused her with cold water. Soon—whatever her mother's decisions—she'd be back at Raleigh College, preparing for a new fall term, proofreading her new book, picking up with Rob where they'd left off. How had she let this charming Texan, a stranger, turn her head?

Those thoughts melted away as Max drew closer and ran his fingers across her brow, sweeping her windblown hair back out of her face. He leaned toward her and, with his other hand, lifted her chin so that his lips met hers in perfect sync.

The kiss was both hot with longing and gentle, somehow wistful, she felt—each of them restrained for their own private reasons. But Dee also realized it was like no other kiss she'd ever experienced.

It was more than just his rough late-afternoon beard on her cheek, the primal scents of outdoors, the pulse of her body next to his. There was something—what?—at once passionate and vulnerable beneath that surface. Dee caught her breath and regained her composure as he smiled and walked away toward his pickup. She deeply, desperately wanted to know more.

16
Old Settlers

*Aim high, shoot low: when earthly matters inevitably
distract you, raise your sights again toward your goal
of publication.*

AT THE LIBRARY the next morning, checking in with Cynthia after logging in to get her e-mail, Dee had to bite her lip to keep from breaking into a giddy grin. But she couldn't avoid saying his name for long. She just had to come on out with it.

"Max Miller—you know Max, the photographer, right? Well, I think Max would be the perfect speaker for next week's Write Stuff program," she practically gushed. "He could really show the group how images can enhance their content, and I don't think it's a secret that he's working on a book of his own, which is under contract with a publisher from Houston, and—"

"Slow down, girl! Are you telling me you just need a break from leading the workshop? No problem—I don't think anybody will mind a substitute. Especially such a good-looking one."

"Oh, no, I—I thought it might help to start diversifying our approach before I have to leave for good . . ."

"You don't seem completely thrilled at the prospect," Cynthia observed, slyly adding, "and I'm guessing it's not Alice Mo-Malice who's holding you back."

"No," Dee admitted, blushing.

"Can I tell you a little something in confidence?"

"Sure, what?"

Cynthia pulled the edges of her knit twin set more tightly toward her collarbone. "There was talk when Max Miller moved to Claxton. Now, everybody deserves a second chance, I'm all for that, but for a while there was a fellow from San Angelo dropping by every so often and asking questions at the coffee shop. Stopped in here one day."

"What are you saying?"

"Nothing except that the circumstances of his wife's . . . how can I put this, demise . . . were sort of hushed up. And people said he was a basket case—maybe still is. You *do* know there was a wife, right?"

Dee nodded, glad that bit of information hadn't blindsided her.

"I'd just be careful if I were you. Even if there was nothing there, you might want to think long and hard about getting involved. And you don't want people talking—if they aren't already."

"You've heard rumors?"

"Librarians are especially good at listening when people don't think they can be heard. We know when they're eating candy bars in the carrels, or talking on their cell phones in the stacks, or rendezvousing in the restrooms. Yes, if you must know, that does happen. And no, I haven't heard any gossip since your swimsuit episode. Except that Frances told JoAnn that she saw Max's truck pulling into your gate yesterday."

Cynthia's paranoia had her so tangled up that she almost walked out without telling her the most important thing she'd come to say.

"Gosh, I nearly forgot! I had a message from Susan, my editor—she's looked over my Templeton manuscript and sent it to two outside readers, who are planning to review it and get back to her quickly. I've never made it this far in the process before. It's got to be a good sign! I really owe you. I'd never have connected with Elsa Jensen without your help."

"Terrific," said Cynthia. "Fingers crossed, toes crossed, legs crossed, whatever it takes for luck. And I'll call Max and set things up for Tuesday night."

*   *   *

"Max and I are going out in the field for a bit while Teresa's here with you, Mama," Dee told her mother as she opened the screen door for her client that afternoon. Dee hoped Mama and Teresa would be able to patch things up enough to be civil to each other for a few hours.

"Max promised to give me some gun lessons. Didn't you, Max?" She had to find a way to pump him for information somehow.

He looked a little surprised. "Well, I suppose so, if that's what you want to work on first."

"Might sharpen up my accuracy before I take my pencil to your manuscript," she said coolly.

"Dee Anna's never had any interest in that sort of thing before," Mama said.

Dee parceled out her mother's pills and held a glass of water for her to drink. "Staying out here has taught me it might be a valuable skill to have. Mind if I use Daddy's rifle?"

"Just don't mess it up. If I had to, I could still draw a bead on a critter," she said. "Well, maybe not like *this*," she added, raising her casts.

"I bet you'd find a way," Max said to her, smiling wryly.

"Daddy's gun is in that hall closet there. Bullets are on the shelf."

Max poked around in the barn and found some wire and an old aluminum trash can lid, which he hung on the far side of the cow pen. Dee and Cori kept their distance, watching while he rigged the target.

"Well, you've certainly done an about-face," he said to Dee as he checked and loaded the .22. "You always change your mind this quickly?"

"Just giving myself options," she answered.

He handed her the gun and moved beside her, showing her how to hold it. With his hand on her bare arm it took all her determination to stay calm. "Make sure the stock is firmly pressed against your shoulder . . . now line up your sight with the exact center of the target."

She concentrated on the lesson and forced the image of his lips from her mind. Appearing to take her at her word, he continued his instruction in a professional tone. "Slowly breathe in and release some air until you are relaxed, and gently squeeze the trigger until the charge goes off."

Dee followed Max's directions and fired the rifle. It kicked her shoulder and hurt. She missed the makeshift target entirely. This was a different skill from peppering a Coke can with buckshot, she could see.

He laid his hand on her shoulder and rubbed lightly where the gunstock had bruised it, and her resolve nearly melted. "Try again," he said. "It's the only way you learn how. Remember how you learned to adjust to the shotgun."

"I'm learning to adjust to a lot of things, thank you," she shot back.

He was incredibly patient, guiding her grip and stance. She steeled herself to ignore the tingling from head to toe each time he moved close to her—which he did with annoying smoothness.

"So tell me," Dee asked him as he guided her to load the ammunition and line up her next shot. "Did your wife go hunting and photographing with you? Did she like outdoors stuff too?"

He turned to look at her quizzically. "You do change directions abruptly."

"Sorry to be so blunt. I just wondered what she was like."

"No, no, and only if it was a lounge chair by a swimming pool."

Dee braced herself for the recoil and pulled the trigger. She hit the bull's-eye this time. "Does it still hurt?"

He let out a long rush of air between his teeth. "So that's what this is all about. This sudden chill in the air."

"I only realized that I'd been kissed by someone I'd worked side by side with for two weeks and still didn't have a clue about. Surely you can appreciate that."

"Yeah. Maybe I just gave in, in the moment."

When he declined to offer further insight, she tried a different line of questioning. "Did you—do you—have kids?"

"Nope, we weren't that lucky," he replied when the air was quiet again. He let her reload and go through all the steps on her own.

"I'm beat," Dee said after a few more shots. "Let's take a rest."

They walked up to the front porch to sit.

Teresa miraculously and silently appeared with glasses of lemonade for them both, and then went back inside.

In the distance, they could see Hector out on the tractor. A turboprop cruised overhead, and a hummingbird darted in and out of the hollyhocks.

"It's beautiful here," Max said.

"It is, in its own way, isn't it?" Dee said. "I don't think I ever appreciated any of the good things about this place. I could never get away from it fast enough."

"So, my turn for questions. Is there someone back home—someone you're eager to get back to?" he said.

"Sort of," Dee said candidly. "It's . . . complicated."

"Well, then, I'm glad the competition is six states away." He turned his gray eyes on her and she started to feel that tingling again. Talk about complicated.

"How about you?" Dee teased. "You and Miss February looked awfully cozy at the style show."

"Miss February is a blue-haired floozy twenty years my senior, and I couldn't keep up with her if I tried," Max said, laughing.

Damn, he was hard to pin down. Deciding she wasn't going to get anything more revealing than that, Dee motioned him to come in out of the heat and take a look at the progress she'd made on the book. There wouldn't be many more chances.

*   *   *

"I'd cross my fingers for luck if I could," Mama told Dee, sitting stoically in the waiting room on Friday morning and staring down at her plaster casts, which were soiled and scuffed but still rigid, "but you're going to have to do it for me." Eight weeks to the day since Dr. Kim had first set Mama's fractured wrists, they both had high hopes for the results of the newest X-rays.

"Maybe this'll be the day, Mama. Let's send positive energy out into the universe."

"The minute these casts come off they're gonna think I've gone Holy Roller—I'll be waving my arms in the air in praise."

They'd been biding their time for nearly an hour in the wood-frame chairs when the technician returned. "Are you ready for some good news, Mrs. Bennett?"

"Darn tootin' I am. You got your saw ready?"

"Well, not that fast . . . but come on back and we'll talk about what's going to happen next."

Healing had been slow but sufficient, the technician explained, and Dr. Kim was scheduling Mama for cast removal and a special session of evaluation and therapy the following Thursday.

"You can expect a period of readjustment afterwards," he cautioned her, "and you shouldn't try to return to full activity too fast. Your strength and range of motion will greatly depend on how vigorously you've been doing your physical therapy."

Mama might've stretched the truth a bit when she swore how dedicated she'd been. But she seemed sincere in pledging extra cooperation over the remaining few days. The end was in sight, and the future suddenly looked a lot brighter.

They'd been gone a good part of the day by the time they pulled back up to the gate, and an afternoon thunderstorm had brewed up. Stopping at the mailbox, Dee hopped out to retrieve the day's haul of circulars and envelopes. She hadn't thought to bring an umbrella and wasn't eager to get soaked opening the gate. But she didn't have to. It was standing wide open, a strange event on a day when no visitor had been expected. As she drove through and closed it again, she spotted wide tracks in the recently moistened earth, heading off in the direction of the perimeter of the cotton field. She'd have to talk to Hector if he was being so careless.

Inside, after changing into dry clothes and setting soup on the stove to warm for dinner, Dee and Mama watched the lightning crackle and the rain beat against the windows. Sweet relief was in sight for both of them. Dee marked the doctor appointment on the calendar—July 3. She began to relish the prospect of her own restored freedom as much as Mama did hers.

Dee sorted through the stack of mail, opening a large envelope with a Roscoe return address. "Ah—from our friend Mr. Jerrell, Mama. Send some more positive energy."

Mama skimmed over each page of the appraisal report, her expression hardening to stone.

"Everything okay?"

"Here, you look," Mama said in dismay. "Might as well just give the place away if this is all that fool thinks it's worth." Dee took a look at the figures. Even if the valuation wasn't much, it was well out of Dee's own budget. She saw no way to offer help. Mama laid the envelope down on the table and looked away into the distance, her eyes fixed on nothing in particular. "All those years of working the land, and this is what it comes down to."

"Mama, you can't think of it that way," urged Dee. "You know—just because you got an appraisal doesn't mean you have to act on it. Why don't you just put it right back in that envelope and stick it in a drawer, and see how you feel about it next week after you're back in full form?"

Mama seemed to give that some thought. For once, Dee felt she'd come up with the right response at the right time. "Now here's something a lot more fun," Dee said, picking a colorful flyer from the pile of mail. "Did you see this?"

"The Old Settlers' Reunion," said Mama, a hint of a smile on her face. "You remember going, when you all were kids?"

"Of course! With the square dance and the fiddling contest and the community melodrama? It was even better than Christmas."

"I don't guess we been for a dozen years," said Mama. "But we used to get together with Donna and Rupert and go for the whole day—starting out with the Fourth of July parade and the fishing tournament, and coming back for the dance and the fireworks. People showed up from a hundred miles around. What a production it was!"

Dee thought back to the thrill of those sights and sounds and smells from her childhood. What could be more joyous than the brightly colored floats and tractors, the majestic horses and riders in their finery, the carnival music, the roasted corn and candy apples, the fireworks shooting high in the air over the courthouse spire? For one pure, sweet day, everyone set aside farm work and house chores and gathered on the town square to celebrate freedom. It was magic.

"I've got an idea," Mama pronounced.

Dee could see the disappointment at Mr. Jerrell's report recede from her mother's face, replaced by a rising spirit of determination.

"We are going to have our own reunion," she said. "Our own honest-to-goodness family reunion, right out here on the home place. We ain't had nothin' like that in all the years we've lived here, and it's high time we did. Let's make it a blowout celebration."

"You mean it? I think it's a grand plan, if you're sure you're up for it."

"Why, yes, I mean it. We'll invite every aunt and uncle and cousin on both sides . . . Ruby Lee and Barge can round up the Poplar Grove folks, and the East Texas bunch can come and stay overnight in town, and there'll be Penny's family, and Buddy's, and you can even see if Abby can come back. We'll make it a all-day affair."

Dee didn't know whether Mama's sudden inspiration was a ploy to demonstrate to everyone her ability to continue living by herself—or whether she sensed this might be the last opportunity. Either way, there would be no talking her out of it. "Well, Mama, it sounds like you've got your mind set. What do I need to do?"

*   *   *

Dee had her plate so full with Mama's reunion preparations that she hardly had a spare thought for Max, and he didn't call, either. Mama had Teresa and Dee working overtime to get the house spic-and-span, not to mention the extra effort she was devoting to her muscle toning exercises. Dee's assignments included calling every family member in Mama's address book, making up the considerable list of provisions, and pre-ordering the twenty pounds of sliced beef brisket, ten pounds of German sausage, and five pounds of smoked turkey they would pick up from Buck's Barbecue Barn the day before the event. Mama wasn't one to risk running out.

By Tuesday, though, it was time for Dee to do some careful planning of her own. At the library that morning, she checked airline deals on the Internet and booked her ticket home for Saturday the nineteenth. The firm reality of that date sank in as she composed an e-mail to Rob, who she hoped would pick her up at the airport—and be ready to pick up their relationship where they'd left off two months earlier. A reply popped into her mailbox almost as soon as she'd hit Send, and she eagerly clicked it open.

I will be out of the office until Monday, July 7 . . . what was up with that? Rob wasn't the sort to take an impromptu vacation, and he hadn't mentioned anything about work travel or borrowing the kayak again. She hastily logged off—dodging an encounter with Cynthia, whose inquisitive chat she didn't feel like facing today—and stepped outside to call him instead. After half a dozen rings the call went to voicemail. Well, shoot, she thought, but left an upbeat message anyhow.

Next stop, the Baptist church, where two deacons loaded up Daddy's pickup with the folding tables and chairs Mama had arranged to borrow for the event. "Hope Miss Alice'll soon be back with us on Sunday mornings," one of them said. "We keep her on our regular prayer list, with all the shut-ins."

Shut-ins, Dee mused. That's what they'd both become. Shut in by circumstance and geography. Well, they were about to fling open the doors this time, and it wouldn't be long till she could fly away.

*   *   *

"That is *such* good news for your mother!" Pauline Sandifer gave Dee a sympathetic pat on the shoulder as she accompanied Mama down the hallway before the Write Stuff meeting got under way. Mama intended to be fully rested up before her doctor visit on Thursday. "I know it's going to be a big day and a big week for everbody," said Pauline.

J. D. pulled up a seat at one of the big folding tables beside his compatriots and took out his notebook. Dee had taken advantage of the borrowed tables to give Max lots of room for visuals, and the writers were eager to see what he'd brought.

"Friends, we have a rare treat this evening," said Cynthia, pleased to be introducing a celebrity. "Max Miller's work is known to many of us through magazines and book jackets. He's covered the Lone Star State from the piney woods to the Panhandle, and now we're honored to claim him as a Claxtonite. He's here to show us something about pairing images with words, and to talk about some technical and business aspects of photography for publication. Let's give him a big hand!"

Max's presentation lived up to its billing. He had the Write Stuff members enthralled with his accounts of sneaking up on coyotes in the brush, photographing raptors in flight, waiting cautiously in thunderstorms with the tripod set up inside his truck cab to capture the instant of lightning. His expansive, evocative landscapes had them reaching for words to describe what Texas meant to them, what made their state different. His listeners waxed sentimental about old windmills against sunsets, though they weren't so sure how they felt about the new ones.

"I've seen some of those big turbines up close," said Wendell. "Down there near Abilene, you look out by the interstate and they're lined up on the ridge. But as you drive toward 'em they're as big as a microwave tower with a mobile home sitting on top."

JoAnn said she'd read about opposition from environmental groups, who had filed injunction suits in some states. No one seemed to be certain what the giant turbines' effect might be on flocks of birds, or on humans for that matter.

"They do change the skyline dramatically, that's for sure," said Max. "Here's a shot I did for a corporate calendar." Against a cerulean sky a field of white towers stood in ranks like a futuristic army, the twirling of their precision three-blade weapons frozen in mid-rotation. The company's caption described the scene with a neighborly spin. The group passed each sample around the table.

"Thank you so much, Max!" said Cynthia as the closing hour drew near. "Let's give him a special round of applause for sharing his talents."

"I for one have learned a lot," said Wendell. "I haven't used a camera since my military days, but this makes me want to go out and try one of those fancy digital models."

Cynthia agreed. "And now there's another bit of business we need to take care of," she added. "I'm sure you all know by now that our gracious host and teacher will be leaving us in a couple of weeks to return to her *real* writing life, and we want to thank her properly. Some of us have been talking about the most appropriate sendoff we can give Dr. Dee, and here's what we propose: a farewell party with a "graduation" reading on our last evening together, July 15. What do you think?"

The idea met with approval all around—with one caveat. "I'm all for it," said Frances, "but if I'm going to stand up and read in front of all y'all, I'd better start practicing tomorrow!"

Dee was touched at their enthusiasm and agreed to provide tips on reading for an audience. She was also impressed with how far they'd come in their writing. The participants began discussing details on the way out. Summer Jones made it a point to invite Teresa to attend— assuming Alice would be able to make do by herself by then, of course.

Max, Dee noticed, appeared subdued as he gathered up his materials. When the last of the guests had departed, Mama was tucked into bed, and Teresa closed the door behind her, Dee helped him carry the large portfolios out to his truck.

The sky was clear at late dusk, with only the tiniest hint of a moon, and the stars and planets switched on one by one like porch lights from the distant heavens. Max slipped his arm around Dee's waist and drew her close. "Just two more weeks? I guess I'm the last to hear the news."

She turned away. "There's no need in pursuing this, Max. It was always going to happen—I just didn't know exactly when. I have to be realistic."

"Then our time really is short . . . I'm sorry I won't be here for the writers' shindig, since I'm heading up to Colorado for a photo shoot next week after the Old Settler's Reunion—and I guess that means I won't be here to see you off, either." He seemed genuinely dismayed.

She reached up and laid her hand on his cheek. "Max, I—I'll miss your friendship. What if we could have our own going-away party, just you and me?"

He perked up. "What did you have in mind?"

"I've had such a wonderful time tramping around fields and creeks, seeing the world through your eyes. The wind farm pictures you showed us tonight were amazing. Could we go out there, to see the real thing, before I leave?"

"You got it." He placed a kiss on her forehead. "Anything."

She let him go as darkness fell. She might never again cross paths with such a gentleman, such a gentle man, she knew. But she had made other tough decisions recently, and she'd stick to this one too.

17
I Love a Parade

Do not let your plot stall; keep the action rolling.

RUBY LEE AND BARGE were the first to arrive on the afternoon after Mama's long-awaited appointment to have her casts removed. They were there waiting, in fact, when Dee and Teresa pulled up beside the porch steps in the hundred-degree heat and stepped out, weary as Mama from the doctor's testing and probing and flexing.

"Hooray and welcome home!" Ruby Lee gushed, reaching out to hug Mama. "We figured you'd be about wore out, and we're here to help."

Mama, who still required assistance to get out of the back seat, raised a skeletal arm as high as she could manage. "Well, you're right about the wore out part, so come on in and set in front of the fan with us."

"Oh, we already did, Auntie. We knew you wouldn't mind if we just let ourselves in."

Barge held the door for them. Mama stopped immediately inside the door, leaving Dee to wonder what she was gawking at. "Oh, my word!" was all Mama could say.

The ceilings had been decked out in red, white, and blue streamers gathered in the center, and an enormous arrangement of carnations with miniature American flags adorned the breakfast table. A sheet cake was inscribed "Happy Independence Day" and a large banner taped to the paneled dining room wall proclaimed "Freedom!"

"Lord have mercy, Ruby Lee," said Mama, reeling from the sensory onslaught as she made her way to the recliner. "You didn't have to go to all that trouble."

"It's our contribution to the reunion! We wanted everything to be festive for you."

"Well, I think you did it. Right now, I might just need a glass of water. And some rest."

Mama slept right through dinner, and Dee began to wonder if she hadn't seriously overreached. Maybe it wasn't too late to call things off. But Ruby Lee and Barge pitched in to get the yard and garden in shape, tackling the big jobs that Dee hadn't had any assistance with since Ian and Abby had left. Ruby Lee was a genius when it came to staging, inside and out, and when she was done Dee had to admit the home place had truly never looked so good.

After a purchasing expedition to town, Ruby Lee returned with brightly colored paper goods to complement the white Chinet plates Mama had bought, electric party lanterns that she had Barge string up in the peach tree, plus misting fans for outdoors and portable air conditioning units for inside. "Honey, by about three o'clock tomorrow that'll make all the difference between happiness and misery," she assured Dee, "and I imagine you'll agree with me that Auntie Alice is the only one in the family who's any good at misery." Dee agreed, indeed. She also noticed that Ruby Lee had laid in a supply from Buck's Beverage Barn, which she guessed would be served *sub rosa* out in the Bennett barn.

Dee checked in on her mother several times during the evening, after Ruby Lee and Barge had left to meet the rest of the arriving kinfolk at the Stagecoach Inn, and was pleased to see her resting soundly. For the first time since her arrival in Claxton, her own sleep was not disturbed by the ringing of the cowbell; to Dee's great relief, the only sound she heard in the night was that of the toilet flushing, reassuring her that Mama was up and able to take care of that matter by herself.

She left Mama sleeping at four a.m. and drove to town to meet Abby and Ian's bus. She'd grown to like the streets of Claxton at that early hour, when slowly passing each darkened house and empty storefront allowed her to muse about the potential of the day to come. On this morning, the barricades were already in place for the parade and the grandstands stood empty, waiting. Yards of draped bunting lent the viable shops an air of importance and hid the sadness of the vacant ones. Yes, it was going to be an excellent day.

*   *   *

Ian helped Dee get Mama situated in a folding chair in the shade, a commodity in short supply along the parade route by midmorning. Buddy and his kids had gone early to secure the desirable spot and set out chairs for the Bennett-Schmidt group, while Penny and her crew brought donuts out to the farm for breakfast and helped Mama get dressed for the big day. None too thrilled to see how cannily Ruby Lee had stolen the glory for décor, Penny'd had to admit the portable climate control was nothing short of a miracle.

The procession kicked off at ten with a flotilla of bicycles, tricycles, and Big Wheels. Parents with little tikes pulled them in Flexible Flyers. Behind the children came the American Legion Jeeps and the beauty queens and political candidates in convertibles, then the Shriners in their funny cars, and tractors and riding mowers of all makes and eras. Cheerleaders and ballplayers tossed wrapped candy from the shiny fire trucks, and a county commissioner up for reelection, dressed as Uncle Sam on stilts, passed out emery boards with his name and the word CONSERVATIVE imprinted on the smooth side. In food stands covering the courthouse square, church groups, school clubs, and ladies' auxiliaries peddled everything from sausage on a stick to breakfast burritos to fried Mr. Goodbars.

"It's so good to see you out and about, Alice!" shouted Dianne Turlock, who was passing out brochures and miniature flags for the League of Women Voters.

"Heat's about to get to me, but I'm just glad to be here," replied Mama, who gamely waved her flag a couple of times.

Dee caught sight of the library's float, "Bring Reading to Life," which featured an ornately detailed desk piled high with fake books, and the Write Stuff members costumed as literary characters. She recognized Cynthia as Scarlett O'Hara. Wilbur and J. D. made a convincing Sherlock Holmes and Watson. JoAnn, Frances, and Margaret were pretty racy Witches of Eastwick. Wendell stood tall and proud as George Washington.

Summer drove the pickup that pulled the flatbed. Dee felt a professorial pang of pride as she waved heartily at her adopted scribes.

About midway through the convoy of floats, one enormous trailer captured everyone's attention. Buck Turlock's Sun Spots Tanning Salon had created a mobile beach, complete with white sand and plastic palm trees surrounding a water-filled kiddie pool. Woven grass curtains draped the truck bed to complete the tropical effect. Bikini-clad beauties cavorted with hula hoops and waved at bystanders from lounge chairs. Stacey, Mama's new ten-year-old neighbor, splashed in the pool with a beach ball. Hunky guys in Speedos practiced bodybuilder poses. At the very back, a bronze-skinned beauty queen perched on a makeshift lifeguard stand tossed miniature Frisbees into the eager crowd.

"Lord-a-mercy," said Mama as the rolling beach approached their spot. "Looks like to me the only freedom they're celebratin' is from their clothing."

Buddy was too enthralled with the lifeguard to hear her. His wife, Roxanne, elbowed him and told him he'd better pay more attention to his mother.

Max Miller, following the route on foot, didn't waste any time getting the best angles, either. But Dee was determined not to let Ruby Lee see she'd noticed. He was coming their way, facing the line of floats with camera in one hand and Chester on a leash in the other. Turning to look over his shoulder, he caught Dee's eye and started to wave when Chester suddenly took advantage of his master's relaxed grip.

In a flash the dog was off toward the back of the beach float. Dee wondered what must have captured his interest, but it quickly became apparent. Chester leapt into the air in an attempt to catch one of the flying disks in his mouth. He missed one and went for the next, snagging it right beside the float but tearing off part of the trailer's grass skirting in the process.

The parade halted temporarily so Max could retrieve the retriever. Buck Turlock came running with duct tape, swiftly covering up the trailer again and sending it on its way. "When you gonna teach that dog some sense, Max?" he shouted irritably. "He nearly got hisself run over!"

Max hauled the chastised Chester to the sidelines, where Ruby Lee offered to hold the leash while Max finished his photo assignment. Abby took the opportunity to relate the story of Chester's earlier escapade with Coriander, and Ruby Lee was greatly amused.

As the parade was winding down forty-five minutes later, Max returned to the Bennett camp for Chester.

"Set a few minutes in the shade with us if you like, Max," said Mama, clearly in fine fettle as matriarch, hostess, and bona fide Old Settler. "And you're welcome to join us for a bite out at the home place. I imagine there'll be plenty of barbecue."

Max hated to decline on both counts, he said, as he thanked them for dog-sitting. "I am truly sorry I can't take you up on your invitation, Mrs. Bennett—but I'm still on photo duty for the rest of the parade—*and* the tractor pull, the horseshoe toss, the carnival, and the fireworks."

"Look—here comes the Sheriff's Posse!" shouted Buddy's youngest son, Whit, pointing at the end of the procession. Older brother Web chimed in, "Wow, look at that beautiful Palomino!"

"You remember the year someone had the bright idea to *start* the parade with the mounted patrol, Mama?" Buddy asked.

Mama got a good laugh out of the recollection. "Wasn't that also the year Penny was head baton twirler, right behind them?"

Penny rolled her eyes. "You cannot imagine how gross it was."

"'Horse hockey from head to toe,' is how your daddy loved to describe it," said Mama. "*Horse hockey from head to toe!*"

*   *   *

Wilton Bennett's name was invoked fondly and often during the ensuing afternoon and evening. The later the hour grew, it seemed to Dee, the taller the tales. How had she forgotten what simple pleasure there could be in a paper plate full of mouth-watering beef brisket, spicy beans, deviled eggs, and coleslaw shared outdoors in folding chairs with a score of aunts and uncles and a dozen cousins and their offspring? How could she forget their quips and stories?

"Now Mary Alice, that is a fine stand of cotton, if I do say so," proclaimed Uncle Rupert, Wilton's older brother and complete opposite in personality, in a voice he meant everyone, not just Mama, to hear. "A *fine* stand. Wouldn't be surprised if it brung two bales to the acre come fall. That is, if the weather holds. I'm mighty glad to be out of that game myself."

Mama started to thank her brother-in-law for the compliment, but his wife piped up first. "Rupert Bennett, you ain't had to worry about a cotton crop since Eisenhower was president, and you wouldn't know a fine stand if it bit you on the—"

"He don't mean nothin' by it, Donna," Mama cackled. "Wasn't his fault neither one of them Bennett boys could tell a boll from a bowling ball. Their daddy didn't teach 'em nothing but lassoin' steers and stringin' bob war. Why, when we first come out here to plant in '53, Wilton couldn't tell which end of the mule to hitch the plow to!"

They all appreciated the humor in that.

"Well, you cured him of cowboyin' in a hurry, Mary Alice," said Uncle Rupert. "He never left Caprock County again once y'all settled on Granddaddy Bennett's land."

"Nope, it was Penny who done that," countered Mama. "Wilton was so taken with his baby girl, he got over wantin' to leave all the time. Then Buddy come along, and all *he* ever learnt was farming—and football."

"Now, Dee Anna is quite a bit younger than the other two, isn't she?" asked Aunt Donna, who knew the answer full well. Dee listened in, over the noise of the young folks shooting off firecrackers in the field, while she pretended to nibble on a brownie.

"Nine years younger than Penny, seven years younger'n Buddy. Let's say her arrival was a unlooked-for blessing." The older generation chuckled as Mama added, "Now, you remember the night of that big far at the gin?" and told the story Dee had heard repeated many, many times.

"Well," said Aunt Donna when Mama had finished, "it's a good thing you all decided to settle down out here. So many folks don't have any stability these days, but you picked a wonderful place to raise a family."

"You're right, Donna. That's what was important to us. But now that the kids have all moved away, I don't know what's going to happen. Don't know if any of this'll matter to them, or their young'uns either."

As if to emphasize Mama's point, a Roman candle burst overhead, scattering sparks into the dusk. "You kids keep those firecrackers pointed out at the field and away from the house," Roxanne warned. "Dry as it is out here, you don't want to be starting a wildfire!"

They watched the colors explode one after the other until full dark, when on the horizon came a louder boom, followed by a sparkle that lit up the night over the distant city of Claxton. As the big fireworks display continued, young and old alike fell silent, enveloped in the warmth of the July breeze. Dee watched the silhouettes of Abby and Ian against the faraway bursts of illumination, and the shadow of her mother, seated in the aluminum chair surrounded by everything and everyone familiar. Beyond them the nightscape spread out to the staccato grand finale in Claxton Park, where Dee pictured Max at his tripod capturing the light, to every small town in Texas, and beyond, where other watchers were celebrating in this same tradition. Past and future, near and far, were linked in this moment, and Dee understood — just a little — why it was her parents had never wanted to leave.

18
Turkey Run

*Outlining your plot can be a breeze, if you first set up a
grid of characters, setting, and events.*

MONDAY MORNING BROUGHT a brisk wind across the hilltop.
The day before, all had been quiet; Dee and Mama had both rested
all afternoon after the throngs of visitors departed. The reunion had been
a great success all the way around, and with Abby, Ian, and Coriander
delivered to the bus station in the wee hours, cleanup chores done, and
Mama napping, Dee had enjoyed the first day of her entire summer
free of responsibility for any other living being.

Coffee cup in hand, Dee stepped out on the porch. Her hair blew
willy-nilly into her face. Back in North Carolina, a wind like this would
be strong enough to kick up whitecaps on the lake. *The lake* . . . how long
since she'd thought about her cabin? Or the water?

She was still standing there in her reverie, watching the branches
flutter, when she heard Max's truck turn off the road, pause at the gate,
and rumble up the drive. She recalled that, when she was a child and
kinfolks like Ruby Lee and Pearl would visit, from the porch you'd
have plenty of advance notice—enough time to run back to your room
and finish making the bed or put away the dust cloth before company
knocked on the door.

Leaving Teresa to look after Mama's few needs, Dee grabbed up
the folder with Max's completed manuscript and disk to turn over to

him. She gathered the bag with her own notebook and camera, along with bug spray, sunscreen, and an old straw hat of Daddy's. Mama had offered Granny Schmidt's calico sunbonnet—but Dee's vanity wouldn't let her go that far.

"Morning, Dr. Dee—you ready for your field trip?" Max called out as he stepped out of the pickup. "Got your milk money and your backpack?"

"You bet I'm ready. First time I've left the county since—well, since that world-class event at Poplar Grove!" Dee was giddy as a Girl Scout at the prospect of today's outing. The idea of an outdoor excursion had made her realize just how constricted her boundaries had been on the farm, as though she were once again an eight-year-old who'd never explored her home state. She regretted that she was just now going to range farther afield when it was time to leave.

They climbed into Max's truck and were on their way, with Chester seated happily between them.

"What is that wonderful aroma?" Dee asked.

"Sourdough bread and oatmeal cookies, fresh from Wilson's Bakery," Max replied. "I hope you don't mind a picnic for lunch—where we're going, there aren't any restaurants, although you can't beat the ambience. There's a great view of the river from up on the canyon rim. So I brought a basket full of the best delicacies Claxton has to offer. Along with Mrs. Vu's homemade dog biscuits for Chester."

"That all sounds great," Dee said. Water—she *would* get to see water again! Bread and water suddenly started to sound like heaven.

She rolled down her window halfway to enjoy the breeze in her face. As they left the farm-to-market roads of Caprock County behind and turned onto the four-lane, the long, flat miles rolled by at seventy-plus, and soon they were making southerly tracks toward Abilene. Lush fields of knee-high cotton surrounded them in regular rows, often irrigated by enormous center-pivot systems pumping water from the aquifer far underground. Old-fashioned windmills like the one on the Bennett farm stood at intervals next to broken-down frame houses or newer brick ones, but these were only minor landmarks among the continuous pattern of vast ranches and agricultural sections.

When they crossed the river Dee could make out in the far distance a row of white posts topped by regularly turning blades, arrayed across a cliff like sentries, or children's pinwheel toys stuck into the earth.

The closer they came, the more fully Dee could discern their unique shapes. Each gleaming, slender white tower, as tall as a skyscraper, supported a large box from which radiated a trio of armlike blades spinning perpendicular to the ground.

"They make me think of the Dallas Cowboys Cheerleaders," observed Dee with delight, "all in a row, twirling their pom-poms!"

"I hadn't thought of that myself," remarked Max as they turned off the highway again, taking a dirt road around the base of the cliff and then, in a gut-wrenching series of hairpin turns, right up its side. The towers loomed above them like gantries. Dee held tight to the grab bar above the truck door.

"That road wasn't a lot of fun last winter, when I came down here to photograph the project in a foot of snow," said Max, as they surmounted the cliff edge and emerged on the high plateau. The vista from the heights was amazing.

"You have to come here in weather like that?"

"That's one of my assignments—to capture scenic views of the project in every month of the year, for a wall calendar that goes out to the shareholders."

"You do a lot of pinups, do you?" she teased.

"Well, you can't beat the pay. Turkey Run will be the largest wind power operation in North America when they finish this phase next year, and the company's putting plenty of money into it. There are more than a hundred windmills out here just like the ones you're sitting under—generating enough electricity to power fifty thousand homes for a year. The company has had a huge public relations challenge, to convince residents that the turbines aren't harming wildlife, they're safe to humans, and they're cheaper and cleaner than fossil fuels."

"That sounds like a tall order in Texas. Folks out here love 'em some oil and gas."

"Yeah, but farmers who haven't benefited from oil and gas leases are catching onto wind energy in a hurry. They can continue raising their crops like always, while the kilowatts are generated right above their heads."

"Pretty impressive, I must say."

Max turned the truck onto a side road that led right up to the base of a newly erected turbine, where he stopped and turned off the engine.

The whirring of the windmills—low and steady, and not bothersome, at least to Dee's mind—was the only sound they could hear on the deserted cliff edge. A construction sign proclaimed the site "A Green Generation Project of Texas Star Energy." The company's logo, a large blue-and-green star with a capital "T" superimposed, was emblazoned on the sign as well as on the base of the tower. "Let's hop out here," Max suggested. "The crew has finished with this turbine and moved on, and we'll have the view all to ourselves."

Chester gladly escaped the close confines of the cab and bounded across the sandy soil, where new grass was starting to come up. Dee got her phone camera and pointed it up at the blades directly overhead, producing a dramatically foreshortened composition with the sun, almost at its noon zenith, obscured by the boxlike structure at the top of the tower.

"What's that thing the blades are attached to?" she asked Max.

"That housing contains the transformer that converts wind energy into electricity," he explained. "It's computer-controlled, so that the blades can change angle to capture the greatest amount of wind current. It also shuts down the rotation completely if the wind gets too high—if there's a big storm—to keep the blades from spinning out of control."

"I don't think I'd want to be underneath one of these things in a gale." As it was, the steady breeze kept the ranks of windmills turning in a smooth, almost hypnotic motion.

"I'll tell you something else interesting," Max offered, reaching behind the truck seat to get the picnic basket and cooler. "Everything about these turbines is precisely scientific, from the height of the tower in relation to any other trees or structures around, to the exact placement to produce the most energy. Those blades up there—with that twist in them that makes them look like high-tech aircraft propellers—are designed to perform best at wind speeds of exactly twenty-four miles per hour. That's how the company initially decides where to install a wind farm—where climate data shows the greatest number of days annually that the wind blows at that speed."

"Wow, how do you know all this?"

"The engineers talk to me while I'm working. Plus, I'm just nosy. I ask a lot of questions."

"Well, I want to ask you some," she said, smiling, as he unfolded an old patchwork quilt on the grass and opened up the lunch basket. "Friend to friend."

They sat facing the valley, and as Dee closed her eyes and rubbed coconut-scented sunscreen over her face and bare arms and legs, she could almost imagine they were at the beach, the blue sky surrounding them like the ocean, the soothing hum of the windmills like the sound of the surf.

"Go ahead, shoot. Just let me get our feast prepared. Here we go: sliced brisket or honey glazed ham. Make yourself a sandwich on that sourdough if you like, and here's your choice of mayonnaise or brown mustard. Dill pickles my mother put up last summer. Cold iced tea. And potato salad that I made myself, the way Mama taught me."

"You are a man of diverse talents, Mr. Miller." She took two slices of the loaf and spread mayo on them. "So—have you always been so adept with technical things? You realize this is coming from someone who can't tell a wrench from a potato peeler and has never been very good with either."

"Growing up in a military family, I about couldn't help it. My dad was an army engineer. He could fix anything with gears, levers, switches, or wires—or make it if it didn't already exist. Sort of MacGyver with medals. I learned a lot from him, because you didn't want to *not* measure up to a guy like that."

"You said you grew up in Texas?"

"Yes, in every corner of it from El Paso to the Red River. But then I joined the Air Force myself, stationed in San Antonio and San Angelo. Of course, freelance work takes me all over the West now. This trip to Colorado—I'll be working for a rancher who has a huge spread near Gunnison with exotic game. Guys like that put together high-dollar packages for hunters and tourists. It ought to be something."

"Mmm," Dee said, taking another bite of the sandwich. "How'd you get into it?"

"Photography? That's what I did in the military. Digital imaging. Everything from technical documentation to infrared photography."

"Sounds like espionage!"

"Nah, other departments handled the cloak-and-dagger stuff. I just had the knack for taking accurate pictures. I did a lot of aerial work and night photography—things that come in handy when you want to shoot nature and wildlife, too. When I got out of the service it was just a natural step to commercial photography. And from there to fine art, like I'm getting into now."

"Sort of the way my journalism assignments prepared me for creative writing," she said, contemplating that. "I'd like to think that if you can capture any scene or character with precision, you can turn that talent into something more—*lasting* and influential, I guess. Something that people want to hold on to."

"That's a good way to put it."

They finished their lunch, threw Chester the last scrap of brisket, and went for a walk along the rim. At midday the sun cast no interesting shadows, and the colors of the hills were flat and wan, but against the dramatic sky the windmills appeared majestic, Dee thought. She held out her arms and let the breeze move against them, feeling with fuller appreciation the invisible force that lifted airplanes, moved sails, and, here on the dusty plains of West Texas, brought light and cool and warmth to the miniscule humans living and working this very moment in communities out there, too far away for her to see.

Max came and stood beside her, anchoring his thumbs in the belt loops of his jeans. "Storm's coming. Can you feel it?"

"My daddy used to say he could smell rain twenty-four hours ahead of time. I never had that knack."

"I suppose we'd better get back. It's a long drive to Gunnison—isn't it, Chester?"

She let her arms drop to her side but could still feel the power of the wind against her face. Max reached over to rest an arm on her shoulders.

"I have to let you out of my heart, Max Miller," she said, not looking into his eyes, "but I promise, I won't let you out of my mind. When I come back next time I'll genuinely look forward to it—with a better appreciation for the place. I could almost say I love it. You made that happen."

"So it's *hasta luego* and not *adios*," he said. "I could almost say . . . but I won't."

19
Stormy Weather

*The climax of your story is the single turning point that
brings conflict into sharp focus.*

MAMA'S MOOD WAS AS FOUL as the gray sky. "My bones just seem
to hurt worse'n they did when they was all bound up," she told Dee the
next morning, sitting at the breakfast table in her bathrobe. "And I hardly
have the strength to lift my nightgown over my head." Though able to
get up and down and around without aid again, she was discovering
that daily life still had its challenges.

"It'll get better, Mama—Dr. Kim said it would take a while to build
your muscle tone back up," Dee reminded her. "Why don't you go ahead
and let me pick up that pain prescription for you when Teresa gets here?
Come on, I'll help you get dressed."

Grumpy and achy, Mama acquiesced. "But you get back here before
lunchtime. I don't want no more a' them burritos she brought—I think
she's tryin' to give me food poisoning."

"Mama, please," said Dee. "Give it a rest. I ate them too, and I'm fine."
The nineteenth just couldn't come fast enough. She didn't know how
much more of the moaning and groaning she could take.

*　　　*　　　*

It was sprinkling rain when Dee left the farm, but by the time she'd
gone to the bank, waited in line for the Walmart pharmacist, and gassed

up the car, the sky had turned the color of charcoal and the wind was gusting in fits. She pulled into the drive-through at the Lot-a-Burger, hoping that if she brought cheeseburgers for lunch Mama would lay off her for being late.

The rain started in earnest as she flew home down the highway, taking the slick pavement as fast as she dared. The wind bent the trees, pushed the clouds swiftly toward the east, and propelled tumbleweeds across the road. Prairie dogs scurried for cover and birds darted into tangled branches.

When she reached the driveway, the bar ditch had turned into a small creek, flowing swiftly. And the damned gate was standing open again. But what on earth would Hector have been doing out there on a day like this? She just left it as it was, to avoid getting drenched herself.

She could hardly see to avoid the ruts in the driveway as she headed up the hill, it was raining so hard. She went mostly by memory but hit one particularly hard and had to gun the engine to get back on the path again. She parked beside the house, as close as she could get, and dashed in with the burgers and medicine bags. She'd forgotten it could ever rain in West Texas with such ferocity.

It took her a few minutes, standing dripping on the linoleum, to realize there was no one home. She called Mama's name, and then Teresa's, but heard no answer. She walked to the end of the hallway, calling into each room. Still no response. The lights were on, just as when she'd left; the front door was shut, as it had been. She returned to the kitchen and threw open the door again, and saw what she had not noticed before, in the downpour. Daddy's pickup was gone.

Had there been an emergency? Had Teresa needed to take Mama in the truck? And the open gate . . . but no, she recalled, Teresa had driven her own father's truck to the farm that morning. *Dear God,* she thought. She ran to the phone but before she could dial 911 — or any other number that might occur to her — she heard wheels come to a stop beside the car.

Teresa stepped out into the mud and came running, but she stopped at the edge of the porch. "Oh, *Jesús bendito,* I'm glad you're back," she said to Dee. "I heard on the radio —"

"Teresa! Where's my mother?"

Teresa stood in the rain and looked past Dee through the doorway, puzzled. "She not here with you? She was right there in her chair when I left, and —"

Again, Dee, fully panicked now, didn't let her finish. "You *left?*"

Teresa broke down in tears. "She—oh, Dee, Miz Bennett send me away. She tell me never to come back. I turned around when I hear the tornado watch on the radio. I was afraid she might not be able to get to the storm cell—storm cell—"

"Oh, God, the storm cellar!" Dee was out the door before Teresa could say more. She splashed through puddles to reach the back side of the house. The handles of the side-by-side cellar doors were still held shut by the one-by-four that Daddy had used to latch them, but Dee slid it out and lifted one of the heavy metal doors anyway. The cellar was unoccupied, and she let the door fall back with a clang.

As Dee darted back into the house, she found Teresa, soaking wet, standing beside the kitchen table. In her hand was the empty vase that had held Ruby Lee's flowers.

"What, what?"

"I think I know where she gone." Teresa took Dee's arm and led her to the grandfather clock in the hallway. "*Su padre. Su papa,*" was all she could get out. She pointed at the brass plaque on the clock that she had dusted routinely each week: *To Wilton and Alice Bennett on their 50th Wedding Anniversary, July 8, 2000.*

"Oh shit, Teresa—if she tried to drive to the cemetery in this weather, there's no telling what might've happened. Would you stay here while I go look for her? It's not far—but if she came back . . . would you, please? Turn on the TV to watch the weather. And go to the cellar if you need to."

Whatever spat had taken place between Mama and Teresa, it could wait. For now she had to find her mother and get her to shelter before she caught pneumonia, or worse.

Dee slipped and slid down the hill in the Ford, then splashed through the bar ditch up to the running board before turning onto the road. She tuned the radio to the clearest channel she could get and listened for storm warnings.

The community cemetery was only a mile west, situated on a rise in the shadow of several working pumpjacks and surrounded by a line of overgrown cedars. The trees at first hid the gravesites from view as Dee approached, but when she turned down the dirt road she could see it. Her father's truck, parked beside the iron railing that surrounded the Bennett plot.

She skidded to a halt right beside the pickup and jumped out, then scrambled in on the passenger side of the cab when she saw her mother in the driver's seat, dry and unharmed.

"I thought I could do it," Mama said to Dee flatly. "But I forgot how hard it is to shift this durn thing. I didn't have the strength to get it back in gear again."

Dee flung her arms around her mother's neck and cried, "I don't care. I'm just glad you're okay." The rising wind rocked the truck, and a branch fell from a cedar tree onto the hood. "Come on, let's get home while we still can." She helped Mama to the Crown Vic, and they rode back to the house, not speaking. Dee battled unsteady gusts to keep the car in the lane and struggled to get it up the hill again.

She turned over the list of resolutions in her mind. First off, they were going to get Mama one of those life alert pendants—one of those 'I've fallen and I can't get up' systems. And make her wear it. Second, whatever it took, they were going to keep Teresa on. Third, she was taking the keys to the car *and* the truck.

Teresa was waiting, pacing by the kitchen door, when they returned. The windowpanes hummed as the wind whistled through every crack in the framing. "Your brother called and said go to the cellar," she said. "He hear the tornado warning too."

Mama turned to Dee. "What is she still doing here?" she demanded. "She stole money from me."

Without another word, Teresa fled back out in the storm, fighting the wind to get back to her truck.

Dee shouted after her. "Wait—you can't go! It's not safe—come to the cellar with us." But the wind howled over her words, and Teresa did not look back.

The power flickered and failed, and Dee grabbed a flashlight from the kitchen cabinet. She guided Mama around to the cellar and once again heaved the metal door back. Her mother's arms seemed frail as kite sticks against the blast. They descended the stairs into pitch dark as she managed to pull the door shut and let it drop overhead.

The flashlight's batteries weren't fresh—they surely hadn't been changed lately, Dee guessed—but they provided enough light to check for spiders and snakes. Dee shivered as much from that thought as from the chill of her wet clothes, and she was sure her mother must be miserable too. They sat apart on the muddy canvas cot that Dee remembered sleeping on when a long-ago storm forced all the Bennetts to the cellar during the night.

As Dee's eyes adjusted to the dim light, she noted the jars of peas, corn, and jelly that Mama and Daddy had dutifully put up, labeled with masking-tape strips in Daddy's scrawled penmanship. She rummaged around and found a kerosene lamp but no matches. She gently shook the dust from a couple of old blankets for each of them to wrap around their shoulders.

"I had to go talk to Wilton today," Mama said, barely loud enough to be heard over the rain and wind. "I know that may sound crazy to someone as educated and hifalutin as you, Dee Anna, but I had to."

"Mama, please," Dee said wearily, "don't try to explain."

"I was beginning to come to the conclusion that the farm was too much for me."

"But we were starting to bring the place back, and keep you living here on your own."

"It's funny," Mama said, "if I go to the cemetery with something on my heart, and I ask your father what would be the right thing to do, it comes to me. 'Course it sort of messed me up when I went to the cookie jar to get some money to buy flowers with, and found it was eighty dollars short."

"You don't really think Teresa would've stolen money?"

"Any of 'em would, if they needed it bad enough." Dee just shook her head in the dark. She didn't know how they would replace Teresa. She only hoped that she was safe—and that her mother had been mistaken.

Mama ignored Dee's defense of Teresa. "But I didn't really get my answer until just now." They could hear thunder rumbling amid a rising noise above them like marbles being poured into a jar. "Hail," said Mama. A louder crash shook the doors, and Mama waited for a second before continuing.

"Dee Anna, I couldn't have gotten into the storm cellar by myself," she admitted. "I couldn't even have opened them doors. My wrists are just a-throbbing and killing me with the pain as it is."

"Mama," Dee said, "your arms look swollen." Best she could tell by the glow of the flashlight, Mama must be hurting considerably.

"I guess that's why the doctor said I wasn't supposed to drive for two weeks."

"I would have taken you to the cemetery."

"It wouldn't have been the same," Mama replied. "But I'm going to have to learn to make some adjustments, I guess. I've made up my mind to let y'all sell the place. It'll make Penny and Buddy happy and keep 'em from worrying about it. And it'll free you up. You've got your own life. Abby and the other kids too."

"Mama, don't give up if you're not ready to." Why did Dee find herself on this side of the argument, in light of what they were going through? She felt a wave of nauseous unease coming on. Her face felt clammy, in the close quarters.

"You're one to talk," Mama muttered.

Dee wasn't sure she'd heard right. "What do you mean?"

"About giving up. On your husband and family," Mama replied sourly. "You just rolled over and let your own daughter go away with that—"

Dee forced down the sick feeling. "That guy who divorced *me*? Sure, Mama, I could have followed Jake to Boston like a puppy dog. I could have thrown away every scrap of self-esteem and hard work. And still have come out with nothing."

"You could have fought for Abby." There it was, dropped between them like a lit firecracker. The judgment her family had passed on her, the life sentence they'd imposed.

"You know that was her choice."

"You think it was right to let a child decide?"

"I have to tell you something, Mama," Dee said, looking her in the eye in the near-dark. "Because I am done blaming myself, and I am done second-guessing my actions. And done having them thrown up in my face."

Mama shut up, and all they could hear was the noise of the wind. Dee raised her voice to be heard over it. "Yes, I let Abby have her way. Of course I talked with her. She came back from the summer with her dad all excited about living in Boston, seeing new things in the big city. Maybe she hoped Jake and I would still get back together. But I didn't exactly get a vote in that, either. And I thought she was better off—better than being dragged into a court battle against her will. I thought all these years *I* was the lousy parent, the one who couldn't have managed alone. Financially, logistically, or otherwise."

"Well?" Clearly Mama thought so too.

"Jake got out because he had to leave. I didn't find out until a few months ago."

"He had to leave? What do you mean?"

"He had an affair, Mama. With a student. He thought *she* was going to follow him." Dee practically had to shout the words to be heard over the wind.

"Oh," said Mama in dismay. "What a jerk."

"He sure had me fooled, but it turned out the joke was on him. He cut me out of his life—but ended up jilted himself. I learned about it completely by accident, on a camping trip with a group who didn't realize who I was."

Mama remained quiet and let her continue. "But of course Abby had turned eighteen by then, and custody didn't matter anymore. So why even bring it up? There was no reason to challenge Jake now, or upset his current marriage."

"I never trusted him to begin with."

"Would I have done things differently if I'd known? You bet. But I did look for a way to spend more time with Abby for once, and really try to understand her experience, and be a better mom. It's one of the reasons I looked into the Berkshires Fellowship."

"Well, I sure am sorry how that worked out."

"It's okay. I wouldn't trade it now."

Mama moved over on the cot and reached a weakened arm with some difficulty to lay it across Dee's shoulder. She lifted the other one and stroked Dee's mussed hair, something that stirred a long-ago impression in Dee's mind.

Dee could not have said she ever remembered such an action on her mother's part, but the sensation evoked a color of light, a time of day, a season. The smell of plowed earth. An apple crate. She began crying in huge sobs that took some moments to subside.

"That . . . that *bastard*," said Mama.

"You on those drugs again?" Dee asked, wiping her face on her sleeve.

"I apologize for sayin' those things, about giving up. I'm sure Abby will be all right, and you just keep on after your dreams."

The wind pulled at the chain of the storm cellar door and lifted it a couple of inches before slamming it down again.

"I'll manage, though. I think it's high time I moved into one-a-them patio homes Penny was talkin' about," Mama said. "That's assuming there's anything left to sell when we get out of here."

Dee put her head in her hands and stared at the dark dirt floor of the cellar as hard as she could.

"Are you feeling okay?" Mama asked.

"My stomach's a little upset," Dee replied.

"I told you! I told you it was them burritos."

*   *   *

Half an hour later the hammering of the hail tapered off, and the rush of the wind quieted and then died down altogether. Thin shards of sunlight sliced through the opening between the doors. But when she tried to get a look out, Dee found the doors much harder to push than they had been to pull. She couldn't get them to budge more than an inch.

"Can you see out at all?" Mama asked.

"Nothing but hailstones on the ground everywhere." Dee climbed to a higher step so she could wedge her shoulder against the door, still with little effect. She wondered how long it might be before someone thought to check on them.

Finally, by pushing repeatedly on the loosest side, Dee shook the obstacle loose and was able to squeeze through. The house appeared relatively unfazed, but a huge limb from the mulberry tree had fallen across the cellar opening.

Finding a hoe to use as a lever, she was working to move it when she heard a large vehicle approaching from the highway. An oilfield truck? The fire department? She managed to shift the branch far enough over to pull the other side of the door open.

Dee helped her mother back up, and they picked their way through scattered limbs and lawn chairs to the front of the house. Hailstones still covered the ground like snow in midsummer. Off to the east the wall of clouds was dark and multicolored, while in the clearing sky to the west the sun cast an ethereal gold over the house and barn and damaged windmill. The largest peach tree, split in half, seemed to have suffered most, though the grape arbor was in shambles and the vegetable garden — so lush and well tended a few hours before — had been flattened by the hail. In the cool air hung the overpowering scent of bruised sage.

The diesel engine sound moved closer until they could see, at the bottom of the hill, a yellow school bus parting the floodwaters like

Moses in the Red Sea. The bus turned into the driveway and chugged up the hill with some difficulty. As it topped the rise Dee could read the lettering on the side: Darrell I.S.D.

The bus stopped beside Daddy's truck, and the door opened. Buddy, in his burnt-orange coach's polo shirt, stepped out and embraced his mother and sister with relief.

"I was in Midland delivering the bus to the shop when I heard the weather report," he explained. "When I couldn't get you back on the phone, I came right on."

"Well, it looks like you missed the excitement," said Mama wearily. Dee and Buddy helped her up the steps to the porch and brought out a kitchen chair for her to sit in.

"I had to pull under a gas station awning down around Big Spring—ran into hail the size of golf balls. I was lucky to find a place to get out of it," he said. "Looks like y'all got some of it too."

"You think the cotton is okay, Mama?" Dee asked.

"Nothing to do but wait and see," she replied. "Now I don't know about you, but I could sure use some rest." Dee and Buddy helped her up from the chair and steered her through the nearly dark house by flashlight to find her bed. She lay down without changing her damp clothes and was almost instantly asleep.

Dee and Buddy sat on the porch looking out over the chaos in the yard. She told him about the events that had preceded the storm. "What do you think about Teresa, Buddy? How do we know who's telling the truth here? Or Mama could've been wrong about how much money was in the jar."

"Well, it's not like her not to account for every penny."

"I know—that's what bothers me. But Teresa doesn't seem like the kind to steal, either."

"Let's not dwell on it," Buddy said. "Mama was going to need more than part-time help anyhow."

Dee had no answers at the moment. She, too, was weary to the core. "Look, whatever you think we need to do about the farm, I'll go along."

Buddy went to find the oil lamps from the pantry and set them out so they could see to make sandwiches for supper. About that time Dee detected the sound of another vehicle splashing through the floodwaters and turning at their gate.

"What in tarnation is that?" asked Buddy, spotting the camouflage-patterned high-clearance truck crossing the ditch and taking the hill as smoothly as the Autobahn. They watched as the armored monster came to a stop behind the school bus.

"Well, I made it," said Wendell Grover, jumping down from the driver's perch and slamming the door. He gave the front corner of the hood a friendly slap. "Old Humvee doesn't see any action except hunting these days, but she sure got me here on time. You guys haven't started the workshop without me, have you?"

20
Empty Nesters

*Be merciless in cutting anything that does not
contribute to your story.*

"IT'S NOT AS BAD as it sounds, Penny, I swear," Dee assured her sister
the next morning. "Really, Mama made it through the storm just fine.
The power came back on during the night, too. We have plenty of food
and water. You don't need to drop everything and rush out here."

"That's not how she told it," said Penny over the receiver. "She
said y'all were lucky to be alive. And that home helper? There's no
telling what she has helped herself to, either." Dee kicked herself for
letting Mama get to the phone first. They'd been sitting on the sofa
with their coffee, watching the local news coverage while Buddy went
out to meet Hector in the field, and Dee had forgotten how easily Mama
could now reach over and pick it up. Before she knew it, Mama's full-
blown soap opera account was unfolding.

The damage in Caprock and surrounding counties had been considerable.
Dozens of roofs and barns had been blown away, a flash flood had washed
out a bridge in the southern part of Claxton, a utility pole had fallen
across the entrance of Jesse Jane's Roadhouse, and a car had been swept
downstream at a low-water crossing, though the driver had managed
to escape first. The biggest concern on everyone's mind, however, was
the fate of the cotton crop. Insurance adjusters were already in the fields,
Channel 11 reported.

Mama's house had escaped with only some damaged shingles and shutters, as far as Buddy had been able to tell. The barn was missing a section of roof, and one of its doors was swinging loose, hanging from a single hinge. They'd been lucky: the tornado itself had passed within a mile of them, and another had touched down in Poplar Grove, where a trailer park had been hit hard.

Mama had given Penny the full rundown—and her blessing, so long withheld, to put the place on the market.

"You're right about one thing, though," continued Dee, walking around the corner with the phone so Mama couldn't hear. "Without help, it'll be nearly impossible for Mama to manage out here. We all realized that last night. We'll do what we have to do."

"Well, I'm glad to hear that you've come around," Penny said. "I'm going to fax you and Buddy a form to sign today, and if you can send it right back, I can post a listing immediately. And we can discuss what repairs need to be made after Mama hears about the insurance."

Dee hung up with a deep sadness. Buddy drove into town to pick up tarps and a new chain saw—if he was lucky and got there before supplies were depleted—and Penny's fax.

Dee left Mama to switch the channels for herself and went out to the barn to get a rake. The sun was well up in the brilliant azure sky, bathing the beaten and drenched landscape in rich color and illuminating corners of the barn like a Vermeer painting. Meadowlarks sang in the fields. Dee could appreciate none of it. She took out her own blues on the limbs and leaves, pouring her energy into cleanup chores.

The ground was covered with windfall peaches among the downed branches, and soon Dee had filled a bushel basket of the nearly ripe fruit. Mama was pleased at what Dee had salvaged. "Put 'em in grocery sacks in the window sill, and in a couple of days they'll be soft enough to eat," she instructed. "Maybe we can put up preserves, too." They gathered what squash and tomatoes the hail hadn't bruised too badly and left the hard green grapes, too early for picking, for the birds.

*   *   *

Mark Sturgis from the Farmers' Mutual Bureau wasted no time. He arrived in his white Ford Focus late that afternoon, about the time

Dee and Buddy finished piling up a tower of limbs worthy of a bonfire. "We're writing up claims as fast as we can and printing out checks on the spot," Sturgis told them. "I'll do a visual on your roof and check out the rest of the property, and I'll let you know what I find."

After half an hour of inspecting the structures and taking notes on his clipboard, Sturgis knocked on the door. Mama got there first. "Since I can't get an Internet connection to print you a check, Mrs. Bennett, we'll have a settlement letter to you later in the week," he said. "But it looks to me like you've lost quite a few shingles and some flashing around the chimney, and you want to take care of that before it causes a leak. And the hail has really beat up the paint on the east side of the house. You're looking at about twenty-five hundred dollars to help cover repairs, after your deductible. A few bucks more for the loss on the barn, which wasn't in great shape to begin with."

"What about the crop?" Buddy asked, as Mama signed the claim form with some difficulty. "I went out with our farm manager this morning, and it didn't look good."

"Well, that's a different department, but I just want to warn you: we're already seeing total losses around the county. You might start giving some thought to plowing it up and putting in sorghum for the fall."

Mama watched Sturgis pick his way down the rutted hill in his little car. "Sorghum? Ain't never planted sorghum, don't know a thing about it. But we never lost a crop this late in the season before. I just don't know."

* * *

Dee was peering into the bubbling forty-quart canner full of freshly made preserves in Ball jars the following afternoon, her reading glasses steaming over, when the phone rang. Mama was struggling to stir sugar into the next batch of peaches on the adjacent burner.

"I'll get it," said Dee, hoping to hear back from the multiple messages she'd left for Abby and Teresa. Without Teresa's help, it seemed that every task took triple the effort. But even more important to Dee, her continued absence was troubling.

"Don't let them jars process too long," said Mama, who had given instructions for every step with the precision of a drill sergeant.

"Hello?" said Dee expectantly, receiver in one hand and tongs in the other.

"Dee Anna, it's Penny, and I have good news!"

"What's up? We could use some."

"Well, it's only been twenty-four hours since our MLS listing went live, but we've got an offer! I had a call just now."

"No kidding? Does the buyer have a clue how many repairs have to be done?"

"This buyer says it doesn't matter."

Dee turned to Mama. "Go pick up the phone by your chair, Mama. Penny's on the line and she's got a commission to earn."

Mama removed her apron and sat down in the recliner. "What do you know, Penny?"

"Mama—we have an As-Is offer from a local buyer! Now, it's ten thousand less than our asking price, but we can work on that. The great thing is, you wouldn't have to fix anything before selling. You wouldn't even have to do any staging or show the house. And it's a cash deal, to close within ten days. Wouldn't that be wonderful?"

"Let me guess, Penny," said Mama, no fool. "This buyer's already familiar with the place."

"Why—well, yes, since you mention. How did you know?"

"Tell me what else Buck Turlock said."

Dee, still on the line, bit her lip to keep from bursting out laughing, and kept stirring and listening to Penny make her case. "Mama, it's the best situation we're likely to run into, especially after the storm damage. You might get a little more money down the road, but you don't have the luxury of time."

"Now, *how* long did you date him?"

"He was five years older than me, Mama! He had already graduated. And it never was a real date. He was just sweet on me. I think I can still use that to our advantage."

Dee weighed in. "With all due respect to your professional expertise, Penny, I think you're the *worst* kind of seller right now—a motivated one. Isn't that what they call it in your line of business, when you have a property you can't wait to unload?"

"Now that's not fair—I've put a lot of research into this. You don't think I know how to wring every nickel out of a sale? I already got him to agree to take that old farm equipment in the deal."

"Oh, and how much allowance are you giving him for hauling it off?" said Dee acidly.

"Girls," Mama said, forcefully interrupting, "quit bickering. Dee Anna, I imagine Penny is right—I could sit there in them senior homes and bide my time for a year before another buyer comes along, and go broke doin' it. But Penny, I'm trusting you—we're all trusting you—to make a fair deal for us. Now you go back to Buck and tell 'im if he can't come up with the full appraisal price he can just find hisself another farm to buy, and we'll call up ever' one of his hunting buddies and tell them there's a prime lease available this fall right next door to his."

*　　*　　*

Things moved swiftly once the contract was signed, and Dee had to admit she was glad for the whole business to be done with. She was sure Mama felt the same way. Penny scheduled the closing for the following Friday morning, the day before Dee's departure, to give them a week to pack. It wouldn't be hard—Mama's furnishings were basic and her other possessions sparse.

Dee left the apartment-hunting to Penny, who came out to Claxton for a couple of days to help with the lease and the transition. Buddy would return next week to oversee the actual move, so she didn't need to worry about that either. Instead she went to visit Mitzi at Helping Hands, with two important objectives.

"We need to line up some help at my mother's new place, Mitzi," Dee explained. "Someone who can make sure she continues her strength exercises, do light housework and lifting, watch for any trouble signs. And who's licensed to drive clients around town."

"Yes, I understand—many of our clients reach that point in their lives. They always want to keep driving, but the family has to put their foot down! We keep a list of volunteers—church members and the like—to drive the elderly. Why don't I check into it and let you know?"

"That's good. And we'll be glad to keep paying for general help even when Mama's medical benefits run out." She fished for information. "That is, if Teresa is still available."

"About Teresa Rivera, I haven't seen her since the afternoon of the big storm," Mitzi said. "She came by to turn in her resignation, without notice. Said it was a family matter. But I am glad to hear that your mother is mobile again, and I'll start looking for a replacement."

So at least Mama hadn't called and gotten Teresa fired — that was something — although the missing money still hadn't turned up. "I'm really eager to reach her, Mitzi. We didn't get a chance to give her a token of our appreciation."

"Well, that's not necessary; Helping Hands has a policy prohibiting employees from accepting gratuities," she replied. "But she may be in to pick up her final paycheck next week, and if I hear from her I'll pass along your thanks."

Leaving empty-handed, Dee tried to think of another angle. Should she ask Hector and Flora if they knew the Riveras? She had already scanned the entries in the phone book and hadn't found one that matched. And she never had known Teresa's address; she'd assumed Teresa lived with her father but she had not been nosy enough to ask. She considered driving street by street through the Hispanic neighborhood on the east side of town in search of the Toyota truck, but that would look pretty conspicuous. And what would she say when she did locate Teresa? She wasn't sure.

Abby hadn't returned her calls, either, and that really worried her. How had she let her eighteen-year-old daughter simply leave with a strange man — however nice he seemed — without learning his full name or contact information? She could be so dense sometimes. But she and Abby had gone for longer stretches than this without talking, and she wanted to give her the space she needed. If she could stand it.

*   *   *

Calendars came down and family photos went into banana boxes from the grocery store. Pots and pans were packed with canned goods, dishes were stacked between towels, clothing and accessories were folded into suitcases. The oil painting one of Alice's church friends had done, of a windmill and stock tank, was wrapped in a quilt to be moved in the car. Penny finished packing boxes under Mama's direction.

Dee was amazed at the things her mother had squirreled away over the years. Items she'd never seen before emerged from drawers. "Mama, what's this in the buffet? Looks like you've got enough flatware for a whole dinner party."

"Oh, that . . . that set belonged to my grandmother back in East Texas. It always seemed too fancy to put on the table out here." Dee shook her head in amazement. All the years they'd eaten meals with dime-store forks and spoons, and here was a treasure that never saw the light of day.

Mama, despite her disdain for sentimentality, seemed also to have collected a considerable number of family photographs. "Who's this, Mama?" Dee asked, picking up a Polaroid dated 1968.

"Hmmph. Lucinda Smathers . . . your daddy's cousin that ran off with the Methodist preacher in the early seventies. Reverend what's-his-name went all Jesus Freak or something, and he and Lucinda lit out for California. Oh, it was a huge scandal. She was married — left her husband and all."

"Were they disowned or excommunicated?" asked Penny.

"No, Methodists don't really excommunicate anyone — they just kept prayin' for their souls. And it was a long time before they hired a pastor fresh out of seminary again. Lucy came back to Claxton with that preacher on a revival tour years later — like people would've forgotten."

Mama picked up a hand-tinted photograph in a leatherette folder and opened it to show her daughters. "Now here's one you may not remember," she said. "This here's your great-grandfather, William Travis Bennett, about the time he married Ella Wilton in 1900 — back before there was even a town in Caprock County. Nothing but bob-war and a dugout house on this place back then."

Dee recalled stories of her forebears who staked their claim here in the nineteenth century, but she was fuzzy on the details.

"Will and Ella were the first ones to farm the place, but it was actually his father who got the land for fighting in the Civil War." Mama couldn't shed any more light than that, except the intriguing tidbit that Will had been a doctor and Ella a nurse when they came west. In the photo Will Bennett was tall and dapper, dressed in a dark suit and tie; Ella was shorter and clearly some years younger, her brown hair topped by a gaudily feathered hat and her head cocked merrily to one side. Dee could hardly imagine these ancestors eking out a living on the plains. Surely there was a story there.

Penny set out a photo album they had all perused at family reunions and holidays. There was Wilton and Alice's wedding portrait, a sharp-contrast black-and-white. Wilton on horseback, in his chaps and dark felt cowboy hat. Various snapshots of the farm, and the barn and house—already well weathered by the 1950s—and sites around Claxton. Pictures of some of the same aunts and uncles they'd seen days ago, in faded fashions of earlier eras. School pictures of the Bennett children. Dee thought she caught a moment of wistfulness on her mother's face. She wished they could tell tales all afternoon, but there was still work to do.

They finished almost all of the packing by Monday, when Penny had to return to Dallas for a closing and a consultation with Madison's wedding florist. The farm house had been stripped to its last-minute essentials, the yard mowed, the canning completed, the kitchen stocked with paper plates and sandwich ingredients to get Mama and Dee through the week.

So much was over and done with, Dee thought. Past tense. So much yet to happen. Infinitive. By the end of the week, more would be over and done with soon. Future tense? Future perfect? Completed, crossed off, like the X's on the calendar they had now packed away.

*   *   *

She drove to town that afternoon with Mama to take care of a long list of small errands. A checkup with Dr. Taylor. The auto inspection to be renewed on the Ford. Thank-you notes from the card store. Utilities to be set up for the apartment. Boxes of Daddy's clothes to be donated to the charity thrift store. Printouts of her final notes for the Write Stuff members, since they'd missed a week. Drafts of her fall class plans, which she would review on the plane.

In the midst of this last task at the library, while Mama waited in the car, Dee read the message that sent her spiraling back to past tense. Square one, or might as well be. She drew in her breath and read the e-mail over again, in case she hadn't parsed the sentences correctly the first time.

Dear Dee,

I've had your revised Templeton manuscript in hand for several weeks now, and I was so impressed with your excellent work and progress that I have been hesitant to write you about today's developments at the Press. I would have preferred to call, but since you've been out of pocket, I must go ahead and spell out via e-mail the good news and not-so-good news.

On the strength of positive peer reviews—which we turned around speedily to stay on schedule—our editorial committee has approved your manuscript for publication with only a few recommended revisions. I'm attaching a summary of their responses; they are particularly impressed with your book's potential for shedding light on little-understood aspects of twentieth-century literary history. Our editor-in-chief likewise gives your project his unqualified support.

However, fiscal events outside our control have forced some changes to this year's publishing schedule. I won't burden you with the details, but the upshot is that we have no choice but to postpone publication indefinitely, perhaps a year or more. While you are no longer under immediate pressure to deliver your revisions to us by August 31, per your contract, I hope your tenure committee will be understanding.

I realize this development must dilute the effect of my heartfelt congratulations. I am sorry to convey this mixed message so impersonally; let's talk as soon as you are available.

Sincerely,
Susan

Understanding? Susan didn't know Pritchard. *Fiscal events outside our control?* What the hell was that supposed to mean? Could they really do that, randomly delay the book your whole career depended on?

She shut the program down and made her way to the farthest corner of the library stacks, to Philosophy, where she knew few patrons ventured, and took out her cell phone.

Yes, Susan said, there'd been a huge round of budget reductions the end of June. People had lost jobs. Manufacturing and marketing resources had been cut. Editors fought for their authors' manuscripts, but in the end there was no option but to publish fewer books next year. Projects already in the pipeline got priority.

Dee hung up. Would it be enough? Would the center hold, for another year? She'd need time to think it through. She slunk—slank?—slinked?—oh, God, who cared—*slid* down the metal bookcase until her tailbone hit the floor. She buried her head between her knees until she could catch her breath. But self-pity wasn't an option, either. Mama was waiting.

21
Adios Farewell Goodbye Good Luck So Long

Let your writing take inspiration from your dreams,
both literal and figurative.

WHEN THE WRITING GROUP members assembled in the Bennett living room Tuesday night for their farewell event, their voices resonated in the empty chamber as though in a great hall. The colors of the sunset through uncurtained windows reflected off empty walls and shone on the banner Wendell and J. D. had hung, which read "We've Got the Write Stuff!" The sofa had been pushed back in the corner, an assortment of chairs had been arranged in rows, and the free-standing cabinet Mama used for storing her pickles and preserves had been brought in to serve as a lectern. Refreshments had been set up on the bare kitchen counters.

You couldn't keep these Texans down for long, thought Dee. Here they were, every one of them touched by some hardship or other as a result of the storm—but they were taking a respite from their cares to celebrate a minor milestone. Or did their writing mean that much to them? Maybe she just had to put her woes aside too.

Pauline Sandifer had come along to support her husband. Several newcomers joined the audience as well: with Cynthia's husband, Drew Philpott; and Margaret's, John Strickland; Summer's boyfriend, Scott Silsbee; and Mama seated in the audience, the evening felt to Dee like a graduation ceremony with seven valedictorians.

Only one of their usual number was missing. In the crowd and excitement Dee hoped Teresa's absence might escape notice, but Cynthia motioned her aside with a question.

"No," Dee answered vaguely, "I haven't talked with Teresa since she finished up her assignment with us. Why do you ask?"

"I have a surprise," Cynthia whispered, just as mysteriously. "It can wait."

As mistress of ceremonies Cynthia, resplendent in a coral-colored sundress and loads of faux-turquoise jewelry, welcomed them all. "We're in for a treat this evening as we hear from all of our dedicated writers. And I want you to especially thank our generous host, Alice Bennett, for putting up with us for so long. Mrs. Bennett, we're sure glad you're on the mend, but I have to say we couldn't have done this if it hadn't been for your mishap to start with!"

Wendell placed a friendly arm around Mama's shoulder as the group applauded, Dee noted.

"Now, we'll start in alphabetical order, with each writer telling you a little about their work and reading a brief selection. So without further ado, let's welcome Frances Echols."

Frances stepped to the improvised reading stand with her pages, her hands shaking. When she read her voice shook, too. *Come on*, Dee thought, *you can do it.* Most of these writers had never spoken in public like this, she guessed. Maybe in church, maybe at a Rotary luncheon, but not when their original writing had been under scrutiny. She certainly understood the pressure, even when you were among friends.

"Never in my wildest dreams, when my husband and I were planting cotton across the road there," said Frances, "did I imagine that one day I would be standing in the Bennetts' parlor reading part of a novel I wrote myself." Her listeners applauded, and that seemed to lend her the strength she needed. "But y'all know, it is nothing short of a miracle, what's happened here. Dee Anna Bennett, you were just a tiny baby back when I first started thinking about this story, but you have sure shown me that it's never too late to make your dreams a reality!"

Dee felt a catch in her throat. She smiled, nodded, and fought the impulse. *Never too late.* Frances plunged into a passage from her story and soon found her stride. When she finished, the audience murmured and clapped with genuine admiration.

As other readers followed in turn, the hours quickly passed. Margaret finished up with a first-person account, "Why I Write," and the ovation she received was extended to all.

"Friends," said Cynthia, motioning for the writers and guests to take their seats again, "I have an announcement and a presentation to make." She pulled a page from her briefcase, and cleared her throat. "Several of you entered the Texas Writers Online competition this year, and we've been eagerly awaiting the results. Well, I received this press release today, which I will post in our newsletter, but I wanted to go ahead and share it with you now."

"Did I win second place in a beauty contest again?" asked J. D.

"Oh, shut up and let her read," said his wife.

"Well, actually, I'm pleased to report that our own JoAnn Rinehart has won third place for her story 'The Cowpoke Needed Killing.' Way to go, JoAnn! And—drum roll—the top honors go to another entry from Claxton—'The Swimming Lesson' by Teresa Rivera!"

The room went quiet. Then Summer spoke. "You mean Mrs. Bennett's Teresa? *Our* Teresa? How cool is that?!" The group followed Summer's lead in clapping politely.

"The awards will be presented at the annual conference in Abilene in September," Cynthia confirmed. "Let's give both our winners a hand!" Mama sat tight-lipped in her recliner amid the applause. Dee just prayed she'd continue to keep quiet.

"And now, I think J. D. and Wendell want to say a few words in closing," said Cynthia. "Come on up, gentlemen."

Wendell drew out a box from the cabinet and set it on top, still closed.

J. D. took a piece of paper from his pocket, adjusted his specs, and spoke with high drama. "You all are aware how much of a sentimental fool I am about crops and cattle and ridin' and ropin'," he began. Heads nodded all around. "Well, you know, the writin' life is not so different—it's a great big world of words and ideas out there, but none of it means much without care and cultivation. You have to have discipline. You have to work at it. Like breakin' sod, or breakin' horses. That's what we've been doing, right?"

They were all poised, waiting. "Dr. Dee, this is for you."

> "I once wrote a story
> Of which I was proud—
> But that was before
> I fell in with this crowd.

"I brought my new novel,
Convinced it was grand—
But I learned some new lessons
On this plot of land.

"Out here in this country
Where the buffalo roam
They're a tough bunch of critics,
As hard as they come.

"They'll break your bad habits,
They'll critique and expose—
They'll rein in your clichés
And rope in your prose.

"They'll lasso your language,
They'll wrangle your words;
They'll cut out your adverbs
And thin out the herd.

"When your stories roam wild
They're riding the fences,
Roundin' up danglers
And fixin' verb tenses.

"My friends and companions,
Keep writing, take heart—
Let's count ourselves lucky
Although we must part.

"When we're finally published,
We'll look back and give thanks
For the things that we learned
At the Paragraph Ranch."

He closed with a salute, as everyone laughed and applauded, then Wendell lifted the lid of the box to reveal a wrought-iron sign set upright on a flat wooden plaque. It was the cutout of a paragraph mark—the double-stroked, backwards "P" known to typesetters and copy editors— which the Write Stuff members had seen often on Dee's marked drafts.

"We thought that made more sense than Delete or Insert," said Wendell. "Put it on your desk when you get back—and think of us when we all win Pulitzers!"

"Wow, how delightful," Dee said, still dabbing at her eyes. "Clever, clever. I'll treasure the poem and the memento!" It was all the speech she could muster. How could she ever express so eloquently what *they* had taught *her*?

Cynthia stuck around longer than the others, to help clean up. But after Mama had turned in, the other members had waved good-bye, and the procession of taillights had descended the hill, she called Dee aside in the kitchen. "I had another reason for lingering, too," she confessed. "I have a little something for a remembrance and a personal thanks."

"Cynthia, you didn't need to do that. I'm the one in your debt."

Cynthia handed her a flat package about the size of a mail-order circular. "Open it now if you like. You're going to need this the next time you return to Claxton in search of an Internet connection!"

Dee unwrapped the package to find a plastic placard bearing vinyl letters on one side reading "Reserved VIP Parking, Caprock Public Library." The back side was signed on the back by all the staff—even Gladys.

"Ha—how right you are! And it'll slip inside my suitcase with no trouble at all. Thank you—I won't leave home without it."

"It's been an amazing summer. Who knew what adventures we would all go through together?" Cynthia hugged Dee, and Dee found herself returning the embrace despite herself. "In case I don't see you again before you leave, now, don't be a stranger when you come back. And you let me know the minute you hear anything from your publisher!"

Dee exhaled. "About that," she said, "I'm glad you stayed for a minute. I need to tell you a couple of things." She motioned toward two chairs in the dining room, and both of them sat.

"I had a message from my editor this morning," Dee said. "She loved the manuscript, thinks it's ready to go after only a few changes. But the news wasn't all good. I might have to find another publisher."

"No! Why?!"

"Budget cutbacks . . . a lack of funds. Can you believe it, after getting this far? Doesn't matter right now—what I wanted to say is how much I will always value your help on my project. You made it possible for me to finish the story, and I seriously doubt I would have done as well on my own if I had gone through with the fellowship. I didn't think I could fully express that by e-mail."

"Oh, Dee, there's no justice in the world. But you'll land another publisher in no time! And if you ever need help in the future, well, I'll put every resource I have at your disposal."

"That's the second thing I need to talk about. I've hit a dead end on something even more important."

"What could be more—?"

"Teresa Rivera. My mother fired her a week ago, and she's missing. I need you to help me find her."

"Oh, my—you don't think there's been—foul play?"

"Don't go overboard with the whodunit stuff, Cynthia," Dee replied. "I just think she wasn't treated fairly, and I want to find out for sure. And now, there's this writing award you need to let her know about. So do you think you and I could put our heads together?"

"Oh, absolutely If Teresa submitted an application to the writing competition, then she had to provide a mailing address. I'll track that down first thing in the morning. Meet me at the library tomorrow at oh-nine-hundred, and we'll go from there. And don't forget your parking permit."

*   *   *

Cynthia's source at Texas Writers Online didn't mind revealing to a fellow board member the Claxton address Teresa had provided on her membership application. She also told Cynthia that notification letters had gone out on Friday, with checks enclosed, so Teresa should expect hers any day. Cynthia hadn't said why she was asking.

Cynthia and Dee drove down Third Street toward the east side of town, passing Max's studio on their way.

"By the way," Cynthia asked, catching Dee looking in that direction, "I hope I'm not being too nosy, but—"

Dee laughed. "You can assure all your cronies that Max Miller and I are just friends," she offered. "Good friends. I enjoyed working with him professionally, and that's all."

Past the abandoned railroad depot and the Phillips 66 station, they turned onto a dirt side street crowded with small houses of all sizes and materials—wood frame, asbestos shingle, old brick. "Pecan Street, right?" Dee asked.

Cynthia checked the paper. "We're looking for number 584. Should be on the right . . . keep going a little farther."

They slowed down in the 500 block and spotted a house that stood out from the others on account of its brick façade and a masonry-and-iron fence enclosing a magnificent apple tree. The place appeared extraordinarily well cared for, if hardly luxurious in size. They parked beside the fence and Dee looked around, hoping to spot the Toyota pickup.

Dee and Cynthia opened the front gate and went to the door together. Dee wondered, as she rang the bell, if she might be mistaken for a Jehovah's Witness on a weekday canvass. A toddler playing in the dirt yard next door stopped what was he was doing and peered through the fence pickets at them. Inside the house, a dog began yapping at the sound of the bell.

The door opened only as far as the security chain would allow. A stooped, gray-haired Hispanic woman peeked through the gap. She shooed the dog away.

Dee spoke first. "Good morning—we're looking for our friend Teresa Rivera. Does she live here?"

"No," the woman replied, but she didn't turn them away. "*Qué quieren?*"

"Teresa is in our—writers' group," Cynthia answered in halting Spanish.

The woman called out behind her, and a girl who looked to be about ten or eleven came to the door beside her. The woman whispered to her and then let her do the talking.

"Mrs. Hernandez would like to know who you are and why you are here," she said with clear English diction, still behind the chain.

Dee tried to give out the right mix of information. "I'm Dee Bennett, and this is Cynthia Philpott, who is the librarian in Claxton. Teresa Rivera read a wonderful story in our writing workshop, and it won an award." Dee looked at Cynthia, who nodded confirmation. "But we missed her at our meeting last night, and we wanted to make sure she knew about it."

The girl conveyed this information to the older woman, then turned back to the open door with another question. "Which one of you is the college teacher?"

Dee answered, relieved. So they were at the right place. The woman slid back the chain and opened the door wider.

"Mrs. Hernandez asks if you can come in for a minute," said the girl.

The older woman spoke, pointing to herself, then to the child. "Lupe Hernandez. *Y mi amiga chica,* Linda Rivera." Dee and Cynthia were shown into a narrow living room furnished in a Victorian mode and offered seats on a velvet sofa.

"*Muchas gracias*," said Cynthia. "Is Teresa here, by any chance? We'd really like to talk to her."

The girl, who had taken a seat on a hassock next to the woman's wingback chair, translated both ways. The white Chihuahua stood behind the chair, growling warily. "Teresa talked a lot about your writers' group," said Linda. "She would come in with her notebook and tell us all about the lessons and the other writers."

"That's so good to hear. She's okay, isn't she?" said Dee.

Their hosts conferred again before the girl answered, measuring her words with care. "Teresa is away right now. She said not to worry. She has some business to take care of."

Dee thought this over. "We came to tell her that the writing award is a very high honor. And it comes with a cash prize. We wanted to make sure she gets the full recognition she deserves for her story."

At this Mrs. Hernandez almost cried, and the girl patted her arm. Suddenly the woman's sentences flowed in a torrent of Spanish. The girl put her arms around her until she finished, and when Mrs. Hernandez nodded *Si, si*, she turned back to their guests.

"Mrs. Hernandez is very concerned about my sister Teresa, but she doesn't know whom she should trust. There was some trouble with *la migra*—the, how do you say, immigration police—at the construction job where our father was working, at the hospital in Claxton."

"I remember reading about that in the paper last week," Cynthia said to Dee. "Didn't they detain several workers?" Cynthia had the tact to avoid the term *illegal aliens*.

"My father was one of them," Linda said. "But we don't know why, because he has a green card. Teresa went right away to find a lawyer and look for him—she left her job and everything. Our cousin told us she might need to go in person to the burro—excuse me, *bureau*—in Dallas. But that was more than a week ago, and we don't know where they are."

"And what about your mother?"

"My mother passed away when I was little. It's just the three of us."

Dee saw Cynthia redden, and she changed tacks. "Teresa has a cell phone, doesn't she?" she asked.

"Yes, but that's what has us concerned—she's not answering it. Teresa made me promise not to worry. She told me to stay with Mrs. Hernandez until we heard from her. But what if she's run out of money, or gotten in trouble?"

Dee reached over to take the girl's hand. She put aside the notion that flashed through her mind about Teresa's need for money. "Please tell us what we can do to help. We want to know she's safe, too. We have friends who might be able to get some answers."

Mrs. Hernandez spoke to the girl again in Spanish. Linda looked as though she might choke up too, but she held her composure. Pretty impressive for a ten-year-old, thought Dee.

"Mrs. Hernandez also wants you to know how grateful she is that you let Teresa take part in your group," said Linda. "She apologizes for being suspicious, but she was afraid the immigration agents would come here. Teresa and I stay with Mrs. Hernandez often, and she lets Teresa use her address for mail. Especially for things Papa does not approve of." She lowered her voice. "Papa would be furious if he knew . . ."

"Thank you for trusting us," said Cynthia. "I'm going to tell you something that should prove our good intentions. You watch for the mail—and when that envelope comes for Teresa, it will contain a check for three hundred dollars. When she opens it, you'll remember that we told you the truth. But right now, if you want to come to the library with us, we can look for information. And our friends can help too."

*   *   *

The group—Dee, Cynthia, Lupe Hernandez, and Linda Rivera, along with JoAnn and Margaret—assembled in the privacy of Cynthia's office. "Now, let's start with that newspaper story from last week," said Cynthia. "It says here that Claxton's Sheriff Joe Kreidler cooperated with Citizenship and Immigration Services to question and arrest fourteen workers at the hospital, where the new wing had been under construction since spring, but it doesn't provide any other details. JoAnn, what's the best way to confirm whether Linda and Teresa's father was among them, and where the detainees were taken?"

"I'll call my buddy in the sheriff's office right now," she said. "What's your father's name, Linda?"

"Jésus Martinez Rivera," she replied, after getting the nod from Mrs. Hernandez.

"And do you mind telling me where he was born?" asked JoAnn.

Linda, concerned, translated the question and again looked to Mrs. Hernandez before answering. "In Mexico. But Mrs. Hernandez says I should tell you my father has been in the United States for many years legally, long before I was born. She thinks there must have been some mistake with his papers."

"I'll be discreet," JoAnn assured them.

Dee and her cohorts pieced together more about Jésus Rivera from the background Linda was able to give them. Because he'd been steadily employed in agriculture in the U.S., he had obtained a green card by amnesty in 1987, the year after crossing the Rio Grande into the Texas desert with his pregnant wife. Teresa, born in Laredo, was an American citizen, as was Linda, born at Dallas's Parkland Hospital ten years later, but their mother had never qualified for a visa. The family moved with the crop seasons, and though Jésus Rivera sought better work and eventually settled down in Claxton as a bricklayer, he lived in fear of immigration authorities. Only after the death of his wife, when Linda was six, did he feel safe in enrolling his daughters in U.S. schools. It was their neighbor, Mrs. Hernandez, who had taken the girls under her wing and insisted on that. Linda, with the benefit of public-school education from the outset, learned to speak English much more readily than Teresa, who had such a late start.

"But Teresa always had a gift for writing things down," Linda said, translating from Mrs. Hernandez's part of the story. "In eighth grade her teacher told her, 'If you're having trouble saying it, just write it in your notebook.' And that's what she has been doing ever since."

Dee knew they'd been granted a rare glimpse into a life she knew little about. She pledged what help she could give in the time she had left.

"Margaret," Cynthia directed, "your job is to visit Mitzi at Helping Hands and see if you can learn more. Maybe she'll tell you something she didn't tell me or Dee. And I'm going to see what I can uncover in Citizen and Immigration Services records."

Dee read back over Teresa's drafts for any possible personal clues. But her missing-person search was turning out to be harder than expected. Their leads were few, and they had to be careful. If a bunch of Anglo women went nosing around asking questions door to door, they'd risk stirring up wrong ideas—or even unintentionally drawing unwanted attention to Teresa and her family.

It didn't take long for JoAnn's source to confirm that Jésus Rivera had been arrested at the hospital job site and jailed overnight along with a dozen other workers and their American employer. Cynthia's sleuthing in a beta version of a CIS database confirmed only that Rivera had not been deported, although two undocumented workers with criminal histories had been. Margaret managed to learn that Helping Hands distributed payroll checks every other Friday. They would call when anyone knew more than that. Dee would have to leave it in their hands, at least for now.

22
Closing Time

*Weave together contrasting human emotions—
joy and sorrow, love and loathing, hope and
disappointment—and through all, desire.*

BUDDY ARRIVED EARLY the next morning with the U-Haul and three beefy football players to help move the big furniture. Mama cooked a breakfast like she would've done before a day's work on the farm — generous portions of bacon, scrambled eggs, home fries, and biscuits — and Dee washed and packed the last of the pans. But no one took time to sit down to the table; everyone fixed a paper plate and helped themselves, nibbling on the run. It took a few trips back and forth, but soon the rooms stood vacant.

As dusk fell, Buddy loaded the last of Wilton's old tools onto the trailer, packed the Dust Devils into the van, and headed slowly down the hill. Dee watched the taillights at the gate as he stopped to close it behind him one last time. She really didn't know how he felt about losing the place—Buddy never showed much emotion except on the football field. But she suspected he wasn't going to relish tomorrow's closing any more than she was. Penny had already gone to spend the night with Mama at the new place in town, to help her get settled in. Dee would drive the pickup and stay at the Stagecoach, attend the closing in the morning, and catch a ride to Dallas afterward with Penny.

Dee sat alone on the edge of the back porch, dangling her legs over the beat-up garden and looking out at the fading colors of the sky. Already

Venus had risen, a jewel set in a field of velvet blue. Doves cooed, sheltered in the evening branches, as a soft wind blew across the ridge.

Soon the summer would end and another cycle of academic life would come around. It would certainly be different going back this time, thought Dee. Even if she'd missed out on the fellowship, she had managed to get her manuscript across the finish line—and she would start right in on a list of likely publishers as soon as she got to North Carolina. She was still in possession of an unused airline ticket to Massachusetts, too, and maybe she could visit Abby during fall break. She'd made new friends in an old familiar place. And she'd gathered new experiences to bring to her teaching. It was shaping up to be a fruitful year—she could feel it in the air.

As for Rob . . . it irked her that she could be gone for nearly three months and merit nothing more than a few phone calls and an occasional message from him. What was up with that? But surely she could make a fresh start on that, too.

She stood and went inside, to give the place one final walk-through. She let the screen door slam behind her. Her boots made larger-than-life echoes on the bare hall floor. It reminded her of the movie scene where the gunslinger strides into the ghost town, glancing around to see if hidden eyes are watching.

She hoped the only ghosts here were satisfied ones. An entire family's experiences and memories had lived here in these empty rooms—half a century's good times and bad. And Daddy's spirit . . . was he content with the decisions they'd made?

Dee heard a vehicle coming up the drive and could see the bouncing glow from its headlights. Had Buddy forgotten something? A pickup pulled to a stop beside the porch. She looked out the window to see Max Miller removing several items from his truck and setting them on the porch steps. Chester stood in the truck bed, tail wagging expectantly.

Her heart leapt with an unbidden joy, which she hoped she was successful in concealing. She swung open the screen door as casually as she could manage. She flipped the porch light switch to illuminate Max's unshaven face. "So, what's a desperado like you doing on my land?" she teased him as she leaned against the porch post. "I warn you, I know how to shoot a gun."

He tipped the brim of his gray hat, playing along. "Well, ma'am, seein' as how it's your land only for another few hours, I thought you might like to spend your last night on it under the stars."

"Max, are you serious? What an idea!"

"I've got bedrolls and backpacks for both of us. Go get a jacket—it gets cool at night."

Dee returned with warmer clothes from her suitcase. "I didn't think you'd be back from Colorado," she said.

"Left early yesterday and stopped over in Albuquerque. Chester and I have been on the road since six this morning."

"Must've been some big deadline."

"Ruby Lee called and told me about everything—the storm and your mother moving and all. I changed my plans."

By flashlight they made their way down the path over the breaks, sending pebbles scurrying down the hillside. Max held Dee's hand firmly to help her find her way in the dark. At last on more level ground, they picked a campsite sheltered by mesquites but well up the slope from the bottom of the draw. Dee gathered large rocks from the creek bed to make a fire ring, and Max scoured the area for deadwood. Soon they had a cozy blaze going and a pot of coffee perking.

"Did you ever camp out here as a kid?" Max asked Dee.

"Never! I don't think it ever would've occurred to me. Buddy had a scout tent, and I think he set it up in the yard some nights . . . but I guess Mama wouldn't have considered camping very sensible."

"Look up there . . . you can really appreciate the stars, when you're out away from the house lights."

"I know—I've camped on the Outer Banks, up in the Smoky Mountains, even way up in the Adirondacks one time. I love lying on my back and picking out the constellations."

"You go camping by yourself?"

"We used to take Abby when she was little. And then there's this friend—this guy I told you about—I was supposed to take a kayak camping trip with before all this."

"Sounds like a pretty cozy friend."

She didn't meet his eyes. "We'll see."

They peered up at the stars for a while, identifying the ones they could see through the break in the stubby trees. Max leaned over to stir the coals and eke out the fire's last bit of warmth and light. He refolded his blanket and sat closer to Dee. "Look, I came back to tell you something important," he began.

"If you wanted to make an offer on the place you're too late," she deadpanned. "Buck Turlock's beat you to it."

"I'm serious."

"Go ahead, then, I'm listening."

Max seemed to choose his words carefully. "There are realities I haven't faced . . . since my wife's death. Hard issues."

"Such as?"

"I know I've dodged your questions. That was churlish of me. Selfish. It wasn't just you—I've hidden the truth from everyone. I guess I thought if I ignored all the bad stuff, it would just go away."

Dee softened a little toward him; it was obvious he found the subject painful. "I understand alcohol was—an issue."

"So you did hear rumors."

She nodded.

"I expect so. I expect people said I had a drinking problem."

"Not in so many words, but—"

"They might've been partly right, but that wasn't the worst of it. Celeste and I had a very public fight one evening at a party where we'd both had too much to drink—we went to a lot of arts events and fundraisers in San Antonio, her family was big society—and she left without me. An hour later she drove her Lexus off the bridge into the river."

Dee drew in a quiet breath. "How horrible."

"It was. For me, for her parents, everybody . . . it was in the news. People blamed me, of course. As they should have."

"Blamed you? For her drunk-driving accident?"

"There is something I never told anyone. I didn't want her memory tarnished in any way. I'd rather everyone think what they wanted to about *me*, about what an irresponsible husband I was, always on the road, how Celeste had married beneath her, how we fought, whatever." Dee could see even in the low light that he was struggling to find words. "I was the only one who knew. When I got home, there was a note." He paused again. "It was intentional."

"I'm so sorry . . . for you both," Dee said, searching his face in the shadows.

"It was such a senseless loss. She was lovely in every way, and loved. I should have been better to her."

"You couldn't have been the source of all her troubles."

"Maybe, maybe not. But I'm the only one who read the letter. And I thought by destroying it I could wipe it all out. Make it like it never happened."

So there it was. He'd withdrawn into solitary pursuits and carried the burden himself rather than have his wife branded a suicide. Could Dee trust he was telling her the truth—or should she be worried about being out here alone with him, far from any phone?

She looked into his eyes, which glinted gray and gold in the dying firelight, and met his tone evenly. "Tell me what it's been like to live with that."

He stood and retrieved another log for the fire. "I don't like the dishonesty. There was an autopsy and investigation—people wanted answers. But once I'd burned the letter, who'd've believed me if I'd come clean about it?"

"I see what you mean," said Dee.

"I haven't let myself get close to anyone else. It didn't seem fair to drag others into my worries."

Dee nodded. They watched as the log crackled and split in two, sending up a shower of sparks.

"But then, you kind of yanked me out of my self-pity. Gave me someone else's situation to think about."

"I must have seemed pretty absorbed in my own woes," she admitted.

Max smiled, and the twinkle returned to his eye. "I rather enjoyed coming to your rescue on occasion. Although something tells me you'd be just fine left to your own devices anyway."

"Well, we'll see, won't we?" she said with tinge of remorse. Why was it she'd been in such a rush to go? So determined to leave? Suddenly she couldn't remember

She felt the warmth of his arm around her waist and his lips on her forehead. "You'll be fine," he said. "And I'll expect you back when it's time to sign books. Yours and mine both."

"You're a good man, Max."

He leaned back on the pillow of his bedroll and gathered her fully in his arms. The moon had risen, brilliant and round, over the line of trees, and they watched it until weariness overtook them. The campfire crackled and popped until only embers remained, and they slept as Venus made its nightly circuit and the Summer Triangle wheeled above them.

*   *   *

Dee woke at dawn as a breeze began to pick up in the east. She was thirsty, and she also needed a few moments of privacy down at the spring before Max awakened. She left him snoring in his sleeping bag and slipped quietly out of hers. Chester opened one eye but settled right back down. No fool about the snakes, Dee stepped into her boots and picked up the shotgun just to be on the safe side.

She made her way carefully down the slope, watching every step in the dim light. It was not difficult to keep to the path worn by cattle and wildlife, but the bent shapes of mesquite trees and hackberry bushes looked a lot spookier than in full daylight. She found a trickle of water and cupped her hands to drink from it.

As she stood and turned back the way she'd come, she heard a rustling in the brush a few yards away. Startled, she picked up the gun and raised it slowly. It couldn't be Max—the campsite was in the opposite direction, over the rise. Deer? A coyote? She remembered what Max had told her about staying downwind of your prey, and she backed slowly down the draw. But before she could reach better cover a portly man suddenly emerged on the path, and she instinctively trained the gun on the shadowy figure before recognizing him.

"Buck Turlock? Good God, what are you doing here? I nearly shot you!" Dee said as she lowered the barrel.

"I—I just come out to look things over and check a boundary marker. But what are you—"

A second man then appeared on the path behind Buck—a good-looking, clean-cut, thirty-something guy Dee couldn't place but who seemed familiar to her. He carried a flashlight and a clipboard with papers, and he wore a green T-shirt and a baseball cap bearing a large "T" within a star, sort of like the Texas Rangers emblem.

Like Nolan Ryan, Mama had said. And Dee realized in a flash where she had seen that logo before.

She raised the shotgun again and pointed it directly at Buck. "You sonofabitch."

"Now, little lady, I don't know what's got you so riled all of a sudden, but I assure you we don't mean any trouble."

"You goddamned sonofabitch!" she repeated, gritting her teeth.

"We apologize if we accidentally stepped onto your land," pleaded Buck. "Just put the gun down, and—"

Both men moved to cover their faces. Nolan Ryan held up the clipboard in both hands.

Dee was taken aback—she didn't think she'd inspired *that* kind of fear.

"Whoa, don't shoot—" Buck shouted.

Dee hadn't intended to pull the trigger at all. She heard a clicking sound behind her and, in the growing light, looked over her shoulder to see Max with the Nikon trained on the men, one of whom was going to great trouble to cover the logo on his cap.

The flash went off as the camera's autodrive shutter captured frame after frame of the men trespassing on Bennett land. "I don't think your company is ready for this publicity just yet," said Max coolly. Chester stood behind his master, teeth bared.

"Look, it's all just a misunderstanding," said Buck in an attempt to gloss things over. "Like I told your girlfriend here, we was just out checkin' some property lines, and sometimes it's hard to find the markers."

Dee held the gun steady and looked over her shoulder at Max. "And you—you've been working for these guys?"

"I promise you, I had no idea," he said sincerely. "But this fellow—haven't I seen you on the work crew down at Turkey Run?"

Before the Nolan Ryan lookalike could say anything further, a third man stepped up behind the hapless pair. He wore a big brown scruffy hat—like Festus on *Gunsmoke*, Dee had to agree—and a serious expression. "Put the gun down, sweetheart." He reached for his shoulder holster and drew a pistol. "And hand over the camera, Miller."

Dee shifted the shotgun's sight from Buck to Festus. Buck, moving faster than anyone gave him credit for, seized the opportunity and fled through the brush, with Chester barking in pursuit.

Dee realized this could get ugly. She thought fast. "Snake!" she yelled, directing her gaze toward the man's feet. She aimed the gun well right of his boot and squeezed the trigger.

Festus dropped his handgun in shock. Max quickly retrieved it, and with Dee's help had the two men covered.

"Shit, lady, you nearly blew my foot off!"

"I'll blow off more than that if you don't tell me what you're doing on my mother's property."

"Like Mr. Turlock said, we're just helpin' him check boundaries. Don't he have a legal contract to purchase the place?"

"Not if he's been talking to you about energy rights behind our backs." Dee turned to the younger man. "Do you drive a green pickup?"

"Why, yes, ma'am," he said. "Why do you ask?"

"Give me the keys."

He looked stunned. "What?"

"I said, hand me your keys. And that clipboard."

"Miss Bennett—Miss Dee—we was working in good faith," said Festus.

"That's *Doctor* Bennett to you. And just one more thing."

"What's that?" said Nolan Ryan, who looked like he was about to wet his pants.

"Take off your boots." The two men looked at each other quizzically, but after deciding there was no telling what this madwoman might do, they complied and removed their work boots.

"Okay, back to back, guys."

She instructed Max to pull the laces out of the boots and tie the pair's hands together behind their backs. "Hurry, there's not much time!" Chester came bounding back down the hill and stood guard, growling like he meant it.

Max hurled the boots one at a time into the brush, and they left the men there to fend for themselves. "Oh, and when you do get those knots undone," he told them, "just in case you were wondering—your cell phones don't work out here."

*   *   *

The appointment for the closing was fast approaching, and Buck had had a good head start on them. Dee and Max ran pell-mell up the draw towards the green truck, guns and camera flying. Max hid the guns in the brush before revving the engine and speeding toward town.

As they pulled up at the curb beside the Caprock State Bank, on the south side of the town square, the courthouse clock chimed the quarter hour. Max flung open the heavy brass door and the pair rushed into the lobby. In the mirrored pillar Dee caught a glimpse of her matted hair, full of cedar sprigs, and her rumpled clothes. Max, in a two-day beard and a checked flannel shirt, looked like a mountain man come down out of the wild.

Dee gasped for air as she stopped at the customer service desk. "Where—where is the Bennett closing?"

"Give me just a minute and I'll look that up," said the clerk calmly. "They're expecting you?" She eyed her visitors as though she might reach for that secret alarm button any second.

"Sort of," said Dee. "But we—brought something my mother needs."

The clerk consulted her computer screen. "Let me go tell them you're here."

Without waiting to be announced, Dee and Max tailed the clerk down the hall to the conference room.

"Mr. Foster?" the clerk asked the bank's vice president, who was seated at the head of the table. "There are additional parties here for the Bennett–Turlock appointment."

Dee and Max burst into the room, pushing her aside.

"Mama," said Dee breathlessly, "Don't sign that! We can't sell."

Penny, Buddy, Mama, and Buck Turlock, all seated at the table where papers were stacked in neat piles, turned and stared.

"Dee Anna Bennett, what on God's green earth?" asked Mama.

"Mr. Miller, so good to see you," said the puzzled banker, always eager to please.

"What is going on?" Penny demanded.

"Have you lost your mind?" Mama said. "And where have you been? You look like you just come in from a huntin' trip or something."

"In a manner of speaking," Dee said more calmly. On the table in front of the group, she caught sight of the document with every signature but hers already inked in. She reached for it and ripped it in half as they all looked on.

Buck started to speak first. "Just wait a minute there—"

But all Max had to do was lay his Nikon and the truck's mileage log on the table in front of him, and Buck shut up in a hurry.

Penny burst out in a rage at Dee. "Now look what you've done! Everything was all neat and tidy and ready to go, and you've screwed it up and I'm going to have to come back out here and do this all again!"

"You want to know what your buyer here has been up to? I'll bet if you checked the courthouse records down in Sweetwater and Abilene, you might find Mr. Turlock's name on some very interesting leases. And I'll bet he doesn't plan to farm the Echols place for much longer, either—any more than he does yours, Mama."

Buddy jumped in. "I don't think he intended to—"

"Shut up, Buddy. What is my sister talking about, Buck?" asked Penny, turning her full ire in his direction.

He crumbled under the force of her wrath. "I thought I was doin' y'all a favor, Penny. It'd be a win-win all the way around, seein' as how your mama didn't need to be out there in the country by herself and all."

"What's Buck's not saying," explained Dee, "is that he's been talking to the Texas Star Energy Corporation about wind turbine leases on land in Caprock County—before anybody else even knew they were coming here."

"Why, that's just business, Miss Dee," Buck argued. "Just a little side deal, in case cotton don't work out."

"Side deal, huh? I did some research after Max took me out to the Turkey Run project last week. Seems those turbines can pay landowners ten thousand a year in royalties, not counting the initial lease."

"Well, that's if everything works out with steady winds and all," he said. "Could be a lot less—it's a big gamble."

"For a gamble, you shore seem to know a lot about it," said Mama.

"I'm guessing he knows a lot more than that," said Dee. "Judging from what I saw at Turkey Run, this company doesn't just go in on a hunch. They do a great deal of advance analysis on average wind speed, rainfall, and topography—as well as studies of property access so they can be sure those huge construction trailers and cranes can get to the turbine sites. I'm pretty sure Texas Star has already had its crews and test trailers out here in Caprock County the past few months, isn't that right, Buck?"

Max added his two cents' worth. "You'll pardon me for saying I feel like I've been duped, Buck—I thought you were just being kind, letting me access your property to shoot wildlife in exchange for those prints. But I think you've got more than you bargained for in that camera now."

At that moment two other parties joined the proceedings, ushered in by Mr. Foster's clerk in even worse shape than Dee and Max. Their feet were bare, their faces and arms were cut by briars, and the younger man's left pants leg was ripped off at the knee.

"Whatever deal you got goin' here, Turlock, count us out," said Festus, removing his brown hat and brushing it off. "This job don't provide for hazard pay."

Mama's eyes opened wide at the sight of the two men, and Dee didn't fail to notice.

"Mama," she said, "these gentlemen are employed as landmen for the Texas Star Energy Corporation, and they just happen to drive a green pickup truck on their scouting expeditions. Their notes are all right here in this log—dates and routes and everything." She turned to face the men. "I didn't get either of your names, but perhaps you'd like to introduce yourselves to my mother, Alice Bennett, and to apologize for running her off the road beside our farm a couple of months ago. And one of you forgot to close our gate when you left, too."

Nolan Ryan spoke up. "That wasn't us, it must of been Jason tryin' out our trailer," he blurted out.

"Quiet, McFarland," Buck snapped.

"I'm Bo Bohannon and this here's my assistant, Trent McFarland. I am indeed sorry if we've caused you any trouble, Mrs. Bennett," said Festus. "But this was just all exploratory, and Mr. Turlock never let on he didn't have your permission. As for Miller here, well, he's been shootin' pictures for me out at Turkey Run all year, but he don't know anything about the company's future plans." He turned in Max's direction. "I got just two things to say to you, son," he said irritably, pointing toward his colleague's missing pants leg. "One, you're fired. And two, you have got to get control of that damn dog. He liked to have kept us from hitching a ride to town."

Banker Foster, who stood to lose a tidy sum in fees if things fell apart, had finally recovered his equilibrium. "Why don't we, ah, postpone this closing for another day, when all parties have had time to reconsider and come to amended terms?"

"Postpone my foot," said Alice Bennett. "Dee Anna is right, we ain't selling."

"But Mama, you've already leased the patio home. We've got to do something," whispered Penny, taking her mother's hand and helping her to her feet. "I don't know that we could even cover the expenses, without a crop this year."

"Maybe Ruby Lee or somebody will be interested, to keep it in the family," Mama sighed as they turned to go. "But I ain't selling our farm to no double-crossing crook."

Dee placed her palm on the table suddenly. "No. I know what we're going to do."

Penny pursed her lips. "What now?"

"Just give me a few hours. I've got to get hold of Rob—and Jacob."

"Rob the boyfriend?" asked Max, turning to her quizzically.

"The Jew from Jersey?" asked Mama.

"Hush, Mama," Dee answered. "Penny, if you could be so kind as to give me a ride back to the farm, I'll tell you my plan." Max grabbed his camera and the five of them headed for the door, leaving the frazzled banker, his clerk, his would-be client, and the two Texas Star agents standing speechless in their wake.

"Oh, and I guess you'll need a way to see yourselves back across the county line," Dee said to McFarland, tossing him the keys to his truck. "Happy trails, y'all."

23
Wheeling and Dealing

*Characters have a way of taking events in directions
their author has not foreseen.*

DEE, SHOWERED AND RESTORED to presentability before dashing
back to town, used the privacy of Cynthia's office to make calls on her
cell phone while Cynthia, always up for a research challenge, searched
and printed background articles and public documents.

Dee reached Rob in his campus office that afternoon. "I'm going to
ask you a favor," she said, "and if it seems bizarre, just hear me out
before you answer." How quickly could he find out for her what her cabin
and lake property might bring from one of those hot-to-trot developers?
She told him all about the near-sale of the farm.

Engage him in financial questions, she thought, and suddenly he
was downright chatty. Not to mention suspiciously helpful.

"But didn't you just say," Rob replied, "that your father had already
conveyed a third interest in the property to you? If that's the case, you
don't need a cash down payment up front to buy out the others. Use
yours as collateral. All you need to cover are the closing costs and any
unpaid taxes. Just take out a short-term loan and pay it back when
your own house sells."

Of course—how simple. It hadn't even occurred to her. "You're a
genius, Rob—truly a genius! Now, just one more thing . . . what would
you do in this situation, if you were me?"

"Well, if it were *me*—I'd leverage my considerable savings instead and invest the lake proceeds in energy stocks, but hey, it's your money." What he didn't say told her all she needed to know. Not a word of "Wow, what about us?" or "I'd sure hate to see you go."

"There's someone else, isn't there?"

He waited a beat too long to answer. "Why don't we talk tomorrow when I pick you up from the airport?"

"Save your breath, Ducky. I'll get a cab." One click of the End button, and that was that.

*   *   *

Her next call was trickier. Jake's wife, Melissa, answered, and Dee had to listen to a not-quite-muffled "Honey, you have a call from Abigail's mother" before her ex picked up.

"Dee?" he said. "Haven't heard from you in ages. What's up? You still in Texas?"

"She told you, I guess."

"Yeah, about having to renege on the fellowship. Must've been brutal."

"It's spilt milk now. I did the right thing," she said. "And that's why I'm calling. You know I've never asked for anything from you."

"Yes, that's true," he said warily.

"Years ago you and I put aside a fund for Abby's future. Education or whatever. Well, I'm investing in her future now. I need three thousand dollars of it. Short-term loan, I'll pay it back within the year."

He seemed to mull that over. "You do know that Abby's dropped out?"

"Yes—and I don't know what to do about that any more than you do."

"Oh, I *know* what to do," he replied. "And I imagine it won't be long before she reconsiders this short-sighted AmeriCorps idea. And the slacker boyfriend."

The reality dawned on her. Why was she always so dense about these matters? And Jake—had he completely forgotten what it was like to be young, carefree, and idealistic? "You cut her off, didn't you?"

"In a heartbeat. Tough love. Something you never appreciated," he said. "She called me a couple of weeks ago when her iPhone was about to be disconnected. I told her too bad, switch to a prepaid plan and budget it out until her next paycheck. And I know those AmeriCorps folks provide housing and meals, so it's not like she's destitute."

"Maybe not destitute, but desperate," Dee countered, seething. "Get a pen and paper, because we're going to trade some numbers here. I'm going to give you my checking account information for a wire transfer, and you're going to give me Abby's new phone number."

"What? What did I say?"

He just didn't get it, that thing between mothers and daughters, regardless of how many miles separated them. Never had.

*   *   *

Cynthia had a sizeable stack of documents waiting for her, all neatly paper-clipped. "In case you need to make photocopies," she explained helpfully. "I was able to get some of these faxed from other counties."

"SuperLibrarian!" Dee said in genuine admiration.

"And there's something else. Frances and JoAnn have been staking out Helping Hands all day, and they called to say that Teresa just pulled up there in the truck—alone."

"You don't think she'll disappear again, do you? I need to talk to her—but there's something I have to take care of first."

Dee took the folder of papers and drove straight to her mother's new patio home, where Max met her with documents of his own. They found Mama seated at the dining table while Buddy hung pictures and Penny unpacked boxes in the tiny kitchen.

"Lord have mercy, come in here and tell me what all happened. Hadn't moved out for twenty-four hours and the whole world's gone crazy over one sorry half-section farm."

Everyone gathered around the table, where Dee spread out the sales figures, deeds, leases, and studies that indicated a pattern. She pointed to the map Cynthia had marked. "It looks like our farm was only one of dozens targeted for lowball offers," Dee suggested. "Anyone with inside information would be able to make deals before the company even held a public hearing. It wasn't hard to see once you knew what to look for."

Max pulled out a folio of the photos he'd produced for Texas Star. The logo on the signs was indeed the same as that on the cap McFarland had been wearing that morning.

In Max's stylish industrial photography, the massive white components of wind turbines—blades, tower sections, controllers—looked like contemporary art. Mama pointed to one view of a rectangular contraption, big as a house trailer, mounted for transport on an oversized green flatbed. "That's it!" she cried.

"What's it?" asked Buddy. Dee immediately knew where she'd seen the flatbed truck before, too—when Chester had pulled back the covering on Buck Turlock's parade float.

"*That* thang, that's what nearly gave me a heart attack when I ran off the road," Mama said with certainty, jabbing her finger at the picture. "I was just tellin' Penny and Buddy how it all came back to me. Them two men at the bank this morning, well, they come speeding over the hill that day blinded by the sun, and I jerked the car over on the shoulder to get out of their way and ran in the ditch."

"And was that when you fell?" asked Dee.

"I was just getting out to see if the car was okay, when this contraption comin' along behind 'em nearly blew me away. I was so startled, I remember—I tripped and tried to catch myself from falling. You don't want to fall at my age, you know. Next thing I knew, I was layin' there with ants all over me and Hector was callin' my name."

"Well, it's a good thing Hector came along when he did," said Dee.

"I'm grateful to him. And I don't guess I say this enough, but I appreciate ever' one of my kids for looking after me, too. Dee Anna, I'm thankful you stuck by me through this whole ordeal—and you were so smart to figure out the mystery."

"I wouldn't have put two and two together until it was too late, if Max hadn't come by and suggested the campout. But there's one other mystery that needs solving before I leave, so Mama, can you come with me for a minute?" They left the others to pore over the papers while she guided Mama out to the small brick patio out front, where Buddy had placed the rocking chairs.

"I believe there's an injustice to be set right," Dee explained as she punched the speed-dial on her phone. "I'm going to put this on speaker in just a second."

Mama screwed up her face with her sour-lemon look. "I wouldn't know how to talk on one-a-them cell phones."

"You'll get the hang of it." The phone rang a few more times, and Abby answered.

"Hello?"

"Hey, honey," said Dee. "I hope I'm not catching you up on a roof or anything."

"Nope, in fact, it's water break time. Is something wrong?"

"No, nothing like that. I just hadn't had a call from you since you left, and, well, I got concerned and called your dad."

"Oh."

"You know, my flight leaves for North Carolina in the morning, and I was saying good-bye to Gramma Alice. I'm going to put this on speaker for both of us. Is there something you want to say to her?" Dee punched the key, and Abby's voice came over the phone loud and clear.

"Uh—hi, Gramma, I hope you're still getting better."

"Much better, thank you, but there shore has been a lot of excitement around here," Mama replied, leaning in and shouting at the phone.

"There has?"

"We had a big hail storm and lost the cotton crop. And most of your garden."

"Oh, wow, that's awful . . . but you and Mom and Teresa are doing okay?"

Dee replied this time. "Abby, Teresa was accused of taking something that didn't belong to her. It was a real shame she got fired." She paused to make her point clear, and spoke slowly. "But I'm sure Gramma Alice would forgive anyone who was big enough to confess."

Mama drew back and looked at Dee. "What do you mean? I ain't forgiving that thieving Meskin."

Abby's voice came over the speaker. "I—am—sooooooo—sorry . . ."

"Sorry for what?" asked Mama.

"Oh, Gramma Alice, I was going to send it back to you as soon as I got paid. But then my paycheck wasn't enough, and—oh, I am *so* sorry if I've gotten Teresa in trouble. I—I was flat broke when I got ready to come back to New Mexico, and we had to have meals and cat food, and I didn't want Mom to lecture me." There was a pause and an audible gulp. "I knew you kept your rainy-day money in the cookie jar. I—I took eighty dollars out of it."

Mama absorbed what she'd just heard. "Well," she said with a sigh, "a rainy day come along."

"What can I do to make it up? I'll get a second job, I'll—"

"Mama and I will work out amends for now," Dee said. "You can pay back the money later. I'm asking only one thing of you."

"What? Anything. I'm so ashamed."

"Get yourself back to school this fall. I'm sending you money and a bus ticket. There are going to be some big changes—we'll talk later."

"Oh-kay, maybe you're right." Dee and Mama leaned in closer. Abby was starting to cry. "Gramma Alice, I never meant to hurt anyone. Can you ever forgive me? And what can I do to make it up to Teresa?"

"People can make wrong choices when they're in a pinch," said Mama. "Do like your mother says—and don't give this another thought. About Teresa, I guess I have to eat some crow myself."

*   *   *

Dee and Mama pulled up in front of the house on Pecan Street and parked behind the Toyota truck. Dee hoped that was a good sign. Cynthia's car was there, too.

"Is *this* where she lives?' Mama asked, surprised.

"Not exactly, but I want you to meet someone." Dee knew she had to proceed with the skill of a diplomat. "Can you wait here for a minute?"

Linda answered the door this time.

"Teresa's here?" Dee asked expectantly. "And I hope she's okay?"

"Yes, come in and tell her yourself. Your writer friends are trying to help our father."

There was no empty seat in Mrs. Hernandez's crowded living room. JoAnn and Cynthia took up the velvet sofa on either side of Teresa, who was drying her eyes with a tissue. Margaret had her reporter's notebook out. Mrs. Hernandez was holding the Chihuahua dog in her lap.

"We've all missed you, Teresa," Dee said. "I'm so relieved you're safe!"

"I've been so afraid—I—didn't want to come back without Papa, I—"

"Well, you're here with friends now," said JoAnn, "and you did the right thing. Do you want us to tell Dee what's happened?"

Teresa nodded.

Dee said, "I want to hear all about it, but Teresa, can you come with me for a minute first?" Dee motioned toward the door, and Teresa followed, skeptical.

Teresa displayed even more reluctance when she saw Mama waiting in the driveway with the car window rolled down. But Dee urged her closer. "Teresa, my mother has something to tell you that I think you'll want to hear."

Mama did not look directly at Teresa, but she began, "I found out an hour ago that I have wrongly accused you of stealing, Teresa." Teresa stood and waited. "The good book says we must not bear false witness, and I owe you my deepest apology."

Teresa nodded in appreciation.

"But Dee Anna also tells me that you stuck by me the day of the storm even when you had family worries of your own, and for that, I owe you thanks." She reached through the window with some difficulty and grasped Teresa's arm.

"*Mi padre* . . . my father—"

"I know. You do what you have to do. Your family is the most important thing."

"Would you like to come in?"

Mama looked at Dee, who opened the car door and helped her out. As she assisted her up the walkway and into the foyer, Dee was pretty sure it was the first time in her life Alice Bennett had ever set foot inside the home of someone whose skin color was not the same as her own.

*   *   *

Teresa let JoAnn do the talking. Giving up her seat for Mama, the paralegal shared everything they knew so far. Jésus Rivera, while treated well and allowed to see Teresa, was still behind bars in Dallas. She'd found him, after choosing to pay the retainer of an Irving *abogado* rather than her cell phone bill, but the attorney turned up one technical offense that still required attention before he could negotiate a release. Jésus had forgotten to renew his visa the previous year—something he'd had to do only once before, more than a decade earlier. Teresa spent the last of her cash on gas to return home for paperwork and bail money.

But JoAnn had even better news for Teresa when she and Margaret intercepted her at the Helping Hands office. She'd talked with a lawyer friend who specialized in immigration issues—and who asked one very important question. Had Teresa reached age twenty-one?

"So, guess what?" Teresa interjected, as animated as Dee had ever seen her. "After my birthday next month, I can spon—sponsor *my own father* for United States citen—citizenship!"

They all applauded and wished her and Linda well.

Lupe Hernandez had a special word for Mama before letting her go. She asked Linda to translate. "Mrs. Hernandez says she is so grateful to you, Mrs. Bennett. If you had not let these writers use your home . . . we do not know where we'd be today."

Mama acknowledged the sentiment. "I'm glad for you. Now, I guess we best be goin'—Dr. Dee's got some big plans to work out before she catches her plane."

24
The Paragraph Ranch

Always leave your readers wanting more.

"CAREFUL WITH THAT END," Abby shouted up at Max, who was standing at the top of the extension ladder he'd propped against the tall post. In the searing heat of the August dusk they were sweating like linebackers. The bystanders looked up and shielded their eyes. "Don't let it slide off—but push it back to the right about four more inches," said J. D.

Ian, whose ladder was set up similarly on the latch side of the gate, maneuvered his end of the old telephone pole into the notch of the upright and fastened it temporarily with a couple of long screws. "Got it. Won't be any uninvited flatbeds coming this way again!"

Jésus Rivera inspected the brick bases he'd made for the new gate and tested the clearance.

"Good going," said Max as he secured his side and scrambled down, wiping his forehead on his sleeve. "So, Dr. Dee, you want to do the honors?"

She got up her courage. Ian moved his ladder to the center, propping it against the horizontal beam, and she ascended one rung at a time with the iron sign, hammer, and nails in a bag slung over her shoulder. Ian and Hector steadied the ladder and Abby watched, along with the crowd of well-wishers who had gathered at the foot of the driveway. Max focused his camera in Dee's direction.

When she had climbed high enough to rest the iron base of the sign on the beam, she methodically slipped the eight-penny nail into the first slot, just as Ian had showed her, and let the hammer fly. A few strokes, repeat on the other side, and it was done. Wendell's iron sculpture had found its new home.

She struck a brief pose. The Write Stuff members, along with Mama, Hector, Teresa and her family, and two newcomers who'd read about the writing group in the paper and asked to join, applauded at the close of the impromptu ceremony. She scrambled down before she could succumb to vertigo.

"Well, it ain't fancy as Texas estates go," joked Dee, thankful to be standing on solid ground again, "but it'll do for now." She brushed the dust off her hands and wiped her face with a bandana. "Welcome to the Paragraph Ranch!"

"It's so good to have you back," gushed Frances. "But what about your job?"

"Well, there are writers and books everywhere, aren't there?" said Dee. She was still savoring the look of shock on Pritchard's face when she'd given notice. Or was it dread at the thought of having to teach the grammar and editing courses himself?

The Write Stuff gang helped take down the ladders and load them into the trucks, and one by one they followed Ian and Abby up the hill to the house. Dee waited until last, to hitch a ride with Max.

She stared up at the sign. *Hers.*

The sale of her Carolina cabin, to her great surprise, had brought more than enough to cover the mortgage on the home place. Enough, in fact, to cover her basic living expenses for a while. Until she figured out where the next chapter in her life was headed.

When word got around that Dee Bennett was returning to Claxton—with a moving van this time—the phone calls and e-mails piled up like tumbleweeds against a fence in a storm.

From the Texas Writers Online staff: would she be willing to lead a seminar at their fall conference, for a modest honorarium?

From Ruby Lee Bargeron, who wanted to pencil in the home place for her fall fashion show. Outdoors, with a rustic theme.

From Hector Ortiz, who wanted to know if he should go ahead and plant a sorghum crop.

From Dr. Kim, who was checking to see how Mama's healing was progressing.

From Abby, who planned to stop over with Ian after their AmeriCorps stint was over, on their way back to Massachusetts.

From an agent who'd heard about Dee's book from Susan Sterns and wanted to read the manuscript.

From Elsa Jensen, inviting her to come visit her in California soon and meet Gineva Holland Templeton's kin in person.

From her neighbors, Stacey's parents Jason and Cheryl Woodberry, who said she was welcome to drop by anytime she needed a cup of sugar.

From Buddy, who wanted to make sure she didn't get rid of the tractor, and then from Penny, who just wanted to make sure she hadn't changed her mind about Buck Turlock's offer.

When she'd heard nothing further from Rob the accountant, she put an ad in the campus newspaper. Ocean kayak for sale, blue, eleven-foot tandem, fore and aft gear hatches. Paddles, PFDs, and trail maps included, $500 OBO. A student had snapped it up the following day.

Mama, who had worked with the county extension agent to learn everything she could about farming sorghum, had settled in to the senior community with an ease that amazed her children. "There's a beauty shop right here in the complex," she told Dee. "And a van that takes folks to church and Walmart, and a 42 dominoes group that meets ever' day at lunch. I don't know why in the world I hung around out there in the country for so long."

A corporate representative of Texas Star Energy had come calling at her patio home with an enormous fruit basket the first week after the Turlock sale fell through, Mama reported. He had no idea they'd been part of a shady deal, and certainly no awareness that they had run an elderly woman off the road. They hoped it would be okay if they approached the new owner about a wind energy lease once all the transfer documents were finalized. Mama figured he was making a preemptive strike against being sued.

With some deep background provided by Max Miller and Cynthia Philpott, Margaret Strickland had come out of retirement to break the story in the *Claxton Courier* of Texas Star's local explorations. She was on a roll the following week with a carefully researched enterprise piece about the unfair treatment of Mexican immigrant workers on the hospital construction project.

Max lifted the toolbox over the side of the pickup and shut the tailgate. Chester leapt out and dashed into the mesquite scrub after a flash of motion that was not apparent to his master.

"Nickel for your thoughts?" Max asked Dee. "Inflation, you know."

Dee continued to gaze up at the newly turned fields, the sorghum sprouts tinting the red-brown furrows with a hint of green. Just above the tree line she could make out the brand-new metal roof, the gap where the large peach tree used to stand, the old windmill turning in the breeze. The setting sun reflected a pink-orange off of the porch posts, highlighting the hailstorm scars. The weathered barn anchored its corner of the hill like a castle keep.

"If I had a nickel for every time I made a wish to leave this place, I'd be rich as T. Boone Pickens himself," she said. "So who knew I'd go and plow everything I owned into coming back?"

"Go figure," said Max. "But I guess it all depends on how you define rich."

She looked into his eyes, and reached up to kiss him long and hard. "Maybe it does. So, you think it might be time to start earning some interest?"

"I think you can count on it, Dr. Dee."

"I will, Miller."

"Let's go, then. Your stable of writers is waiting."

Acknowledgments

WE OWE A GREAT DEAL of thanks to the many readers who lent a hand at the Paragraph Ranch: especially to Cathey, Lori, and Kara, who were unfailingly supportive and helpful; to the Write Right Critique Group and the Ad Hoc Writers' Group of Lubbock, Texas, whose members provided invaluable feedback; to Ginger and Ad, who responded to this work and others in progress; to our Booktrope publishing and marketing team Kenneth Shear, Katherine Sears, Jesse James Freeman, and book designer Kelsey Wong, and our extraordinary Booktrope creative team, book manager Stephanie Konat, designer Greg Simanson, and proofreader Cecile Jagodzinksi; and to other friends and family members who have cheered us along. To the late Stanley Colbert, we lift a vodka gimlet in gratitude. We appreciate all the real institutions, the towns, the people, and the events that inspired the fictional landscape in which *The Paragraph Ranch* is situated. We hope our truest love and respect for them shine through.

More Great Reads from Booktrope

Spirit Warriors: The Concealing by **D.E.L. Connor** (Fiction) Suspenseful, romantic, and awash in Native American magic, *Spirit Warriors* captures the tragic enchantment of the American West—and confirms the power of friendship.

One Day in Lubbock by **Daniel Lance Wright** (Fiction) William Dillinger despises how he spent his life and has one day to find out if rekindling love can change it.

Taxicab to Wichita by **Aaron Asselstine** (Fiction) Quinn Jacob is a drug-addicted taxi driver with no options, no money, and no destination. Rocky is a thief with no getaway car, no driver, and no time. In the gathering darkness of a perfect storm, can they trust each other, risk it all, and recreate themselves on the high-wire roads to Wichita?

Biking Uphill by **Arleen Williams** (Contemporary Fiction) Sometimes the best family is the one we build ourselves. A heartwarming story of enduring friendship.

The Graduation Present by **J.T. Twissel** (Action and Adventure) An unexpected gift. An unforgettable adventure. A young woman's eyes and heart are opened.

Swimming Upstream by **Ruth Mancini** (Fiction) A life-affirming and often humorous story about a young woman's pursuit of happiness.

Discover more books and learn about our new approach to publishing at www.booktrope.com